Time & Again
Upon A Time
Book Two
By
Stella May

I0672645

Copyright

Editor: Sloane Taylor

Cover Artist: Justine Alley Dowsett

Published by Draft2Digital

1. https://www.myidentifiers.com/title_registration?isbn=978-1-7376474-2-3&icon_type=New

2. https://www.myidentifiers.com/title_registration?isbn=978-1-7376474-3-0&icon_type=New

Table of Contents

To my husband Leo, my best friend, my rock, the center of my universe.

CHAPTER ONE

And so, it was done. The Coleman house, the most challenging restoration project *Before & After, Inc.* had ever taken on, was finished.

The result was, hands down, spectacular. Nika glanced around the entry hall as she walked farther into the old manor. Yes, it was indeed a brilliant job, if she said so herself. A whiff of fresh paint tickled her nose and a brief smile touched her lips.

Every ounce of her skill, every drop of her sweat and blood, was invested into the project. She and her crew labored for ten brutal months to restore the mansion, and awaken this great sleeping beauty.

She trailed her right-hand fingertips along the glossy walnut banister as she continued to the formal living room. Memories flooded her mind with every step.

The longest and most difficult time of her life. Ten moths she lived and slept right here, on the site, working like a woman possessed. She ran herself and everybody ragged, acquired a few enemies along the way, but more good friends.

And at the end, she made good on her promise.

Never mind that she made that promise to the *house*. To Nika, a promise was a promise. She chuckled, as she recalled that day, when she first stepped inside the Coleman house. Brimming with joy, she was impatient to start on her dream-come-true job. So elated, so in a rush, Nika almost salivated at the prospect of getting her hands on the house at last. Since she first laid eyes on the house it became her obsession. She fought for the privilege to own it, but to no avail. All attempts from her cousin and business partner Alex to make an offer met with resolute denial from its current owners. Then, one day, out of the blue, their company, *Before & After, Inc.,* was presented with an offer they couldn't refuse: *carte blanche* to restore the Coleman house.

The circumstances of that offer were most remarkable and unorthodox. But the opportunity was just too irresistible to pass up, especially for her, the professional House Whisperer, who dreamt about this once posh residence for three long years.

Reluctant at first, Nika soon became driven. After her phantasmagorical journey through time and her unexpected return, she simply had no choice.

She plunged ahead, single-minded, and unwavering. Even the most devastating pandemic that swept along, disintegrating the world, didn't put a hitch in her stride. Left with a skeleton crew, Nika refused to stop. The suggestion of the local authorities to pause the renovations was met with her resolute defiance.

She continued her work even when Abby got ill with COVID-19. And that was the hardest challenge of them all. For twenty devastating days, alone and isolated, Abby fought that viscous virus in the hospital, the very same that her brother had built and donated to the city some hundred plus years prior.

Nika shuddered. The memories of the night Abby was taken to the hospital were still fresh in her mind. Fear, anger, helplessness.

They coped differently. Alex made donations to the various labs working on a vaccine. Their grandmother *Verochka* prayed and kept vigils. Nika drove herself harder.

She raged and raved and cursed fate, but never stopped restoring Abby's childhood home.

Well, all of that was behind them now, and the Coleman house was finished.

At last.

There was nothing more for Nika to do but turn the keys to its legal owner Senator Lauder. In a few days he would fly in to take over.

Just a few short days...

Not enough time to get used to the idea that the most challenging and unusual project of her career was completed. Finished. Done with. Period.

Sad and lost, Nika glanced around for the last time. The spacious foyer, the staircase, the floors, and walls, and ceiling...Everything gleamed, and shone, and pleased the eye. The perfectionist in her rejoiced, while the woman wept in silence.

Hollowed out, mind and body, she was so tired and... empty. Deflated.

Was it like postpartum depression? Probably. No, worse, because the 'baby' she labored very hard to bring to life was never hers to begin with.

The Coleman house belonged to strangers, and she was just a surrogate mother to it for almost a year. But for the next few days, the house was all hers.

Nika swept her eyes around one more time before she turned to the object of her greatest fear and hope: the infamous Coleman's heirloom, the grandfather clock. The sentry of the house, as she dubbed it, stood six feet tall, domineering the space. Restored and cleaned to its original perfection after half a century of neglect, this English masterpiece circa 1827 was one magnificent creation that always adorned the Coleman household. Carved out of dark mahogany, its case was warm as velvet and soft to the touch, while its face and arms, inlaid with 18th carat gold, sparkled and gleamed like a mirror.

Now, all polished and spiffed up, it ticked out time in a dignified and solemn manner, like the superb *object d'art* it was. This clock, however, was one of a kind in more ways than one. Wound up by a small brass key, it transformed into a portal between times. That key, three inches in length, plain and ordinary, etched into Nika's memory forever. But, like a clock, it too was unique.

The special hiding place on the back of the clock's panel was another mystery she uncovered a year ago, urged by the letter written to her in 1909. She knew each word by heart.

Find the key. You know where it is. Hurry, for goodness' sake!

Lo and behold, she found it. Prompted by some invisible force, Nika inserted that key into the clock's slot, and was transported a hundred and ten years back.

To 1909.

On the patch of a dirt road, thunderstruck and stunned, she met the one and only Elijah B. Coleman, the author of that cryptic letter, and the master of the Coleman house.

Talk about weird. Or amazing.

Nika's hand rested on the ring she wore on a chain around her neck. The day Eli proposed, on November 7, 1909, he put it on her finger. His grandmother's heirloom amethyst that reminded him of her unusual violet-blue eyes he said.

Since her return, Nika couldn't bear to see it on her hand as a constant reminder of her loss. But neither could she part with it. So, she put it on a chain, and wore it close to her heart, drawing from it her strength, and hope. And patience.

When she was low on all three, she would go to the old cemetery, *Bosque Bello,* and visit two graves, and remind herself that one day she, indeed, would find her way back. Because the second, smaller headstone, the one she called *Daisy's* in her own mind, with missing a birthdate and an odd inscription 'the timeless miracle', was her own.

There was no doubt in her mind that she'd find her way back. The million-dollar question was when. Because, as she discovered, the physics of time didn't apply equally to the different dimensions. She lived in 1909 for almost three months, but in her own century it amounted to just three days, so her family didn't even notice her absence.

Talk about irony.

Today marked fourteen months since she and Abby made their infamous journey to the present time. Nika was afraid to apply the same math, because the answer was daunting. She glanced again at the grandfather clock, and reached out to touch the gleaming surface. Then, as was her habit, she squeezed her hand between the wall and the clock's backside, fingering a barely-there small button that opened the hidden panel. Nika held her breath as she reached inside the tiny place, but her fingers encountered the empty space. She swore under her breath.

"Dammit, Coleman, for someone so smart, you could've figure it out long time ago!"

The mysterious sentry of the Coleman household refused any and all key copies she acquired. No matter how well it fit inside the slot, the clock never turned back to life. The only solution was to get the original key, the one that she dropped in 1909 during her return trip. But how? Nika was losing her patience, along with her sanity, when the answer, simple as day, dawned on her. To get her hands on the original key here and now, Eli must put it in its hiding place then and there. If he did it once, he must do it again. He must!

He will.

He'd figured it out the same way she did.

Every night for the past ten months, exhausted after full day of work, she sat before the grandfather clock, and waited. To no avail.

She refused to entertain the notion that Eli deliberately withheld the key. He was a hard man, a proud one, but never cruel. And he loved her.

But would a proud man wait fourteen years for his runaway bride?

He would. He did. The two graves at the *Bosque Bello* were her proof.

"Come on, Eli. Don't make me wait any longer. Put the damn key back in its hiding place!"

Her desperate shout reverberated through the vast emptiness of the mansion.

"Okay, you stubborn moron," Nika's shoulders slumped in resignation. "And that goes for you too." She frowned at the grandfather clock. "Wouldn't hurt you to help me a little, now, would it? Time's running out, you know. In a few days I will turn the house to its owner. So, it's up to you now. I did what I could. I upheld my side of the bargain. Now the ball is in your court."

Without looking back, Nika walked down the hallway.

The eerie silence of the empty house was interrupted by a sudden loud *bong* of the antique clock just as she closed the front door.

CHAPTER TWO

Eli failed to get his wits about him. Three days now since he had learned the truth. He still grappled with the implications. His friend, his cousin-in-law, the man he knew for a better part of his life, had lied to him, deceived him. Betrayed him. How do you reconcile it with the fact that the same man also saved your life? He was mortally wounded in the accident then died in Eli's, stead.

If William hadn't pushed him out of the way, it would be him buried under that pile of loose lumber that crashed down.

If William had died instantly, instead of clinging to life for an agonizing few hours, Eli would never have learned the truth about Daisy's disappearance and his friend's sinister role in it.

He still was too dumbfounded and yes, hurt, dammit, to fully grasp the meaning of the uncovered facts.

But the main thing was, Daisy hadn't run away. Nor lied to him. Or abandon him. Most important—she hadn't stolen a single thing. The proof was spread out in front of him. He gently fingered the contents of the jewelry box that once belonged to his first wife. William had kept it as a memento of his late cousin.

All the items William claimed Daisy purloined, were strewn on his bed where Eli dumped them. His grandmother's pearls, his father's golden watch, his mother's sapphires, wads of cash, and many other things, including a peculiar long-billed hat with embroidered golden letters *B&A*.

"Oh, William." Eli shut his eyes, and pressed his fingers against the sockets. "Why? Why did you hate her? What had she done to you?"

Those were the important questions his friend refused to answer in his last hours. He had stared at Eli with mournful eyes glazed with pain until the good Lord took mercy on his soul.

Today, after his best friend— and his worst enemy— was laid to rest, Eli at last gathered the courage to search his room. He found everything exactly where William said it was. On his deathbed, badly broken but conscious, he confessed to everything: urging Daisy to travel back to visit her family, stealing the key from its hiding spot inside the fireplace, and then hiding all the valuables in order to accuse Daisy of thievery. He even admitted to his initial inclination to damage the clock to prevent her from coming back, but Abby's unexpected intervention caused Daisy to drop the key. Without it, she was not coming back. William simply returned the key to its proper hiding place then dusted his hands of the affair.

When Eli came home, he had the audacity to console him, offering his loyalty and friendship. All the while Eli was insane with grief, drinking and blaming himself for being a fool and an easy mark for a clever con-artist, his best friend, the man he considered a family, hid the damnable truth: he was the major culprit in this disaster.

Daisy was innocent. Her only fault was that of loving her family too much, and wanting to bring them consolation and peace. She was going to come back to him.

She loved him.

In face of William's death and his shocking deception, the thought of her was the only thing that kept Eli sane, the only source of strength and courage.

Daisy, my Daisy, my wildflower, my wondrous time-traveler.

When he was able to function and think clearly again, Eli realized that his only solution was to get her back. One way or another.

And how can you accomplish that, Coleman?

She was as far away from him as the moon. Even farther, all things considering.

A sudden movement announced the presence of another person in the room.

His anger ignited. Eli turned, ready to give a tongue lashing to whomever dared disobey his order not to be disturbed.

The rage dissipated as soon as he recognized the disobedient soul, the only one who could brave his anger.

"Hello, Belle. Well, come in, girl. Don't be shy now." He motioned to the dog with his right hand.

Belle, her huge shaggy head cocked askew, lolled her tongue, then approached him, curious and happy. She rubbed her massive body against his leg in lieu of a greeting, or consolation.

"Thank you, Belle, I needed it." A fleeting smile alleviated a bit of his sorrow. He stooped and scratched her head between the ears, one upright, the second hanging permanently to the side. Truth be told, the dog was so ugly, it was painful sometimes to look at it. Hence, the name *Belle* that Abby gave the creature, to balance in some fashion the scale of nature's cruelty. But what this mutt lacked in the beauty department, it compensated in spades in more important qualities, such as love, loyalty and kindness. And smarts. She was a smart one! If only she could talk.

Eli almost heard the dog's thoughts at times, so eloquent were her eyes. Especially when she looked at him direct and calm, like right now.

He stopped wondering *how* he understood what the dog conveyed to him in silence. He accepted it as fact. On some primitive level, they *felt* each other.

And they adopted each other.

After Daisy's disappearance, the dog was in bad shape. When Eli found her near the stables, she was half-starved, and motionless. He was afraid Belle had perished. Then she opened her eyes and moaned. That sound of human-like agony chilled his soul. The stable hand had even offered to shoot the dog to relieve it from its misery. Eli turned to face the sorry youth and stabbed him with a look. The boy turned white and backed out of the stable.

Belle was Daisy's dog, and she was mourning, just like he was. They both sought death, but in a different manner. He drank himself into a stupor while Belle refused to eat or drink. A broken heart was hard to mend, be it human or canine.

A loss of a loved one was irreversible. A tragedy that left a permanent mark on one's soul. Like looking in a mirror, his own grief was reflected in the dog's shattered eyes.

Eli vowed there and then to nurse Daisy's dog back to life, even if it was the last thing he did. And so, he scooped the malnourished dog into his arms, unmindful of dirt and flees, and carried her into the house.

They saved each other. Her ugly appearance ceased to bother him, because the inner beauty of her soul was infinite. He was the lucky one to have this marvelous creature in his life. Eli smiled at her now, and rubbed her nose. Cold, wet. Thank God, the dog recovered, and was healthy and strong. Belle butted her head against his leg. Then she made a quiet inquisitive sound, as if prodding him to carry on. Eli heaved a deep sigh.

"He saved my life, but he lied to me. And what am I supposed to do now?"

In response, Belle tilted her head, then made another small sound.

"Yes. He confessed to everything. Why? I still can't wrap my brain around it. He was my best friend."

She let out a long groan, and hung her shaggy head.

"It's the mystery we will never uncover, I'm afraid. And now, girl," he framed Belle's head with both hands, and searched her eyes, "I must get her back. But how?"

Daisy's favorite hat caught the dog's attention. Belle sniffed at it, then burrowed her nose deep into the material. After some time, she gazed up at him, barked once, and shook her head. Eli could swear he heard her saying 'are you really that obtuse?' Then she jumped to her feet, and moved to the door, where she paused and barked again, loud and stern-like.

"You want me to follow you, is that it? Okay."

Curious now, Eli grabbed Daisy's hat, unwilling to part with it even for a moment, and followed in Belle's footsteps. The dog bounced to the staircase, and soon brought him to the hidden door that led to his tower. She barked again, clearly ordering him to open it.

"Okay, girl. I hear you loud and clear." Eli mastered the hidden lock and opened the door. Belle bulleted in, then stopped before the elevator with her head cocked on a side. The message 'what are you waiting for? This elevator won't open by itself' was written all over her face.

Eli smiled at the dog's antics, then opened the elevator door and allowed Belle to precede him inside.

"All the way up?" He asked the dog, half-mocking.

Instead of a reply, Belle plopped her butt on the floor, all patience now, and stared at Eli as if he were a stupid human.

Once inside his tower office, Eli allowed her the lead. Why did she bring him here? What was on her mind? Belle didn't make him wait long. She went straight to the stone fireplace crafted as an open lion's mouth, put her nose inside, and barked a few times.

And then it hit him, the key! He asked Belle how he could bring Daisy back, and she brought him here, giving him the answer. The key was the only answer.

"Oh, my God, Belle. You are so right."

Eli reached inside the fireplace, felt around then grabbed the key to the grandfather clock.

The small brass item on his palm was heavy and cold to the touch. Such an innocuous, plain thing. Was it possible that it held the tremendous power of opening the curtain of time?

"Well, there is only one way to find out."

Belle gazed up at him. The silent question 'anything else I can help you with?' in her liquid brown eyes wasn't hard to interpret.

"No, girl. You helped enough. Now's my turn. I promise, she shall be back, our Daisy. Soon."

I hope.

Belle let out a deep sigh, then lolled her enormous tongue and seemed to smiled.

"Thank you, my girl. I will never forget it." He kissed the dog's cold wet snout, making her sneeze. In lieu of a response, she heaved her big body upward, put her front paws on his shoulders, and licked his face.

"Okay, alright." Eli endured one last mighty lick of dog's tongue, then chuckled, and stepped back. "Enough, Belle. I have preparations to make."

Impatient now, he moved with a purpose toward the door, and exited his office, the priceless key clutched in his hand. Daisy claimed she had found the key inside the clock, in its special place on the back panel no one knew about but him.

It was still a mystery to Eli how she managed to discover that hidden space. He was determined to solve it, among other things, as soon as he had a chance.

As soon as Daisy is back where she belonged.

Fortified by that thought, Eli descended the stairs. The peculiar hat with its golden embroidered letters *B&A* was still in his hand. To take it with him, or not?

After a moment of inner debate, he decided to leave it there, just in case something went awry.

Don't be a pessimist, Coleman. If a slip of a girl can do it twice, you'll manage just fine.

But still, he placed Daisy's favorite hat onto the newel post—for safe-keeping—and approached his family's most cherished heirloom, the old English grandfather clock.

CHAPTER THREE

N ika drove, unhurried and relaxed, through the historic downtown of Fernandina Beach. The quaint and picturesque section of town was her favorite. She was familiar with the history behind each building listed on the National Register of Historic Places. The downtown was unique not only because of its age and a charming small seaport village ambience, but also because it was forever and unapologetically suspended in the Victorian era. Thanks to Henry Flagler and his railroad venture, in 1890s all the wealthy tourists were drawn to the most southern parts of Florida state, bypassing Amelia Island. The result was a blessing in disguise. On one hand, the modern world ignored the tiny speck of a land, on the other—it left it untouched and unblemished, and as authentic as the day Jean Ribault stepped his foot on it in 1562.

Well, maybe not *that* much authentic, but close. To Nika, Amelia Island was a fairytale land forever locked in an enchanted time bubble.

A warm smile tweaked her lips at the little boy who skipped along the sidewalk, dressed as a pirate, and brandishing his tiny saber.

Was it any wonder she was fascinated with her hometown, its turbulent history, captivating beauty, free-spirited people? But most of all, she was in love with His Majesty, the ocean that ruled it all for ages.

Should she go to the office for a few hours? She had a ton of paperwork that needed her attention and gazillions of phone messages to sift through, not to mention emails that sat in her mailbox unattended for God knew how long. Nika braked, looked from the car window at the building that housed the offices of *Before & After, Inc.*, then pressed on the gas pedal, and drove away.

Tomorrow, I promise.

Tomorrow was soon enough to deal with paperwork, and messages and everything else, but not right now.

"I'll get to it tomorrow," she murmured under her breath.

Okay, Scarlett, and what'll change tomorrow?

Nika shrugged, and tried to ignore her inner bitch that always popped up when she was least welcomed.

"Tomorrow is another day."

And that highly scientific data is significant because...?

"Get lost, will you." Nika grumbled, turning into her driveway. Traffic was light, so she made it home quickly.

She had no heart to deal with anything right now, her inner bitchy self-included. Almost on autopilot she parked her truck in its space and noted the absence of Alex's car. She was home alone. Good. Because she really wasn't fit company right now. Detached, Nika climbed the stairs to the second story of the house she and her cousin owned together. The bluish-grey building sat on reinforced wooden stilts. Nika always thought of them as mythological Atlases, weightless and fanciful. Because of its hexagon shape, it was often called round. The main living space was on the second floor, whereas the first one was a huge five-car garage. The winding staircase hugged the house from both sides like two gigantic wings.

Thanks to the unique structure, both Alex and her had their own separate entrances and living quarters. Privacy was a commodity they both valued and respected. Was it because their childhoods lacked that precious commodity altogether? Maybe. Probably. But even though most often they spent their time in the company of each other, the privacy of their own space was precious and non-negotiable. It yielded only to freedom that both had fought for tooth and nail, and achieved by running away from home right after college.

Best friends since they were in diapers, Nika and Alex recognized early on that they were different from the rest of the Morris clan ruled by two mega rich, tyrannical fathers who happened to be identical twins.

Even as children, they embraced the 'black sheep of the family' status, and did everything possible, and sometimes impossible, to live up to its meaning, and the low expectations of others.

They were comfortable with each other even in silence. Familiar with their own quirks and pet peeves, they complimented each other's strengths and weaknesses.

They were best friends, confidants, and partners in a business they started from scratch in Fernandina Beach. Nine years since their secondhand car had broken down in the middle of the tiny town. Nine years as they found themselves, penniless, but free and happy, stranded on beautiful Amelia Island.

Those nine years seemed like nine minutes. Funny how time always affected her. When she was home on college breaks time crawled by. Yet all the years they'd been on the Island, time flew. Strange how time always seemed to pass to suit her mood.

Nika shrugged off her thoughts and opened the door then stepped inside. Now what should she do? Was she hungry? Did she want something to drink? Standing in the middle of the kitchen, motionless, she listened to the reassuring sounds of the house. The hum of the oversized fridge, the tick-tock of the wall clock, a murmur from the AC. Suddenly it all felt so out of place.

While working in the Coleman house, she had no time to think 'what's next.'

She had no time for anything except her unyielding determination to finish the project as soon as possible. No time to eat or sleep properly or wonder. No time, period.

Now, the restorations were over. She had all the time in the world on her hands. The avalanche of thoughts, memories, and feelings slammed into her, pressing, pushing, pulling, tearing her apart.

What's now? What's next?

No idea. She was dead sure that the solution was inside the Coleman house, and as soon as it was fully restored, she'd find it.

Stupid, so stupid!

She padded to the family room, then slumped onto the sofa. Her only wish right now was to curl into a small ball and sleep for ages.

Time's awasting!

So what? Who cares? Not the Coleman house. And not the stubborn moron who lived there. *Eli.*

All he had to do was put the damned key into its hiding place inside the grandfather clock. But did he do it? Oh, no! He was nursing his wounded pride, playing martyr, punishing her. William must have confessed. He must have found the key and told Eli everything. After all, the young man was honorable and loyal to Eli. He was probably scared out of his wits, too, seeing as she and Abby just puffed into a thin air and disappeared.

William couldn't lie about any of it. Even if the brunt of Eli's wrath was swift and horrible. William would never betray his friend.

So, why was it taking so long for Eli to figure the simple answer?

Maybe because he still didn't forgive you.

All this time? Was he really that mad at me?

Maybe he doesn't want you to come back.

Nika refused to consider that possibility.

"I will be back. I have proof."

A grave in the cemetery? So what? Maybe he found another Daisy.

"And how many Daisies ran around Fernandina circa 1909?" She fired back, repeating Alex's words from ten months ago.

No, she *did* return. One day, Nika will find her way to get back to the stubborn proud man she fell in love with a hundred and ten years ago. With or without his help, she'll be back, and then she'll give him a piece of her mind, and demand an explanation. She closed her fingers around his ring she wore on a chain.

"I swear I will be back, Eli Coleman, whether you forgave me or not. One day, I will look into your eyes, and ask you what the hell has taken you so long."

At last, exhaustion won the battle of wills. With her fingers wrapped tight around the pulsating ring, Nika drifted to sleep.

CHAPTER FOUR

The aroma hit him first. Freshly brewed coffee and something...yeasty and sweet like... pastries. Then the noises. Music and voices. So many voices... laughing, talking, barking...*Barking?*

Disoriented, lightheaded, Eli blinked a few times. His vision was blurred with a gray mist around the edges. He shut his eyes, pressed his fingers into the sockets, then open them again, trying to bring the scene before him into focus. The colors brightened, the wobbly images sharpened. Eli found himself standing. Just barely, he realized, because his legs were weak as two noodles. He was on a corner between two vaguely familiar buildings. He looked up. The sun was bearing down in the east. Not quite high in the sky so he figured it must still be morning. The temperature was comfortably warm for which he was grateful otherwise his wool 3-piece suit would have been unbearable.

Where am I?

Eli glanced around. The area looked familiar but in such a strange way: tall buildings, some kind of metal objects racing along the street, ladies in the strangest attire with their knees bare. He looked up again. The color of that special glorious Florida blue couldn't be mistaken for anything else.

But where in Florida? Eli squinted against the glare of sun, and turned to look at the nearby sign post. *Centre Street.* He must be in Fernandina.

Thank goodness.

The strange sounds drew his attention again, and again he wondered at the loud barking from all sides. Still unsteady, and with great care, Eli turned around.

A strong of people, some with some kind of a contraptions on wheels with little children strapped in, some with strange conical *things* they brought to their mouths and... *drank from?*

And almost all of them accompanied by dogs of various sizes. Even in buggies! *So many dogs!* No wonder so much barking was going around. Eli shook his foggy head in a poor attempt to clear it.

Unsteady, bewildered, he staggered backward on his wobbly legs. The utter embarrassment of his predicament knifed through his fuzzy brain.

Thunderation. A gentleman cannot become weak and lightheaded, no matter what!

Had he traveled through centuries? He was a grown man of four and thirty. He must behave according to his status. After all, he did manage to accomplish what he wished for: he jumped through time, and landed in Fernandina Beach somewhere in the future.

Weak as a babe, and scared. Eli cursed under his breath.

Yes, he admitted, he was a bit frightened. Okay, a lot frightened.

Take stock and decide on the course of action.

He already established he must be in Fernandina from the street sign and its cross street, but *when*? What day? What year? *What century?*

That's why Daisy was so muddleheaded at first, and acting in such a peculiar manner. She was scared from the tips of her painted toes to the end of her sunny ringlets. Eli curved his lips in a smile. If God was merciful, and he arrived at the right time and place, she was here, in this city, somewhere.

The knowledge warmed his heart, and multiplied his resolve. He was so close to his destination he could almost taste it.

Just please, God, let me be on time.

The thought that he may have arrived much later, and Daisy could be a married lady by now was unacceptable. But what about if she was an *old* lady? What if he landed in a much later period of her time? No. He shook his head and refused to think that.

Stay positive, Coleman. Concentrate on finding her, first and foremost.

That was the most important thing right now.

You won't accomplish that by standing and gazing around.

He had to move. *Do* something. Eli took a tentative step, and barely held himself from falling on his face. He gritted his teeth, and tried again. And failed.

If not for the iron bench nearby, his ass would have plopped down onto the paved street. Instead, he managed to fall onto the wrought-iron seat. He huffed a breath when his behind met the unyielding metal. Infuriated, Eli let out a set of rude curses.

A high-pitched barking from underneath the bench almost stopped his heart. He managed to suppress a yelp as he glanced down. The first thing he noticed was a tiny pink tongue. It was attached to the tiny creature with the furry long ears. That *thing* crawled from underneath the bench, the hairless body confronted Eli. The tiny black beady eyes were full of unabashed curiously. The odd thing—was it a dog? — jumped back, then took a couple of tentative steps forward, and cocked its funny, long-haired ears before giving a string of sonorous yelps. Yes, the creature was a dog, indeed. Even though it more resembled a rat.

"Hello, little fella."

Eli bent forward to pet the tiny dog, but his head revolted. He closed his eyes, and sat motionless for a moment waiting for the dizziness to pass. When the swirling behind his eyes stopped, Eli cracked a smile. The tiny peculiar creature held its ground, but started to shake from its hairy ears to its pointy tail.

"Don't be afraid, little fella, I won't hurt you."

He wanted to touch the dog, just to assure the brave little pipsqueak that he was not a threat to it, but that entailed bending forward. He tried that already, and look where it got him. Instead, Eli cautiously offered his hand to the dog to sniff at.

"He's not afraid, just curious."

A cheerful statement from somewhere behind him caught Eli off guard. More surprised than alert, he turned to face the owner of that piping tenor. The man was boyishly thin, almost slender, clad in some wide pants of undetermined color, pink shirt, and strange shoes with no tops and sturdy soles. What was they called? Oh, yes, sandals, a popular footwear in Greece and Japan. Obviously, they started to wear them in Florida too. Eli scanned the bare toes to the bright red hair of the newcomer. The fashion of hair must have undergone a revolution. How else would one explain such a bizarre style: long sweeping locks on top and shaved temples and nape? Fascinated, Eli finally dragged his eyes from the man's hair to his face. Long and thin as the rest of him, it was sporting a short reddish goatee and a huge innocent smile. But the cornflower-blue eyes were shrewd and direct. Their measured gaze was aimed at Eli.

"Aren't you, Maximilian?" The Red winked, and plopped his skinny behind on the bench across.

Eli frowned. He searched around for someone named Maximilian whose arrival he somehow missed. With a snort he realized Red was addressing the tiny dog.

"His name is...Maximilian?"

"Yep. And don't you make a mistake by calling him Max or Maxie. He gets insulted," Red whispered to Eli out of the corner of his mouth.

"I would not dream of it," Eli replied, amused despite his current predicament.

"Vic." Red offered his hand. "It's actually Victor, but I prefer Vic. Short and sweet, don't you think?" And he winked again, this time at Eli. "And you are, handsome?"

"Ahh..." Eli's jaw opened and closed, before he found his voice, "Elijah."
Handsome? Did this youth just call me handsome?

"Uh-oh, a mouthful." Red chuckled, and clapped his hands.

"I'll call you Eli. Yes, much better," he said, as if pleased with himself. "So, Maximilian," he glanced at the tiny dog, "come say hello to our new friend Eli."

The strange-looking creature scooted closer to Eli, sniffed at his trousers, and then jumped up, and landed on Eli's knees. Then it sat, and licked Eli's hand.

"Aww," Vic crooned, delighted, "he likes you! He really likes you!"

"Well, I like him, too."

Still not in a full command of all his faculties, Eli scratched the little fellow between his enormous furry ears. The dog purred, and closed his round buttons eyes in canine bliss.

"Are you a dog owner or just a dog lover?"

Vic crossed his legs, fluidly, propped his elbow on his knee and put his face on the palm of his right hand. He was a picture of a curious ginger cat.

"I have a dog. She's called Belle."

"Beautiful name. What breed is she? No, let me guess. A tall, dark, and quiet type like yourself will most likely to go for a... Great Dane? No, no, a Russian Borzoi, right? Am I right?"

"Almost." Eli cracked a smile. "I suppose, she could be all that, and then some."

"Pardon me?" Vic's ginger brows curved into elegant arches.

"A mutt. She's a mutt. The best breed there is."

"Hmm," Vic shifted his legs, changed his position, then declared, "You know what, Eli, you're so right."

"And what breed is Maximilian?" Eli really wanted to know, because he had never encounter a dog like this one.

"He's a Hairless Chinese Crested. Marvelous breed, if a bit high-strung. Beautiful, isn't he?"

Eli would probably choke before calling this dog *beautiful*, but the beauty was in the eye of a beholder for sure. And who would know better than him?

"He is really...unique."

Pleased, Vic smiled. His gaze, though, was speculative, guarded.

"Well, my new friend Eli, tell me how can I help you?"

It was Eli's turn to arch his brows.

"I beg your pardon?"

"You're new here, obviously. No offence, but you look... different." Vic pointed at Eli with a long, elegant index finger. "Suite, vest, tie. Wingtips. Beautiful shoes, by the way." He nodded at Eli's feet. "So, you're a new guy on the block. And as such, you're either looking for someone, or something." Vic smiled again, flashing his perfectly straight, white teeth. "Tell me what can I help you with? I know everybody around here."

Eli thought for a moment. Silly not to use help when it presented itself. After all, he really needed guidance on how to proceed.

Cautiously, buddy, very cautiously.

"I'm looking for someone. I'm looking for a lady."

"Of course you are." Vic sighed, then turned to address his dog, "I've never had a chance, Maximilian. Oh, well."

"I'm sorry, what?"

"Tall, dark and oh, so handsome," Vic murmured, sighing again. "Not a chance."

In the next instant, his mood shifted. Mischief danced in his eyes as he asked, "So, who is she, your lady? What's her name? Come on, tell Vic everything! As I said, I know everybody on this island."

"Everybody?"

"Absolutely! And if I don't recognize the name which I highly doubt, there are people who know people. And if that failed, there's always Google, but as the very last resort. You agree?"

"I... yes." He had no foggiest idea *who* was that *Google*, and *what* he just agreed to, but it was too late to backpedal.

"So?"

"So?"

"The name?"

"The name?" *Thunderation, I'm acting like a parrot. Or a fool.*

"The name of your lady?"

"Oh. Daisy. Miss Daisy Morris."

Vic knitted his ginger brows. "I know Nika Morris, but not Daisy."

"Nika!" His heart gave one heavy thump. *Of course!* She was called Nika here, or Veronika, named after her grandmother. "That is, Veronika Morris. You know of her?"

"Do we know *of her*, Maximilian?" Vic rolled his eyes dramatically. The funny dog gave two short yelps, and happily lolled his tiny tongue. "Not only do we know *of her*— we know her very well."

Eli's hackles soared.

"How well?"

Despite his deliberate attempt at nonchalance, he obviously failed, because Vic appeared to be surprised, then confused. Then he chuckled, and slapped Eli's knee in a playful fashion.

"Oh, goodness, Maximilian, I think Eli's jealous."

Am I that transparent? Thunderation.

"Relax, Eli. If anything, I'd like to know her cousin Alex *that* well, but..." He shrugged his bony shoulders, "Alex is straight as an arrow, if you get my drift."

And what the hell was that supposed to mean?

Absolutely befuddled now, Eli was afraid he lost the young man along with his drift.

"To each his own, I suppose. His loss." Vic shrugged again.

Eli didn't care at the moment about Alex, or Vic's grieving for him. All he cared about was finding the woman he loved, and discovering whether or not he was on time. Eli curbed his impatience. In a cool and polite manner, he addressed his new acquaintance, "Can you kindly tell me if Miss Daisy... if Miss Nika is presently in town?"

"You are in luck, my friend. Not only she's in town, she's presently in her office." Vic's his chin pointed toward the closest building to Eli's left. "Her car is on the parking lot. See that little jazzy number?"

"I beg your pardon?"

"No need. I mean, that sexy as hell cherry-red convertible. See?"

Eli glanced over. Some red contraption on four wheels...Automobile? But where was its roof? Was it a *jazzy number, sexy as hell, cherry-red convertible*?

What the hell was *he talking about?*

Eli shrugged it aside. Doesn't matter. What matters was that Daisy was here, just around the corner, just in the house next door. Impatient, excited, Eli stared at it, afraid to hope.

Was is possible? Am I going to see her soon? So, what are you waiting for? Go, man, just stand up and move.

Startled, Eli pulled out of his reverie.

Vic's head was tilted, and he stared at Eli.

"What? I apologize, did you ask something?"

"I asked, what do you need with our famous House Whisperer? Have a house to renovate?"

"Yes, precisely. A house."

Daisy was in the business of fixing houses with her cousin Alex. He decided to pretend to be a new client. After all, he did have a house, so it was not an outright lie.

"There are none better than our Nika," Vic agreed. "She just finished an enormously important project, the Coleman house. Have you heard of it?"

"What? What did you say?"

"The Coleman house. Oh, man, there is such a scrumptious history behind it, let me tell you. The rich and aloof owner, the beautiful sister who disappeared just before her wedding, the terrible dark secrets—the whole nine yards. The house was shut tight for a half century, after the last owner passed away, and the family moved out of state. And a really sad sight it was! Until our Nika. Rumors have it, she made it exactly as it was in its hey-day. I haven't seen it yet, but sure hope she would agree to give her old friend a private tour, before the good Senator from Massachusetts comes to claim his inheritance."

"What senator?"

A vague memory tried to push through his stupor. What was it, for goodness' sake? Something Daisy mentioned...something about his descendant who commissioned *Before & After, Inc.,* to restore his house. Who gave her the letter supposedly written by him. He had brushed it off then, and didn't take it seriously.

Was afraid to take it seriously.

"Senator Lauder," Vic's words cut into his reverie, "the descendant of our famous town citizen, the original owner of the house, Elijah Coleman."

The Coleman house. The senator. Vic and Maximilian.

All of a sudden, it was too much. Like he was dropped into another dimension. Or another world. Which, in a way, he was.

The trick was not to think about it.

Think about Daisy.

First order of things was Daisy. Eli focused at Vic.

"May I bother you with a question?"

"Sure, anything." The young man scooped his dog from Eli's knees. "You look kinda funny, my friend. Like you've seen a ghost."

You have no idea.

"What day is it?"

If Vic was surprised, he hid it well. Very seriously he answered: "Friday. November twentieth."

The relief was enormous. So, it was the right month, and the right day. He left home at the same day, November twentieth. Good. That was very fortunate.

Suspicious, Vic watched him in silence. Then he added: "Twenty-twenty."

"Twenty-twenty...as a..."

"As a year. 2020."

Hadn't Daisy told him she came from 2019? No problem. Maybe, he was mistaken. Just one year. It was such a small detail, after all. The main point was, he arrived at the *almost* right time, to the right place.

And Daisy was just around the corner.

Eli rose from the bench, unable to wait a minute longer. Pleased that his legs held steady at last, clearheaded and determined, he turn to his unusual companion.

"Thank you very much, Vic, for all your help and your pleasant company. I appreciate it greatly."

"Never mind that," Vic chuckled. "If someone helped, it was Maximilian. He found you, after all."

"Thank you, Maximilian." Working up a smile, Eli rubbed the tiny dog between his furry ears, which earned his hand another lick. "Well, I must be off."

"Tell Nika hi from us."

Despite his impatience, Eli stopped and turned to Vic once again.

"Where are my manners? I'm sorry, I didn't introduce myself. That was very rude of me, and I apologize." He nodded formally: "Elijah... Benjamin, industrialist, at your service."

On the spur of the moment, he decided to omit his surname. *Coleman* would ring the bell for sure, and that was the last thing he wanted. "I'm very pleased to make your acquaintance. Both of you."

"Industrialist, huh?"

"Yes. And you, sir?"

"Victor Malone, Esquire," Vic answered, mimicking Eli's formal way of introduction down to the head-nodding. Then he rose, and drew a small card out of his shirt pocket. "If you're ever in need of an attorney, Mr. Industrialist, I'm your guy."

"Attorney?" Eli blanched. For the life of him he couldn't reconcile the image of this peculiar red-haired boy with that of a man of law.

"Yep, a corporate attorney of Malone, Schroder & Smith." Vic chuckled, rather delighted than offended. "You should see the look on your face, my friend. Many a person made that mistake, but," he moved closer, picked an imaginary speck of lint from Eli's shoulder, and gazed at him with eyes as hard as crystals, "they lived to regret it. I promise you that."

Eli didn't doubt it for a second.

"I will never make such a regrettable mistake." Eli held Vic's stare as he pocketed the business card. "And if I ever in need of an attorney, I'll call on you, Mr. Malone."

After an imperceptible nod, the young man pointed to the building on his right.

"What are you waiting for, my friend Eli? Go, go." He made a shooing motion with his right hand while his left held tight to a squirming Maximilian. "Nika might pick up the next client, and leave you and your project waiting in line till next year."

His confusion was brief, until it hit him: house renovations. But of course. He told Vic he was looking for Daisy to renovate his imaginary house. He quite forgot about that fib. Annoyed with himself, because he hated any lies, even a necessary as this one, Eli nodded and lifted his hand, only to realize that in his haste he forgot his hat at home, in 1909. He nodded again, hatless and embarrassed, and then turned and walked toward the building where Daisy made her office.

"See you around, Mr. Industrialist," Vic called after him in lieu of a farewell.

"I highly doubt it," Eli murmured under his breath.

In the next second, he forgot all about the strange skinny man and his dog.

The door sign *Before& After, Inc.* was painted in bold gold letters. Eli took a moment to steady himself. Then he opened the door and walked inside.

CHAPTER FIVE

Nika slapped her pen against her desktop. She hated this part of her work: being cooped up in the office, answering emails, or, God forbid, returning phone calls.

Thank God, meeting with clients was Alex's job. She was able to handle some phone conversations, or an occasional Skype conference, but not face-to-face. No way, no how. Alex was much better at handling people, making them feel comfortable and relaxed. A superb conversationalist, he chatted easily with friends and strangers alike. It was some kind of a talent. Alex was friendly and easy-going, a likable guy, a people's person. Her? Not so much. She was friendly enough with those she knew and liked, but strangers? Nope. Never a diplomat, she could— and did, many times over—blurt something that offended people. And not because she was insensitive by nature, or rude, or mean. The thing was, Nika had zero tolerance for verbal pleasantries, a total waste of time, and preferred actions to words. Give her a distressed property any day, and she was in her private paradise. But to actually *talk* about it, or meet with the owner— and she was ready to pull her hair out. Literally.

She scowled at her computer, turned her gaze to the stack of sticky notes with the names of people whose calls she needed to return, and blew an irritated breath. Why did so many people insisted on contacting her? Why her, and not Alex? Why did she have to spend the best part of her morning answering emails and returning calls?

Annoyed at her cousin and the world in general, Nika plopped her feet up onto her desk, and looked at the ceiling. She was brooding, and bored out of her mind.

And deflated. And, yes, irritated, dammit!

What was taking Eli so long?

Didn't he realize she was on the brink of her patience? Maybe, while she was sitting here, he already put the key inside the clock? Maybe, it was already there, waiting for her? Another run to the Coleman house was a must. Just in case.

You checked it this morning, and it wasn't there.

"So, I'll check it again, and again, and again," she muttered stubbornly.

And after you turn the house back to the Senator? How will you manage it?

"I'll think of something."

Well, think fast, because you're almost out of time.

"Don't harp. I have time yet."

Just two and a half days, but still.

Unable to sit and wait a minute longer, she swung her legs from the desk, and jumped from the chair. In her haste, she struck the coffee cup with her elbow. As Murphy Law would have it, that stupid cup hit the floor with a sickening noise, and broke into a million pieces.

Be grateful it was empty.

"Dammit!" That's all she needed. What did *Verochka* say? China breaks for luck. Nika hoped her grandmother was right, because she was fresh out of that commodity for the long stretch. She figured she was well overdue. With a deep growl, Nika bent and started picking up the bigger pieces, careful not to cut herself.

The smaller shards were trickier. They spread all over the floor, and emitted an irritating crunching sound whenever Nika stepped on them.

Clumsy idiot.

She could already have been on her way to the Coleman house, but no! She just has to jump and break the stupid cup into a gazillion stupid pieces. Nika grabbed the portable Vacuum cleaner from her tiny closet. That thing was small, but powerful, and sucked the mess off with the force of a tornado. Done. Nika was in a process of checking the floor for the leftover shards, when her intercom buzzed.

"Jeez, just leave me alone!"

Cursing the inanimate object was a waste of time and energy. Nika indulged anyway. When she ran out of curse words, she pushed the intercom button.

"Yes, what?"

"Ah, Ms. Morris? There is someone in the lobby wishing to see you."

Their secretary's voice was all business, which means that whoever just came in through the door was a stranger, a walk-in without a prior appointment. On top of it, Sue called Nika 'Ms. Morris', that only confirmed the fact.

"Sue, I'm ready to head out. Can Alex handle it?"

"Ah, this gentleman asked for you specifically, and insists on seeing you."

"Insists?"

"That is correct, Ms. Morris."

"A gentleman?"

"Affirmative."

Affirmative?

There was something in Sue's voice and her careful pronunciation of every word that made Nika's hackles go up.

"Sue? What's going on?" Maybe, some sicko came in, carrying a gun, and Sue was trying to convey some urgent message to Nika. "Is he threatening you? Is it a robber? Should I call the police?"

"No! God, no," Sue exclaimed, then lowered her voice, "He's just looking kind of...unusual, and he asked to see you. Very politely, but firmly. He called you 'Ms. Veronika Morris'."

What the heck?

"Unusual? How do you mean?"

"Well, he's wearing black suit with vest and tie," Sue whispered, obviously careful not to be overheard. "And you should hear his voice. Deep and rich like an opera singer."

Chills started to run up and down Nika's spine. Only one man had a voice like that.

"What...what does he look like?" Her own voice was now a hoarse whisper.

"Tall, very tall," Sue replied. "Even taller than Alex. Black gorgeous hair, pale grey eyes, deep cleft in his chin."

Nika was running before her brain had a chance to catch up. Her mad dash from the second-floor office to the lobby took no more than a few seconds. But even that seemed an eternity.

"W-where is h-he?" Breathless from the run, shaking from hope and fright—God, what if she was mistaken— Nika rounded on Sue.

"Mr. Benjamin is waiting for you, Ms. Morris."

Seated behind the counter, all business, with her no-nonsense up-do and thick framed glasses, Sue gestured to the row of chairs in the lobby. Her eyes behind the lenses, however, were sparkling and alight with excitement. She rolled them at Nika, then batted her lashes. If Nika wouldn't be so wound up, she'd have laughed.

And then it hit her: *Mr. Benjamin.* Disappointment swept through her like a tidal wave. She was mistaken, after all.

And what did you expect? A miracle?

With a sinking feeling, Nika turned her head, and looked in the direction Sue pointed.

Her heart stopped. Her vision blurred. Everything dimmed.

Then, in a flash, all her senses snapped back. Her heartbeat drummed against her ribcage like a trapped bird, desperate to escape.

No, she was not mistaken. Eli Coleman, all six feet-five gorgeous inches of him, stood in her lobby, larger than life, and more handsome than any man had a right to be. The love of her life, the center of her universe. The miracle she was afraid to believe in. *He was here.*

Instead of placing the key inside the clock, he made a journey through time by himself, coming for her. Her heart trembled.

The bravest, honorable, incredible man. Was it any wonder she was so in love with him? Overwhelmed, Nika stared at him, afraid to believe, unable to tear her eyes away.

The stubborn, irritating, indolent moron!

A sudden blast of anger burst the bubble of her euphoria. Enraged, Nika marched up to Eli, and hit him in the chest. Her fists pelleted his broad torso again and again and again, until she was breathless.

"What took you so long?"

Then she started to cry.

Eli hadn't expected this reaction.

He had no idea what he expected from Daisy, but definitely not this.

The maddening wench.

She hit him—actually hit him—and quite painfully too, and then she dissolved in tears. If the first action was shocking, the second simply unmanned him. Eli never saw Daisy cry, not even when she was pretending to be a boy, afraid and lost and totally alone in his time, where everything and everybody was unfamiliar and alien. And yes, unfriendly.

His brave little bride, the one that was always standing up to him, challenging him, calling him names and accusing him of tyranny and God knows what else, was now weeping her heart out. Because of him. Was she mad at him? She clearly was. But why? Was she so unhappy with his arrival? Did she really hope to escape from him for good? Has she fallen out of love with him?

Stop it.

Easier said than have to obey his own command. He reminded himself that Daisy was not a shy sort. If she was unhappy, and didn't love him anymore, she would tell him. As soon as she stopped crying, and was able to carry out a simple conversation that is. She was so miserable, so broken to pieces, Eli couldn't bear it.

Thunderation.

Hurting for her, cursing under his breath, he scooped Daisy off her feet, cradling her against his chest. Even if she no longer loved him, he could give her the simple comfort of a friend.

Friend, my ass.

"Here, here, *ma petite*, don't cry." He kissed the top of her head, which made her cry even harder. Helpless, Eli crooned to her, all the while his own heart was breaking from guilt and grief.

The older woman who manned the office offered a glass of water, pointing to Daisy. Eli shook his head, but mimicked his thanks. She stepped back, but hovered nearby, concerned and frowning. He dismissed her, and concentrated on his precious charge. She was so tiny in his arms, fragile and lighter than a feather.

Goddamit, she lost weight.

At last, Daisy quieted in his arms. Eli let go of his breath, and relaxed a bit. But his tranquility was short-lived.

"What's going on here?"

The newcomer was tall, bald as an egg, and sported a deep scowl that put Eli on immediate alert.

"Alex, thank God!" The exclamation came from the older woman. "I didn't know what to do, so I buzzed you."

So, this is Alex, Daisy's cousin.

Daisy hiccupped, and made an attempt to disengage herself from his arms, but Eli tightened his grip.

"Nika? What the hell?"

The bald man marched forward, all the while glaring at him.

"Who the hell are you, and why are you holding my cousin? And why is she crying? Nika never cries. What did you do? And, I repeat, who the *hell* are you?"

"Alex, stop," Daisy managed to turn sideways inside the tight circle of Eli's arms. "I'm okay, and he didn't do anything. Well, except popping up. *Finally.*"

The last word was addressed to Eli, accompanied by a sizzling glare.

He noticed Daisy used a gentler tone of voice with her cousin than with him. Oh, yes, she was definitely angry at him. The million-dollar question was, what exactly for?

"Why are you so angry at me, *ma petite*?" He must learn the truth, or go mad. What could he do, being centuries away, to make her so vexed with him?

Uncovering this mystery took a precedence to everything. Eli dismissed the unwelcomed audience of the female secretary, and Daisy's cousin.

"Why am I angry? Oh, that's just so rich, Coleman!"

CHAPTER SIX

C*oleman?* Alex blinked. So, that was the famous Elijah Coleman.
Unsure of what he was feeling—shock? amazement? —Alex
studied the man he never met but knew and heard so much about. He
harbored mix feelings about Coleman. On one hand, he was a local hero,
almost a legend, a most prominent and admired citizen of Fernandina Beach
of the last century.

On the other, he made two women very dear to Alex miserable. In Nika's
case he couldn't blame the man. It wasn't Coleman's fault Nika decided to
visit her family and lost the key in a process. In Abby's situation the rat
bastard was guilty as charged, and then some.

Alex frowned, then came out of his reverie when he realized that Sue
tapped him on the shoulder.

"Sorry, what?"

"I said, do you know him? I mean, he looks so distinguished and polite,
but then..." She pointed at Nika who was still enclosed in the man's arms. "I
wanted to call the police, then decided to call you first."

"You did the right thing, Sue, and yes, I know him. Don't worry,
everything is fine. Nika's just...overjoyed."

A quick glance at his cousin contradicted his statement. Overjoyed she
looked not. As a matter of fact, his cousin was so mad she was about to
explode. By the wary expression on Coleman's face, he had figured it out, too.

That's my girl.

But Sue was unconvinced.

"Oh, so you mean she hit him because she was happy to see him?"

"She hit him?" He couldn't be prouder of Nika. Grinning, Alex silently
cheered her on. *Give him hell, baby.*

"Yes, several times. Then she started to cry. Nika never cries."

"Don't worry. He's, ah... a long-lost relative. It's kinda complicated."

Yeah, the understatement of the century.

And how to explain it all to Sue without spooking her? To tell her the truth was out of the question, because she'd think, and rightfully so, that both her bosses went bonkers. To lie was against all his beliefs and ethics. "You know what? Why don't you go home?"

"But...but it's not even lunchtime."

"It's okay, we're obviously won't do anything productive today." He pointed at Nika and Eli. "Consider it your afternoon off. With pay."

"Well, if you're sure." Sue flashed a quick glance at the pair nearby. "Okay. Thanks, boss." With an uncertain smile, she swept her purse from the bottom desk drawer. "Oh, one more thing. He said his name was Benjamin, Mr. Benjamin. But Nika just called him Coleman. Strange, isn't it?"

As soon as door closed behind her, Alex turned his attention back to the couple.

Mr. Benjamin, huh? Interesting.

A loud argument interrupted his musings. It seemed that his cousin was on a roll.

Alex chuckled, folded his hands over his chest, leaned against the doorjamb ready to be entertained.

"I'm mad! I'm so pissed at you, Coleman."

"But why?"

"Why? You're asking why? Can't you think of a single reason?"

"I wouldn't ask if I could. If someone should be mad, it is me."

"Oh, really? And why is that?"

"Because you left! You just went behind my back and left!"

"William knew everything. He helped me. He gave me the key. He knew I was coming back, but then Abby...and the key...and..." Nika's exasperated breath accompanied her hands wind-milling gesture. "Oh, let me down, will you? I can't argue with you like that."

"Like what?"

"Like...like...Just put me down already."

About to comply, Eli stopped in mid-motion and gasped:

"Dear Lord! What did you do to your hair?"

"I..." Nika touched her hair. "I treated it with keratin."

Alex grinned. His cousin obviously forgot about her latest trip to a salon. As the result, Nika was presently sporting a neat bob. Classy, sleek, and beautifully straight. Alex hated it. He missed her messy mop, and couldn't wait until she washed away all that classy sleekness.

"Well, un-treat them, because I don't like it!"

Alex reared up at Eli's outcry of indignation.

The nerve of the bastard.

"Well, I do." Nika all but spat it. "And that's all that counts." She squirmed, and pushed against Coleman's chest, to no avail. "Oh, for goodness' sake, put me down this instant."

"Daisy."

"Eli."

They glared at each other.

Alex had enough.

Time to butt in, or they'll argue until the next century.

His cousin was stubborn as a thousand mules. Coleman proved to be a good match in that department. Whistling or clapping? Alex settled on the latter.

"Children, children. That's enough. Time out."

Two faces with the identical expressions of exasperation turned in unison.

Coleman came to his senses first. Stiff and aloof, he inclined his head.

"I apologize for this unfortunate scene, sir, and for disturbing your place of business. Daisy and I will take our leave immediately."

"We will?" Nika rounded on him. Her eyes narrowed to slits. "Says who?"

"Daisy, be reasonable. We need to return back home."

"I don't know about you, Coleman, but my home is right here."

"You home is by my side, woman! And nowhere else." He glared at her. "I came to fetch you and bring you back where you belong."

Alex rubbed the top of his head. As much as it galled him, this round went to Eli. Even though his teeth were grinded to a powder by now, Coleman still managed to hold his temper. The sheer will of the man was admirable. Nika could tempt a saint. Who should know better than him?

"*Woman? By your side?* Huh! Came to *fetch* me, did you? You weren't in a hurry to do that for more than a year. Fourteen months, Coleman! What made you decide to 'fetch' me after all this time, all of a sudden?"

"What are you taking about? I came as soon as I learned the truth, two weeks after your disappearance."

"What?" Still suspended in Eli's hands, Nika blinked, then stammered, "W-what?"

"Fourteen days." Eli repeated, "it's been fourteen hellish days since I returned home and found you and Abby gone."

"F-fourteen *days?*"

"That's what I said."

"Oh, God! Oh, my God."

When Nika's fist banged against her forehead for the third time, Alex decided he had to do something. Eli's hands were occupied, so it was up to him to stop her from damaging permanently that stubborn noggin she called a head.

He feigned a loud cough.

"In case you forgot—again—I'm still here."

"Alex," Nika's eyes were filled with misery, "it's been just fourteen days there!"

"Yeah, I got it, Cuz."

Time moved differently, here and there. He was afraid of that. Afraid that it was fourteen *years* there comparing to fourteen months here. But apparently it was reverse. Fourteen month here equal fourteen days there. Somehow, it made it even worse.

Son of a bitch.

Apparently Nika came to the same conclusion.

"Just fourteen fucking days, Alex! Can you believe this shit?"

Eli's jaw dropped. "Daisy! Such inappropriate language!"

Alex barely suppressed his chuckle. Yeah, that Coleman was a gentleman, alright. Even at a crazy time like this, he was worried about proprieties.

"Shut up. I'm having a revelation moment here."

"You can have it without using dirty words, young lady. Although, you are not a lady, and I told you so many a time."

But despite his stern lecture, his eyes were full of such naked tenderness, that Alex swallowed his angry retort. It was clear as day that the guy was crazy about his cousin. Crazy enough to jump through time to find her.

"I like him, Nika. Sort of." *And I would like him even more, if not for Abby.* "He's something, alright."

"*He* is standing right here, and can hear you."

Coleman's reply was cold enough to freeze blood.

"Fair enough." The rebuke was well deserved. "Well, put her down, and let's make the formal introductions."

Being on his own turf gave Alex an advantage, plus he couldn't blame the man. The welcome he got from his bride, from both of them, sucked. *Verochka* would be outraged. Alex stepped forward and offered his hand. "Alexander Morris, Nika's cousin, and business partner. You can call me Alex."

After glancing at his outstretched hand, Coleman gently positioned Nika on her feet.

"Elijah Benjamin Coleman, Daisy's groom, soon to be husband. You can call me Eli."

He accepted Alex's hand with a firm clasp.

They pumped hands for quite some time, and by the grimace on Eli's face, Nika gathered that Alex's squeeze was brutal. Intentionally so. A sarcastic smile played on his face, but his eyes shot fire. Eli's face remained expressionless during this silent exchange, except that first initial grimace. Calm and unruffled, he stared back at Alex, more surprised that angry.

Why was Alex acting like a jerk? Was he deliberately baiting Eli?

Men! Time to put a stop to their foolishness.

"If you two finished comparing your dicks," Nika said primly. "Then may I suggest closing this joint and going home? We have a lot to talk about."

"I told you once, and I'm repeating again, you are not a lady, Daisy," Eli replied, but his eyes were glued to Alex's face.

"Hey, watch it, pal. You're talking to my cousin here."

"I'm talking to my bride here, *pal*. And in case it has slipped your attention, she is not a proper, traditional lady. Thank the merciful Lord."

CHAPTER SEVEN

"So, that's your home."

A symphony of emotions—curiosity, astonishment, bewilderment—played across Eli's face. Nika could only imagine what passed through his mind at seeing the modern structure, especially her hexagon mini mansion. Nika pressed her lips tight as the image of his expression popped into her mind. She knew she shouldn't laugh. After all, Eli had never seen Jaguars, Ferraris, or other luxury vehicles. Of course, her driving twenty miles over the speed limit didn't help his confidence. Served him right, the domineering bastard.

And it came on top of his first experience of driving in a modern car through the twenty-first century version of the city he called home once upon a time, no less.

Nika reached over to tap on her favorite smooth jazz station. She glanced at Eli, and realized he would never handle music, let alone jazz, coming from a dashboard. She drew her hand back to the steering wheel. Time enough to introduce him to her modern society.

Eli's befuddled expression during the short trip told the whole story. He failed to recognize his own hometown. No surprise there. The city had changed. Maybe not drastically. It still maintained the flavor and charm of a small Victorian village. No matter how stubbornly it clung to traditions, progress and time take over.

I wonder what he thinks, what he feels.

For a reason she couldn't explain she wanted him to like her version of their hometown. It was imperative to her.

Nika was quiet during their drive, allowing Eli to absorb everything on his own, to sort his conflicting emotions. To steady himself.

Who could understand his turmoil better than her? Just a year ago, she was in the same situation, so to speak, confused and baffled by Fernandina Beach circa 1909.

It was an experience she would never forget.

The perception of looking at the familiar images through the distorted glasses was eerie. Everything was dim and opaque, and out of focus. Like a comparison of a modern digital picture and daguerreotype of the same object. The recollection was disturbing even after all this time.

Was it like that for Eli, only in reverse? Did everything feel brighter, sharper, more vivid? It could be daunting, even intimidating. And definitely unsettling.

But most overwhelming was fear. No, Nika corrected herself. She hadn't felt so much *afraid* as totally and abysmally alone. And lost like Alice in a parallel universe of her own version of Wonderland. She shuddered, and stole a quick glance at Eli. No matter how confused he was, he was not lost like she was then.

Unlike hers, his trip here was intentional, and carried a specific purpose.

Granted, it's not like she stepped inside the Coleman house a year ago without specific intention or purpose, but her single goal was preliminary inspections. That's all. Instead, she ended up being thrown back to the last century by the trick of the grandfather clock. Or the whim of the Universe.

Sprawled in a middle of a dirt road, winded and confused, trying to catch her breath, when a monster of a black stallion almost trampled her.

And then its rider, enraged and mortified, yelling, manhandling her, calling her a 'pile of rags,' and an 'imbecile boy.'

Blindsided and dumbfounded, Nika was mesmerized by the pair of them. The horse and the rider were so much alike, both dark, huge, and impossibly beautiful.

That was the first time she laid eyes on Elijah Coleman.

Then Abby came along, shaming her older brother for scaring the 'poor little thing,' comforting Nika, taking 'the boy' under her wing.

The next thing she remembered was waking up in a beautiful, unfamiliar room, tended by the funny little man she had mistaken for Santa Claus.

Doc Schmidt, the family physician to the almighty Carnegies, was the first person who uncovered her real gender, but true to his word, he kept it in secret.

Oh, the confusion of those first days!

A smile tugged at Nika's lips as a tiny ping of nostalgia stirred her memories.

True, it was easy now to think about it with humor and amusement, but then...

Then, and for quite some time, she was afraid for her sanity. And her safety.

One thing led to another, and soon she was living in the Coleman household, accepted as the 'boy who dropped out of the blue sky.'

She didn't remember when she had fallen in love with the aloof and infuriating owner of the Coleman house. From the very first moment? Probably. But loved him she did. Desperately, helplessly. Absolutely.

She never felt that way before, didn't know that it was possible. Or that she could.

Her whole life split on before and after, and no, her company name had no relevance whatsoever. Eli was her destiny, her timeless miracle, her one and only.

And he jumped through time for you.

It was still hard to believe that he was here; that she could simply touch him, hear his voice, smell his unique scent.

Fourteen impossibly long months she had waited for this moment, longed for it, dreamt of it. Gazillions of different scenarios played in her mind. Agonizing over it, she practiced every word, every expression, every glance.

But when her most sacred dream finally came true, she panicked.

No, you chocked on it. You fumbled, and you chocked.

Yeah, I did.

Look at you, reluctant, hesitant, unsure. Coward.

Her inner bitch was brutal, almost vicious. But she was right.

As crazy as it sounded, despite all her scenarios, Nika found herself unprepared.

Emotionally, mentally. Even physically.

She wished Alex was here to play a buffer. Her ever-considerate cousin opted out of the reunion, allowing Eli and Nika privacy.

Tongue-tied like a schoolgirl on her first date, uncomfortable and uneasy, Nika struggled for composure, all the while watching Eli.

He stood nearby, proudly erect, unfazed, and calmly surveyed her home. The funny and most ridiculous thing was, even dressed in his old-fashioned clothes, he fit right in. His commanding stance and domineering presence was as obvious as ever.

If he was unsettled in any way, it wasn't visible. Tall and absurdly handsome, he managed to look right at home in her time and place. As if he belonged here.

For some reason it irritated the hell out of her, even as her heart melted at the sight of him.

You are a complete nut job, girl.

Look who's talking.

At least I know my loonies from my toonies. Do you?

Shut up.

Eli's gaze trailed up, then paused on the wooded stilts.

"Clever," he muttered under his breath.

Despite everything, he found himself to be genuinely curious about Daisy's home. What a marvelous structure! It was unique, peculiar looking, and mindboggling. Like everything else today.

I'll be darn. The sheer power of a progress in unbelievable.

"What material is that?" He pointed a well-manicured finger toward the stilts.

"Reinforced wood."

"And the staircase?"

"Concrete."

"Huh."

The second floor was fluid and appeared to be weightless. The engineer in him was mesmerized.

"Amazing. Simply amazing. Did you build it?"

"No, we bought it, but made a few adjustments."

If Daisy was annoyed at his endless questions, she didn't let it show.

"What's there?"

"A garage."

Garage? His expression might have been as blank as his thoughts, because Daisy made a point to clarify the word. "We keep our cars in there. It's like a stable, only for...automobiles."

Automobiles? Plural?

"How many do you own?"

"I have two. Alex has one car and a bike—motorcycle. And when *Verochka,* that's our grandmother, visits, she sometimes uses a rental car. So, do the math."

"Your grandmother can operate an automobile?"

CHAPTER EIGHT

Wide-eyed, Eli gaped at her. For the past couple of hours, this perpetual bewilderment had become his normal facial expression. It was kinda cute.

"My grandmother can fly an airplane, so a car is child's play."

"You are jesting!" After a long stare, he concluded, "You are not, are you?"

She shook her head.

"Now I know who you take after in your family."

His quiet voice, that deep baritone she remembered so well, sent shivers down her spine.

"I wish." Despite her turmoil, Nika found herself grinning. "*Verochka* is simply amazing."

"So are you," Eli answered matter-of-factly, then, before she even grasped the meaning of his last words, he turned his attention back to the house.

Like she wasn't even here, like the most important thing, after jumping forward a century, was to learn about her house. That irked.

"How many people are living under this roof?"

Damn it, the man could try the patience of a saint.

"Just the two of us. Well, three now."

He rubbed his chin. And the gesture was so dear and familiar, Nika's heart squeezed. More than anything she wished to touch him, to dip her finger into that adorable cleft, and then to kiss it.

Well, what's stopping you? Here he is, in all his glory. Just make the first step.

I can't.

Why ever not?

Just...can't.

Coward.

She had no explanation why she was reluctant to take that first step. Mad at herself, unsure and unsettled, Nika cursed under her breath.

I'm not a coward.

Prove it.

Without notice Eli's demeanor changed. His posture became stiff as concrete, his eyes frosted over, his hands balled into fists.

Jeez, what was that all about? The mystery was solved as soon as Eli asked his next question:

"Three? Has Alex married recently?"

"No."

Son of a bitch. Will he dare to ask?

"And...you?"

He dared indeed. *The bastard!*

Nika allowed herself a moment to breath, to settle. To calm down. If he was behaving like an adolescent jerk, it was not a reason for her to—

Oh, the hell with that!

"If you can ask me that question, Coleman," she managed through clenched teeth, "then you're not only an ass, you're a stupid bastard, a conceited dickhead, a total shit, and a fucking moron!"

Her impressive vocal crescendo would have made an opera diva green with envy.

Eli let go the breath he held. So, nothing had changed in Daisy's personal life.

Thank God.

Even though it was more than a year she had lived in her time, she was still alone. And when he mentioned her marital status, she almost bit his head off. So, she must still love him. That's all he needed to know. She called him a *fucking moron*. With an enormous effort Eli swallowed his chuckle. He must be really demented if her cursed words sounded like music to his ears. But the bothersome thought, the very same one that prompted his unfortunate question, remained: *why wasn't she wearing her engagement ring?*

That was the first thing he noticed about her. No, Eli corrected himself, the first thing was her hair, that shiny, slick, disgusting hairdo that replaced his favorite curls. The ring was the second thing he noticed. But there was time to find out about it. As soon as he satisfied his curiosity about her living arrangements. After all, *someone* besides her and Alex lived here.

"Then who's the third person living here? Your grandmother?"

"My grandmother owns more properties around the world than you have fingers on both hands," she retorted with a glare. "She doesn't live permanently anywhere. She's a travel junky."

Huh. Whatever that means.

She wanted him to play a guessing game? Infuriating female.

But then Daisy drew in a breath that seemed to calm her, and replied, "Your sister, Abby lives here, too."

If Daisy expected some sort of a reaction from him, she was doomed to disappointment. Eli kept his gaze straight, his expression intentionally blank. It cost him greatly, more than he was willing to admit.

But no one was allowed to know the fury building inside him.

Not even Daisy.

After what seemed like an eternity, Eli finally asked, "How is she?"

"She is happy. She's okay. Healthy. Now."

She didn't meat to alert him, but her tone of voice, or choice of words, grabbed his attention. Eli's brows knitted in silent question. Dammit, she knew that look.

"Maybe we'd better go up inside."

Without a second glance at him, Nika turned toward the staircase.

Already inside, Eli focused his full attention on her, without even the cursory glance at his surroundings.

"My sister, Daisy. Is she alright?"

Nika took her time to deposit the keys on the counter, and drop her purse on the chair.

"You are stalling."

Yes, she was. Well, she better tell him the truth.

"Abby was very ill, Eli. She's fine now, but it was serious. Very serious."

His face darkened, but his troubled eyes never left her face. Only once she witnessed that mutinous expression on Eli's face: when he thought that he hurt 'the boy' sprawled in the middle of the dirty road.

He blamed himself, even though it wasn't his fault. Not then, and not now.

But try to explain that to the man who carried the world on his shoulders.

Go to him, you idiot. A simple hug of comfort wouldn't hurt you.

But still she hesitated. Something stopped her. Maybe, the closed off expression on his face, or the silver glint in his eyes.

Nika cleared her throat.

"You see, we had a pandemic throughout the world. Corona virus, or COVID. Millions of people died. So much loss. So much suffering."

Her voice broke. It all was still too fresh, too painful, too cruel. *Incomprehensible.*

After a long moment, the horrific images etched into her memory faded, leaving her shaky. They were still sneaking up upon her when she least expected it. Less often now, but still.

"Abby was in the hospital, the same that you built and donated to the city long ago. In a way, you helped to save your sister, along with the doctors and nurses. She's strong, resilient, and stubborn, just like her older brother."

Nika tried to smile, but her lips trembled. "And Abby is young. That all played in her favor. She recovered, thank God, and is totally healthy now. You don't have to worry."

Her tremulous smile died as soon as she heard his sharp, cold reply, "That's settles it. I'm taking Abigail back with me."

Nika's hackled soared. She slammed her hand onto her hips. "You and what army?"

"I beg your pardon?"

"Stuff it, Coleman. I'm taking Abigail back! Listen to yourself. Do you ever learn?"

Old resentment boiled over, dredging up the bitter taste of all their previous arguments. Obviously, nothing had changed since she left the Coleman house circa 1909. Eli still had the same attitude where Abby was concern.

He's taking Abby back. Ha! We'll see about that.

Nika was smart enough to know with a man like Coleman anger would get her nowhere. It was a sure way to aggravate him further. As much as she hated it, her best course of action was to retreat.

Patience, Nika. Patience.

She clamped her jaw, and took a deep breath.

"Your sister is healed and healthy as a horse, Eli. And she's really lucky because my grandmother appointed herself as her guardian angel. Abby had all the care in the world."

"That's beside the point—"

That does it.

Her patience snapped like a dry twig.

"That precisely *is* the point, Coleman! She's healthy, she's happy, and she has people who care about her. It might surprise you, but your baby sister is a force to be recon with. And my *Verochka*..." Nika's snort accompanied by the eye roll was deliberately rude, "let's just say, two of them together? You have no chance in hell to do anything they don't want you to."

"We'll see about that," Eli countered coolly. "Where is she? Please call her down this instant. I want to see for myself that Abigail's unharmed and well."

"She's not here, so I can't call her *down*, but I can arrange for you to see and talk to her via Skype."

"What— or should I ask who— in blue blazes is this *Skype*? And what do you mean, she's not here? You told me she lives here. Where is my sister, Daisy?"

"Skype is 'what', not 'who', and it's..." *What?* How on earth to describe in layman's term the miracle of a modern technology to a guy that considered a horse the best mode of transportation? Nika let out an exasperated breath.

"I'll explain it later. And Abby? She's where she always wanted to be: in Paris."

"Paris? As in France?"

"Congratulations, Coleman, you know your geography. Yes, Paris, France."

"Don't mock me, Daisy. I'm on the very brink of my patience as it is!"

His already disheveled hair was subjected to a rough finger-rake.

"What the hell is Abby doing in Paris? And why did you let her go alone?"

Take a deep breath, Nika, count to five, then let it out. Slowly.

"Eli, please pay attention, because I'm going to tell this only once. Your sister's in Paris, because the whole point of her running away from home was to go to France. She's an artist, in case you forgot, a very talented one, and she's quite determined to make a name for herself. I'm not finished!" Nika barked when Eli opened his mouth to reply.

"Abby is a free human being," she continued, "an independent woman, so no one can *let* her do— or don't do— anything. She decides for herself. Got it?"

"She's barely twenty years old."

"Surprise! She turned twenty-one, so she's of legal age in this and your century. You forgot, yet again, Coleman, that more than a year passed *here* while you spent just fourteen short days *there*, doing nothing, absolutely not a fucking thing to fix this mistake."

"And what mistake would that be, pray tell?"

CHAPTER NINE

Quite irritated and yes, damn it, hurt, Eli barely contained his temper.

It galled him that Daisy was right. Abby was of legal age to do what she pleased, especially in this unbelievable, amazing time she lived in now.

It grated on his nerves, and his conscience, even though it was not his fault that time had such a peculiar way of *flowing*. How could he possibly know that fourteen days in his time could equate to fourteen *months* in here?!

Dear God!

How did Daisy manage it? How did she survive? He would lose his mind for sure. He almost did. She must be stronger than him. He admired her for that. But it irked him that she blamed him for twiddling his thumbs, doing nothing. He almost died. If not for Belle...

But her next words stopped him cold.

"The lost key! Instead of putting it in its hidden place inside the grandfather clock so I can find it and return, you were nursing your wounded pride, punishing me!"

Unbelievable!

Insulted, Eli lost the tenuous grip on his famous control, and exploded, "I did nothing of the sort! How can you even think that?"

"What was I supposed to think?"

"Anything, but this."

Somehow, they ended up nose-to-nose, glaring and yelling at each other.

Eli was first to recover. They would accomplish nothing by continuing this argument, except wounding each other deeper. They both needed to calm down, and talk. In a civilized manner. But God, it was so hard to keep his composure when the woman he loved thought so little of him. After everything they had been through.

The insufferable creature.

CHAPTER TEN

"Let us just be clear. You thought that I was intentionally withdrawing that blasted key so you could not return."

It wasn't a question.

Unsure and uneasy, Nika clenched her hands, praying she didn't squirm. "Yes."

Eli held her gaze, his disappointment and hurt almost palpable.

Nika flinched. Ashamed. She wished to take back her angry words, but the damage was done. His pain cut deep like it was her own.

"What was I supposed to think?"

Her desperate cry went unanswered. Silence grew, oppressive, overwhelming. Those few feet that separated them stretched and spread, until it became a chasm.

What the hell are you waiting for, Nika-Daisy?

That inner voice Nika was cursed—or blessed with—screamed in her head, snapping her back to reality.

Your silence will accomplish nothing! You need to talk. Now.

"Do you have any idea what it did to me? The guilt? The remorse? The fear of never seeing you again? I felt so...so helpless. It broke me to pieces. I wanted to die. If not for Alex, and the Coleman house restorations, I probably would have. For ten months, I lived in that house, never stepping foot outside. Because I was afraid to. You see, I was waiting for you to put the key back."

Eli's facial expression remained closed and impassive. As much as she tried to, Nika couldn't read it, and it scared the bejesus out her. Unable to tear her eyes from Eli, she took a broken breath. She hated to be placed in a position of explaining herself, but Eli deserved the truth. Condemning, painful, uncomfortable truth. She owed him that much.

"Day after day, night after night, I waited, checking that stupid back panel. Even in the middle of the work, I would run to the clock and check.

Of course, my crew noticed, and start joking about 'boss's folly.' It was embarrassing, but I didn't care. Some nights, when I couldn't sleep, I sat in front of the clock, hoping for a miracle. But nothing happened. For months. For long, miserable months." A lone tear rolled down her face, but Nika ignored it. "I even prayed! Can you believe it?"

But again, silence was her only answer. After what seems like an eternity, Eli drew a deep breath.

"I can see how you might come to this conclusion, Daisy, but, honestly, did you think so little of me? Look at me."

At last, he breached the chasm of those few separating feet, and came to stand in front of her.

"Look at me, *ma petite*. Did you really think I would do something as deplorable as that?"

The censure in his voice was unmistakable. Damning. He was disappointed in her. Unbearably sad, unbelievably tired, Nika lifted her eyes.

"I didn't know what to think. I knew for sure that one day we would be together again. And that's what was holding me up. But the wait..."

She broke his heart. He could see clearly the picture she painted with her words: Daisy, his darling girl, sitting in the dark, in that huge house, amidst the construction chaos, staring at the grandfather clock, waiting, hoping, praying for a miracle. The images were killing him.

She was so pale, so tiny and fragile, he imagined he could see right through her. Her broken sigh stabbed him in the heart.

"I truly am sorry, Eli. I'm so sorry I decided to accept William's offer. I'm sorry I lost that damn key. But I was so sure you would understand and forgive me when you learned the truth. Why did you make me wait so long?"

"Because I didn't know that you lost the key. I didn't know you left to visit your family. I didn't know any of that, I swear, Daisy."

"What?" Confusion clouded her amethyst eyes "But...I don't understand. Didn't William explain? Didn't he find the key I dropped?"

"He did. Found the key that is. But he didn't confess to me until..." He still had trouble believing, much less talking about it. "Until three days ago."

"But why? I don't get it. Why? And what happened three days ago?"

"The accident."

"Tell me." She laid her right hand on his arm. Her touch was hesitant and light and so familiar. Oh, God, how he missed their physical closeness! Craving it more than his next breath, Eli grabbed her hand, squeezed, then brought it to his face.

Daisy. Her smell, her touch…

And just like that, the floodgate was shattered. Words poured out, unabridged, and uncensored.

…Every detail of that horrible day was etched into his memory. The salty smell of the ocean, the cerulean blue of the sky, the brilliant gold of the leaves—nothing predicted disaster on that nice Autumn morning. A regular visit to the docks may have been his last, if William hadn't insisted on accompany Eli. They just arrived at the scene, and was about to talk to the steward regarding the latest shipment, when something alerted Eli. Curious, but unperturbed, he turned around. He remembered a sudden sound, odd and ghastly, and William's stricken face as he looked over his shoulder. Eli was about to make an inquiry but found himself pushed sideways, stumbling, falling. That fall knocked the breath out of him, temporarily rendering him immobile. Then, incensed, Eli reared back. The thought that William dared to physically assault him barely formed in his mind as the horrific image of his friend, bloody and broken, and buried under the enormous logs, cut through the haze of his anger. The horror of that picture was so enormous, so unbelievable, Eli froze. And the truth dawned. William pushed him away from the rolling logs, and saved his life. Still alive, his friend grabbed his hand. The confession tumbled from William's lips in a garbled and confused slur. At first, Eli took it for delirium. But then, as comprehension dawned, the rage replaced his sorrow. He flung aside the hand of the dying man, shaking in impotent fury.

"Why? Damn you, man, why?"

But William just stared at him, unblinking, mute, as his tortured eyes has slowly glazed with death.

After his sad tale was finished, there was nothing left inside but guilt. Heavy and dark. And sorrow. He just confessed to Daisy that for some time he believed her to be a liar and thief.

How's that for thinking so little of the person you love?

Silence stretched, dense, oppressive. How did they ended up sitting on a sofa? For the life of him, he couldn't remember. At last, he gathered the courage to ask, "You must hate him."

Quiet, unmoving, Daisy gazed at some invisible spot on the floor. She resembled a statue. At some point, even her breathing became shallow and weak. Eli couldn't tear his gaze away from her. What was going on in that brain of hers? What was she thinking?

Dear God, why didn't she say something? Anything!

He was beside himself with frustration. Daisy took a deep breath and turned to face him. Her amethyst eyes were awash with sadness.

"I don't. I can't. He saved your life, and for that I will be forever grateful to him. He slandered me, but I don't care. He exchanged his life for yours, Eli. I'll cherish his memory, and mourn him until my last day."

Undone, Eli allowed himself a moment before he could trust his voice.

"You astonish me, Daisy."

"I just love you."

There were no words to describe his jubilation. Something hot pressed against his eyes. Unbearable tightness in his gut slowly eased, allowing him a first free breath.

"But you," she continued quietly, "how could you believe that I can leave you, or steal from you? Did you think so little of me?"

The question he asked her earlier found its mark. *I deserve it.*

"What was I supposed to think?" he replied, echoing her words.

When Daisy averted her eyes, Eli's heart sunk.

Did he managed to lose her after all? Will she ever forgive him?

More than anything he wanted to touch her, to take her in his arms, and never let go. But he was afraid that she wouldn't let him.

They were slowly drifting apart, or did he imagine it? The suspense was killing him.

I cannot stand it.

"So, what's now?"

What now indeed.

And now, my girl, you have to decide what's more important: your pride or your happiness.

It was such a no brainer, but she'd be damned if she let him off the hook that easily. From her arsenal of weapons against the opposite sex, Nika pulled a stern look, and aimed it at Eli.

"And now, Coleman, we must make a pact."

His silver eyes clouded with suspicion.

Perfect. Let him stew a little.

"What kind of a pact?"

Her voice held firm, which pleased Nika because her nerves were dancing a jig.

"Let's make a promise to each other that we will never, under any circumstances, believe the worst about each other, no matter how convincing the facts. That we will always talk to each other face to face, openly and candidly."

"Agreed."

His quick reply was accompanied by an enthusiastic nod. Relief was written all over Eli's face. The picture was almost comical. Nika swallowed her bubbling laughter.

"And if we won't be able to have a face-to-face, heart-to heart discussion immediately, we'll wait—"

"Wholeheartedly agreed."

"Even if we have to wait fourteen days, or fourteen months."

"Even if we have to wait fourteen centuries."

They moved together, and finally she was in his arms. Nika closed her eyes, pressed her cheek against his thumping heart, and held on for dear life.

"God, not centuries, please! I barely survived this year."

"I almost didn't survive fourteen days, if not for Belle."

"Belle? Oh, my God, Eli!" Excited, Nika pulled back from the embrace. "How is she? Is she okay? Do they treat her decently in the stables?"

"She's more than okay. And she lives in the main house now, not stables, and gets treated as royalty." Eli smiled. "But you'll soon see for yourself. She misses you terribly."

"I'm miss her too! And Mrs. Smith, and Sultan, and—" her voice broke.

"And?"

"Oh, damn you, Coleman, I missed you so darn much, it's not even funny!"

With that, Nika reared up, straddled Eli, and captured his mouth with hers.

The kiss went on and on. Eli was too pleased and stunned to do anything but enjoy being devoured. Soon, however, the passive role ceased to be enough, and he took charge of the kiss, returning her favor with eagerness.

Their mouths fused, their tongues battled, entwining, while their hearts melted and their blood churned.

"Daisy, my Daisy," he chanted, planting hungry kisses all over her face. "My very own wild flower." His hands became busy, molding her breasts, shaping her ass, all the while wrapping her tighter in his arms, until they all but became one body.

"Eli." She became busy too, kissing her way up from his chin to his forehead, her own hands hungry, exploring. "Eli, please..."

When she started to unbutton his shirt, his sanity decided to resurface. *Thunderation.*

"Daisy, wait, we can't, darling." Somehow, he found himself on the sofa with his beloved Daisy on his lap.

With the last morsel of his resolve, Eli lifted his head and pulled back. For the life of him, he couldn't form the coherent thought in his brain as to *why* they couldn't just tear their clothes away and enjoy each other. He just knew the time was wrong.

"Why not?"

"Because."

Her pouting mouth was his undoing. Dropping the fast hard kiss onto it, Eli untangled her vise-like grip on his neck. Or tried to. "It is not the place, nor time."

"It's the perfect place. And if you ask me, we're long overdue."

"I agree, but—"

"Don't you want me?"

"Only as much as my next breath."

"Then, I repeat, why?"

"It's the middle of a day, Daisy."

"That's never stopped you before."

"Yes, but then we were home."

"We're home now. *Me casa, su casa*, Coleman."

"But this *casa* also belongs to your cousin. What if he returns?"

"So what? It's not like Alex never saw people kissing. Or do you think he's under the impression that we were playing chess all the time I was at your place?"

Heat crawled across his cheeks. Damn if she didn't make him blush. *The wench!*

"Be that as it may, but I feel rather uncomfortable."

"Okay, let's go to my bedroom."

"Daisy."

She was killing him, sitting astride, disheveled, mussed, with her mouth red and swollen from his kisses. His pants tightened more when she performed a seductive wiggle. "I would cut my right arm right now for the privilege to have you, but..." Eli drew a broken breath. "I just can't."

A deep scowl marred her forehead, as her eyes sparkled with irritation.

"Fine, be that way."

Nika made a production of sliding off his lap, huffing and pouting. To make sure that she was not alone in her misery, she rubbed her thigh against the most vulnerable part of him, and rejoiced when he winced.

"I hope you're not aiming at a full-blown celibacy route while you're here. Or do you plan to wait until we go back in 1909?"

"I honored by your high opinion of my self-control, Daisy, but even I couldn't manage that." He gave her a crooked, half-pained smile. "Although I'd rather prefer to wait until we're back home. But it seems like we shall stay here for a while." His smile slipped off his face, replaced by a deep frown. "As much as I wish to return, first I must see Abigail. I have to make sure that she's alright and not wanted for anything. And ...I wish to speak with her, to ask—"

"Ask what?"

His expression turned grim, almost haunted.

"Ask for her forgiveness. If not for my cruelty, she'd never succumb to such an extreme measure as jumping through time."

"Eli." Nika went with her heart, and framed his face with her hands. "You're not cruel, far from it, my darling."

"I drove my baby sister away, Daisy. From her home, from everything familiar and dear, from the security of her position in society. What is that if not the act of an astonishing cruelty?"

"A great love. Yes, love," she added when he shook his head in denial, "blind and unwise, maybe. Tough and high-handled, definitely. But love nevertheless. And I'm sure Abby understands it. Or she will, with time and more experience. She's not wanted for anything, I promise you that. With the amount of gold she managed to stash and carry over here, she's set for life, and then some."

The infamous satchel Abby brought with her turned out to be full of gold bars. Nika chuckled as she remembered the dumfounded expression on her family's faces when she finally revealed its contents. The ever-resourceful Coleman heiress, as it happened, had emptied her bank account in secret, in preparation for her journey. God only knows how she managed it, being so closely supervised. But Abby was her brother's sister. Nothing stopped the Colemans siblings if they wanted something bad enough. No obstacle was high or hard enough to overcome.

Not even time.

"Still, I wish to talk to my sister. I want to see for myself how she's fairing in this wondrous time of yours before I can go back. Before *we* go back."

Eli focused his searching eyes on her.

"You are coming with me, aren't you?"

"If you really think I'll let you out of my sight now, when I finally got you back, then you are a moron, Coleman."

"But you have so much here: your business, your house, your family."

"You are my family, first and foremost."

"As you are mine." Eli laid his forehead against hers, and let out a long sigh.

"You are my whole world, Daisy. You are my everything."

"And you are mine. I love you, Elijah Benjamin Coleman. More than I can say. So much that it hurts."

"You humble me. Profoundly."

For several heartbeats their breathing was the only sound in a hushed silence of the room. Because she was close to a meltdown, Nika drew back.

"Humble looks good on you."

And just like she hoped, Eli smiled, and the somber mood dissipated.

Laughter danced in his eyes when they met hers. *My, oh my*. She almost forgot the lethal power of those silver eyes and that high-voltage smile.

"So." She ignored her screaming hormones. For now. "If you absolutely refuse to indulge your second basic instinct, let me try to indulge the first one."

Eli paled, and swallowed audibly. Was it low of her to enjoy his confusion so much? Yep, it was, but she couldn't help it. To add to his discomfort, she patted Eli's cheek. Now naked panic was written all over his face. Priceless.

"Ah, Daisy? What exactly are you talking about?"

Enough was enough. Nika grinned, and jumped to her feet.

"Relax, Coleman. I'm talking about feeding you. Nothing kinky, I swear. Just food."

"That's what I thought."

Was it relief or disappointment she heard in his voice? Probably both.

And he was not alone. Nika, too, was disappointed, but if she was honest with herself, she had to admit that putting on the brakes for now was smart. Frustrating as hell, but smart. Passion was prone to muddy a brain, not to mention common sense. Her brain was muddy enough already. She needed to keep her wits sharp and her mind clear. At the moment, however, she couldn't come up with a single reason why. Her gaze flickered to the sofa, as if the answer to her dilemma was hiding somewhere between the cushions. If Eli didn't keep his cool, dammit it all to hell and back, they would be rolling on that sofa right now, naked and sweaty, and—

Get your head out of the gutter, girl.

"Damned logic."

"Pardon me?"

"Ah, nothing."

Flustered, properly chastised by her own inner voice (*bitch*), embarrassed to be caught talking to herself, Nika blew out a few strands of hair out of her face.

Why was she standing in the middle of the kitchen?

Her brain was fuzzier than she thought, because for a moment she drew a blank. Then it hit her: food. Okay, alright. She promised to feed him. Something simple, but homey. Right. Her mind zipped her back to her first meal at the Coleman house. And wasn't that an elaborate affair. A fancy seven course dinner, no less. She wouldn't dream to compete with that, of course, but an omelet and a salad? She can definitely pull that off. She hopped.

Nika's heart sank as soon as she surveyed the contests of their fridge. Dammit, they were long overdue for grocery shopping. As of right now, she was a proud owner of one egg, a couple of sad and tired apples, and a solitary bottle of Heineken.

Alex, you skunk, you miserable stinky skunk.

Her cousin was the one in charge of the groceries, but he slaked on his duties as of recently. Come to think of it, Alex was slaking in other areas as well.

Because Alex's heart was not in any of it. His heart was somewhere else, period.

Like in Paris.

Irked and irritated, Nika fumed in silence. When Abby was living with them, he stuffed the cabinets and fridge with food like they were supplying a third world country. There were always cold meats, fruits and veggies, spreads and bagels, not to mention Abby's favorite whipped cream. Now it was back to the old way of things. He totally ignored the fact that Nika must eat in order to survive, too, the bastard. The message was clear as day: she must fend for herself.

We'll see about that.

As soon as the miserable skunk got home, so help her God, she was going to give him a piece of her mind. Then she was going to strangle the lazy bastard for embarrassing her.

Simple, but homey meal, my ass.

In a desperate hope of a miracle, Nika kept rummaging inside of a fridge, but to no avail. Pulling her hair out or cursing wouldn't help either. Resigned, Nika slammed the fridge then yanked open the door of the one cabinet where they kept food. She shook both cereal boxes to find them empty. No canned goods whatsoever unless you wanted lima beans. Why on Earth would Alex ever buy lima beans? In utter disgust and humiliation, she turned to Eli.

"Sorry. It seems like we're running low on some essentials, so the homemade meal has to be postponed. What do you say about ordering in? Pizza, or Chinese? Or...or I can call for sushi."

"Don't trouble yourself, Daisy. I'm not all that hungry, really, just thirsty. A glass of lemonade, maybe?"

If the earth could open up and swallow her alive, she figured it would be much less than she deserved. The man hurtled through time, all the way from the last century, and not only she couldn't slap a simple PB&J together, she didn't even offer him a drink. *Verochka* would simply die from shame.

C'est dommage!

Embarrassed, frustrated, mad at Alex (*oh, you're so in trouble, Cousin*) Nika cursed under her breath.

"I am so sorry, Eli. I have much better manners than that, I promise. It's just..." She flicked her wrist "Never mind. Can I offer you a glass of Bordeaux? We have an excellent vintage from *Verochka's* prized cellar. Or whiskey? Or if you prefer cognac—"

"Relax, *ma petite*, a glass of water would do nicely."

"We have a Heineken." Nika managed a half-smile. "Alex is a fan. Somehow, he missed one bottle in a fridge. Wanna try it?"

"What's a Heineken?"

"A beer. According to my skunk of a cousin, it's the drink of the Gods."

"If he loves it so much, and you have only one bottle left, then we should save it for him. The water is perfectly fine."

It might be fine, but they were out of bottled water as well. Nika would die before she offered him tap water.

Please God, help.

And, like an answer to her desperate plea, the inspiration struck.

An Evian!

She always carried a bottle or two in the truck. Her legs were moving before she could register it. "Be back in a flash. Wait here."

"Where are you going?"

"To the garage. I'll return in a jiff."

CHAPTER ELEVEN

Daisy ran off. Eli was left alone in the strange space that seemed as alien as the moon. There were some items he recognized, furniture, pots and pans, and rugs, but that was the extent of it. The clock on the wall, he supposed it was a clock, was a round disk with red glowing numbers. What he assumed was the stove had a shiny black surface with a front glass door and a kettle perched on it. A strange noise that surrounded him—some humming, clucking, even whooshing— added to his discomfort. He should be insanely curious, but God help him, he was just weary. And, to be honest, a bit nervous.

When was Daisy coming back?

A strange small apparatus laying on the table became alive with a peculiar chime.

Now what? Thunderation.

Eli observed the little object while his uneasiness grew, but then, thank the good Lord, the door burst open.

There she is. His relief was so overwhelming, Eli almost sagged with it.

"I knew I had it! I usually have a few bottles stashed in my truck." Like some kind of a prize, two small bottles were held high in Daisy's hands. She presented one to him. "Here it is!"

"What is that?" He accepted the offering, uneasy but curious. The pink label was pretty, the bottle itself much lighter that it appeared. And it was soft, made out of some transparent material.

"A water."

"A water? In a bottle?"

"Yep. And not just any water, Coleman." She gave him a wink. "It's the best damn water in the hemisphere, according to the company that makes it."

Eli gazed at the peculiar bottle for a long time. Was he losing his mind?

"How do you make a water?"

"Well, they're not exactly making it. They just bottle it. From the spring."

"A Natural Spring Water made by the French Alps." Eli couldn't believe the words he just read out loud. "What rubbish. How do you know it was gathered near French Alps? And why not Swiss Alps? Or—"

"Hey, do you want that drink or not?"

Visibly irked by his argument, Daisy knitted her brows.

A full minute passed before Eli capitulated. "I beg your pardon, *ma petite*. Sure, I'd love some water."

Must be looking like a damned fool.

Daisy didn't seem to mind. With a shiny smile on her face she made a picture, she truly did. He would be more than happy to just bask in that smile all day long, but Eli's thirst increased tenfold.

"Ah, Daisy?"

"What?"

"A glass? If it's not too much trouble. And the instruction of how to open this, please."

That prompted her into action. In a moment, a tall crystal glass was in his hand. He passed back the bottle. A quick twist of Daisy's hand uncapped the bottle.

Water poured into the glass. She held it out. "Sorry I forgot that some things are different here."

Eli emptied a full glass in a couple of gulps. Daisy uncapped the second bottle and poured again.

"Thank you. This Evian water is quite tasty. But I really wonder how—"

Another chime interrupted his musings.

"Oh, there it is again. It was playing that melody when you ran for the water. What is that thing? Some kind of a gramophone?"

Daisy snatched up the peculiar devise.

"No, it's a phone, just a phone."

"A phone? What does it do?"

"A lot of things. I'll show you later."

"And this music?"

But the strange chiming had stopped.

"A Skype ring-tone. Probably *Verochka* was trying to call me."

"What? But...how?"

"Relax, Eli, I'll explain and show you everything. I promised you a Skype call to your sister, and I'll keep my word, but for now, we must order something to eat. I'm not sure about you, but I am totally famished."

Eli watched in a wondrous stupor as Daisy tapped a few times on that strange little devise she called *phone*, and placing it to her ear, started talking. After a minute or two of that conversation with an invisible stranger, she removed that thing from her ear. "Okay, give me a moment to text that idiot cousin of mine."

She continued tapping the screen with both fingers in a rapid succession, muttering all the while. Eli thought he hear the word 'skunk' and 'stinker', but he could have been mistaken.

The food was ordered. It wasn't much, just a pizza, but it was the best darn pizza in this part of town. When they first moved here, *Moon River Pizza* became their favorite. To this day, it continued to be an essential part of their daily nutrition. Of course, whether Eli would like it or not was another matter altogether, but Nika didn't— couldn't— stop to think about it. She was jittery enough as it was. And, besides, who doesn't like pizza?

Nika wasn't hungry. But she knew that Eli has to be on the last leg of his endurance. He always had the appetite of a healthy, big guy. And boy, was he a big one.

Nika considered Alex to be a giant, with his lanky six-one to her puny five-and-change, but compared to Eli even he looked like a squirt.

Then again, many men did.

"Okay, three loaded pizza pies will be here in forty minutes. Alex has been warned about grocery shopping, or else. So..." trying to switch gears, Nika drew a deep breath, and glanced at the clock. "We have enough time to Skype Paris. There is six-hour difference in time, so they must be home by now."

"They? Who are they? And what's in the blue blazes is that *Skype* of yours?"

"They, Coleman, are *Verochka* and Abby. Remember I told you that my grandmother became Abby's guardian angel? Two of them live in *Verochka's* place. And Skype is an amazing invention that I'd rather show you than try to explain, because, honestly, I'm not tech savvy enough. You'll see." Nika glanced at Eli then nodded her head, "There's something you should know before we Skype so you're not surprised."

Eli's face paled.

"No, don't worry. Isn't not a bad thing. It's just that *Verochka* has always called me Daisy or Daisy-girl since I was a toddler. She said my mass of unruly hair and its ungodly yellow color reminded her of wild daises."

Relief spread across his face. Nika took his hand and gave it a warm squeeze.

CHAPTER TWELVE

Dumbfounded, Eli watched as Daisy picked up her little device again and tapped a few times. But she didn't put it against her ear. Instead, she held it before her face. In a moment, an unfamiliar female voice, smooth, cultured, and sonorous, filled the room. To his utter astonishment, the sound was coming from that little *phone*.

"Well, hello-hello, Daisy-girl. How's my favorite flower?"

Daisy smiled at her devise, and even sent it an air kiss.

What in blue blazes...?

"I'm fine, *Verochka*. Really fine. And how are you? Looking smashing as always."

The voice coming from the phone laughed, a rich and marvelous sound that was oddly and uncomfortably erotic. To add insult to injury, Eli's face became hot as a furnace.

My Lord, am I blushing again?

Meanwhile, that voice continued quite cheerfully,

"Oh, thank you, my darling. Tried to call you a few times, but you were incommunicado. Is everything alright?"

"Everything is wonderful. I just..." she spared him a quick glance, "just couldn't take your call earlier, sorry."

"Well, then, tell me everything. Alex said you finished the restorations."

"Yes. It's done."

"Finally! I'm dying to see it."

"I can do a Face Time, or Skype tour for you."

"We can do better than that: Abby and I decided to fly home for Thanksgiving. Well, aren't you happy? In a couple of days, we'll all see each other again."

No matter how befuddled Eli was at the moment, one thing penetrated his fuzzy brain, and became crystal clear: Abby would be here soon. So, he would see his sister, and stop agonizing how on earth he would be able to secure a passage to France. The matter of transportation notwithstanding, there was more a pressing, and quite humiliating, problem: a financial one. Stupid of him not to think of funds when he first set on his journey. Then again, who would? He was so excited, he didn't think of anything. Not even his safety.

But, alas, he was here, safe and sound, and so would Abby, in a few days. Thank God. Eli let out a sigh of relief, and concentrated on Daisy, as his mood lightened considerably.

The full implication of her grandmother's words hit Nika between the eyes.

"Oh, wow. Wow! Wait, *Verochka*, wait. Home? Here?"

"Well, my dear, Abby and I consider Amelia Island home. Why? Any objections? Did you and Alex have some other plans?"

"No, no. No plans. And it will be absolutely wonderful if you both come here. But…"

"But? Daisy-girl, another moment, and I would think you don't want us to come. Is everything alright?"

And just like that, *Verochka's* eyes lost their laughing shine.

Uh-oh.

"Of course, I want you to come. Are you kidding? I missed you both so much. It's just…"

"Just?"

What the heck are you doing, Nika-Daisy? Get on with it, tell her the truth.

"Just wonderful, but unexpected. It is such a surprise. It just threw me off for a moment, that's all. Alex will be ecstatic. Wait till he hears it."

"That's better. For a second here you gave me a pause. I almost thought—"

"Well, you thought wrong. Tomorrow we'll buy a huge turkey. And on Thursday we're going to celebrate a true Thanksgiving. Like a family, a complete family. At last."

Her last words were for Verochka, but her eyes sought Eli, and held his gaze.

"... you have so much here: your business, your house, your family."

"You are my family, first and foremost."

"As you are mine." ...

"Daisy-girl? You're talking in riddles. A *complete* family at last?" *Verochka's* voice lost all its playfulness.

"Nika? What is going on? What are you hiding from me?"

"Not what." Shifting closer to Eli, Nika angled her phone. Now they both were visible on the screen. "Who. *Verochka*, meet Elijah Benjamin Coleman."

A string of French and Russian words, all of them unsuitable for the general audience, followed her announcement. After a moment, *Verochka* fell into a shocked silence.

The first thing Eli noticed was the eyes. The shape of them, but especially the color. That amazing amethyst shade was unmistakable. They were Daisy's eyes. For some reason, it made his anxiety disappear, and settled his equilibrium. Once again, Eli was calm and in control. More than that: he was quite happy.

"I am honored to make your acquaintance, Madam."

He added a formal nod to his words, trying not to think how peculiar it was conversing with the image on the small screen.

The woman who was Daisy's grandmother, and now his sister's guardian angel was a stunning beauty. She gazed back at him with something close to fear in her mesmerizing eyes. Her mouth moved, but no words came out.

"Is something wrong with that devise?"

"No."

"Then, why can't I hear anything?"

"Because she's in a stupor."

"My Lord, that's a very serious condition! Is she prone to that? Shall we call a doctor?"

"Doctor?"

Daisy squinted at him in confusion, but then she chuckled. "No, no. She's not in stupor as in *stupor*, Eli. She's just in shock."

"Why?"

"Why do you think?" Daisy's grandmother quipped in a playful manner. "Not every day a woman meets such a gorgeous hunk as yourself, Mr. Coleman. *And* from another century, no less."

Was she joking with him? Although her lips were curved in a smile, her eyes were quite serious. Daisy shouldered him aside.

"I'm sorry, *Verochka*. I should've prepared you better, but—"

"Don't mind me." *Verochka* as she'd been called, brushed off an apology. "But I'm glad Abby isn't around. That would be way too much for her."

"Where is she, by the way?"

"At Marie's. She's at the studio, working day and night. Didn't I tell you? Marie managed to arrange the first official showing of Abby's paintings in Rostoff gallery."

"That's awesome!" Daisy exclaimed. "When?"

"In December, right after Christmas."

"Oh, wow! So soon? Abby must be ecstatic!"

"And then some. So, she's crazy excited, as you can imagine, and she really doesn't need an additional stress right now." *Verochka's* elegant brow furrowed in concern. "Maybe we should postpone our Thanksgiving trip? The girl is a nervous wreck as it is."

"With all due respect, Madam, but I must see my sister, no matter what."

Despite the politeness of his words, his reply was curt. Both women gapped at him.

"So, if you won't come to Amelia Island, I will find a way to come to you. But before I return back home, before Daisy and I take out leave, I shall have a private talk with Abigail."

Daisy's grandmother furrowed her brow.

"Even if she doesn't want to talk to you?"

"Even then."

"Mr. Coleman—"

"Eli, please. After all, we are a family."

Eli's smile could stop a woman's heart. Nika's own skipped a bit. *Verochka*, obviously, was not immune either. Visibly torn, she returned the smile, but her face was still a bit strained.

"Eli, then. Can I ask you the reason? Why do you need to talk to Abby?"

"To beg her forgiveness."

That simple reply was just the right answer. *Verochka's* face relaxed.

"You're a true gentleman, Elijah Benjamin Coleman, and I am pleased to call you family."

"The pleasure is all mine, Madam."

"Oh, stop that Madam nonsense. It makes me feel ancient. You must call me *Verochka*."

"Then I shall, Mad...*Verochka*. I hope you won't take it as frivolous statement, but you are one very beautiful and unique lady I have the privilege to know. And you don't look like a grandmother."

"My dear boy, you can make frivolous statements like that to me every day."

Verochka's pleasure shone through her laughing eyes.

Her amusement, however, was short lived, and once again that stunning face turned serious.

"Okay, kids. Here is the plan. Abby and I will come home for Thanksgiving, but I won't tell her about you, Eli. When we are there, it's up to you how you want to play it. Take my suggestion." She squinted, and pointed her finger at him. "Grovel, buddy."

CHAPTER THIRTEEN

"**W**ell, what do you think?"

Between their Skype call and pizza delivery, Eli was suspiciously closemouthed.

"About?"

"About my grandmother, for one; about this new world around you. The pizza." Nika was about to explode from curiosity. After all, it was not every day you asked a guest from the last century about his impressions. Eli was not forthcoming. They sat at the kitchen table, devouring their impromptu meal with gusto. Nika's worries about dinner dissipated as soon as Eli bit into his first slice. His orgasmic groan of pleasure was akin to a highly erotic version of halleluiah.

Currently he was on his fifth slice. She would bet her prized toolbelt that it wouldn't be his last. After he chewed thoroughly and swallowed another bite, Eli granted her a short reply.

"The pizza is very tasty indeed."

That's it? That's all he has to say?

He wiped his mouth with a napkin, then cleaned his fingers. A stalling tactic if she'd ever seen one.

Okay, we'll do it your way.

After a while, he cleared his throat.

"I doubt, though, that this kind of a meal is very healthy."

Her derisive snort broke free, rude and unladylike.

But, hey, I'm not a lady.

"Who cares?"

"I do, and so should you, my sweet. After all, you'll be bearing my children, and I am very much in favor for them to be healthy."

That statement shut her up. Eli's smile was that of a Cheshire cat who just snatched a fat, tasty canary.

Nothing he said could surprise her more. The subject of children was a taboo at the Coleman household. His tragedy of losing his first wife and their unborn child was heartbreaking. But Eli has never talked to her about it. Whatever she learned, came from Abby. This was the first time he brought it out in the open.

Her throat was so dry, Nika doubted she could squeeze a single word out. The water she gulped from the bottle went the wrong way, prompting a violent cough. Eli leaned over and tugged at the ends of her hair.

"Look up, *ma petite*, and breathe. That's it. That's the way, Daisy. By the way, I still hate the hair."

"Don't worry, it'll wash off."

"I can hardly wait."

Between her coughing bout and her surprise, Nika had a hard time concentrating.

After dropping a bomb like that, all he cares about is my hair?

A slow journey of his fingers through her keratin treated, slick as rain hair was such a sensual experience, it was almost erotic. Shaky, Nika let out a delighted purr, but then his fingers withdrew.

Damnation. This guy is maddening.

"But to answer your question."

Eli's voice sounded so cool and normal, Nika almost screamed in frustration.

"Your grandmother is...a very interesting woman. I don't quite know what to make of her, or how to describe her in mere words, but she is one of a kind."

"You got that right."

"I think I'm a bit terrified of her."

"Really? Why is that?"

"She is like an ocean: beautiful and tranquil, with a perfect storm brewing in its infinite depth. And you never know when this perfect storm is going to arrive."

"Huh. You know what? I think you just hit a bullseye. A perfect storm. *Verochka* would love that."

"If you say so."

After a moment of contemplating, Eli continued, "Regarding your world...I'm quite in awe with the accomplishments of the human brain. All these amazing inventions like your phone, and automobiles, and this," he pointed to the black screen on the that hums wall, "whatever this thing is—all this quite frankly takes my breath away, and boggles the mind. Just a hundred-year difference, Daisy, but the changes are absolutely miraculous."

"Hundred and eleven." Her gruff response burst out on autopilot.

"What?"

"Never mind. And this thing on the wall? It's called TV, or television."

"What does it do? Play music?"

"That, too. I'll demonstrate later."

"I can hardly wait."

Another slice of pizza found its way onto Eli's plate.

"What do you know, I was hungry after all."

His smile was half-joking, half-apologetic.

"I could never tell."

Nika's smile tugged at her lips, even as her heart thudded in her chest. After his earlier bombshell, Eli was still evading the subject of children.

Enough was enough. If he wouldn't talk about it, she would. All she has to do is prod him a little. Just a tad. Smooth and gentle.

"So, you want children?"

Nika cringed. *Smooth, very smooth, Nika.*

"Of course. Don't you?"

"Of course, I want children."

"Well?"

"Well, what?"

"Why did it surprise you so much when I brought up the subject?"

"I don't know. I guess, we never talked about it, that's all."

"We've never talked about many things, *ma petite*, but we will. As soon as we are back home."

But she has to know. Needed to know. Now.

"You never talked about... your first wife and your unborn baby. Abby told me. And I thought that maybe... you don't want any more children."

His eyes flashed for a brief moment, then the shutters closed again.

For as long as she lived, Nika would never forget that excruciating, raw pain she glimpsed in his eyes. It scorched her skin.

"You thought wrong. Yes, I never told you about Mary. It's painful for me. Very. For a longest time, I couldn't see a child, or a pregnant woman, without hurting. It took me years to heal, to forgive."

"Forgive? What?"

"Not what, but who. Myself first, God second."

"That wasn't your fault, Eli. It happens, unfortunately. Even today, when medicine is much more advance. Some things just go wrong."

"I understand. Now. But then..."

The cloud of those painful memories darkened his face. Eli was suddenly so far away, fear of losing him overwhelmed her.

Silly, Nika, he's sitting right beside you.

But silly or not, she laid a hand on his arm, squeezed gently. That brought him around.

"I was shattered, Daisy. The guilt was too heavy for me to carry. I couldn't live with myself. I cursed God, drunk myself to stupor, thought about ending my misery. Ending my life."

Nika was shocked, and appalled. Her heart was breaking for him, for his poor young wife, for the baby who never took its first breath. Tears burned her eyes, but she struggled to keep them at bay. He didn't need her tears, or her pity—even her kindness. She knew from personal experience that kindness in the pivotal moments could bring a person to a complete meltdown. No, he didn't need that. What he really needed was a kick in the ass, and she was more than happy, not to mention capable, to administer it. Bracing inwardly, Nika glared at Eli.

"I would never take you for a coward, Coleman. Ending your misery? Really? Do you think it would have brought Mary back? Or your baby? Do you think she would have wanted you to die, too?"

Eli was surprised and a bit hurt at her harsh words. Didn't she understand? Didn't she hear what he just said, what he confessed?

Then it dawned at him: she was not attacking him. She was fighting for him, for that poor misguided youth he used to be, trapped in a jail of tragedy.

Eli's heart trembled as his soul soured. Had she said something kind, something nice and soothing, it would have belittled him.

Unmanned him.

"I love you too, my sweet wild flower." Moved beyond words, he gently kissed her hand. "Thank you."

"What for?"

"For being you. For loving me. For everything."

He kissed hand palm again. He touched her wrist where her pulse thundered, true and hot. Then he pressed her hand against his cheek.

"I am so fortunate to have had you drop from the sky onto my path."

And wasn't he just? What would have happened to his life if she hadn't stepped inside his house and found the key? What would have happened if she ignored that letter she insisted he wrote to her?

The letter.

That reminded him: as soon as he back home, he must write those words— what did she say?

Find the key. You know where it is—and seal the envelope. Then he will give it to his solicitor for safekeeping. That is the first thing he would do. The next thing...

Eli's fantasy conjured the image of the bedroom with his oversized bed. Oh, yes, he would take her inside that bedroom, strip her to skin, and keep her there for as long as was humanly possible. His blood heated, churned. His pulse thundered in his ears.

Thunderation.

If he didn't get his hands on her soon, he would surely explode.

Patience, Eli, patience.

"I am very fortunate you stopped Sultan in time, and didn't let him stomp me."

Her voice, rough and husky, sent shivers along his spine.

Lust stabbed his gut like a knife. Deep quivers broke throughout his body. Another moment, and he'd be shaking like a stallion that sensed a filly. Patience? What jest!

Eli moved his plate aside, cleared his throat, and stared at Daisy. She returned his gaze. For a long breathless moment their eyes clashed, held...

And the sudden pinging sound hacked into an electrifying silence with all the finesse of a pirate's axe.

They sprang apart, and the moment was broken.

CHAPTER FOURTEEN

Both relived and disappointed at the interruption, Nika grabbed her phone and tapped the face.

"Oh, it's a text from that skunk of a cousin of mine."

"Text? What is a text?"

She glanced at Eli. "It's like a note, or a short message."

"You can send a note on that thing?"

"You sure do."

"Marvelous. How?" His brow furrowed.

"Sorry, how what?"

"How do you write a note on that thing?"

"Oh, that's simple enough." She turned the phone so he could see the screen. "You press on this app, open up your text screen, then chose a contact, and type."

"Okay." Eli eyed the small screen with mix of fascination and apprehension.

"So, what is it your cousin wrote to you on that devise?"

"That he would be home very late, if not tomorrow morning, because he decided to join a poker game at a friend's."

"Is he a good poker player?"

"He's the worst poker player in the whole wide world, and I have no idea why he..."

Then it hit her: Alex left them alone, to allow them a complete privacy.

Her heart melted.

The skunk. The most wonderful skunk in the world.

"I like your cousin."

"Yeah? So do I. He's the best. Loyal, and funny, kind and smart. He's..." And how to describe in a few words the most important person in your life? "He's... Alex."

And that said it all. Uncomfortable with Eli's narrow gaze, she grabbed another slice of pizza she didn't want.

"He loves you."

"And I love him right back."

"It would hurt you to leave him behind. And your grandmother."

It wasn't a question. Abandoning all pretense of eating, Nika drew a deep sigh and dropped the soggy slice onto her plate.

"Yes, it would. But it would hurt me even more to leave you behind. No," she corrected herself, "it would completely destroy me. This year I survived *only* because I believed—I knew— that one day we will be together again. But without that belief I would be shattered. I would not survive."

"You said that before. That you knew we would be reunited one day. How did you know that?"

After a long-charged moment, she came to a decision.

"Let's go."

"Go? Now? But...where?"

"You'll see."

And before she lost her resolve, Nika grabbed her car keys.

To say that Eli was thrown off balance was the understatement of his and her centuries combine.

Damn vixen.

One moment she was gazing at him with an unguarded passion in her eyes, and set his blood on fire, the next—she was moving away, gathering items and tucking them into her various pockets with precise movements of a person on a mission.

Baffled and confused, Eli attributed his current stupor to a maddening switch in Daisy's behavior. But since she left him no choice, he pulled the remnants of his wits together, and, cursing under his breath, followed her out. What on earth prompted him to ask her that last question? Why couldn't he keep his mouth shut? If not for that, they would already be engaged in much more pleasant activities than hurrying pell-mell the devil only knew where.

Thunderation.

The trip in the red automobile Daisy called a *convertible* was breathtaking, even if a little unsettling. Eli still didn't know their destination, but he didn't care. After all, they had a whole night ahead of them, so why not try to enjoy himself? He was granted such an amazing, unbelievable, once-in-a-lifetime experience, it would be unwise to waste it on brooding.

It proved to be very entertaining to move at such a breakneck speed.

And to observe the scenery. Everything changed. The buildings, the streets, the people. Everything was somehow brighter and larger. But the things that mattered most, the sky and the ocean, didn't change a bit.

He was home. He would know it anywhere.

Eli squinted at Daisy. She navigated the streets in her *convertible* (how did Vic call it? Oh, yes, a *red jazzy number*) with the sure hand of an expert.

Yes, he was home, as long as she was by his side. Happy and carefree for the first time since he left his own century this morning, Eli smiled and his mood lightened considerably.

"You operate an automotive brilliantly, Daisy. I admire your panache."

"Geez, Coleman, you're something else. Panache? Really?"

"Was it a wrong way to put it?"

"It is a very fine way to put it. But it's called driving, driving a car."

"I'll remember that." He covered her hand on the wheel with his and held it there. "Will you teach me to operate— to drive it?" He corrected himself, and grinned at her.

"Seriously? Let you drive my Coco?" She speared him an incredulous glance out of those bewitching amethyst eyes of hers.

"Coco? Who is Coco?"

"This car. She's Coco."

"Really? Your car has a name?"

"So?"

That gave him a pause. Unbelievable. She named an automobile like a...horse, or a pet. Hmm. "So, would you let me drive your... Coco?"

"Coleman, I don't *ever* let anyone touch my baby, never mind driving her. But I'm willing to let you try my truck."

"Truck? What is a truck?"

"A car, only much bigger one. You'll like it."

"If you think so."

He glanced through the side window and frowned. The landmark they were approaching became more apparent. Not a superstitious man, nonetheless he didn't care for cemeteries.

"We're here." The automobile stopped.

"Here? At *Bosque Bello*? Daisy, you do realize that this is a cemetery?"

"Yes."

"Then why—"

"You asked me how I knew that we will be together again. The answer is right here."

"But—"

"Trust me, Eli. Please."

Without another word, she exited the car, and walked through the open gates to the cemetery.

Reluctant, Eli left the confinement of the luxurious automobile, and followed.

The memory of his most recent visit to *Bosque Bello* was still vivid in his mind. Just three days ago he lay to rest William O'Brien, his best friend.

His worst enemy.

The pain was still fresh and sharp. Eli's soul still bled from the betrayal.

But worst of all was guilt, heavy as led, black as a nightmare. Because William died in his stead. Deliberately, purposely. Just three short days ago. No, not three days, but one hundred and eleven years and three days.

How flabbergasting was that?

Daisy moved ahead with a purposeful stride to a destination unknown to him.

Better hurry up, Eli.

She said she wanted to show him something. But what? Uncomfortable and uneasy, Eli tried to avoid looking around, but that proved to be difficult. All these headstones— some elaborate, some very primitive—were graves. Old graves.

He concentrated on the trees. They were magnificent. For the last hundred years, the live oaks didn't change a bit. Like sentries, those ancient trees stood in proud formation, guarding their territory. Spanish moss hung from the long branches like intricate silver lace.

The breeze was comfortable, light and gentle. Peace. Tranquility. *Sorrow.*

Something stirred in his memory, like a soft whisper. A sudden waive of chill washed over him as the images of a burial swam before his eyes.

...Flowers, there were so much flowers, and all of them were daisies. The smell of them was intoxicating. Such a warm day it was, sunny and quiet. The sky was cloudless and clear, and so blue it hurt his eyes. And up ahead was a fresh grave...

In the next instant, the images flickered away, and once again, he was in the middle of the path adorned by the live oak trees.

What was it? Was his imagination playing tricks on him? And whose funeral services he just glimpsed? Not William's. The weather then was miserable and rainy, and the flowers were carnations. Eli shook his head, then shut his eyes, and pressed both thumbs against his sockets. He was queasy, almost nauseated.

Thunderation. Get a grip, man.

"Eli?" Daisy called from somewhere ahead. "Where are you?"

"Right here." His voice sounded unsteady to his own ears. Right now he wished to be anywhere but here. And why in the blue blazes had Daisy brought him to *Bosque Bello* Cemetery?

CHAPTER FIFTEEN

Partially hidden by the tall headstone, Daisy motioned for him to approach closer.

Silence, eerie and dense, struck Eli first. The air didn't stir, even though the breeze was strong enough to lift Spanish moss from the nearby tree. But at the spot where Daisy stood the quiet was absolute.

The time stood still.

Where did that come from? Unnerved, Eli examined the place with his eyes. Isolated, but well-tended, sheltered by live oaks trees.

Whose resting place was it? There were several graves, but only two sat close together. Against his will, Eli moved to those two graves. He sent Daisy a questioning glance, but her face was averted. Eli followed her eyes.

The grey headstone was quite tall, simple, and dignified. He came closer, read the inscription:

Elijah Benjamin Coleman,
a great man, beloved husband and father.
December 7th 1873 - March 29th 1954.

"Dear Lord..."

Eli froze. Shock, swift and frigid, clouded his senses. His head swam, his vision blurred.

Am I really standing before my own grave? Impossible.

He closed his eyes, shook his head in denial.

A dream. Just a dream.

But when he dragged his eyes open, the big gray headstone was still there, stately and solemn, and somehow...proud.

Not a dream.

With a peculiar detachment, Eli gazed upon his resting place. His final destination. He wondered who chose that particular stone, and that inscription.

Probably, Daisy. She would know that I would prefer something simple, but dignified. Somber but not drab.

He was about to ask her, when his eyes landed on the other headstone that sat close to his grave. Smaller in size, lighter in color, almost powdery-blue, but identical in shape and form. He squinted at it, read the inscription.

Daisy Coleman
beloved wife and mother, the timeless miracle
Died January 29th, 1954.

And his world went dark.

Someone screamed in agony. An anguished chant 'No! No! No!" cut through the silence.

"Ssh. Eli, stop, darling, I'm okay, I'm right here. Please stop."

And two strong arms encircled him, held tight. Like a wise. Or an anchor.

Through the haze of grief, with red mist exploding behind his eyes, Eli fought that embrace, desperate to break free.

Daisy!

"I'm here, baby, I'm right here. Please, stop. Please!"

If she lived a thousand years, Nika wouldn't forget this moment. Or forgive herself. Eli's grief was so raw, it was impossible to watch. She never heard him scream before. She wished she never had. The sound was almost inhuman. He howled in pain like a wounded animal. Nika hugged him hard. In shock, Eli thrashed against her, trying to escape. Big and strong and wild in his grief, he was no match for her. With every ounce of her will, Nika held on for dear life. She mumbled words of comfort, desperate to drag him out of his shock to no avail.

Her fault. She should have prepared him, should have told him before she brought him here.

Too late to dwell on what should've, you idiot.

"Shut up. Shut up. Shut the hell up!"

Her unexpected on top of your lungs yell broke the spell of Eli's shock.

At last, his desperate thrashing subsided, as he quieted in her arms. Inch by torturous inch, his back straightened, and he withdrew from the protective circle of her arms. With dark haunted eyes in the bloodless face, he resembled a mask from the ancient Greek theatre. A tragedy mask.

"Daisy. You're alive, you're here."

"I am, my darling. And I'm so sorry, I should have told you, but—"

"*You are alive.*"

That hoarse, anguished whisper was more than she could bear. Nika hugged him again, now more for her own comfort rather than his. Eli's arms enveloped her, all but squeezed the breath from her, but Nika didn't mind.

"I am alive, and well, and all in one piece." She nuzzled his chest, inhaled his familiar smell. "You scared me. Scared the bejesus out of me. Don't do that again, Coleman."

Still shaken, Eli brought her close, held her tight and fast. She was here, with him. They were together. Until that damned January of 1954, they would be together.

That's how she knew. That's how Daisy survived.

He stole a quick glance over his shoulder at the two headstones. This time the shock was akin to a mild jolt of electricity. He was still sad, incredibly so, but not shattered. A silent prayer he offered to Almighty held more gratitude than any religious significance. And how unbelievable was that, praying for his and Daisy's souls when they were entwined in each other arms, alive and well?

Incredible. Unthinkable. Improbable. And still...

The woman in his arms drew a deep breath and furrowed her little nose into his chest.

My Daisy. My timeless miracle.

The great bard was right: there *were* more things in heaven and Earth.

More things indeed.

And the woman snuggled tightly in his arms was the living proof of that.

Eli wasn't sure how long they stood near the graves, holding each other, drawing comfort from each other, but when they finally exited the cemetery, the day was waning. The drive to Daisy's home was uneventful. Eli kept quiet. What was there to say? Words were useless. He learned the truth, but wished with all his might to forget it. What was the purpose of him leaning that she passed away first? That he followed her two months later? That they both died on the 29th? Sometimes the truth was more painful than ignorance.

Eli stole a quick glance at Daisy. Alive. She was alive. She was here. And she loved him. For now, it was enough.

Daisy didn't utter a single word during their return trip, as if giving him time to adjust. And, sweet Lord, he needed it! All in the course of a single day, he jumped through time, found Daisy, met her cousin, and underwent through the most earth-shattering experience of his life. Confused? Hell, yes, he was confused. And blindsided, and bewildered, and... terrified. But she was beside him. She was alive and well. That's all that mattered. He'll deal with everything else later. As soon as he managed to herd his unbridled emotions under control.

CHAPTER SIXTEEN

Why didn't he say something? Anything? His silence was killing her.

Then again, Nika still remembered her own reaction when Alex first brought her to the cemetery and showed her those two headstones. Shock. Denial. Sorrow.

And overwhelming grief.

She slanted a glance at Eli. Quiet, pensive, but alive, and oh, dear God, so handsome! And he was all hers. Forever.

Not forever, but until the winter of 1954.

Oh, how she hated that tiny voice sometimes.

It's a gazillion years ahead, and nobody asked your opinion.

Or sixty-six years before.

"Shut up, you stupid bitch."

"I beg your pardon?" Eli's voice interrupted her inner-self argument.

"Ahh...nothing. I was just talking to myself."

"Are you in a habit to call yourself names, then?"

"Yeah, sometimes." She shot him a crooked smile. "When I misbehave."

"Do you misbehave often?"

"Not if I can help it, but once in a while I've been known to say something without thinking it through first. Or act rashly. Like today. I'm sorry, Eli."

"For?"

"For bringing you to the cemetery without preparing you first."

"Nothing could have prepared me for that, Daisy."

His voice was flat and vacant like his eyes. He was right, of course. No words could prepare for *that* experience.

"I know. It was such a shock for me, too. When Alex showed it to me a year ago."

"Alex? So, he was the one." Eli plucked at his chin absentmindedly. "Remind me to thank him. It seems that I owe him a lot."

"Owe him? What are you talking about? You don't owe Alex anything."

"Oh, but I do. For taking care of Abby; for finding that headstones, and giving you hope; for not punching me in the face this morning," he finished with a ghost of a smile. "He wanted to do it so badly, I could feel it. I'm not sure why, but he wanted to hit me."

"Yeah, well, you don't have to worry about that. Alex is a peaceful sort, unlike me. He would never act rashly."

But Alex's combative stance, and his open resentment and animosity toward Eli was still fresh in her memory. Her cousin was an easygoing, laidback, and even-tempered guy. Nothing short of a disaster could shake Alex's composure and his sometimes infuriating sunny disposition. So, what happened to make his anger flare and his fangs bare?

What gives, Cuz?

For the life of her, Nika couldn't think of a single reason. Resigned, she pushed it out of her mind for a moment.

Later. I'll grill Alex later.

And just like that, they were smack in the middle of her own driveway. How did they arrive home? How long were they sitting in the idling car, anyway?

Unsure of her next step, Nika turned off the engine.

Now what?

Almost on autopilot, her hand came to touch the engagement ring hidden under her shirt. Inside the car, the silence was disturbed by a faint murmur of the ocean and soft cries of seagulls. Enough was enough. Another moment of silence and she would burst at the seams. She cleared her throat.

"How did you find me?"

Eli's time-traveling experience seemed like a safe subject. And Nika was really curious about it. Come to think of it, *how* did he find her? Granted, Fernandina Beach was a small town, but still.

"It was easy. I turned the key in the clock, and it brought me here."

"Here where?"

"Remember when I asked you how was it possible that you turned the key inside my house in Fernandina, but ended up on Cumberland Island, where I was visiting at that moment?"

"I remember, yes."

"Remember what you told me? The only explanation you had was that we are connected, deeply, internally. Throughout time. Now I know that for sure, because I turned the key inside the grandfather clock, and found myself on the street corner near your office. Near you. Eventually, I would have found you on my own, but I was fortunate to meet Vic and Maximilian, and get their assistance."

"Vic? You met Vic?"

As fate would have it, her flamboyant gay friend was the first person to greet Eli into the twenty-first century. Talk about culture shock.

"I did indeed. And his trusty little companion."

Eli was serious, but his silver eyes were sparkled with humor. They slowly cleared, losing that haunted faraway look. Thank God. Her mood shifted from pensive to humorous.

"I wish I could see that. So, what did you think of him?"

"He is one fine and funny fellow, although peculiar looking."

"Are you talking about Vic or Maximilian?"

"Both, I guess."

"Funny, but true. And what did you tell him?"

"I told him that I'm looking for Veronika Morris, and he pointed me toward your office. He called you a 'House Whisperer.'"

"Well, I'm known for restoring old houses. Remember my tool belt?"

"How can I ever forget?"

His low, intimate murmur carried a dark edge, and just like that, the atmosphere in the car became charged with sensuality. Without so much as touching her, with his voice alone, Eli made her shiver, and shot her heart rate to the stratosphere.

"Vic also informed me that you just finish the big job on the Coleman house."

For some stupid reason, Nika blushed, feeling annoyed and embarrassed. Here she was, all hot and bothered, and he was talking about the house. Moron.

"Y-yes."

She shrugged. "I told you before that I was hired by your descendant to restore your home. That's how I ended up in your time in the first place."

"I remember. Did you really finish it?"

"Yes. I did." Pure nerves fluttered close to the surface. Would Eli like it? It was imperative for her that he approved of her job, that he be proud of her. After all, she did it for him.

Nika recovered quickly, masking her nerves under the layer of false bravado. "And I did it splendidly, if I say so myself. They don't call me a House Whisperer for nothing, Coleman. So, the senator is flying down on Monday, to accept the finished project. But I'll show it to you before—"

"Do you realize what that means, Daisy?" With grave impatience ringing in his voice, Eli interrupted her in mid-sentence.

"No. What?"

"We must return before he comes. Even if that means I won't see Abigail." His face clouded with regret. "But we *must* go, Daisy. Immediately."

"But I can't! Not right now. I have to be there when the senator arrives. I have to show him the finished project, and officially relinquish the house."

"Can Alex do it in your stead?"

She could say no, but it would be a lie.

"He can, but, Eli, it's my restoration, my job, and I have to do it myself. I need to. My crew and I spent ten months on the site, working day and night. It was grueling work, sometimes brutal, but we did it. We restored the old house to its magnificent self. And I must see it through. I have to finish it. Call it professional pride, call it ego, if you will. Or duty. But that's for me to do."

"I understand your reasoning, and appreciate your professional ethics, Daisy. More, I admire you for that. But, *ma petite*, if you turn the house back to the Senator, and relinquish the rights, how will we get inside? We must enter it to get to the clock, and return back home."

"And we will. I promise."

"But how?"

"I'll find a way. Please trust me, Eli. I'll think of something."

He was still reluctant. When Eli started to rub his chin with two fingers, Nika rushed ahead, "The main point, you have the key, right? The key from the grandfather clock?"

"I do."

Eli pulled a leather cord from underneath his shirt and showed her the familiar little key that he wore like a pendant. Nika sucked in a breath.

She would know it anywhere. From the hundreds of copies she made, she recognized it instantly. The form of it, the color, the muted sheen of patina was unmistakable. This key was one of a kind. She dreamt about it so many times she lost count. If she hadn't dropped it last time...

Unable to resist, Nika touched it lightly with her index finger, and felt a sudden jolt. Startled, she jerked back her hand, but her finger still smarted, like after a bee sting.

What the heck?

Something to puzzle over, for sure, but later. Rubbing her tingling hand, she concentrated on Eli.

"We will get inside and go back, you have my word on it. In two days, *Verochka* and Abby will be here. You will make amends with your sister, and we will have our first and last Thanksgiving as a family. Then, the next day, I'll say my goodbyes, and we will return. I promise."

For a long moment, Eli was silent. After what seemed like an eternity to her, he nodded. "Until the day after Thanksgiving, then."

"Until Friday."

And like an echo, her words reverberated in her mind, again and again, in an endless, infinite loop. Why did she feel so lost and deflated all of a sudden?

Unsettled, Nika pushed the door open, and stepped out of the car. She lived this past year in hope, waiting for the day when she was finally reunited with Eli, and go back to his time. And now, when the date was set— next Friday, just a week from today—she was unsure, and yes, dammit, afraid. And a little sad. Okay, a *lot* sad.

The reality of the looming deadline crashed her spirit, flooding her with doubt. Was she doing the right thing? Was she brave enough to do it?

Absurd!

Her place was beside Eli, her beloved, her future husband. And yes, she was brave enough— audacious enough—to do what she wanted. What was *meant*.

They were meant. They were two halves of a whole. If the past year had taught her anything, it was the lesson that she was miserable without him. Half alive, barely trudging through life without purpose or destination.

But her other place was right here, in this time, with her grandmother, and her cousin, and the business they built, and home they made together—

Snap out of it, girl, you have a whole week ahead of you, so make the best of the time allotted.

"I will. I'll try."

Try harder. Remember Margaret? The baby who's waiting to be born, your daughter? And don't screw up!

"I won't," she murmured, whipping a single renegade tear from her face.

She feigned a smile at Eli who came to stand nearby.

"Were you taking to yourself again, *ma petite*?"

"Yes, I was."

"You were miles away, so sad and pensive. Are you alright?"

"I am." She took his hand and pressed it against her wet cheek. "I am now."

"Do you want to stay here?" He asked quietly. A somber expression filled his face.

Oh, he knew her too well. She allowed herself to drown in his somber silver eyes.

"No. My place is beside you." A simple truth.

"And mine is beside you," he said quietly. "So if you are in doubt, and decide to stay here, I will stay, too."

"You... you will stay? Here? In my time? Giving up everything?"

"I would give up my life for you."

Sincerity of his statement stole her breath away. Her heart trembled, then melted.

Any indecision, any confusion she harbored, was wiped clean. Joy, quiet and sweet, fluttered in the pit of her stomach, then surged up, filling her to the brim.

Nika's eyes overflowed with tears. No matter how many times she swiped them away they continued to stream down her cheeks.

"I love you, Eli. More than anything in the world. And next Friday, we will return together to your time and place." She smiled through a sheen of tears. "To *our* time and place."

"Are you sure, Daisy?"

"Absolutely, positively. We'll start our life together in the Coleman house and live happily ever after." Nika finally succeeded in wiping tears from her face and gripped Eli's hand. "There's the hospital you need to build, and Belle who's waiting for us, and Sultan, who's getting fat and bored. Not to mention Mrs. Smith, who'd be mightily pissed at me for keeping you here, and let me tell you, her wrath is scarier than hell." She shook her head. "We are getting back. You can bet your last cent on that."

"You are one of a kind, Daisy," Eli murmured, bringing their joined hands to his heart. "One of a kind."

"I am indeed." And to switch the mood, she winked at him. "But I'm afraid I've been the worst kind of a hostess so far. And since I failed to welcome you properly this morning, I'll try to redeem myself now."

"What do you have in mind?"

"Oh, you'll like it, Coleman. I promise." She gave him her best sexy smile. "Trust me."

CHAPTER SEVENTEEN

He liked her version of welcome.

What red-blooded man wouldn't?

Eli smiled, as he laid in the soft bed, atop the smooth silky sheets with Daisy's butt snuggled firmly against his groin in a fashion she called spooning.

Only if he is a dead one, he answered his own question.

As soon as they were inside, Daisy all but attacked him, tearing his clothes off, scattering them all over the house. By the time they reached her bedroom, he was naked as a newborn babe. Eli let her have an upper hand because he was enjoying it too much. Frankly, being ravaged was a novel experience for him, and he found that he liked it rather tremendously. But soon he took the lead. All his pent-up frustration surged upward, ending in a mating so fierce, he was afraid he had hurt her. But afterward she smiled up at him like a Cheshire cat who slurped a bowl of fresh cream. She even licked her lips, the wench. Eli smiled, as his mind took him to the first time they made love in his bed, at his house in 1909.

...They didn't utter a single word on the way toward his bedroom. Gently he propelled her inside and shut the door. Then he locked it, and turned to her. Still silent, he closed the distance between them and in one sweep pulled her shirt over her head, and then her pants down her legs. She stood completely naked in front of him, carefree and brazen. Her body was slim and petite, with a boyish build and no curves to speak of, but her legs were long, her small breasts were round and high, and her overall muscle tone was excellent.

"You are exquisite, simply glorious." His whisper was raw and harsh.

Daisy smiled and pointed at his chest. "I'm at a disadvantage here. Do you think you could lose a few layers?"

"Do you wish to see a naked gentleman, ma petite?"

"Not just any gentleman. Just you."

He could almost feel the steam as it poured out of his nostrils.

"Well?" Her smile was wicked.

"I knew you were not a lady," he rebuked, but shed his clothing with great enthusiasm.

"Are you by any chance complaining?"

"What I'm doing, is giving praise to all the saints."

"Oh, my, oh, my, oh, my!" She all but salivated. "Oh, sweet baby Jesus! Look at that!"

"So, I take it you like what you see?"

"Love it!" she murmured. "You are beautiful! You, Eli Coleman, are absolutely beautiful!"

She stepped in front of him and touched his chest. Eli couldn't prevent a growling sound if his life depended on it. He almost lost it, there and then.

"A gentleman cannot be beautiful," he countered through his clenched teeth. He was burning, hurting, from the clawing hunger. If she didn't stop touching him like this, or looking at him like this, he was afraid he wouldn't be able to keep the beast chained much longer.

"I don't know about 'a gentleman,' I don't care about 'a gentleman.'" She circled him once, then twice, all the while her fingers were busy touching the various parts of him. The most intimate parts. "But you are truly and seriously beautiful."

She lifted her smoldering eyes and licked her sinful lips. All the blood rushed down from his head to his shaft. Throbbing, straining against the confinement of his own skin, it demanded release.

"You are playing with fire, ma petite."

"Oh, I hope so." Her reckless smile had a bite of a smugness. "I really, truly hope so."

And just like that, the chain snapped and the beast burst free.

He grabbed her, or she jumped into his arms, and the madness began...

He remembered being pleasantly surprised when his little street urchin proved to be a true courtesan in bed. Uninhibited, unselfish, even naughty, Daisy was a dream lover every man fantasized about since the dawn of time. She delighted him and bewitched him, and made him a raving, insatiable lunatic.

And wasn't that an embarrassment to him, a gentleman of a ripe age of four and thirty. But he wasn't embarrassed tonight. If anything, Eli was delirious. She went in flames as soon as he touched her. She scorched him, burned him alive, all but destroyed him. Yes, she was one of a kind, his Daisy, in and out of the bedroom. And wasn't he the luckiest son-of-a-bitch alive to have such a woman? And was it any wonder he risked everything, his very life included, to find her again, in another time, another realm, another world? And he'd do it again, in a snap.

Daisy stirred, rubbing her delightful little behind against his most sensitive parts, and sent his juices flowing. Instantly aroused, Eli marveled at his own prowess.

Tonight, hungry and randy as a pair of youngsters, they almost did away with each other. He expected to be half-dead by now, but instead, he was alert and energized, and ready. Eager for the next round.

They left her bed just once, to freshen themselves— to take a shower, as it was called here—only to end up making love under the steamy sprays that came crashing down from that amazing invention, the waterfall shower.

He was baffled at first when at the flick of her hand the bathroom came awash in different shades of color, pulsing with blues and greens. Laughing, she explained that it was a modern invention for mood enhancement. Well, it definitely enhanced his mood, and sent his desire, not to mention that other part of him, into an overdrive. The recollection of it now made him hard as iron.

Impatient, Eli pressed his throbbing shaft against her soft ass, and blew gently at Daisy's exposed nape. She muttered something in her sleep, shuddered delicately, and made him chuckle. And when she turned around, sleepy and warm and oh, so kissable, Eli's heart trembled from the wonder of her.

With great care, he wound one of her springy curls onto his finger. Oh, how he adored those messy ringlets! Thank God, all of them came back after the washing, as she promised. Daisy never breaks her promises. Overwhelmed, Eli leaned over and kissed first her perky little nose, then her eyes, then her pointy stubborn chin.

"I simply adore you, *ma petite,*" he whispered.

"Yeah? Show me," she said with the smile of a harlot.

His laughter turned into a moan once she straddled him like a stallion, and took him inside of her. She was hot as a furnace, smooth as satin, wet as rain. She was his salvation, his redemption, his destiny. His woman.

"Show me." A demand, urgent, desperate. "Now." A plea, soft and quiet.

What choice did he have but to show her? And one he welcomed like a starving man at a banquet.

Much later, Eli left sleeping Daisy in bed, and went in search of his clothes. He picked them up, one piece after another, and dressed. And not a moment too soon. Startled, he almost jumped when the door burst open, and Alex walked in, carrying what seemed like a small mountain of parcels and packages in both hands.

"Well, good morning to you, Mr. Benjamin," he drawled, arching his brow.

"Good morning to you too, Mr. Morris."

Eli did his best to look unruffled and composed, but was gravely afraid that he failed.

Here he was, dressed in rumpled clothes, still aglow from the marathon of sex, and blushing, if the heat in his face was any indication.

Thunderation.

"Help me, will you?" With that, Alex dropped, without ceremony, a mountain of packages into Eli's hands. Eli grabbed them, and stood, frowning, unsure of his next move. To say that he was baffled would be an understatement.

"Well? Haul them to the kitchen, and put everything on the table." Daisy's cousin instructed. "Then come with me, as there's more of them."

Without uttering a word, Eli deposited everything on the kitchen table, and ventured out.

Alex was rummaging inside the automobile, and what an incredible beauty that one was, muttering something under his breath. Eli's attention was glued to the automobile—no, car, he corrected himself, so he missed Alex's question.

"What? I beg your pardon. I was busy admiring your car." He stood a little straighter, proud of himself to use the correct vernacular.

"Beautiful, isn't it?"

"It is for sure. What is it called?"

"The manufacturer calls this model Tycan Turbo S, but I just call her Baby. Isn't she sweet?" Alex caressed the car with his free hand like a lover to his mistress.

"She is magnificent." Eli had no desire to hide his awe and admiration. Sensually curved and gleaming with chrome, this car indeed reminded him of a female, a stunningly beautiful and tempestuous one.

Eli's voice held a note of a pure reverence that only another male understood and appreciated. Because of that, Alex's demeanor softened toward the poor bastard. But he wasn't ready to let him off the hook. Not yet, anyway.

Alex watched the newcomer out of the corner of his eyes. If he hadn't known better, he would never have pegged him for a traveler from the last century.

Geez, that sounded as asinine as the day Nika introduced the subject a year ago.

The very idea of traveling through time made Alex twitchy. But there was Abby, and Nika's famous letter, and the two graves at the old cemetery...

Only a fool would argue against the reality of it all. Alex was no fool. Far from it.

And twitchy or not, he accepted the unacceptable, even though he still couldn't wrap his brain around it. He slanted a glance at Elijah Benjamin Coleman.

Tall, lithe, with broad shoulders and long legs, he was built like an athlete. Any basketball team in the country would sign him.

A touch of aloofness in his demeanor, a regal posture and a proud grace he carried himself with reminded him of Abby. Alex's heart squeezed.

Don't, he ordered himself. *Don't even go there.*

But it was hard not to when Abby's eyes looked at him from the face of a stranger. Alex swore under his breath.

Put a muzzle on it, buddy. The lady is not for you.

With tremendous effort, he shoved the thoughts of Abby into the back of his mind, and turned toward the older Coleman sibling.

Would you look at him, almost shaking in his wingtips, salivating over a Porsche?

Half-amused, half-irritated, Alex followed Eli with his eyes.

Dressed in clothes that belonged in a history museum, and badly rumpled on top of that, he should be looking ridiculous, or at least out of place. Instead, Elijah B. Coleman looked like he belonged in this picture.

The tyrant, the jerk, the controlling asshole.

The bastard!

Alex flexed his hands. No, he was not ready to forget and forgive. Not even for Nika's sake.

Sorry, Cuz, but this is a guy thing.

"Wanna spin?"

"I beg your pardon?"

"I meant, do you want a ride?"

"Inside this automobile? I mean, car?"

"Yep. Just a short one, mind you, because otherwise Nika will have my hide. She's mad at me as it is."

"Oh, yes. I would absolutely love a ride, even if a short one."

A naked delight on Eli's face made Alex feel guilty. *Almost.*

"Why is she mad at you?"

"She thinks I'm slacking on my household duties and chores." Alex picked up another full bag, hefted it on his hip. "She's right. As always. But don't tell her I said that. And so, I'm trying to get into my cousin's good graces. Hence, the grocery shopping."

"Grocery shopping? Like marketing? For produce and food?"

"Yeah, something like that."

"Why do you need so much food, and all at once? Won't it spoil?"

"To answer your second question, no it won't spoil because we have such a convenience as a refrigerator." He pointed to his left. "The big steel thingy in the kitchen. That's the one. It's like a cold box, only electric. As to why so much of it? Buddy, it's a Thanksgiving week. And the family is coming to town, I hear. So, we need a lot of this and that, and one big-ass turkey."

Alex tagged something huge and round from the car, and held it by an attached cord. "Grab the bird, will ya?"

The mystery thing was quite heavy, dense, and cold, and required the use of both hands to hold it.

"What...what is this?"

"Why, the turkey, of course."

"But...but it is hard as a rock."

"As it supposed to be, because it's frozen."

"Oh." As if that cleared the matter. Was Alex joking? Or did they really freeze Thanksgiving turkeys in this century? But how?

Why the devil for?

Eli had no time to wonder about it, as Alex aimed another one of his white-toothed smiles at him that didn't fool him for a second. The man was after his blood, and that shark's grin was just another proof of that.

"It's going to be a true family dinner, with all of us together. Aren't you excited?"

The slap on the back was so forceful, it almost sent Eli face first to the ground, turkey and all.

Alex did it on purpose. Eli was sure of that.

So, he was not mistaken after all. The little bastard. Daisy's cousin did harbor animosity toward him. The million-dollar question was, why?

"So, *Mr. Benjamin,*" Alex flashed him another fake grin, "help me transfer all these groceries upstairs, and I'll give you the ride of your life."

With that promise, Alex grabbed another handful of parcels from the open space in the back of a car. Puzzled, but elated with the prospect of a ride, Eli put the subject of Alex's grudge on the back of his mind for a time being. He was determined to get to the bottom of it, sooner or later. After three more trips up and down the stairs, they managed to transport all the groceries to the kitchen.

And at last, Eli found himself inside the marvelous invention called *car.*

He tried not to gape, and not to touch anything, but it was rather impossible.

He was behaving like a child, but Eli couldn't help himself.

Sweet Jesus, everything is so fascinating.

Of course, he was familiar with Mr. Ford's automobiles. He had seen it, even driven some of the models, but never was tempted to own one. Now, this car? Eli would die to purchase one of those.

Impossible. Not for a hundred years yet.

Resigned, he settled deeper into the leather seat, to enjoy himself while he could.

Daisy's cousin drove fast, very fast, with the effortless skill of a true master. But not without care. Eli admired that and had no fear.

"I wish I could operate a car and drive like you." His confession earned him a surprised look from the younger man.

"What's the problem? I'll teach you."

"You...will? Really?"

"Sure, why not? I bet it wouldn't be as hard as teaching Abby to drive."

Eli drew a sharp breath and fixed Alex with a steely glare.

"You...taught my sister to drive?"

"Sure did. Among other things."

A myriad of unpleasant pictures sprung to mind. His blood froze in his veins.

"And what might those 'other things' be?"

"Let's see. To fix breakfast, to do laundry, to work on a computer—"

"My sister washed her own clothes?"

All his fears of something nefarious Alex might have taught his baby sister were replaced by an outrage.

Abby did the washing? His Abby?

In their home, Abby had never have done anything more strenuous than pour tea. Washing? They had servants for that, for crying out loud.

"Well, the washing machine did the actual work, but yeah. Why? Any objections?"

Eli mulled that for a moment. New times, new rules. New life.

"Not at all." He averted his gaze, and looked out of the window.

Thunderation.

"I am in your debt, Mr. Morris," he said after a while. "And owe you a world of thanks." That earned him another surprised look out of the violet eyes identical to Daisy's, and a puzzled frown.

"Whatever for, Mr. Benjamin?"

"Oh, stop that Mr. Benjamin nonsense, and call me Eli, will you?" Eli snapped.

"Okay. Then you stop that Mr. Morris crap, and call me Alex."

"Alright. Alex. I want to thank you."

"For?"

"For my sister. Daisy tells me you and your grandmother took care of Abigail when she came here first, and later, when she became sick. I appreciate that sincerely. More than I can say. I understand it was a huge burden on you."

"Now you're going to piss me off. As a matter of fact, I was pissed at you from the beginning, and wanted to give you a piece of my mind for a long time."

Ah, finally. The truth.

"Why are you upset with me? I couldn't help but notice it. What have I done to displease you? And please go ahead and give me that piece of your mind, as you put it. I'm at your disposal."

"Oh, are you, now?" Alex scowled at him. "Well, where to start?"

"At the beginning would be the best."

"You are a piece of work, Elijah Benjamin. By the way, why Benjamin? Why not your real name?"

"It seemed like a thing at the time."

"Okay, whatever." The younger man shrugged, and stopped the car. "Your business. Well, from the beginning, then."

And in a lightning strike move, he punched Eli in the face.

CHAPTER EIGHTEEN

Golden sunrays teased her closed eyelids. Nika stirred. Was it morning? Already? It couldn't be...or could it? She shielded her eyes with one hand, and squinted through the splayed fingers. Yep. It was morning, alright. Ridiculously pleased, she flopped onto her back, and couldn't suppress a wince as pains and aches from last night's passion fest zipped through her body. The beautiful memories of the previous night flooded in a rush, and Nika came completely awake.

Eli.

No wonder she was sore. Smug and happy, Nika rolled onto her stomach. The faint murmur of the ocean drifted inside. She reached out to Eli's side of the bed. Warm. Empty. Where was he? Nika strained her ears. Not a sound. Huh. Did he wander outside? So what? He was home, well, sort off, and he was a big boy.

Oh, God was he ever!

Big, and strong, and...

And you're getting all hot and bothered again. Damn.

Nika blinked the remnant of her sleep away, and stretched. She slowly scanned around the room until her gaze landed on the bed. She gaped, and bolted upright.

Sweet baby Jesus!

Her bed resembled a battlefield. The sheets were tangled and twisted, the pillows strewn across the floor, and her heirloom duvet was torn in the middle.

She took a deep breath. Everything smelled of passion. Even her skin. Her lips curved into a satisfied smile.

I smell of Eli.

A thrilling sensation chased away her initial shock. Nika giggled. The heck with the sheets. She was so happy! No, scratch that, she was delirious with joy. Spreading her arms wide, she plopped back onto her abused bed. And smelling Eli, began to drift again. Her mind floated, hazy and languid. Where was she? In her own home, in 2020, or in the Coleman house in 1909?

Does it matter? As long as she was with Eli, she didn't care about a thing.

Still half-asleep, Nika lifted her left hand and brought it closer to her face.

The antique amethyst ring that belonged to Eli's grandmother once again adorned her finger. Her heart trembled. Last night, when he found it on the chain around her neck, Eli unclipped the clasp, slid the ring off, and slid it back onto her finger.

He kissed the back of her hand, then her wrist, then her palm. With his heart in his eyes, he proposed again. And she accepted. Again.

And then he made love to her like she was the most desirable and beautiful woman on earth. So tenderly that she wept. So reverently that she rejoiced.

The intimacy was her undoing. *He* was her undoing. He was her everything.

From the first moment she laid her eyes on him to the moment when Nika realized she was in love with her aloof and forbidding host, Eli was her savior, her anchor, a single stalwart constant in her life.

Their first lovemaking in his tower office was turbulent and uninhibited. Nika was astonished to find that under his polished and cool exterior, Eli was a volcano of passion with the heart of a true romantic sap. Then he all but destroyed her with his fire. But tonight surpassed it ten times over.

They both were wild, hungry and greedy, coming at each other like two starved animals. Guided by pure madness, their first mating was fierce and unapologetically carnal. With his body he claimed her, branded her. With his eyes he cherished her. With his hands and that clever mouth of his, he brought her to the brink of a delirium and then set her free, jumping after her, chanting her name—*Daisy, my Daisy*—like a prayer. But as soon as the initial hunger was satisfied, the true magic began.

Tenderness replaced desperation, urgency gave way to pleasure, and at last, love unveiled its gentle wings, and swept them both to the enchanted place where they stayed throughout the night, spellbound and lost in each other.

Complete melting of souls was something Nika has never experienced before.

Eli, her lover, her timeless miracle...And he was all hers.

God, she felt glorious! All soft and fluid and lazy. She would drift back to her slumberous paradise, if not for the faint annoying twitch in her midsection.

What on earth...?

Since frowning took too much energy, Nika just lay amidst the torn sheets, and focused her mind on her body.

After a while, the mystery of her discomfort was finally solved. Hunger pangs. Unlike her mushy brain, her stomach was fully awake and displeased at being ignored. Time to get up. Reluctant, Nika sat, and ran both hands through the tangled mess she called hair. What time was it, anyway? She squinted at the bedside clock, and yelped in shock.

"Eleven o'clock? How could it possibly be eleven?"

No wonder her stomach issued a note of protest. She never slept past six A.M., and often was up and running even before the sun was up.

But today, for the first time in ages, she overslept.

"I overslept," she muttered, half embarrassed, half amused.

I wonder why, her inner voice piped in, heavy on sarcasm.

"Oh, shut up. You're just jealous."

By her rough estimate, they slept no more than four of hours, if that.

Was it any wonder that some of her body parts were still tender and tingling?

You're sporting some visible love marks, too, girl.

"Good for me." Nika snickered. They were her badges of honor.

After such a marathon of lovemaking, it was a pure miracle that both of them regained their ability to move. Well, Eli did. His clothes were missing, while hers were now accurately folded and left on a chair. Her shoes stood together on the floor, lined up from heals to tips.

"I am crazy about you, Elijah Benjamin Coleman."

She plopped back, reluctant to leave the bed that still smelled of Eli. But lounging wouldn't get her a cup of coffee, nor the more solid sustenance her stomach demanded. Damn. With a groan, Nika wiggled and twisted, and at last managed to pry her body free of the torn sheets. Her tummy let out a warning growl.

"Okay, I hear you. But shower first. And then coffee, and—"

Her planning was rudely interrupted by the loud banging of the door, and the sounds of two angry voices. *Eli and Alex. Uh-oh.*

Alarmed, Nika grabbed her robe. A following racket of breaking furniture kicked her panic into an overdrive. What on earth? Stumbling, belting her robe on the go, Nika and ran out of the bedroom.

The picture that greeted her eyes was so ridiculous, she pinched herself to make sure she wasn't still dreaming.

The chaos ruled. Her living room was in shambles. And in between the broken shards of the lamp and overturned coffee table, her cousin and her fiancé were locked in a parody of an embrace, swearing and cursing like two seasoned sailors.

They pushed and pulled at each other like two rambunctious kids fighting for a toy. Fists flew, muscles bulged, insults bloomed. The war was in progress.

Nika quickly accessed the situation. It was obvious that the honor of stopping this mayhem belonged to her. Well, then. She pursed her lips, and brought two pinkies into her mouth. An ear-splitting whistle shattered the air. Both adversaries sprang apart. Mad enough to chew nails, Nika rounded on the pair of them.

"What the fuck? Have you two lost your mind? Alex?"

"He...he ..."

But that was the extent of his speech. Seething, with his left eye half-closed, and a blood trickle from a scratch over his brow, Alex looked a fright. Appalled, she turned to Eli. He didn't weather any better. His nose was puffy and bloody, and his mouth was misshapen, swollen, and split at the corner.

Nika's first instinct was to kiss and make it better.

Hell, no.

With boys, and who were men if not the boys only larger in size, the more pragmatic approach was required. Like kicking butt. In this case, two butts.

"I repeat, what the hell is going on?" The glare she aimed at the pair of them was hard enough to shatter diamonds. "Alex? Care to explain?"

"No." His curt reply cut the silence like a sharp blade. Stepping away from Eli, he bent, and picked up an overturned chair. By the deep frown marring his injured face and his jerky movements, Nika figured Alex held himself in check by the skin of his teeth. But he clammed up. The skunk.

Okay then. After a couple of deep breaths, she turned to her fiancé.

"Eli? What on earth?"

"Stay out of it, Daisy. It's between him," he sneered and glared at Alex, "and me."

"Since both of you are related to me, and dragged this," she swept her hand over the chaos, "into my home, I'd like to know why you fought like a pair of hooligans. I have a right to know!"

"You want to know?" Alex exploded, and shot his accusing finger at Eli. "He had a nerve to say that in his opinion Abby would be better off married to some pitiful schmuck than, I quote, *'running amok, trying to pursue her folly'.*"

Ah, of course.

Resigned, Nika wondered for the umpteenth time if her cousin was aware that he was in love with Abby. Nope, the poor moron was clueless. Well, then, let him figure it out on his own.

"Can you believe this shit, Nik?"

Alex's disgust erupted in a string of inventive curses. Since Nika was on a receiving end of that same discussion with Eli many a time, she did, indeed, believed that *shit,* as Alex succinctly put it.

"And that's why you two fought? Alex, you jerk, Abby is here—not in 1909—and doing what she loves and wants. She's free and safe and happy. Do you honestly believe that fighting over what might-have-been-once-upon-a-time-if-chips-would-fall-differently is smart? Really?"

"I had to, Cuz. I just had to. Remember how miserable she was when she came here first? How scared, and lost, and—"

"That was over a year ago. She's not scared, or lost anymore. She is exactly where she belongs, with the people who love her, and care about her."

Eli kept his silence. Cool and unruffled, he regained his composure, or as much as it was possible considering his pitiful state.

"And what do you have to say for yourself, Coleman?"

Eli's bruised knuckles crept to his split lip. He winced.

"I was not an aggressor, Daisy," he uttered after a pause. "I was merely defending myself, as best as I could."

Nika sneered at him. "Yeah, I can see you did a great job of it, too."

"He was first to throw a punch. What, did you expect me to do? Sit and let him pound on me?"

Granted, his version of 'he started it' circa 1909 was a bit more mature, and had some finesse to it. But not enough to sway her.

Nika sighed, and shook her head. This situation was so childish she would have laughed if she wasn't so pissed.

"Did you happen to explain that you wanted to talk to Abby face to face, to apologize and make your amends? Or it didn't occur to you?"

"Why should I? She's my sister, and it's strictly between Abigail and I. And if he assumed the worst of me without any reason," Eli sent an arrogant nod in Alex's direction, "then it's his problem. I won't deign to disabuse him of his delusion."

"Deign to...to disabuse?" Alex almost spat, choking on the old-fashioned words. "Why, you pompous piece of sh...work," he finished when Nika sent him a warning glance. "You said she's better off married to a man she didn't love than chasing what you call her *folly*!"

"If you would listen carefully, young man, you would realize that I said I *thought* it would be better. As in past tense. I was mistaken then, and changed my mind on the subject."

"Why? What made you change it so suddenly?"

"Death."

"Death?" Alex frowned, thrown of balance. "Whose death?"

"My best friend's. I realized that life is miserably short, and precious. And each of us have a right to decide our own fate." A hunted expression darkened his eyes.

"So," not fully convinced, Alex pressed for clarification, "you will not pressure Abby to go back with you?"

"Do you think I could? I am many things, young Morris, but a fool is not one of them. And even if I had that power over my sister, I would never pressure her to return to the time and place of her unhappiness. I love Abigail, whether you believe it or not."

But her cousin was not ready to capitulate just yet.

"What about Nika?"

"What about her?"

"Why did you wait so long? Why didn't you jump through time immediately as soon as you found the key? Why did you put Nika through hell? She suffered."

"I know, and I am sorry for it. More than I can express in words. But the problem is, I didn't find the key. William did. And I didn't know that Daisy left for a visit, and was going to return. William knew, but he didn't tell me the truth until three days ago."

"William? The one who died?"

"Yes."

"You lost me. Your best friend knew that Nika left for a short time to say good bye to her family, but lost the key. He found the key. He knew Nika couldn't return without it. And he didn't tell you about it. Why?"

"That's a million-dollar question. I wish I knew the answer. But William took it to his grave." Frustrated, Eli rubbed his chin, then grimaced and touched gingerly his rapidly enlarging nose.

"Nice friend." Alex snorted, and wiped the blood that trickled over his swollen eye.

"Don't judge the man, Morris. He saved my life, and died in my stead. Three days ago. Or rather hundred eleven years, and three days." Eli hitched the corner of his mouth, then flinched.

"Well, hell. Couldn't you explain everything earlier?"

"When? Before, or after you plowed your fist into my face?"

Exasperated, Alex grunted, rubbing his head.

"My sentiments exactly." Eli concluded with a curt nod.

Nika heard enough.

"Okay, you two. Listen up."

Her stern voice cut into the uncomfortable silence.

"I am going to my room, to take a shower and dress. By the time I come back, I expect this mess to be cleaned up, or else." She pointed her finger at the shards and furniture on the floor. "I also expect my coffee. Some breakfast would be nice, too. And Alex? If you as much as touch Eli with your pinky, you'll answer to me. Same goes for you, Coleman."

"Yes, ma'am." Eli inclined his head, but his lips twitched.

"Sure thing, Cuz." With a mock salute, Alex shot her a lopsided grin.

Nika tried to hide her own smile. Just look at them. Bloody, dirty, still pissed, but sliding off the last wave of anger. Did they have any idea how much alike they were? Both proud, brave, and loyal to a fault. Both were larger than life, and handsome as sin. At least they were, before they engaged in a stupid brawl.

And both stubborn like a proverbial mule. Was it any wonder she was crazy about the pair of them?

"Now, boys, what are you waiting for? Time's awasting."

Behind her, she caught Alex's joking voice. "Don't worry, Benjamin, she's not a violent type, our Nika-Daisy."

"That's what she told me about you, Morris."

She grinned. Yep, absolutely positively crazy about them.

First cup of strong black coffee conjured its magic, clearing Nika's brain cells of cobwebs, and revving her up. The second cup was for pure pleasure. As a rich fragrance of Columbian Supreme kicked her olfactory nerve, Nika said a little prayed to a Coffee God. Alert, with all her senses engaged at full throttle, she contemplated the next step. Maybe it was petty of her, but Nika ignored both men, taking her time to enjoy her breakfast. She spared a quick glance at the pair of them, and barely suppressed a snicker.

Just look at those morons, so busy feinting nonchalance, pretending to be engrossed in a task.

Any manual chore was beneath the head of the Coleman household, but Eli assisted Alex without so much as a scowl. More amused than she was willing to admit, Nika watched them out of the corner of her eye. When they finished, she rose from her chair, and took the first-aid kit from the cabinet.

She jerked her head at Eli and pointed with her finger to the bar stool.

"You first." For an extra measure, her command was accompanied by a frown.

"Thank you all the same, but he's hurt more, so don't you think—"

"Coleman, don't make me repeated it twice. Come here, and introduce your butt to the seat, or else."

Eli's brow arched in insolence, but the overall picture was spoiled by his swollen nose and torn, bloody lip. Dammit, she loved that face with its high cheekbones, beautifully carved mouth and clefted chin. If Alex wouldn't be equally hurt, the stinking skunk, she'd punch him herself for ruining that perfect face.

"Or else what?" The owner of that face demanded. Nika's frown deepened.

"You don't want to find out."

With a longsuffering sigh, Eli complied.

Nika gently touched his split lip, dabbed antiseptic on it, then blew at the wound. With hands that shook, she cleaned his face, all the while cringing inside.

She was hurting him, and hurting along with him, for she felt every stab of pain as her own. But Eli took her ministrations stoically. He didn't utter a single sound during the whole procedure.

Alex, on the other hand, hissed, and cursed, and tried grabbing her healing hand. Irritated and mad at him, Nika administer a smart slap at the back of his head. His high-pitched, surprised yelp was like a balm to her heart.

"Don't be a baby, Cuz. Take an example from Coleman. He took it like a man." She delivered her coup de grace, deliberately adding insult to injury.

Alex's reaction was so predictable, Nika smirked. He stopped squirming, sat straighter and aimed a fumigating glare in her direction.

"Do your worst, Brat. See how the *real* man can take it."

"Real-schmeal," she said with a snort. Her taunt was heavy on sarcasm, but her touch was gentle.

For the next half-hour, Nika patched the cuts and treated the scrapes as best as she could. At the end, both men were sporting band aids, deep scowls and similar expressions of mutinous disgust. The strong smell of antiseptic permeated the air.

Nika washed her still shaking hands in the sink. Just some scrapes and cuts, she reminded herself. Nothing to worry about. Heck, who was she kidding? Of course, she worried. She was sick to her stomach.

"Maybe I should still take you both to the clinic, so the real doctor could take a look?"

Her suggestion was met with a stubborn resistance. Men, she huffed in exasperation. So predictable, so childish. Perhaps, she could win this battle of wills, but what was the point? To save the aggravation, Nika capitulated.

"Okay, but if any of you get an infection, don't come running to me."

Alex grunted. Eli merely lifted his brow. Then they exchanged the look, an arrogant between-us-guys look, that Nika supposed was a male equivalent of rolling their eyes. She could almost hear an exasperated oath 'female.'

With a stern scowl on her face, Nika glared at the pair of them, but inside she was rejoicing. Because unconsciously, unwillingly, Alex and Eli started to forge a bond. A tentative one, but a bond nonetheless. For now, it was enough.

CHAPTER NINETEEN

"Listen up, you stubborn fools. You both stink! I would appreciate it if you'd take a shower, then clean up. There's one thing I draw a line at, and that's being dirty." Nika turned to Alex, her hands on her hips. "You'll loan Eli anything and everything he needs, including clothes. And then, my dear cousin, you escort my fiancé to your favorite store and treat him to enough clothes to see him past Thanksgiving." She narrowed her eyes. "Got it?"

Without any complaints, Alex and Eli split in separate directions. Scurried was a better description. Nika grinned at their retreating backs, and poured another cup of coffee.

"Boys."

They were so predictable, even the most complicated of them. Like her Eli.

Would he be able to figure out how to use the shower? Yes, he would. She showed him last night, to his undiluted delight, how to turn on the hot water and the lights. And if he would not, then he can take a cold shower, for all she cared. The idiot.

Let him cool off that fiery temper hidden under the layer of ice. Wouldn't hurt.

The guy was hot as a damn furnace. *Oh, shit.* Her own body temperature flared up to a dangerous level as her imagination conjured the events of the last night. Scattered clothes, twisted sheets, torn bedding...

Eli above her, under her...

Snap out of it, Nika.

When Alex emerged from his room, Nika was still battling her erotic demons. But one look at her cousin, dressed now in clean clothes, was like a dash of cold water.

Eli entered the room, cleaned up and marginally presentable, wearing his rumpled clothes.

He made such a pathetic picture, clad in his old-fashioned three-piece suit, smudge of blood on his high-collared, once white shirt, and dirty wingtips, it was embarrassing.

Son of a bitch.

Guilty, Alex muttered a curse. An honest fistfight was one thing, but humiliation of the opponent was something entirely different. As God was his witness, Alex never intended to embarrass the guy. Just beat him senseless. But it looks like he accomplished both. A parade of Band-Aids all over Eli's face was a testament to his achievement.

Son of a bitching bitch.

Since Nika treated his own cuts and bruises with the same generous hand, Alex's appearance was not much different. As penances go, it was a small one, and no less than he deserved. Plus, the guy managed to plant a couple of good ones on him, too. So, they were even.

Then why do I feel like a skunk?

Alex spared another brief glance at Eli. Hell. If anything, he looked even more pitiful than a minute ago. Whatever his sins, the guy didn't deserve this. He was an aristocrat, for goodness' sake. Now he looked like a homeless person clinging to the last drop of his dignity. And it was all Alex's fault.

A mixture of pity, embarrassment, and guilt was potent enough to made him ashamed of himself. No, Eli didn't deserve this. Resigned, Alex rubbed his scalp with both hands, cursed under his breath. He owed the guy. Alex always paid his debts.

He turned to Nika. Fire shot from her eyes. "I swear we tried some of my things, but they didn't fit." Alex accepted his fate and looked at Eli. "Okay, Benjamin. It seems that you and I are going shopping."

"Shopping? But you bought a lot of food just this morning."

"Not for food, pal, but clothes."

"Oh. Are you in need for some new garments?"

"No, but you are."

That statement was met with horrified indignation. Amused, Alex kept his mouth shut while his cousin pointed out that Eli couldn't parade for days in same wrinkled and torn clothes. Not to mention, a very old-fashioned one.

"You look like a beggar, Coleman. I won't have it."

"Daisy, I don't have any funds, for Pete's sake."

Nika dismissed the problem with a wave of her hand. "No problem, I'll pay for it."

"No way in hell."

"Why the hell not?"

"Because I will not allow it!"

She blanched, then stared at Eli in mute outrage.

"*Allow* it? Did I hear that correctly? You will not *allow* it?"

"That is correct."

With steam pouring out of her every pore, Nika flew off the handle.

"Who the hell do you think you are?"

"Your betrothed, soon to be your husband."

"Well, that could be rectified, Coleman. Very easily."

"Goddamn it, woman, so help me God—"

Distressed, embarrassed, the poor guy finally lost his cool. For the first time Alex heard him raise his voice. His cousin, God bless her stubborn hide, was red in a face, and seriously worked up. Perched on the balls of her feet, Nika was about to leap.

Uh-oh. Time to interfere.

"Hey, Benjamin. Money's no problem. I played a mean game of poker yesterday, so—"

"How much did you lose?" Nurse Ratchet rounded at him.

God, a guy just can't win. Damn if you do, damn if you don't.

"If you want to know, Brat, I won." His indignation was as fake as his winnings. "But even if I lost, hypothetically speaking, I can afford to splurge on some duds. So, Benjamin, let's go shopping."

"Be that as it may, I cannot accept your money, Morris."

Calm and composed once again, Eli's tone of voice brooked no argument.

"Why? You took care of my cousin, didn't you? Fed her, clothed her. I assume you spent a great deal of money on her wardrobe and baubles. Now I want to return the favor."

"It was different. A totally different matter."

"Because I am a woman?" Nika piped in, all innocence.

If Alex didn't know her better, he would buy into her act, too.

"Well, yes."

Alex winced.

Walked right into the trap, Benjamin.

Nika's steely stare was hard enough to drill a hole into a concrete. Alex couldn't help but commiserate with the poor bastard on the receiving end of it.

Bow out while you still can, idiot.

As if prompted by this silent urging, Eli stopped, and focused on Nika. Her murderous gaze was hard to miss, or interpret any differently.

"No, Daisy, not because you are a woman, or *just* because you're a woman, but because..."

"Because?"

"Well, because."

Exasperated, Eli plowed all ten fingers into his hair, grabbing two fistfuls. Poor bastard. He rubbed his chin hard enough to leave marks, and turned to him.

But Alex shook his head in denial. No way was he butting in on this argument.

You're on your own, buddy.

When everything proved to be useless, Eli cursed under his breath and closed his mouth with a loud smack.

"Just shut up, Coleman, and accept the inevitable."

And with a resolute nod of her curly head, Nika closed the subject

"There is no winning with you, is there?"

"Nope."

Her smile was smug, amused, a bit on the sly side, and reminded Alex of Mona Lisa. He always considered Leonardo's masterpiece an epitome of female cunning.

Cursing was a waste of time, but Eli indulged nevertheless.

Thunderation. Just look at those two.

Alex was smirking, the cad. Daisy's mouth was set in that stubborn line he remembered only too well. No, there was no winning with the pair of them.

For the life of him, he couldn't remember the last time he was so embarrassed.

The subject of money was something he had never fretted about. The Coleman family fortune was enormous. Through years, he added a great deal to it with his various business enterprises. Eli's word was as good as gold, his financial trustworthiness unquestionable. But not in his time. A wad of bills Eli always carried on his person, was as useless here as a fifth wheel on his phaeton.

Thunderation.

On top of being embarrassed, he felt frustrated and helpless, and out of his element like fish out of water. He didn't care for the feeling, not one damned bit.

After a moment of inner struggle, he settled on accepting a loan— never a charity. Not even from the woman he loved. Or her cousin.

"Alright," he capitulated, "but I will accept it only under one condition."

"Let's hear it." His stubborn bride demanded.

"I will only agree to a loan, and nothing else."

"A loan?" Alex pursed his lips. "And just how do you plan on repaying it?"

"I...I have this." He pulled at the chain that held his heirloom pocket watch. "If you'll take this, then I will agree to accept a few new garments."

"Hmm," Alex inspected the item he held on his palm. "Swiss, and gold, if I'm not mistaken."

"You are not. This is my father's timepiece. Made in Switzerland. Eighteen carat gold with diamonds and sapphires."

The jab of guilt was akin to a physical pain. Not under any other circumstances would Eli have considered to part with his prized heirloom. But wasn't Coleman pride more important? His father would agree.

"You know, Benjamin, if you'd think for a moment that I could accept it, you are a total moron. Like certifiable." The younger man finished in a quiet voice. "And you are going to piss me off. Again." His eyes glimmered hard as gems.

"But..."

"You are family, you idiot. Family don't repay each other. We might fight on occasion, we might disagree on certain things, but we help each other, no matter what, and never charge for it. So," he curled Eli's fingers around the watch, "don't insult us both."

Eli was moved more than he was willing to admit. Afraid that his voice would betray him, he jerked his head in a curt nod, and pocketed his watch.

"Coleman, you are a piece of work," Daisy muttered. Was it regret, or disapproval in her eyes? No, it was sadness. Deep and profound.

Goddamit.

"I didn't mean any insult. I just..." But the words failed him. What could he say, really?

"Thank you." Was the best he could come up with.

He was grateful, and humbled, and confused. And on top of it, he somehow managed to insult both of them. So, if accepting charity was his punishment, so be it. No, no charity. A gift. From the family. Because, whether he wanted it or not, he was part of their family now. As they were part of his.

Dammit, he was so out of place here! More than anything, he wished to grab Daisy and return to his own time. And the rest be damned. But it would be an act of weakness. There was not much Eli despised more than weakness. His inner turmoil was interrupted by Alex.

"For now, you can wear this." He held out a shirt and short pants to Eli. "And loose the wingtips, brother."

"And what am I supposed to wear? Or should I go barefoot?"

"You could do that, and no one in this town with blink an eye, I promise. But in the spirit of comfort, you should try this." Alex produced a pair of flimsy sandals.

"You propose for me to wear...this?" Dubious, Eli eyed the garments in Alex's hand.

"Why not? I do." And he pointed to his own half-bare legs and feet clad in similar sandals. His naked toes looked even more ridiculous than his legs. For a reason he couldn't name, Eli felt his face flood with color.

"It's very convenient in our weather." The younger man finished nonplussed.

"Thank you, but no. Absolutely not."

With that, Eli took what he assumed was a shirt from Alex's hand, and went to Daisy's quarters with as much dignity as he could master.

Ten minutes later, clad now in pale blue polo shirt tucked neatly into his black old-fashioned pants, Eli entered the room. If not for those trousers and the wingtips, he could easily pass for a regular guy dressed casually, if a bit carelessly, for the day.

"You look terrific," Nika assured him, "if a bit... weird."

"I'm not bearing my legs, Daisy." Eli frowned. "And I'm not wearing those sandals, however convenient they might be, thank you all the same."

"That's a pity." She hid her smile under a mild annoyed look. "Your legs are... spectacular."

"You are deliberately trying to irritate me."

"No, just stating a fact. Okay, boys. Off with you, then."

"Daisy, I still feel..."

"Zip it, Coleman." She interrupted, and dropped a quick kiss on his mouth. That shut him up. "And Alex?" Nika turned to her cousin. "Behave."

"Don't I always?"

With more enthusiasm that was warranted, she shooed them out.

She could—probably should—go along, but Nika figured it would be a good chance for both of them to smooth out any lingering negative feelings toward each other.

Or pound on each other again.

No, they won't repeat their morning performance. For one, they were too civilized for that. And second, they were terrified of her reaction.

Or of the trip to the hospital, more likely.

Nika shrugged. Whatever works.

A shopping trip, according to *Verochka*, was much more than a simple buying expedition. It was an effective medicine from any and all troubles. And a bonding ritual. For the female species that is. Was it the same for the opposite gender?

She'd find out soon enough.

But for now, she was all alone, and had some much-needed thinking time.

Nika surveyed the living room that was, once again, pristine. The pair of hooligans put it to rights, thank goodness. But the lamp was a bust, and so was the beautiful vase *Verochka* brought from China.

Bummer.

Note to herself: order another lamp later.

When she walked into the kitchen, her good mood disappeared in a flash. Nika's gasp of outrage spanned into a litany of curses.

"Alex, you son of a bitch, you miserable skunk, you...you...ahhh!" Frustrated, Nika grabbed two fistfuls of her hair, tugged, and resigned to the inevitable. No point in getting all worked up about something she couldn't change.

To say that it was in shambles was a major understatement. How come the same guy who was almost OCD in life and business matters was such an outrageous slob in the kitchen? Where was his overzealous demands for putting everything in its proper space? Alex's favorite saying 'he who cooks doesn't clean' rang in her mind's ear. Dammit all to hell and back.

"Just roll up your imaginary sleeves, Nika, and get to work."

She was almost done with the chore of cleaning after breakfast mess when Alex and Eli returned.

Either I'm Speedy Gonzalez, or it was one helluva quick shopping.

Suspicious, Nika eyed the results of their trip, which amounted to four bags. But at least, they were from the designer's shops. From the frown on Alex's face and Eli's mutinous expression, their expedition was a bust.

The miniscule quantity of the packages was all the proof she needed. As much as she was itching to, Nika refrained from any pithy remarks.

What was her grandmother's favorite saying? Oh, yeah. *A smart woman always keeps her mouth buttoned.*

So, she kept it buttoned. For just about two minutes. Because a *wise* woman always knows when to unbutton it, and how many buttons to release. So.

"Oh my, did you manage to haul all that merchandise by yourselves? Goodness." She made a production of fanning herself with her hand. "You guys must be much stronger than you look."

"Don't blame me." Alex protested. "Benjamin turned out to be a regular scrooge, and a royal pain in the ass. You should have seen his face in JJ Cooper's."

"It's a plain robbery what they charge for clothes!" Outraged, Eli pointed to his legs and chest. "Two hundred dollars for a pair of jeans? Eighty-five dollars for a shirt? If you could call a tiny scrap of hideous fabric a shirt. Who came up with this nonsense?"

"Ah...designers?" Scratching his head, Alex squinted at Eli.

"Well, they ought to be prosecuted and charged with a crime, the bunch of them."

"Relax, Benjamin. There's always Walmart. And, besides, a dollar nowadays is not what it used to be in your time."

"Obviously not."

Nika cleared her throat.

"So, beside the killer prices, how did it go?"

Alex uttered a noncommittal sound, and dumped the bags on the couch.

In lieu of an answer Eli shrugged, and stuck his hands into the rear pockets of his new jeans.

My oh my.

The way he filled his Calvin Kline's made her mouth water and her skin tingle. If Calvin could get a load of him now, he would fire all his models and beg Eli on his knees to replace them. And when Eli turned, and Nika was presented with an unobscured view of his behind, her heart skipped a bit.

The fantasy of slowly pulling those jeans off his long legs flashed in her mind. *Later,* she vowed, all but vibrating from lust. To distract herself, Nika dragged her eyes from Eli, and addressed her cousin.

"Did you find everything? Shirts, socks, shoes?"

She tried to keep her eyes on Alex's face, but they seemed to develop a will of their own, straying back to the yummy visual of Eli's butt.

"Yes, Mom."

In the manner that always drove her crazy, Alex fluffed her hair. More out of habit than irritation, she batted his hand away, all the while lusting after Eli.

Following her eyes, Alex wiggled his brows and made a hissing sound, mimicking a burned finger. Nika managed to cover her embarrassment with a smoldering glare in his direction. His answer was a milewide grin and a wink.

Clown.

Disarmed and amused, Nika bit the inside of her cheek to hide a smile, and switched her attention back to Eli. His posture was rigid, but she could almost see the waves of indignation—or was it embarrassment? —wracking his body.

"Eli—"

"I am in need of some air." He cut her off, and strode out of the house.

CHAPTER TWENTY

"Jerk," Nika muttered after Eli's retreating back. "And who are you kidding, Coleman?"

He was in need of a solitude, that was as plain as day. Eli wanted to be left alone.

Can you really blame him?

He was so out of his element; it wasn't even funny. Overwhelmed, embarrassed, baffled, lost. Lost in time, literally.

And, let's not forget beaten in a fistfight, her inner bitch supplied with a glee.

No, she couldn't blame him. Who could understand his conflict better? She's been in a similar situation, so she did get it. Totally. And still.

His dismissal hurt. He was fed up with everything and everybody, her included. She wouldn't be surprised if he decided to use the key and return back alone, leaving her to her own devises.

Don't be a moron, Nika. And don't insult him. Eli doesn't deserve that.

Frustrated, she dragged both hands through her hair.

"Don't worry, Cuz. He's just confused, and needs to blow off some steam."

Perceptive as usual, Alex lay a hand on her shoulder, then squeezed it lightly.

"I think I'll keep him company." He winked and fluffed her hair again, twice in a matter of minutes. Under normal circumstances, this would cause a minor war, or at least warranted some bodily harm. As a testament of her pathetically shaky state, Nika gave Alex a wobbly smile, and instead of an elbow jab, kissed his chin.

"Keep company, my butt."

He would trail after Eli, watch over him, keeping him safe. Protecting. Just like he protected Nika when they were growing up, and later, when they ran away from home. Just like he always did with people who matter: *Verochka*, Abby, and now Eli. Because deep down Alex was a protector.

Her own knight minus shiny armor, her best buddy, her partner in crime. "I love you, Cuz. You are the best."

Pressing her nose to the window, Nika focused on two figures down on the beach. Eli plowed ahead, with Alex shadowing at a distance. Nika couldn't imagine her life without either of them.

But she had made her choice. Soon she would return to 1909, leaving her life here behind, leaving people she loved behind. Her heart lurched and squeezed painfully.

How on earth will I stand it?

Nika shut her eyes, willing herself to calm down. She had five days here, she reminded herself. Five days to spend with her family, to enjoy Thanksgiving holiday. To say her goodbyes. And on Friday...

Don't think about that. Just don't. Think about now. You just need to keep busy. Move, Nika, do something. Anything.

But what? Her gaze traveled to the abandoned shopping bags still sitting on the floor. Eli's 21st century wardrobe. Pitiful. His closet at the Coleman house was spectacular and extensive with row after row of natural silk, wool, and cotton along with drawers of gloves, and boxes of hats. And shoes? Nika never suspected a single person could have or need such a collection of footwear.

She looked again at the few bags containing all Eli's modern possessions. Plain pitiful. If only his housekeeper Mrs. Smith could see it! She would no doubt keel over from shame and righteous indignation.

To occupy herself, Nika decided to make space in her closet for Eli's things. Five days or not, he will have his wardrobe such as it was, properly hanged and folded. He deserved that. She had to admit, it was a novel experience for her. Nika never shared her living accommodations with any male besides Alex. Even with him she drew a firm line at sharing her private space.

Yes, it was a totally new experience, but not an unpleasant one.

Soon she will be sharing more than a closet with Eli. She will share her life with him. For better, for worse, for richer, for poorer.

"To love and to cherish."

Amused, and a bit embarrassed, she upended one shopping bag on her bed, and started sorting and folding. She busied her hands, but her mind continued to wander.

The aristocrat industrialist from the nineteen-hundreds and a working girl from the twenty first century. Of course, she was no pauper herself. Her family was considered one of the richest in the modern-day society. But still. One thing was for sure: they were in for one hell of a ride. There will be days full of idyllic bliss, and days when they would fight and argue.

No doubts there, my girl.

They were so different in temperaments and characters, not to mention their origins. The adjustment period was inevitable for her as well as for him. Then again, wasn't it the same for any married couple?

After the vows were taken and promises exchanged, and the short giddy period of honeymoon was over, the sobering reality inevitably stepped in.

Some couples were up to the challenge, but some would wither under its demands, unable to adjust, unwilling to compromise.

Compromise.

Wasn't she the one who proposed it to Eli a year ago?

Or *hundred and eleven* years ago.

Nika smiled as memories of that day played in her mind.

"I wanted to offer you a compromise, and totally forgot about it!"

"A compromise?" Eli gave a short bark of a laughter. *"Darling, I'm afraid the meaning of the word is absolutely foreign to you."*

She argued that it was not, that she could compromise. Would compromise.

And that would be the hardest. Compromises were not her strongest suit, as Eli had noticed even then. But what about him?

They both were strong individuals. Strong willed, to be more accurate. Both were used to giving orders and expect them to be carried out without any qualms. In short, they both were leaders, and neither one of them knew how to follow.

She couldn't explain why she became upset all of a sudden.

You'd better curb your leadership tendencies and learn how to follow, girl.
"Never."
So, you would start making your own rules and try to bend Eli to your will?
Nika snorted. "Eli's not one for bending."
My point exactly.
"And what would you suggest? Meekly follow in his shadow?"
You said it yourself: compromise. After all, how hard could that be?
Nika drew a long breath, let it our noisily. "Very, but for love's sake, I'll try."

She would do her best to adjust to her new position as Eli's wife and the hostess of the Coleman house. She promised herself to learn how to dress and talk properly, how to throw parties, and yes, how to compromise. She opted to make him proud of her, if it was the last thing she did.

But she'd be damned if she became anyone's shadow, even Eli's.

Somewhat pacified by that, Nika bent to pick up a shirt she accidentally dropped, and her eyes landed on her yellow workman's boots.

With a pang of regret, she picked them up, but instead of putting them away, she hugged them to her chest. Her boots, her tool belt, her baseball cap. They were not just mere uniform, but an integral part of her personality. She was a contractor, damn it, one of the best. She loved her job. No, not a job, but a vocation.

What would become of her without it? She honestly didn't know. What she knew for sure was the fact that there wouldn't be any crew for her to command, or any project to oversee, any house to restore.

It seemed that her days as House Whisperer were numbered, and her role as the city's most sought after contractor was coming to an end. Resigned, Nika shoved her boots into the back of her closet and shut the door. She wished she could shut away her regrets that easily.

Nika was about to turn around, when a sudden thought popped into her mind.

What will happen to the company when I'm gone?

She had never given *Before & After, Inc.*, the company she and Alex built from scratch a second thought. A sharp stab of guilt was like a knife in her gut.

She was so busy restoring the Coleman house and waiting for Eli, she never stopped to think what would happen to their company afterward. Never cared to think.

Selfish bitch.

Beating herself over it now, ashamed and disgusted, she wondered if Alex had thought about it. Yes, he probably had, but never said a word to her. Not a word, not a single reproach. He was too busy saving her sanity, and cheering her on.

Protecting.

"Oh, Cuz, I'm so sorry."

Misery and guilt washed over her. Their company was the cornerstone of their lives. They built it from nothing, flying on sheer guts and enthusiasm, pouring their blood, sweat, and dreams into it. They made it into a smashing success. *Before & After, Inc.* today was a well-known and respected company, a multi-million-dollar operation. True, Alex was more than capable of running the real estate part of it. But restorations? Dealing with the workmen crew, architects, engineers, city council, and historic society? He wouldn't know where to begin, or how. Even if he would hire another contractor, it wouldn't be the same. She was the best. Any false modesty aside, it was a fact.

They had a rhythm, and understanding. They depended on each other, trusted each other professionally and personally. They shared a special bond. Without her, that bond would be broken, and the business they built from scratch will cease to exist. In short, she let Alex down, just as simple as that. Devastated by realization, Nika sat on the bed. What have I done?

You fell in love. And it changed everything.

What the hell am I supposed to do now?

You can stay, Eli offered you that choice. He'll stay with you.

But...I can't. He needed back home. I can't ask him to stay. That's unfair.

What about Alex? Is it fair to him?

"Stop, stop, stop!" Nika grabbed her forehead, then slid her hands to cover her ears, but it proved futile. That nagging merciless voice in her mind refused to be shut off. Torn apart, Nika sat amidst the strewn clothes, and brooded. Then she pulled her cell phone and speed dialed the only person who would know how to fix anything.

"What's wrong, Daisy-girl? What is it, baby?"

"Oh, *Verochka,* I don't know what to do. I'm so confused."

"Take a deep breath, and start from the beginning."

As soon as Eli stormed out of the house, he realized his folly. He didn't know where to go. He was a stranger in this place, and even though he was familiar with the city of Fernandina and the island, he was in another time altogether. Like on another planet. Everything was alien. Correction: not everything.

The ocean and sky were still the same, two timeless constants in the variable turbulence of the universe. He looked upward, closed his eyes, and just absorbed the sounds and smells. The noise of the churning sea and cries of seagulls were painfully familiar, and made him steadier. His mood became lighter, and taking a deep breath, Eli started walking toward the ocean.

He needed to think, needed to clear his head, and focus once again on the main goal: Daisy, and their return trip back home.

If it was up to him, he would grab her, get to the newly restored Coleman house and travel back immediately. But she couldn't do it, he understood that, accepted that. And, he admitted, neither could he, no matter how much he wished for it.

Abigail.

Eli skidded to a stop, raked his hand through his hair, and cursed softly. No, he refused to return without making amends with his sister. Even if Daisy agreed to jump through time right this minute, he wouldn't—couldn't—allow himself this luxury. Because it was a coward's way out. He wasn't perfect, and had many shortcomings, but, as God was his witness, cowardice was not one of them. He needed to talk to his sister face to face, ask her forgiveness, he—what did *Verochka* suggest? —grovel, but he and Abby would be on speaking terms once again. And only after that he would be ready to return.

What if she never forgives you?

She will. Abby was a forgiving and generous soul. She could never keep a grudge. She must forgive him, or...Eli sighed, moved forward, stepping onto the wooded plunks of the boardwalk. Or he would never be able to live in peace. They would return, Daisy and him, back in time, but he would never be same.

The thought that he could stay here, in this amazing time, crossed his mind a time or two. Guilty, he was just a man, and these incredible innovations and progress that his fellow countrymen achieved, were rather mindboggling. And for an engineer like him seductive as hell. But...

Eli squinted at Daisy's house, at the row of other structures farther ahead, and admitted that he didn't belong here. No matter what—fantastic progress, miraculous technology—he was product of his time. He could probably be happy here, with Daisy, but he would never be whole. No, he must return.

You did, he reminded himself, as his mind conjured a somber grey stone in the *Bosque Bello* cemetery. And so did she. His Daisy.

They would depart this world in the same year, only month apart. She was destined to be first.

Depressed, unbearably sad, Eli firmed his jaw, stuck both fists into the pockets of his new jeans, and trudged ahead through sand. He barely noticed the ocean on his right, placid and calm, or the dazzling sun.

But he picked up immediately on the strange feeling, like a prickling along his nape. He was been followed. One look over his shoulder proved him right.

There, several paces behind, was Daisy's cousin, trailing after him.

More annoyed than upset, Eli stopped, turned and, and let his adversary see that he spotted him.

"Busted."

A couple of feet away from him, Alex hurried to catch up. His face was rather cheerful, without any sign of embarrassment at being caught.

Annoyed, Eli planted his feet on the wet sand, and faced the younger man.

"May I ask, sir, why are following me?"

"Would you believe me if I said I was just taking a walk along the same path?"

Eli didn't think that question merited an answer, and kept silent.

"Okay, you won't. Well..." Alex rubbed his head, tugged at his earlobe, and shrugged. "Nika is worried about you. You stormed out like your feet were on fire, so..."

"She should not worry. I merely decided to take a walk."

"All by your lonely self?"

"That is correct."

"In the strange time and place, where everything as familiar as a moon crater?"

"The time might be strange, but the place is the same. And despite your opinion of my intelligence, I know what the moon is, and saw some illustrations of its craters."

"That's beside the point, Benjamin, and you know it. Dammit, she's scared."

"Why?"

"Why? For an intelligent guy, you ask a really dumb question. Well, let me enlighten you then. Nika spent more than a year waiting for you, all the while working like a person possessed to finish the restorations of your house. Now, when it's done, you pop up out of the blue, and it all suddenly became real."

Alex shook his head. The frown on his face deepened.

"Her life here is coming to an end, and her future is unclear. She is very close with our grandmother. Hell, man, she became a sister to Abby. And she knows that when she leaves with you next week, she's never going to see them again. Do you think it's easy for her? And what would she do in your century. Have you thought of that? Nika is a career woman who values and loves her profession. She's going to lose that, too. In short, Benjamin, she's losing everything dear by following you back. And you are asking why she's scared? Really?"

"If she's so unsettled, she can stay back. I am not forcing her to return with me."

"You moron, she loves you. More than anything, more than life itself. Do you know that she almost died?"

The question was like a punch in the gut. Guilty, Eli hunched his shoulders, and averted his eyes.

"When she lost the key, and thought that she'd never see you again, she simply folded. She just gave up."

Alex came up closer, so now they stood shoulder to shoulder. Taking a deep breath, Daisy's cousin cursed under his breath, and turn to gaze at the ocean. After a moment, he continued in a quiet voice that somehow reverberated like thunder in Eli's ears.

"She slept hours on end, never leaving her room. We were afraid that one day she would simply slip into dreamland, never to wake up. I was losing my fucking mind, when one day I discovered those graves on the *Bosque Bello* cemetery." A frustrated oath broke free from Alex's lips. He lifted both hands and rubbed his head in a helpless gesture. "And that's what did the trick. The shock of seeing the graves was a therapy that worked. A shock therapy."

Alex's eyes were focused on the horizon, but it was clear as day he didn't see anything. He was lost in his own memories.

"I didn't thank you for finding those graves, and administer that shock therapy. So, thank you, I am sincerely grateful..."

"Oh, stuff it, Benjamin. You don't have to thank me for helping Nika any more than for helping Abby. They are family. They both are important."

Quick as lightning flash of anger on Alex's face was a sign to behold. For the first time since he met him, Eli was allowed a glimpse to a real Alex Morris. There was much more to the young affable man than met the eye. In this split second, Eli was presented with the totally different picture of him. He was a man of strength, of abounded integrity and loyalty. A man who would go hell and back to protect the loved ones. The easygoing, friendly mask had covered the formidable person.

Yes, the young Morris was a strong adversary, but even stronger friend.

Eli allowed himself a moment before he started to talk. "I don't have to, but I want to thank you, Morris. No, don't interrupt." He held up his hand. "You had your say, now let me finish mine. I am grateful to you. For Abigail, and for Daisy. For being the true gentleman. And for lending me money and taking me to shopping, even knowing that I have no means to replay you."

"Oh, come on, Benjamin—"

"And for promising to teach me how to operate your automobile." Alex winced, and Eli failed to hide his smile. "I'll hold you to that promise, young Morris."

"Thought you would."

"But beside all that, I wanted to say this. When I leave, I'll be at peace by knowing that my sister is in good hands, that she has a brother in my stead. I know she will be well cared for, and happy, and protected from any harm.

Because she has you. And I promise to you to care and love your cousin, to cherish and protect her to the last drop of my blood. I promise you to do anything in my power to make her happy. You know very little of me, but I hope you trust me to keep my promise. And I want to say, Morris, I am honored and privileged to be related to you."

Embarrassment was written all over the younger's man face.

"Shit, Benjamin, where I was all worked up and mad at you, you just have to go ahead and say something to make me feel like an idiot."

"Well, you made me feel the same way a few times today, so let's call it a draw."

Eli's offered hand was accepted without hesitation. The handshake was firm, accompanied by a firmer eye contact. For the first time since he landed in this time, the feeling of being like a fish out of water dissipated, uplifting the heavy weight of doubts and confusion from his shoulders. Eli's chest expanded, as he drew a deep, and easy breath of air, smelling the familiar saltiness of the ocean. He was home. With his improved mood came good humor. Cocking his head, Eli eyed the younger man.

"I have one question to ask."

"Ask away."

"When are you going to stop calling me Benjamin, and start using my proper name?"

"When you stop irritating the hell out of me." But Alex's eyes sparkled with laughter.

The cad.

Eli let loose a short chuckle.

"I'll do my best."

And without another word, they turned and headed home.

CHAPTER TWENTY-ONE

For the umpteenth time Nika asked herself why she was so baffled by the opposite sex. After all, she lived with Alex for the past nine years. Before that, she was surrounded by male species all her life: their twin fathers, her two brothers, not mentioning her cousins and uncles on both sides. Nika lost count of how many male relatives she had, as their extensive family was spread all over the US and Europe, and propagated with a single-minded determination and mind-boggling speed.

With so many Y chromosomes in such a close proximity, Nika had an ample opportunity to research the science of male behavior, and considered herself an expert. Or so she thought. She glanced out the window. Eyeing two prime examples of the male species, crouched before Porsche with twin moronic grins on their faces, she came to a disturbing conclusion. She was deluding herself. Not only was she no expert, she was absolutely clueless on the subject.

Whoever said that men and women were from the two different planets was a genius. Amused, and a bit irritated, she watched her cousin and soon to be husband, both animated and excited, as they exchanged high-fives. Since their return from their beach walk, those two became attached at the hip.

Not a lot was said, not in front of Nika anyway, but they were communicating more freely and easily, even if a bit carefully, as if they were still figuring what to make of each other. But ice started to melt.

About time.

Only cuts and bruises on their faces reminded of their turbulent start.

No, she would never comprehend how two people who beat each other bloody could became the bosom buddies in a matter of hours, bonding over a car.

Where was resentment? Or, at the very least, a lingering animosity? Where was the silent treatment and smoldering gazes? Or was she projecting? Probably.

Look at those idiots.

Happy as two puppies with a new chew toy. In this case, a very expensive toy. Alex was absolutely stupid when it came to his new car. Come to think of it, he never let Nika drive it. Drive? She snorted. He never let her as much as touch that gleaming beauty.

"Calls her Baby, the moron."

Look who's talking.

Yeah, so she called her car Coco, so what? She was a girl, she was allowed. And, after all, it was a cherry red convertible. But the man who calls his sleek mean wonder of the German engineering *Baby*? It was more than stupid, it was pathetic.

Oh, God, they were getting into the car, with Eli in the driver seat.

"Oh, no, no! No way. Alex!"

By the time Nika ran out, it was too late. She barely had a brief glimpse of the car's rear end as it zipped through the gates.

"Dammit, Alex, what are you thinking? You can't—"

She was about to follow in pursuit in her own car, then stopped herself.

What was the point? Even if she caught them, what could she do?

Eli was a big boy. He was not a stranger to speed.

Yeah, like galloping on the horse's back could be compared to a sports car speed. Driving on the city road for the first time was dangerous as all get out. And reckless. What if Eli runs over somebody? Or crashes the car? What if he injures both of them?

Oh, God.

As one horrible scenario after another played in her mind, Nika screamed in frustration. "Alex, you moron, what do you think you're doing?"

Don't freak out. He's just teaching Eli how to drive.

"Eli saw a car for the first time just yesterday, for goodness' sake. How can he drive it?"

Let him be. Eli's just having some fun. Leave him alone. He has a few short days to enjoy himself. Don't spoil that fun for him.

Usually, her inner voice irritated the hell out of her, because that bitch who lived inside was argumentative and contrary. But today, all of a sudden, she was serious and quiet, turning into a voice of reason.

"Since when did you became so smart?"

But for once, there was no answer. Deflated, Nika dragged herself upstairs. Nothing to worry about. Alex was an experienced and responsible driver.

If he managed to teach Abby how to drive, he can do the same for her older brother. They'll be back soon. In one piece preferably, please God.

And then she'd give them both a piece of her mind.

And what would be the point? You wanted them to clear the air, to bond. They need it more than you, girl. Both of them.

Again, that voice of reason stopped her bitching. Yes, they both needed it, Alex and Eli. Maybe Alex needed it even more. He would be left behind, with the mess on his hands that Nika's departure would create. Personal and professional mess.

Have you thought how Alex would feel losing you?

"I'm taking care of it. I already contacted our lawyer. All the legalities concerning the company will be squared away."

I'm talking about losing you as a family, not a business partner.

"Oh, God, that was a low blow."

It's not a blow, it's the truth. He's your anchor, but you are his sail. And what is a ship without its sail? Think about it.

"Damn you, damn you. Damn you!"

Damn me all you want, girl, but you know I'm right.

Alex won't be alone. He will have *Verochka* and Abby.

Not alone, no, but sad and unsettled.

"There is nothing I can do about it."

Weighted down with guilt and remorse, she allowed herself a moment of brooding.

She was entitled to a good brood, wasn't she? No one was here to commiserate. No one would understand Nika's feelings, or fears. No one, that is, but another woman. Oh, God, she needed her grandmother, and her best girlfriend, her time traveling companion. But *Verochka* and Abby wouldn't be here until Monday.

So, it's me, myself, and I, girl.

"Yeah, and a big help you turned out to be."

Not sure about help, but I'm about to kick your ass. Time is running out. You have five days left. So, snap out of it, and let's make the best of it.

"You are right." Properly chastised by her own inner self, Nika shook her head, blew away fallen curls out of her face, and stuck her chin out. "And my pity party is officially over."

Annoyed at finding her face wet from tears she didn't feel, Nika squared her shoulders. Time was running out. She needed to make every minute count.

Starting right now.

But first things first. The boys would be back, sooner or later. And what do boys ask after the afternoon spent goofing and playing?

What's for dinner, mom?

Cooking, according to her favorite source of female wisdom, her grandmother, was a soothing and therapeutic exercise. So, Nika decided to test *Verochka's* theory by preparing dinner. Or at least trying to. Now, what should she cook?

"Hmm. Decisions, decisions..."

Eying the contents of their now overflowing refrigerator, Nika contemplated her choices. Something easy, but tasty, something light and healthy, something...

"Who am I kidding? With my culinary deficiency, something eatable would be a huge plus."

Resigned, she pulled packages of pre-marinated chicken breast, pre-cut asparagus, and a frozen bag of quartered potatoes. How hard would it be to preheat the oven, dump everything onto a cooking sheet, and stick it inside? Even someone as culinary impaired like her could do it. All she needed was to drizzle some olive oil over the stuff, and set the timer. Easy-peasy. Now, for setting the table.

This she could definitely pull of, and do it spectacularly, thanks to her grandmother's lessons and the impeccable table etiquette she had drummed early into both Nika and Alex. Not to mention *Verochka's* extravagant collections of good china, crystals, and silverware she imported from all over the world. Since her grandmother never lived permanently anywhere, she considered their house her own private treasure throve where she kept all her precious possessions. Sometimes it came in handy, like today, when Nika decided to set up a table fit for a king.

Or for a Thanksgiving dinner in three days where all of us will sit around the table for the last time.

Depressing as hell, that stray thought was like a proverbial wrench thrown in the middle of action. Off balance, Nika stopped and allowed herself a brief moment of grieving. She was entitled to some. Especially if no one was around to witness it.

"Oh, God, oh, God, oh God."

Her breath hitched, her heart stumbled. Blinking though a sheen of tears, Nika trailed the room with her eyes, trying to take everything in. Soon all of it would be just a distant dream. Her life like she knew it would be just a memory.

The people she loved, her family, everything familiar and dear would be a memory, a figment of her imagination.

On the heels of that came the disturbing question: was she doing the right thing? Was she strong enough? What if she wouldn't be able to get used to her new life? What if she regretted it? What if....?

Get a grip, Nika. Time's running out.

The warning struck like a bolt of lightning.

And just like that, her funk has shattered, and Nika catapulted back to reality.

"Enough!" Her voice lashed out, sharp like a blade, mean like a snake. "Enough of this nonsense. I am strong enough. I am Daisy Coleman, and I better remember that, so help me God."

Swiping at her wet face, Nika took a few deep breaths, fighting for calm.

"Concentrate on here and now. You can do it. Don't think about anything else."

The oven timer gave one cheerful beep, interrupting her self debate. The aroma of roasted garlic infused the air, teasing her nose.

What do you know? She did manage to cook dinner after all. And if it smelled so good, it must taste good too. Fortified with that, Nika returned to the task of setting the table. And if her hands shook a little, there was no one around to notice that.

As to her quivering heart— she chose to ignore it.

By the time Eli and Alex made an appearance, Nika had everything under control, herself included. The table was set, dinner was ready, and the wine was breathing on the counter. Her treacherous heart still trembled, but her hands were steady and sure as a surgeon, and so was her resolve.

She *was* doing the right thing.

If her doubts or fears slithered through like today, she would squash them like pesky gnats. Because she was right to follow her heart.

Because she was Daisy Coleman, and Eli was her destiny. If she was strong enough to acknowledge it, she was strong enough to follow him to the end of the earth. Time and again.

Fate was a fickle bitch, unyielding and ruthless.

But underneath it all, she was just and fair. Fate always gave you choice.

Nika had made hers long ago, in 1909, and she would stick to it, come hell or high water.

No matter how long, or how little time she had left here, she was determined to enjoy every second, and make the most of her allotted time. On Monday, she planned to turn the keys from the restored Coleman house to the senator. On Thursday she promised herself to sit at the dinner table, surrounded by her family for the last time, and say her thanks to fate and the universe. And the next day, she and Eli would return back in time, where both of them belonged. And that was that.

But in the meantime, she had dinner to serve to her adorable moron brigade of two.

One member of that dynamic duo piped a question as soon as he was inside. "What's for dinner?"

She shook her head. Alex always made her laugh.

"Wash your hands first. Then you'll eat this amazing chicken prepared by yours truly, love every tiny morsel, and praise me to the moon and back, or else." Knowing Alex as she did, Nika turned in time to smack his hand before it reached the veggies plate.

"Ohhh, the threats, the violence. I love it when you're in the mood, babe. It's so... invigorating." And the jerk had a gall to wink at her in most salacious manner.

"Stop it, you moron. You made Eli blush."

"Ney, he made of a much tougher stuff, right pal?"

"Ah—"

But whatever Eli was going to say became a mystery, as Alex steam-rolled ahead.

"Hey, tell her about your first driving lesson."

Snatching her opening, Nika turned to her cousin. "Yes, about that lesson—"

Her carefully outlined speech was interrupted by Eli whose excitement overruled all the manners of common etiquette.

"It was splendid, Daisy! Simply marvelous." His sparkling eyes lit up the room. "Morris here is an amazing and patient teacher. I confess, I was hesitant at first, but it was not as hard as I thought it would be. And the speed—"

Now it was her time to interrupt. "Yeah, about that speed. Eli—"

But again, Alex rolled all over. "You are one talented student, Benjamin. Now, your sister? She was squirming and squealing like a girl, but you handled Baby like a pro. You sure you never drove a car before?"

"I am positive, Morris. I have never had the pleasure. This was the very first time, and thanks to you, it went absolutely marvelous."

"You make me proud, my young apprentice." Alex made a production of wiping an imaginary tear from his eye.

"Thank you, my esteemed Master." Eli stooped low in a mocking bow.

More amused than annoyed, Nika eyed the pair of them.

The clowns.

Another moment and they'll be hugging each other, professing unending love and loyalty. It would have been embarrassing if it wasn't so hilarious.

Enough was enough. *This stupid comedy has to stop.*

"Okay, boys." A couple of sharp claps of her hands did the job. "When you are done with your admiration exercises, maybe we can eat dinner before it goes completely cold? Today, preferably?"

"Sorry, Daisy. By all means, let's eat. I am famished."

"Hey, me too, Brat. And let us all pray to survive your cooking."

To avoid her elbow jab, Alex nimbly danced off, then plopped his butt on a chair.

Eli had enough manners to pull her chair out, and wait until she was seated before he took his own sit. Always a gentleman.

Admiring his jean-clad behind, Daisy's mouth watered.

Yummy.

She'd rather sink her teeth into the taught muscles of his backside than her infamous chicken.

Patience, my girl. The night is still young.

Anticipation of dragging those jeans off and jumping Eli made her all hot and bothered. Damn, it was still shy of seven. Maybe she could steal Eli away under the presence of sightseeing?

Yeah? And what didn't he see in the city he was born and raised in?

That was hundred years ago, and many things have changed since then.

But that means leaving Alex alone for hours. With a deep sigh Nika rejected the idea. Soon she would have Eli all to herself for the eternity, but Alex...

One glance at her cousin, and her heart broke all over again. They had just five days left. Just five short days before he became a memory.

No way would she deny herself the pleasure of his company, even for a second.

Eat your dinner, and enjoy the company. And don't think about Friday.

Easier said than done. Lost in her thoughts, Nika failed to notice how quiet it had become. Save the chewing and occasional clinking of the silverware that is.

The chicken turned out to be surprisingly tasty. Twin hums of pleasure from the adorable moron brigade accompanied their first bites.

Considering how fast the potatoes and asparagus disappeared, she managed to pull the dinner off. Cheered by the thought, Nika speared some asparagus with her fork before it too became a distant memory.

Eli broke the silence first. After blotting his lips with a napkin, he addressed Alex. "Did Abigail...was she afraid to operate, ah... to drive an automobile? You mentioned earlier she was...ah, squalling and squirming."

"Oh, boy, did she ever! She even cried a couple of times. Women."

Alex had the grace to blush when he caught Nika's steely glare.

"Some women," he hurried to correct his faux pas. "Present company excluded."

"She better be. But do carry on, Cuz." She flashed him a smile. "You were saying...?"

"Ah...Abby. Yes, she was trying to close her eyes when she saw another car on the road. Like ten miles behind us. Can you imagine? If I had any hair, I swear, it would have turned grey."

"Aren't you lucky you're bald as an egg? Or a baby's bottom?"

Now if was Alex's turn to glare at her. Then he returned his gaze to Eli.

"Anyway, we are all lucky that Abby doesn't have to drive in Paris, because our grandmother employs a chauffeur. I suppose it was an act of self-preservation. Plus, *Verochka* keeps tabs on your sister's comings and goings as much as possible. She's watching over Abby like a hawk. And Marie Dubois plays second fiddle, acting as Abby's surrogate mother. Between them, the Princess is as safe as gold in Fort Knox."

"Do you call my sister Princess?"

"Well, yeah. Why, any objections?"

"Not if you treat her as one. And who is this Marie Dubois? The name was mentioned before. Is she Abigail's French maid?"

Nika choked on her food. Before answering, Alex thumped her back a few times.

"Pal, we don't have maids here, French or local. And Marie Dubois is one of the most prominent artists of this century. She was a mentor to the one and only Kat Rostoff. And since you probably don't know her either, let me enlighten you. Kat Rostoff is the world renown artist and the owner of *the* famous art school. As a rule, Marie Dubois doesn't take any students, but thanks to *Verochka's* friendship, she agreed to take a look at Abby's paintings. The rest, as they say, is history. Your sister is extremely lucky to have Marie as her mentor."

"My sister is extremely lucky to have so many caring people around." He waved his fork at Nika and Alex before continuing, "You, Daisy, your grandmother. And this French artist."

"Add to the list the whole Rostoff clan. Kat, her husband, and her parents."

"I am very grateful to all of them, but especially to your grandmother."

"Yeah, well, *Verochka* is one of kind. Remind me to tell you how she helped me and the brat here to run away from home."

He flashed a reckless grin at Nika, and reached across the table to take her hand.

Nika's heart melted, as the memory of that monumental day revived in her mind.

Was it strange that she remembered the smell of flowers at the restaurant? Or the sound that secondhand car purchased by *Verochka* made when the engine was turned? She didn't remember what she was wearing, but the smells and sounds of that evening had stuck in her memory for nine years.

When her eyes started to sting, she withdrew her hand from Alex.

Maybe Alex read her mind, or her face gave her away. But after a tender smile, he switched his gaze back to Eli.

"My point is, Benjamin, even far away from home, your sister is safe. And she is happy. She has a family, and her art."

"Good. That is a tremendous relief to me." After a moment, he carefully placed his fork down.

Despite his words, Eli's face darkened. Absently, he lifted his fingers to his chin then rubbed it rhythmically. Nika's eyes zipped to Alex. Frowning, she gave a barely perceptive nod in Eli's direction.

Do something.

Alex cleared his throat.

"What *is* a tremendous relief to me, Benjamin, is that Abby doesn't drive. She's a danger on the road. Like a monkey with a grenade. But if you tell her I said that, I will deny it until my last breath."

Eli's chuckle rumbled deep in his throat, as he shot Alex an amused look.

"Your secret is safe with me, young Morris."

"Hey, who are you calling young? I'm the esteemed Master, remember?"

"How can I ever forget."

"And I'm just a couple of years younger than you."

"Alright, my *old* esteemed Master."

"That's better. Anyway, I figured another few lessons, and you will be ready to drive on your own. You are a natural, Benjamin. I swear, a couple of weeks under my tutelage, and you'll be —" Alex's smile faded. "Oh, shit."

CHAPTER TWENTY-TWO

"Rude, but succinct." Eli's conclusion was accompanied by a sage nod and half-grin.

"I guess you don't have a couple of weeks. Just— what is it? — four or five days?"

"Five. Five and a half to be precise."

"Yeah, by all means, let's be precise."

All humor evaporated, as if a switch was suddenly turned off. Shoving aside his plate, Alex surged from the table.

"Shit. Here you are, both of you, breathing, talking, joking, and...and it's so easy to forget that in a few days it's all going to change. You'll be gone. For good. Like you never were here. But you were, you are. It's...it's insane. No, it's fucking unbelievable. Shit."

Alex cursed under his breath, then swept both hands up, rubbing his head, and then cursed some more. His frustration was palpable.

"So, I keep forgetting. No, not true, not forgetting. I don't want to *remember*. I chase it away, because I just don't want to think about the day after Thanksgiving. About saying good-bye, about—"

Unable to keep still any longer, Nika jumped up, but Alex stopped her in mid-motion. With his hands raised, palms-up, he shook his head, then turned his back on her. The message was clear. He didn't want to be touched or tended to. He wanted to be left alone. For once Nika ignored his wishes. She'd be damned if she let him suffer alone. With her arms around his waist, she pressed her cheek to Alex's back. Taut as an arrow, with every muscle quivering, he fought his misery and anger in stubborn solitude.

A futile and doomed battle.

Experience had taught her that lesson the hard way. Either your anger will consume you, or your misery will flatten your spirit, but no matter the outcome, you won't be whole again.

Been there, done that, survived because of you, Cuz. Please don't shut me out.

"I'm sorry, so sorry. I wish I could do something, but...I can't. I'm sorry, Alex."

Her half plea, half apology splintered the silence.

Alex's body relaxed just a fraction. With a deep sigh, he turned around, and lowered his forehead to rest on hers.

"I know, Brat. Doesn't make it any easier. I love you, Nika-Daisy."

Her heart shuttered into million pieces.

"I love you too, Cuz."

"I am sorry, Morris. Sincerely."

My God, she completely forgot about Eli!

With a light kiss on her forehead, Alex released her, but held her gaze a bit longer.

"Not your fault." He glanced at Eli. "But, God, why couldn't you two be born in the same century? Or better yet, why can't you just stay here?"

Weary, Nika shook her head. "Stupid question, Alex."

"Why? Benjamin, come on, your sister is here. Our century is much more advanced than yours. What's holding you there? Why can't you just stay here? And..." He caught Nika's gaze, and stopped in midsentence, "...and I guess it is a stupid question. Sorry, sorry. Forget I said that. I just need a moment."

"Alex—"

But he was already gone. Nika was about to sprint after him, but Eli put his hand on her shoulder, and held her in place.

"Leave him, Daisy. He's hurting. Loosing you is going to be hard on him."

He is your anchor, but you are his sail.

She wondered how many times her heart could be broken and still keep beating.

"I feel so guilty, Eli."

"There is nothing we can do to lessen his pain. And it is not our fault that we were born a century apart. It is fate."

Fury flared within her, hot and vicious. Her hands balled into fists.

"Fate! I'll tell you what you can do with your fate. You can just—"

God knows what irrevocable damage she could've done, flying high on her rage, if not for the sound of a loud knocking. Caught in mid-sentence, Nika glared at the door.

"Who the hell...?"

So, help her God, if the person at the door wasn't bleeding from the mortal wounds, she would kill whoever it was with her own bare hands.

Another knock, more insistent this time.

"Are you expecting guests?" Calm as a rock, Eli lifted one brow in question.

In lieu of an answer, she growled deep in her throat. The menacing sound startled her.

"I will take that as a no." Unperturbed, Eli pointed his elegant hand at the door.

"Well, why don't you go and see?"

Still riding the wave of impotent fury, Nika marched to the front door and flung it open.

The words stuck in her throat, transforming into a gasp of shock.

The person on her doorstep cocked his head in the familiar arrogant manner.

After a charged moment of silence, Nika's tongue finally came unglued, as irritation replaced her initial shock.

"Junior, what the hell are you doing here?"

"It's nice to see you too, Midget."

With that, the newcomer pushed his way into the room, smartly shutting the door. She couldn't believe the gall of the man! Well, maybe she should. Who would know better her childhood tormentor and the bane of her teenage years' existence?

"By all meant, come in. Make yourself at home."

"Thank you, sister dear. Don't mind if I do."

"And if I do mind?"

"Oh, come on, you know deep down you are glad to see me."

"Yeah, so deep down I have trouble digging it out."

He flashed her a milewide grin. If Nika didn't know him better, she might buy that innocent smile. But since she did, her bullshit barometer shot all the way up.

Something was off, way off. Beating around the bush was not her style, so Nika plunged right ahead.

"What brings you to our neck of the woods, Junior, after all these years? And please don't say that you missed me."

Ignoring her, he took his time roaming the room with his eyes.

"Nice digs, Midget. Very nice indeed."

"Aww, I'm all aflutter. And I value your opinion so highly, too."

He had the nerve to frown. "Don't be sarcastic, Veronika."

"Oh, my goodness! You remembered my name. Be still my heart." Nika made a production of swiping an imaginary tear from her eye and thumping her chest.

"You always were a brat. I see time didn't change that."

"You always were a pompous ass. Time didn't change that either."

Their verbal duel was interrupted by Eli's discreet coughing. He stepped closer, put his hand on Nika's shoulder, and drew her to his side. The gesture was hard to misinterpret: Eli was staking his claim. And if a smirk on Junior's face was any indication, he got the message, and was enjoying himself.

The bastard.

"Maybe you'll introduce us, Daisy?" Eli's voice could have frozen hellfire.

Still sizzling, Nika glared at Junior. More than anything she wanted to wipe off that nasty smirk she remembered too well. And maybe slap him for good measure. But manners took over.

I'll deal with the skunk later, in private.

"Eli, meet the Junior aka Pompous Ass, my older brother. Junior, Elijah Coleman, my fiancé."

Always a gentleman, Eli offered his hand first.

"A pleasure, sir." The ice melted, but a tad, just enough to chill blood.

"Likewise. Fiancé, huh?"

"Yes, I am."

"Well, well. And the name is Joseph Charles Morris, or JC."

He shook Eli's hand, and inclined his head, all regal and condescending. The resemblance between him and their father was uncanny.

From the slick mane of dark hair to the arrogant posture of lanky frame, they were a carbon copy of each other, as if they were clones rather than father and son.

Creepy.

"Or simply Junior, since he was named after our dear old dad."

That little barb always got under his skin. Bristling, Junior aimed his annoyed eyes, their father's eyes, in her direction, and almost made her squirm. Like she still was a helpless four-year old, facing her older brother with a cookie in her hand she was not supposed to have. She didn't know why that episode stuck in her memory. But she'd be damned if she squirmed now. She has some ammunition in her arsenal to turn the tables.

Let's see how you like it, asshole.

"You know how I hate to be called Junior. It's demeaning for a grown man, and a bit insulting." Heat crept into his perfectly modulated voice, showing the first crack in composure. Nika's smile was all teeth.

"I know."

"Dammit, Nika. I'm not our father. I just had a misfortune of sharing his name."

More heat accompanied by a dark glare. Junior was unraveling fast, but if failed to bring Nika any satisfaction. Instead, it made her uneasy.

Misfortune? I'm not our father?

Dammit, something was wrong. And asshole or not, Junior was family.

What was going on? Why did he turn up at her door?

The answer was simple: he was in trouble. He would never seek her or Alex out otherwise.

Not unless he was sent by the fathers.

But why? To what purpose? What, after nine years of silent treatment the twins suddenly decided to mend fences with two prodigal offspring? Ridiculous.

Her silent debate was interrupted by Eli.

"I never knew Daisy had a brother."

Did she hear a light censure in his voice? She told him she had a family in New York, didn't she? Yes, she distinctly remembered telling him back in 1909 about the twin brothers that fathered her and Alex, and the bank, but did she mentioned her brothers?

"Huh. Why am I not surprised?" Junior aimed his angry eyes at her.

Another crack. He would never show his true feelings to anyone, less of all me.

Concern replaced her annoyance, making her uneasy. Nika frowned. Something was going on.

Catching her gaze, Junior managed to pull a layer of cool disdain over his face before he turned to Eli.

"Your fiancé happens to have two brothers. I am the oldest and Andrew is the youngest of our triumvirate."

"Well, it is nice to meet one of Daisy's brothers."

"Why do you call her Daisy?"

"Because that's who she is. A flower, tough and wild and beautiful."

"Huh. You must be really smitten, Mr. Coleman, if you consider Midget beautiful." Junior struck both hands into his pockets, as he shot her a little grimace.

Nika never considered herself beautiful, or even pretty, so his barb fell short. But she should have known Eli would voice a different opinion.

"I may be smitten, Mr. Morris," he began in a flat voice, "but I am neither blind, nor stupid. Far from it. I also pride myself of being a gentleman."

In one fluid motion Eli's hands shot out, and grabbed Junior by the lapels. After a rough shake, he let go and patted his sport jacket in place.

"I am not sure what the story is, and frankly, I don't care. But I know this: you came to *her* home, and since you entered the premises, you were deliberately rude and unpleasant to my future bride. You went out of your way to make her feel less, to humiliate and embarrass her. And in front of her soon-to-be husband. You will apologize this instant, or else."

"Or else what?" But Junior had shed his arrogant attitude, and eyed Eli with a combination of surprise and wariness. Nika could swear she also glimpsed a sliver of respect in her brother's expression.

"Believe me, you don't want to find out."

Only an idiot could have interpreted the curve of Eli's lips as a smile. Junior, whatever his shortcomings, was not an idiot. After a charged moment, he switched his eyes from Eli to Nika.

"I am sorry, Veronika. I was rude and disrespectful. I apologize."

"Mr. Morris, you look like a smart man. Maybe you want to think about why your sister cannot stop talking about her cousin Alex, whereas she never mentioned your name to me, not even once?"

As a parting shot went, this one was aimed dead center. Junior jerked as if he was struck in the face, then withered in front of Nika's eyes. He was a pompous ass, but he was also family. Whether she wanted it or not. Nika went with her heart.

"What is it? Why did you really come here?"

"Because I didn't know where else to go."

She had to be blind not to see misery when it stared at her. The cruelty their fathers possessed in abundance was abhorrent to her. Even not liking the person Junior was, Nika couldn't stomach to see him suffer.

"Tell me what happened. Is it dad?"

"Yes and no. I quit."

Nika drew a sharp breath. Who should know better than her the wrath of their twin fathers if one of the children failed to toe the line? "Must've been nasty."

His short burst of laughter was dry and humorless. "Yeah, you might say that."

"Well, what are you going to do?"

Once again, Eli interrupted.

"Daisy, you should offer your brother some supper. He's probably hungry."

"Damn. Of course. Sorry. Are you hungry, JC?"

For the first time in ages, Nika addressed him by his name. She just refused to add to his misery by using the much-hated suffix. If JC was surprised, he didn't let it show. Regaining some of his aplomb, he raised a brow.

"What's on the menu?"

"Chicken Cordon blue, Maine lobster, and Russian caviar."

Junior's eyes widened. "Really?"

"Get real."

With a derisive snort, she punched him in the arm on her way to fetch another plate. While Nika performed her hostess duties, she kept her eyes on the two men.

Eli poured her brother a glass of wine. JC gulped it down like it was water.

Shit.

Without a word, Eli filled the glass again. JC repeated the process. That scene disturbed her more than her brother's words. From what she remembered, he was never one to indulge in alcohol. Then again, nine years was a long time. Things changed, sometimes drastically.

Unperturbed, Eli continued to play bartender, damn his aristocratic hide. Filling up another empty glass for JC, and topping his own, he asked, "What is it exactly do you do, Mr. Morris?"

"I am an attorney, corporate and tax. Or I was until two days ago."

JC fell into silence. Brows knitted over the bridge of his patrician nose, he gazed into his wine glass, brooding.

"So, what is the problem? Good solicitors are always in high demand. You can find another place of employment, or start your own firm."

Encouraged by Eli's statement, her brother perked up.

"I've been leaning in that direction myself."

"Splendid." With a half-smile, Eli lifted his glass, took a small sip, while JC upended yet another one. He was drinking like a man dying from thirst.

Nike frowned, unsure about her brother's tolerance for alcohol.

Even if he inherited *Verochka's* titanium stomach, he was tumbling toward inebriation pretty fast. Time to butt in. Piling his plate with food, Nika plopped it in front of JC, and pointed a finger. "Eat."

"Bossy as always, I see. I'm telling you, Mr....ah, Coleman, is it? nothing has changed. Absolutely n-nothing."

His words began to slur, his lips curved into a lazy grin. Damn, she underestimated JC's state of intoxication. He was well underway of becoming totally wasted. She'd have been amused if she wasn't so nervous. Or embarrassed. Fine way for Eli to meet her family. One member of the Morris clan has beaten him bloody; another was getting stupidly drunk before his eyes.

Nice job, boys.

Speaking of boys, where was Alex? She needed moral support, dammit. Nika eyed JC as he began shoveling the contents on his plate with all the finesse of a five-year old.

Wouldn't be surprised if he licked his fingers, the swine.

"A-and you, Mr.... ah, Coleman? What do you do for a living?"

No grandchild of *Verochka's* would ever dream of asking the question with his or her mouth full. JC broke that cardinal rule with a flourish.

Eli, always the gentleman, ignored her brother's atrocious table manners. "I am an industrialist. I own some businesses, have interest in others."

Even in his state of intoxication, the old-fashioned term gave JC a pause. He pondered it for a moment, then nodded.

"Oh, I get it. An en-entrepreneur, right?"

Without missing a bit, Eli inclined his head: "Ah, yes, precisely."

"Okay. Good. Can I get more wine, p-please?"

"Sorry, JC, we are all out." She demonstrated her statement by lifting the now empty bottle, at the same time as Eli picked up a new one.

Nika plucked it out of his hand, and glared at Eli. For a full measure, she made a swishing hand gesture across her throat. Eli blanched, frowned, then opened his mouth, but Nika shushed him.

"F-funny. You guys are too f-funny together. It's k-kinda cute, really."

Infuriated, Nika turned to her brother. "Funny? You moron, I'll show you funny. I—"

"JC? Is that you?"

Alex sauntered in, and saved the day. Or evening.

"Oh, here you are! Hello, Alex." After a failed attempt to stand up, JC flopped back into the chair. "Damn. Sorry, sorry. So, how are you, my man?"

At Alex's bemused gaze, Nika wiggled her brows in silent warning.

"Ah...fantastic, Cousin. And you?"

"I've been better."

"So, I see. Long way from New York, aren't you? And what brings you to our humble abode?"

"I quit my job, and—"

"And the twins have booted you all the way out, is that it?"

"Well, yeah. Something like that."

"And, being all alone and miserable, you remembered us, the two black sheep of the Morris family, and decided to drop by. After all, who would commiserate better, right?"

All sympathy and understanding, Alex flashed a smile only a blind person or a drunk could mistake for friendly. At the moment, her brother hit the bullseye on all counts.

"Yeah, s-something like that." JC nodded sagely, then spoiled the image with a loud hiccup. "To be perfectly frank, I n-need help."

"You don't say? And what kind of help?"

"Ah...I'm a pariah in New York now. Our fathers...they made sure of it. Thank God, I don't need money, just..."

"Just?"

"Some moral support, I guess. And business connections. You both have plenty, don't you? I was hoping for recommendations, or referrals."

"Were you, now? And why do you think we would do that?"

"Because we're family. We have to help each other."

Pleased with his final argument, JC beamed a thousand volt practiced smile that no doubt won him a lot of cases in court.

CHAPTER TWENTY-THREE

G ood thing she wasn't eating, or Nika would have choked on her food. Astonishing!

The gall of the arrogant son of a bitch. Even drunk as a sailor, JC managed to act as a slimy self-serving bastard she remembered well.

Idiot.

He could care less about family. All JC cared about was himself. Always. Period. The end.

A discreet cough from Eli switched her attention away from her brother. Eli's face transmitted a disgusted expression that probably mirrored her own. Not much was lost on him, even though he was unfamiliar with the undercurrents of the Morris family dynamics. Poor Eli. First pounded on, compliments of her cousin, then exposed to the ugly skeletons of their family closet, compliments of her brother. For the first time, she was glad they were leaving in a few days, so Eli wouldn't have a chance to meet the other members of her infamous clan.

"Well, well, look how the mighty have fallen."

Frigid disdain replaced Alex's fake compassion, hardening his features.

Uh-oh. Familiar with her cousin's moods, Nika cursed under her breath.

Alex's temper, although rarely unleashed, was a sight to behold. It could be hot and swift, or cold and brutal, and always carried a hefty penalty afterward.

So, before he could say something he'll regret later, Nika jumped in. "Alex, for goodness's sake. Don't be an asshole."

The minute those harsh words flew out of her mouth, she wished she could take them back. But it was too late.

Alex's furious glare was hot enough to scorch skin, but what cut Nika to the knees was the hurt written all over his face.

Damn it all to hell and back.

"Really? Really, Nik? Oh, that's rich, especially coming from you. Junior treated you like shit all your life. Did you forget how he tormented you? Lied, snitched, stole?"

"No, it just—"

"Broken toys, new dress cut to ribbons, spiders in your bed. And I'm an asshole?"

"No, Alex, listen—"

"He wouldn't spit on you if you were on fire."

"I w-would too."

JC's drunken protest was nipped in the bud by Nika and Alex's twin snarls, "Shut up!"

Silence dropped like a rock, heavy and oppressive. So much for a quiet dinner at home. Just a perfect finale for the day that started with a fistfight, and progressed from there to the disastrous family reunion.

No use to curse that fickle bitch fate, who chose this particular evening to dump JC on her doorstep, or blame Alex for harboring grudges. And berating herself for doing both wouldn't help either.

Pull yourself together, girl.

With an effort, Nika drew a deep breath. They all needed to calm down, and act like responsible adults. Starting with her. But, God, it proved to be an enormous undertaking. Her heart-rate accelerated to the manic drumbeat. Her stomach twisted into knots. And guilt ate at her like acid. She didn't mean to snap at Alex. The pressure that was building all day, had finally reached its critical point and exploded, spewing its ugly lava at the last person who deserved it. Rats, Alex was more insulted for her than for himself, and she jumped down his throat. And for what? For telling Junior the truth?

Nice job, Nika. Really nice.

Time to make amends.

"Alex, I'm sorry."

But Alex didn't react at all, and kept his eye averted.

"I said I'm sorry, Cuz. I really, truly am."

In lieu of an answer, he shrugged, but didn't make a sound, or eye contact.

Stubborn, insufferable jerk. But he was her jerk, and she just managed to hurt his feelings. Dammit. And damn JC for causing this. Fed up with everything, Nika threw up her hands.

"Jeez, Alex, this is just ridiculous!"

"What exactly?"

At least he was speaking to her. Encouraged, Nika plowed ahead. "Everything. This argument in its entirety is ridiculous. For God's sake, it was a long time ago, and we were children."

"Yeah? What about last nine years? Was he a child when he cut you off from his life? Not once did he make an effort to find you, or call, or text. He didn't even think to invite us to his wedding. Okay, I'm just a cousin, but you? You are his sister. And what crime did you commit to warrant his wrath?"

"Alex—"

"Don't Alex me. Did you know that last year I tried to reach him? And our fathers, and mothers, and the whole merry bunch of fucking Morrises?"

To say that she was shocked was a huge understatement.

"My God, you never told me—"

"Of course, I didn't. Because each and every one of them refused to talk to me. My dear old dad sneered over the phone, saying I won't get a dime out of him even if I was starving. Your dad was singing along the same tune. And JC?" Never talking his eyes off her, Alex pointed his thumb at her brother. "Want to tell Nika what you said to me, cousin dear?"

"I'm sorry."

"No, you told me to never call you again, and to forget that I and Nika have a family. That we were a disgrace, and that we tainted the saint Morris's name. Then you added some colorful expletive, suggesting I engage in anatomically impossible act with myself. Have I cover it all?"

Nika speared a quick glance at JC whose face lost all its color except two patches of scarlet riding high on his cheekbones. As inebriated as he was, he had enough decency to be ashamed. Eyes downcast, JC sat still but erect, like he was waiting for an ax to drop. At that moment, the major difference between him and their father became obvious as morning dew on a bright green lawn. Joseph Sr. would never allow himself to feel embarrassed about anything, least of all himself. Nika doubted the meaning of the word was familiar to him. JC, on the other hand, was a picture of acute and uncomfortable chagrin, and wasn't trying to cover it.

There's hope for him yet. Or am I deluding myself?

Alex's humorless chuckle cut into her thoughts.

"Oh, silly me, I forgot." With the open palm of his left hand he bumped his forehead in an exaggerated mocking gesture. "At the end he informed me that we were as good as dead to him. Now that's all."

"Oh, Alex. Why? Why did you even try?"

"Because...dammit, you suffered. I know you did. We both did. And I thought enough time has passed to reconcile our differences. Especially with this pandemic and all." In his frustration Alex brought both hands to his head then rubbed it a few times. "I thought it was time to reconnect, to mend fences. Yes, we were young, and reckless, and maybe acted stupidly. But we are adults now, and we are family. And, dammit, I wanted to show them all that we succeeded on our own, without any help. Fool that I was, I was hoping our family will be proud of us." Curling his hand into a fist, Alex thumped the table hard enough to rattled glasses. A similar fist clamped around Nika's heart. *Family.* It could be a blessing, or punishment. Some families were tight and nurturing, some selfish and cold.

But you didn't get to choose the family you were born into. Was it fate, or pure luck of the draw? Who decided it? God? Universe? Who knew?

No, she didn't get to choose her parents or siblings, but she was privileged to have *Verochka* and Alex, and now Eli and Abby. They were her true family, and their blessing overbalanced the scales.

Nika turned her eyes toward Eli, and that fist around her heart lessened its grip.

No, you didn't get to choose the family you were born into, but you can choose the one you build.

As if he read her thoughts, Eli took her hand and laced their fingers.

Comfort, understanding, unity. Promise.

And when he smiled at her, Nika let go the disappointments and regrets lingering on the edges of her memory. Free. She was fee at last. Hot tears pressed at the back of her eyes. Happy tears. Sad tears. Tears of acceptance and liberation. Light at heart at last, Nika turned to her cousin.

"You were always the best of us. I love you, Alex."

That teased a half smile out of him.

"Same here, even though I'm still mad at you."

"So noted."

A scraping sound dragged Nika's attention back to her brother.

"What are you doing?"

"T-trying to get up. S-stupid chair...too heavy."

"Or somebody is stupidly drunk."

"Here, Mr. Morris. Let me give you a hand." Gracious as ever, Eli came around and hauled JC to his feet. Her brother staggered for a moment, then slumped against Eli's chest. "Alex? I can use some help here."

After a moment's hesitation, Alex approached the pair. Hefting one of JC's arms onto his shoulder, he squinted at Eli.

"So, does that mean I have to call you by your first name now?"

"Only if I stopped irritating you."

"Hmm. I'll think about it."

"You do that." Eli grimaced as he adjusted JC's other arm onto his own shoulder. "Heavy bastard. And he looks so unimpressively light."

"Deceivingly light, I'd say. Then again, everything about Junior is deceiving."

"Is n-not," came a muffled response. "You just...don't like me. N-never ...have..."

"News flash."

"I...want...t-to go away now."

"Yeah, I want you to go away, too, but it's ain't gonna happen."

Alex shifted JC's weight. A deliberate rough handling prompted a weak sound of protest, but was ignored. "He's too drunk to think straight, much less walk under his own steam. Let's dump him in the guest bedroom for tonight. Tomorrow we'll decide what to do."

That night Nika slept in patches.

Even when Eli joined her in bed and drew her into his arms, she couldn't settle down and empty her mind. They didn't make love that night. She was to wound up mentally and emotionally. The last thing on her mind was sex.

Attuned to each other's moods as they were, she wasn't surprised when Eli kissed her with tenderness rather than passion, and wished her sweet dreams.

Grateful, Nika burrowed her nose into his chest, inhaled his familiar smell, and closed her eyes. But sleep eluded her for the longest time.

Nika dozed, on and off, comforted by Eli's embrace, lulled by his deep breathing, but her dreams were sporadic and scattered, like pictures in a kaleidoscope.

One moment she was in the original Coleman house, dressed in a long skirt and shirtwaist, walking with Belle in the gardens, the next— she was at the construction side, amidst the chaos and noise of the renovations, covered in dust and sweat, wearing her trusty black jeans.

Then she was running along the narrow dirt road at breakneck speed, chased by a huge black stallion, and all the while the old grandfather clock chimed loudly and incessantly, prompting her to hurry, hurry, hurry...

Gasping for air, Nika resurfaced. When she tried to sit up, she found herself unable to move. Something heavy and large was holding her in place, immobilizing the movement of her legs and arms. By the time her panic cleared the last cob-webs of the dream, realization dawned: not something, but someone. Eli.

His embrace was tight and unyielding, with just enough room for her to breathe. One of his legs was draped over hers, pinning her down. No wonder she couldn't move a muscle. Relieved, Nika stopped her mad thrashing, and gulped a few calming breaths. Her heart was about to drum its way out of her ribcage, her legs and arms tingled from the lack of blood circulation, but she was okay. Uncomfortable, scared out of her wits, but otherwise no worse for wear. Turning her head on the pillow, Nika blinked the object of her discomfort into focus. *Eli.* She still couldn't believe that he was here, right here, beside her, in her bed. Her miracle, her gift from the Universe. Her heart lurched, trembled, and then settled, tranquil and content.

Smiling, she let go of the last remnants of her dream, and watched him sleep. Totally defenseless, totally vulnerable. Totally hers. A tidal wave of tenderness surged upward from the very depth of her soul. She wasn't ashamed of the tears that sprung to her eyes, because they were a testament of overwhelming power. The power of love. Afraid of waking him, Nika held herself as still as possible, but Eli slept as he did everything else: with total and absolute concentration.

He was so beautiful. It was almost surreal. That absurdly sensual mouth, that chiseled chin with its deep cleft. What woman could stop herself from touching all that glory? Not this one. Gently her fingertips traced the outline of his lips. Oh, the idea of leaning over and taking a big, juicy bite of that delicious mouth, and then kissing the hell out of it. Tempting, so tempting, but...

Her sigh was a mix of resignation and regret, with a sliver of common sense in between. They both needed rest. Eli needed it even more after his time jump, and all the stress associated with it. Even the big strappy guy like him ought to be wiped out.

Bummer.

The stress-o-meter of yesterday, with one upheaval after another, hit well above the chart. Tomorrow, or already today, promised to be another challenge.

Double bummer.

Her own to-do list was quite impressive, starting with preparations for *Verochka* and Abby's arrival on Monday. Then there was her secret *tete-a-tete* with Vic in his official capacity as her attorney, and the problem of sneaking out of the house without alerting Alex or Eli. And she wanted to drop by the Coleman house, just to check it one more time before the big event on Tuesday. Then there was Thanksgiving dinner to plan, and her and Eli's departure the day after.

Oh, and let's not forget about the little drama with JC. But no pressure.

With her brain in full throttle mode, Nika contemplated her choices. She could get up and start hacking at her to-do list, but... what can she do at this hour? What time was it anyway? Good question. Still pinned under Eli's larger frame, Nika swiveled her head and squinted at the bedside clock. 4:30 a.m. Dammit, way too early. But she was revved and wide awake, so sleep was out of the question. Hmm.

What was the best medicine for insomnia per her clever grandmother?

Grinning, Nika inched closer to Eli.

What about much needed rest?

As usual, her inner bitch poked her nose in, even at this ungodly hour.

"Rest is overrated," Nika whispered before dipping her tongue into deep cleft of Eli's chin.

"Talking to yourself again?"

Without opening his eyes, Eli curved his lips into a crooked smile.

"Mostly arguing."

"What about?"

"Waking you up, or letting you sleep."

"Sleep, *ma petite*, is highly overrated."

Eli drew her closer and cupped her buttocks with his right hand. In a darkness of the room his silver eyes sparkled with devilish mischief.

"We are in a total agreement here." Rolling on top of him, Nika blew her annoying curls out of her eyes before she nipped his lower lip none too gently.

"Ouch! You wench." Strong but a playful swat on her backside shot her rioting libido up through the stratosphere. In a flash, Eli reversed their positions. Now she was trapped under his large and impressive frame. "You must be punished for misbehaving, little floozy."

They were in a total agreement, but Nika wasn't ready to admit it.

"Says who?" Fainting indignation, she glared at him through the curtain of ringlets.

"Your future husband."

Now his eyes sparkled with triumph, even as he gently brushed the hair out of her face. "He also says there are too many barriers between us."

The t-shirt she wore to bed was no challenge for him. Grabbing two fistfuls, he ripped it apart with ease. When her breasts lay bare to his hungry gaze, Eli made a deep, impatient growl and, dipping his head, took one of her nipples into his mouth. A moan that tore from her lips was a mixture of shock and delight. Helpless. Vulnerable.

She was stripped bare— body, mind, soul—and totally at his mercy.

Defenseless, but not afraid. Lost, but not alone. And when Eli gazed at her in silent wonder, she had her answer: he was as lost and vulnerable as she.

They both were lost in each other. They both held power over each other.

Enraptured, she embraced her vulnerability. Emboldened, she accepted her power.

On a long sigh, Nika arched her body in a silent offering.

I'm yours.

Her surrender was an act of absolute trust, an admission of simple truth.

Only you.

"Daisy...my Daisy... you...only you..." Eli's hoarse whisper echoed her silent oath.

"Show me."

His eyes worshipped her. His hands cherished her. His mouth destroyed her. Then, ruthless and quick, he shot her to the first peak, and set her on fire.

Heat, sizzling, unbearable... pleasure, sharp, unimaginable...

Cry—hers? His? — part triumph, part plea...

A shadow of pain danced along her nerve-endings. A tiny bite of danger hinted at something dark and forbidden. She was burning alive, and didn't give a damn. Delirious, Nika surged up, fused her hands in his hair, and demanded, "More!"

"With all my pleasure."

Much later, sheltered inside the cocoon of Eli's embrace, Nika's mind drifted to her earlier dream. Don't have to be Freud to figure that one out, but it left a slight aftertaste in her mouth. And not altogether a pleasant one.

Why was she so unsettled by that dream? Nothing strange in changing scenery and jumping between times, and nothing especially alarming. But she scooted a bit closer to Eli, grateful for his warmth.

CHAPTER TWENTY-FOUR

An earsplitting shriek catapulted Nika from her oblivion to reality.
"What...where—"

Half-comatose from an overload of sex and dreams, she jumped up, fighting to keep her eyes open.

"Oh, dear Lord!"

The voice. Familiar, female. Still befuddled, Nika blinked, trying to focus. Either she was still dreaming, or it was...

"Abby, my dear, please..."

The second woman who entered the room was a dead ringer to her grandmother.

Was she hallucinating? Dragging both hands through her messy hair, Nika shook her head to clear it, then squinted at the two women in her room. No, they were real, flesh and blood, in the middle of her bedroom, both frozen in place.

While Abby's face was a mask of utter shock, *Verochka's* feature were more of a distress and... embarrassment? Why was her grandmother— *if* it was her grandmother— blushing? A whiff of Chloe, *Verochka's* signature perfume, permeated the air. That was all the assurance she needed.

"*Verochka!* Abby!" Still a little groggy, Nika grinned at both of them. "What are you doing here?"

"Sorry, Nika, I couldn't stop her in time. She wanted to surprise you."

"Well, she succeeded, and you too." Fighting with covers, Nika tried to extricate herself from the bedding. "You're really here! I can't believe it! We were expecting you tomorrow. How—"

"Ah...we were planning to, but Rostoffs... they offered us a lift on their plane, so..."

"That's awesome!" Free at last, she was about to jump out of bed, when Abby's mutinous expression stopped her in mid-motion.

"Abs? What's wrong?"

"You are naked! And...and...and there *was* someone in your bed!"

Accusation rang clear in Abby's voice, punctuated by a sharp jab of her finger.

Quick turn in the direction of that pointing finger was all it took to make Nika squirm. Her demolished bed told the story quite eloquently. Damn.

Poor Abby. Even though she lived last fourteen months in the twenty-first century, her manners were still the product of her own time. Blushing furiously, scandalized from the tips of her toes to her uppity nose, Abby all but vibrated from within.

"How could you, Daisy! My brother...he trusted you! I thought...and you... Oh, for pity's sake, cover yourself!"

Nika snatched a sheet from the bed, all the while staring at her grandmother.

"Didn't tell her, did you?"

"No, I...couldn't, sorry, Nika."

"Coward."

"Tell me what?"

"Abby, just please, don't get upset. You see, I was...but then I thought..."

"Abby, what *Verochka* is trying to say—"

But the girl was beyond reasoning.

"Don't Abby me, you traitor. I'm not even talking to you. You see? See that?" Another point at the bed, as she glared at *Verochka*. "She slept with someone!"

So, Abby figured she cheated on Eli. *Geez.* That's all she needed.

And speaking of the devil, where was he?

"A man! In her bed!" Agitated, eyes blazing fire, Abby threw both hands up. "Scandalous!"

Nika swallowed her laughter. She shouldn't be enjoying it so much, but heck, the situation was too absurd not to. Dead serious, she feigned a frown.

"Of course, it was a man. What, did you expect another woman?"

"That's not funny, Daisy!"

"That's a matter of opinion, Abby."

"Girls, girls, please." *Verochka* interrupted. "Nika, get dressed. That sheet barely covers your boobs."

"You saw my boobs before."

"Nevertheless. And you, Abby..."

And that was a far as *Verochka* managed before the bathroom door flew open, and Eli sauntered into the room. So, the mystery was solved. Enamored with her rainfall shower system, he was indulging himself while she was dealing with his sister. The bastard. But one look at him, and Nika's heart trembled, even as her throat went bone dry. My God, he was gorgeous. Illegally so. Like from that time in Cumberland Island, when she lay her eyes on him for the first time, he simply took her breath away. Dear Lord, will that ever change? She sincerely hoped not.

Hair dripping water, naked save for the towel tucked low on his hips, he flashed her one of his dazzling smiles. "Daisy? I thought I heard some commotion."

It should be outlawed for men be so devastatingly handsome, and so early in the morning, too. Hell, it should be illegal at all hours of every day.

"Holly Mother of God!"

"Eli!"

And just like that, her reverie was shattered.

While *Verochka's* exclamation was akin to breathless revelation, Abby's yelp rung closer to a basic shock.

Eli's smile froze. In a flash, his face became a mask of horror. Then, quickly snatching the sheet from Nika, he held it high in front of him like a shield.

"Hey!" Too stunned to be embarrassed, Nika crisscrossed both hands over her chest. But her shriek of protest was ignored by everybody.

Well, two can play this game, buster.

She returned the favor by tugging the towel from his hips, and wrapping it around herself.

Verochka and Abby's eyes were glued to the half-naked rascal.

"Good morning, Madam." Barely decent, but playing it cool, Eli administered a formal, almost regal nod to *Verochka* before addressing his sister, "Abigail, please exit this room at once. We'll talk later."

But instead of obeying his bidding, Abby aimed her sizzling eyes at *Verochka.*

"You...you knew. You knew and didn't tell me! Oh, how could you, Grandmother!"

"Abby, my dear—"

"What's going on...Holly-molly!"

The room became more crowded as Alex and JC piled in. Hollowed eyed, barefoot, and sporting sleep creases all over their faces, both were in different stages of dress, or undress. Alex was in his regular cut-off shorts. JC was clad in trousers and unbuttoned shirt chewed-up beyond recognition.

Jumped right out of their respective beds and ran to the rescue, no doubt.

For some reason this struck her as hilarious. A bubble of laughter burst free despite Nika's best intentions.

As comedy goes, this one is definitely a scene from a sitcom. A cheesy one.

That thought prompted another bout of merriment, which earned her a fish eye from Alex. Then her cousin narrowed his gaze at Eli.

"Benjamin, I would never peg you for a striptease enthusiast. But hey, with the bod like yours you can make a decent living."

This time Nika laughed so hard the towel she had wrapped around herself loosened and slipped away. Something soft smacked her in the face. Alex had tossed her his shirt.

"Cover your excuse for boobs." Alex tossed her his shirt.

Grateful, Nika grabbed it, and tugged it on, and ignored the fact that everybody in the room by now were familiar with the shape of her mammary glands.

Don't flatter yourself. There's not much to see.

Of course, her inner bitch decided to join the party, and add her two cents.

But for once Nika was in agreement with her. Before she had a chance to catch her breath, Alex took control of the situation.

"*Verochka,* my true love, as gorgeous as ever!"

Without a hitch in his stride, he grabbed their grandmother in a tango stance, kissed her on both cheeks, and executed a perfect twirl. "Your Highness," a mocking bow in Abby's direction was accompanied by a lopsided grin, "a pleasure, as always."

"Oh, for pity's sake." On a huff, Abby completed a perfect hundred and eighty, but not before scorching the room in general with her fiery glare.

"Ouch. Was it something I said?"

Rubbing the left side of his chest, Alex squinted at *Verochka*.

"No, dear. It's my fault entirely. I should've told her, prepared her. It's all my fault."

"The fault, Madam, if there's any, is solely mine."

Even in this ridiculous situation, Eli managed to act as a gentleman. If you discounted the fact that he stole her sheet to cover himself, that is.

"Oh, so Abby didn't know that Benjamin popped up?"

"No."

In lieu of an answer Alex whistled, then spared her brother a scalding glance. "JC?"

"Huh?" Like coming out of a trance, he blinked, and unglued his eyes from the direction of Abby's exit. "Wow. Who was that?"

"No one you should be concerned about. Or salivating after."

Was she the only one to catch a warning in Alex's last words? Before Nika had a time to reflect, Alex thumped JC— none too gently— on the back, propelling him forward. "Say hello to your grandmother."

"Hello, *Verochka*."

"Hello, Junior. What are you doing here?

"Well, I—"

"Never mind. I'll talk to you later, but for now..."

And like a commanding general, *Verochka* squared her shoulders, drew a deep breath, and took the reins in her own elegant hands.

"Alex dear... *mon Dieu,* what happened to your face?"

"Ah—"

"Never mind. Sweetheart, please go find Abby, and fetch her back."

When *Verochka* turned to JC, her voice and eyes chilled several degrees.

"Now, Junior, as long as you're here, do something useful and make a pot of coffee."

"But—"

"Beans are in the fridge, water is in the cooler, the coffee machine is in the kitchen. Go."

After shooing Alex and dismissing JC, it was Nika's turn.

"Daisy-girl, do make yourself presentable, please. That shirt does nothing to compliment your complexion, not to mention your modesty. And no eyerolling, young lady. And Mr. Coleman... or is it Benjamin?"

"Coleman, madam. Benjamin is...well, it's a long story."

"I see." A tap of finger against *Verochka's* pursed lips contradicted that statement, but after one elegant shrug, the subject was dropped. "So, Mr. Coleman, what happened to your face?"

"Eli, please. My family calls me Eli, Madam. As to my face, it's...nothing you should concern yourself about."

"Very well. Eli. Please put some clothes on, even though I must admit, it's a crime to cover all that glory." A flash of unabashed and undiluted lust in her grandmother's eyes was impossible to miss. "And by the way, my family calls me *Verochka*."

More amused than appalled, Nika swallowed her chuckle.

"Verochka!"

"What, dear? I'm old, not blind. And the last time I checked, I was still a female."

With a last glance at Eli, her grandmother glided toward the door.

"Hurry up, children. Time is ticking away."

And wasn't that the truth.

CHAPTER TWENTY-FIVE

It didn't take Alex long to locate her. Head high, spine straight, she was marching along the boardwalk, her mile-long legs eating up the distance with careless ease. An angry energy pulsed around her like an electric current.

Wouldn't be surprised to see sparks flying.

As long as those sparks didn't scorch his own skin, Alex was okay.

Abby's temper was hidden deep under layers of class and her Edwardian era upbringing, but when unleashed? Oh, it was a sight to behold. Who should know better, as he was on the receiving end of said temper more times than he cared to count?

They just rubbed each other the wrong way.

Or was it the right way?

Shaking the annoying thought aside, Alex trudged after her. Okay, full disclosure. She unsettled him, made him uncomfortable. Even twitchy. And damn if he didn't like that. No one managed to irritate him like Abby. Not even his illustrious cousin. And, hell, no one stirred his juices like the Princess.

She wasn't even his type, for heaven's sake. He preferred his women to be adventurous, striking, and well over the age of innocence. And blond. Definitely blond. Or so he thought.

Abby was more than striking, but as to the rest? She couldn't flirt if her life depended on it, and her miles of black hair put ravens to shame.

A decade younger—or a century older— she was as innocent as baby in a cradle.

A major pain in his behind, that's who she was. A constant challenge. A damned enigma.

A complication no sane man needed in his life. And still...

What was it about her? When she was near, he went out of his way to alienate her. When she was away, he missed her like an amputated limb.

Damn it all to hell and back.

Despite his pensive mood, Alex cracked a grin when some poor inanimate object that had a misfortune to be in the middle of Abby's path went flying, compliments of her kicking. Even at a distance, he overheard muttering. Was it French? Yep. You don't have to speak the language to be familiar with the meaning of the word *merde*. Oh, yeah, the Princess was pissed. But who could blame her?

The surprise of seeing her brother qualified for a shock of major proportions.

And that's not counting the fact that he was barely decent at the moment of the siblings' rendezvous. She was an artist. She must be familiar with the human anatomy. Probably saw a naked man before. A model? *A lover?*

That thought brought him up short. His blood pressure soared. Dammit, did she have a lover?

"Christ!" What on earth was he thinking? Idiot.

He had more immediate problems at hand, such as catching up with the Princess and bringing her home. Later he planned to corner *Verochka* and grill her about Abby's personal life. And privacy be damn. He was responsible for the girl as much as *Verochka* or Nika. He was the man of the family. Why, only yesterday Eli asked him to watch over his sister in his stead. So, if Abby did have a lover, then...

He'd deal with it. Somehow. As for right now... where was she, anyway?

Abby was quite a distance ahead of him. Those long legs of hers had carried her farther than he anticipated. Picking up his pace, Alex hurried along the path.

Damn, the Princess can really move.

And the energy! Dear Lord. Her anger was palpable, pulsing, dancing, spewing sparks in all the directions. Magnificent! What would it feel like to channel all that energy into more enjoyable, but no less volatile, venue?

Oh, yeah, baby.

Appalled, Alex stopped in his tracks. Was he really fantasizing about sex with Abby? He and Abby?

Fuck.

"No way, no fucking way." He tugged at his tightened shorts, readjusting himself.

If Abby preferred French, Alex always cursed in Russian. Indulging in a string of crude but extremely inventive expletives, he squirmed, rearranging his stance. Embarrassed, thankful for his roomy, baggy shorts, he focused his eyes at the woman ahead.

God Almighty, what a body! Long, lean, rounded in all the right places. Like a perfect hourglass. Mouthwatering. Add the mindboggling face to match that traffic stopping body, and you have a disaster waiting to happen.

"No way. No way in hell."

And if you repeat it often enough, maybe you can convince yourself, buddy.

Defeated, Alex puffed out a breath. Who was he kidding?

From the moment he laid his eyes on her wearing that ridiculous hat, old-fashioned topcoat, and dead-set determination in her pewter eyes she had stolen his breath away.

He had yet to catch it back. And trying to reassure himself otherwise was as futile as his attempt at forgetting her.

Damn it all to hell and back.

Several months they lived apart, in two different countries, on two different continents, but did it do any good? Nope. Not a fucking thing. One look at her, and he was trembling like an addict, grinning like an idiot, and camouflaging his misery under a false bravado. Humiliating? Bet your ass. But...

It was time to admit the truth. He fell for her. Hard and fast.

But admitting the truth was only half of the problem. What was he supposed to do now? That was a totally different ballgame.

And now you have a decision to make. Ignore it, or act on it.

Ignore? A rude snort and another string of Russian curses that would scandalize *Verochka* burst free before Alex could stop himself.

Yeah, so, there you have it, buddy.

His eyes sought and held a lone figure at the edge of the water.

What was she doing? Where was she going, for Christ's sake? God Almighty! She was knee-deep into the ocean.

"Oh, for crying out loud..."

He was running before his brain had a chance to process it.

A mighty warlike cry stopped him in mid-motion.

Abby.

Face upturned, hands fisted, she was now in the water almost to her waist, screaming her heart out. Stumbling, Alex fell. An answering cry of the sea gulls overhead chilled his blood.

"Abby. Abby!"

Did she hear him? Desperate, he kept calling her name, while the pictures of the water swallowing her alive danced in his mind. He was too far. No way was he going to be in time to snatch her from the hungry waves.

"Abby! Get back! Now!"

As if she were mesmerized, she held her gaze on the horizon, ignoring his pleas.

Then, as if coming out of a trance, her body jolted.

With her chin up, Abby squared her shoulders and turned her head.

Their eyes locked. The moment stretched. The roar of the ocean, the cries of the seagulls, the murmur of the breeze—everything faded into silence. The only sound in his ears was the heavy drumbeat of his heart.

CHAPTER TWENTY-SIX

Who moved first? Alex wasn't sure, didn't care. Face-to-face, the water lapping at their feet, they gazed at each other.

Here you are. At last.

The urge to touch her, to kiss that unsmiling mouth was irresistible.

Swamped in tenderness.

In her.

In the moment.

Alex leaned forward and tucked a stray lock of hair behind her ear. An accidental brush of his fingertips against her earlobe was all it took to scramble his brain.

"What happened to your face?"

"Huh?" He blinked. His face? Dumbfounded, Alex touched his cheeks.

Forgot to shave.

Was she referring to his stubble, or the bafflement his face must be projecting at the moment?

"You have bruises here and here."

Her finger pointed up without touching. His skin tingled at the invisible contact.

"Oh, that. Ah...it's nothing. Just a disagreement."

"Did you resolve it?"

"What?"

"The disagreement."

"Oh, yeah. Sure."

"Who won, Eli or you?"

So, the Princess noticed her brother's bruises as well.

"I'd say, it was a draw."

"All is well, then."

"Yeah. We're good, Benjamin and I, we kind of—"

"Benjamin?"

A little frown drew his eyes to her forehead. Pale like marble, smooth as satin. The need to smooth that line between her brows with his fingertips, then kiss it off flashed like a wildfire in his gut.

Damn.

Alex cleared his throat.

"Yeah, it's...a long story, but—"

"What about us?"

Us? Did she say *us?* Like a punch to the solar plexus, all the air whooshed out of his lungs. Abby glared at him with an open accusation. Was it possible?

He must be mistaken, or else he was the biggest fool on the planet.

"Abby, my God, I—"

"I thought we were friends." Her voice shook from the force of her anger. "No, more than friends. I thought of you as my brother!"

For a second time in minutes, she sucker-punched him with her words.

Brother.

That's all he was to her. He would have preferred a slap in the face, but beggars can't be choosers. Hiding his hurt under a mask of a goofy idiot, Alex shrugged.

"I am truly honored, your Highness."

Lightning fast, her eye color changed from silver to pewter.

Fascinating.

"*Merde*, don't you dare to mock me!" Incensed, Abby stomped her foot like a capricious two-year old.

Adorable.

A chuckle burned his throat, but Alex managed to swallow it.

"Wouldn't dream of it. So, tell me, Princess, how did I manage to fall out of your graces?"

"How could you not forewarn me?"

"About?"

"About my brother. Being here, I mean. Not you, not *Verochka*. I can understand Daisy. Her first allegiance is to my brother, but you, Alex! How could you let me stumble into this situation completely blind?"

"And what would you do if you knew?"

"Refused to come here, of course."

"Of course. And you are asking why neither *Verochka*, nor I told you?"

"Don't you turn it around, and make it all my fault."

"I'm not, just pointing out a fact, that's all. Abby, look, your brother popping up here was a surprise, even shock, for everybody. But since he's here, you have to face him. That's inevitable."

"What is inevitable, is that Eli will insist on taking me back. Don't you understand? I was supposed to be married to a member of the Carnegie family."

"So?"

"So? I shamed my brother by running away. I ruined his relationships with his friends. Worse, I ruined his reputation among his peers. He would never forgive me. The only cure to this situation is for him to force me go back, and marry Patrick Carnegie."

"The hell you will!"

His words exploded with such a force that Abby's eyes widened as she took a tentative step back. Poised over a silent 'o,' her mouth showed two rows of perfect pearly whites.

Alex let out a deep breath, then another, all the while cursing silently.

Take it easy, buddy. She's here. She's not going anywhere. And you are scaring her shitless.

"You are not going anywhere." His voice was calm but firm, in a direct contrast with his jittery emotions. "You are where you supposed to be. You belong here."

You belong with me.

"But—"

"No buts." A sudden understanding dawned at him. "That's why you were screaming?"

Her averted gaze and blush that spread across her beautiful face was his answer. Alex took a step closer. Lifting her chin with two fingers, he peered into her eyes. His heart trembled, then sighed. Not his type?

You really are a moron, Alex.

"Don't be afraid, Princess."

"Who said I am?"

Eyes blazing, brows arched, Abby almost managed to pull off a defiance.

God, what a woman! Was it any wonder he was crazy about her?

Chucking, Alex tapped his finger over her stubborn chin. She immediately smacked at his hand.

"Relax, tigress. Your brother has no intention of taking you back."

"And how do you know that?"

"Because he told me. After I asked. Not very politely." Alex pointed at his bruised cheek. "What do you think our disagreement was all about?"

"Me? You hit my brother because of... me?"

"Well, yeah. He treated you like a Neanderthal and I—"

"You fought with Eli over me?" Her voice rose a full octave.

"Yes. Over you, because of you, for you."

"No one ever did. You are my first."

The unintended double entendre hit him between the eyes.

Oh, Lord, have merci.

But when she brushed her lips over his cheek and murmured "thank you," his self-control all but evaporated. Did she have any idea that her innocent kiss almost destroyed him? In his mind he was howling with frustration. Alex mustered all his self-control and cracked a smile.

"You are welcome."

She was close, too close for comfort. Another moment, and he wouldn't be able to stop himself from kissing the hell out of that luscious mouth.

Brother, remember?

To distract himself, he wrenched his eyes off her lips.

Say something, imbecile. Anything.

"Abby?"

"Yes, Alex?"

"You are wet."

For fuck's sake, man, did you really just say that?

CHAPTER TWENTY-SEVEN

Abby's gaze didn't waver, but her lips twitched.

"So are you."

Twin dimples teased to life by her smile twisted his insides into a heavy knot. A fantasy of dipping his tongue into those tiny craters danced across his mind.

You are not helping yourself, pal. Brother, remember? Just brother.

"We're both wet."

And that earth-shattering revelation is important because…?

"What are you doing here?" Like a safety net, her question reeled him back to reality.

"I've been looking for you."

"Why?"

It seems I've been looking for you all my life.

He wasn't sure they both were ready for the answer, so Alex replied with a question, "Why were you going in the water?"

"Maybe I wanted to swim."

"Swim, huh? A bit cold for that, but if you're up to some skinny-dipping, I'm game."

Moron.

Well, if she considered him a brother, he'd oblige by acting *brotherly*.

Abby cocked her head, squinting at him like a curious cat.

"What's a skinny-dipping?"

A bark of laughter broke free despite his current mood.

"How long have you been living in the twenty-first century, Princess?"

"You know very well how long, and I hate when you're calling me that. I have a name."

"So, Abigail Suzanne Coleman, after more than a year living here, you still don't recognize popular slang?"

"So, Alexander Zachariah Morris, what of it?"

"Just boggles the mind, that's all."

"Your mind, my dear sir, is too easily boggled then," She retorted in that haughty tone of voice that drove him crazy.

For some ridiculous reason this usual banter settled him like nothing else, and got his humor back on track.

"Oh, Abby." He looped his arm in a familiar manner around her shoulder. "You'll be the end of me."

She surprised him by curling her arm around his waist.

"I promise to be gentle." Her humorous oath accompanied by dancing devils in her eyes was like a balm to his soul. Or a knife to his gut. God, he had missed her.

The camaraderie between them was more precious than anything, and he'd be damned if he let his libido ruin that. If a big brother role was all she was willing to accept from him, he'd take it. Even if it killed him. Which it probably would.

And who are you kidding, pal?

Alex shrugged that thought aside, and grinned into her smiling eyes.

"Let's go home, Abby. It's time to face the music."

By the time Eli managed to find his new garments and deal with them, he worked up a lather.

Abby was here.

The girl he raised from the time she was in a short dress, was here. At last, he will be able to talk to her, to air their differences.

To beg for her forgiveness.

Instead of a mere fourteen days, an eternity has stretched in between the last time he'd seen his baby sister and today. Fourteen days in 1909 equaled fourteen months in this century.

Thunderation.

So hard to wrap his mind around it. But days or months, one thing was clear to Eli: everything changed. Including Abigail's appearance. A short glimpse before she ran out of the room was that of a stunning beauty he barely recognized. Apparently, her attitude had changed with it, because the young woman Eli remembered from before would never behave and talk in such an unladylike manner. She yelled! She dared to contradicted his order, and then she turned and ran off like a spoiled child.

He expected better of her. And he was determined to point that out to her as soon as he had a chance, and demand...

Demand? Damn it, Coleman, haven't you learn your lesson?

Abigail ran away because he was too busy issuing orders and demands, instead of paying attention and listening to her.

Distressed, he fumbled several times before he managed to zip up his trousers. No, jeans, he corrected himself. A tight, ass-molding, stretchy contraption that was rather embarrassing, even if convenient. Eli grimaced, adjusting his private parts. Every damn portion of his anatomy was on display. How was it possible to maintain one's dignity, parading around in this thing?

Thunderation.

A shirt, even though not body-hugging, was missing both sleeves, so his arms were bare. Self-consciously, Eli tugged at the fabric, trying for a modicum of decency, to no avail. And why was he so concern about his appearances?

He had more pressing matters to worry about, such as an upcoming conversation with Abigail. Eli's fingers curled over his father's pocket watch of their own volition. The familiar shape of the heirloom managed to calm him down a bit. But that constant impression of being out of place remained, no matter what. He suspected it was inevitable until he was back in time and place where he belonged. Until then, he must contain this unpleasant sensation of a fish being out of water, and proceed as best as he could. That means, wearing half-decent clothes.

The hell with it.

Racking both hands through his hair, Eli cursed under his breath. Daisy deserted him to muck through this misadventure on his own. And who could blame her? First, he snatched her sheet, exposing her nakedness, then he snapped at her when she tried to uplift his mood.

I am a complete bastard.

And if the first deed was born out of pure reflex, and could be attributed to his shock, the second was a fully conscious act, a defense mechanism. There was no excuse for his behavior, none whatsoever.

You are a dastardly bastard.

Foreseeing a great deal of groveling in his immediate future, Eli heaved a sigh of resignation. He was confident Daisy would forgive him, after she made his life a living hell, but he harbored a world of doubt about Abby.

What if she refused to talk to him? Or believe his regrets?

No. Impossible.

His sister was a gentle soul without a single cruel bone in her body. She did not have it in her to hurt him by rejecting his apologies. Or did she?

The girl he raised, the young woman she became under his watchful eye was kindhearted, caring, and affectionate.

But what if she had changed? Was it possible fourteen months modified her personality? And the answer was yes. But to what extend?

Well, you are about to find out.

Like a man awaiting an execution, Eli entered the dining room.

The smell of coffee was strong and not altogether pleasant. His nose twitched. Since England, Eli's preference of choice was tea. Coffee in his house was not a popular drink, and tolerated only because of Abby, and later Daisy. The allure was beyond him. But what did he know? A great deal less than he had believed before.

The conversation died as he set foot inside the room.

"Eli, why, my dear, you look fabulous!"

Daisy grandmother's surprise teased a reluctant smile out of him.

"Thank you, Madame...ah, *Verochka.* But if someone is looking fabulous, it is you. Exceptionally stunning, and absolutely radiant. I hope I didn't offend your sensibilities by being so bold."

He flicked a glance at Daisy, when her loud snort and a muttered "suck-up" reached his ears. Still peeved, and so adorable with it. Eli hid his smile.

I'll deal with you later, wench.

"Not at all, my dear." *Verochka* beamed with pleasure, drawing his attention back from his vexed fiancé. "Not at all. I prefer honest and bold men. It is refreshing."

Her offered hand was so small and delicate, Eli was afraid to damage it with his kiss. He opted to brush his lips above her knuckles as gently as possible, inhaling her enchanting perfume. The woman smelled of dreams and mischief.

A pair of unusual violet eyes she passed onto her granddaughter shone with laughter as *Verochka* gazed up at him.

"And if a man is equipped with an excellent body, terrific face, and brave heart, he's every woman's dream come true."

Was she flirting with him, or jesting? A little of both, he deduced. A flutter of lashes, breathless voice, tilted head, and the little devils dancing in her eyes.

Damn, what a woman!

Charmed, amused, Eli found himself grinning back. His sour mood became considerably sweeter.

"If I wouldn't be desperately in love with your granddaughter, *Verochka*, I would beg your permission to court you."

She let out a peal of laughter, before caressing his cheek. His heart melted.

"And I would probably agree, you rascal, even though I'm old enough to be your grandmother."

"You got it wrong, my lady. Have you forgotten how old I am?" His whisper barely reached her ears, as his brain calculated the answer.

Four and thirty, plus hundred and eleven, or one hundred and forty-five.

"Thunderation!" Instantly appalled at cursing if front of a lady, Eli winced, and inclined his head. "I beg your pardon, *Verochka*."

"My dear, I can give you lessons in *real* cursing in three languages, so stop apologizing. Nika? Get Eli a cup of coffee. *Merde*, where are Abby and Alex?"

"Eli prefers tea." Daisy's voice was cold enough to freeze hellfire. But when she addressed her grandmother, her tone warmed several notches. "Alex will find our runaway princess, don't worry, *Verochka*."

A minute later, a steaming cup they called a *mug* was thrust into his hands with all the finesse of a sledgehammer. The smell wafting out of it was more pleasant than coffee, but only by a margin. Eli squinted at a small package swimming in his mug. Why was it attached to a string? What in the name of God was this brew?

After one suspicious sniff, Eli lifted his gaze. A faint aroma of bergamot was unmistakable.

Earl Grey.

Thankfully she wasn't trying to poison him after all.

"Thank you, Daisy." He sipped and his eyes shot open. "This tea is...hot."

The answering missive behind her glare read like the blinking sign he saw on one of his automobile trips: be thankful I didn't pour it over your head. Lord, he was insane about her. A small smile tugged at his lips. She was so alluring when she was mad. But they had an audience, more the pity, so it was time to smooth her feathers.

"*Ma petite*, you are looking exceptionally fetching this morning."

"*Mon ami*," Daisy fluttered her eyelashes in a coquettish manner worthy of any high-priced courtesan, "you are so full of it."

And just like that, his blood was churning and his cock fighting against the restrains of his jeans. She flicked him a knowing smile, and licked her lips.

The steaming mug he forgot all about almost slipped from his fingers.

"Full of... what?"

"'Full of it' is a modern slang, an expression meaning—"

"Shit. It means shit."

That remark snapped him back to the moment.

"Junior!"

Verochka aimed her glare at the younger man, then sent Eli an apologetic smile. "I'm sorry. My grandson is not usually this rude."

Daisy's brother, whom Eli forgot all about, seemed to bounce back to his obnoxious self quite well. Surly and pale, he lounged at the table, nursing a glass of water. The amount of alcohol he indulged in last night would make any man miserable. A headache danced behind his blood-shot eyes, adding a glimmer of mean angst. No wonder JC was in such a crotchety mood. Without a spit of remorse, Eli increased the volume of his voice, "And how are you this morning, Mr. Morris?"

"Fine." His wince, however, contradicted his statement. "I'm fine, Mr...Benjamin, is it?"

"It's Coleman, Elijah Benjamin Coleman."

"Yeah, right. You're my sister's boyfriend, if I'm not mistaken?"

Needling me on purpose, little turd.

"Oh, but you are. I am not a boy, nor am I a friend, but a man and your sister's fiancé."

And you very well know it, you cad.

JC dismissed that, shrugging in a negligent manner.

"You talk kind of strange. Like you are from another planet. Why is that?"

"Because, in a manner of speaking, I am."

"Care to elaborate?"

"No."

"And why the hell not? I want to know—"

"Shut up, JC." Daisy's voice cut through her brother's objections.

"But you are my sister, and I have a right—"

"You have a right to remain silent, Counselor. Or else."

"Uh-oh. Did we miss anything?"

CHAPTER TWENTY-EIGHT

Alex's quip came not a moment too soon. He sauntered into the room, stopping near the bickering siblings. Abby hovered by the entrance, as if reluctant to come all the way inside. The smirk on Alex's face registered with Eli.

"Nika? Reading JC the riot act?"

"Something like that."

"Well, now, don't let me stop you."

Alex sat then crossed his legs and gestured for Daisy to proceed.

"That's ridiculous." JC massaged his forehead.

"Not from where I'm standing," Daisy contradicted coolly.

"Children, may I offer a solution?" *Verochka* cut into the conversation. "Why don't we all take time to cool off our tempers, and leave Abby and Eli alone?"

"Really? Leave him alone with another chick while his fiancé is cooling off her temper? Really, *Verochka*?" A leering smirk disfigured JC's face into a mask of acute derision. A greyish-green pallor of skin added a drop of ugliness to the overall image.

"You moron, this *chick* is his sister," Daisy spat at her brother.

"Oh, sorry. I didn't know."

"And that's why, my man, you're still sitting in this chair with your pretty face intact." Alex clapped JC on the back, almost sending him face first into the table. The grimace passing for a smile on his face was hard enough to cut diamonds.

"I said I was sorry. How would I know?"

"Now you do. Let me introduce you properly, then. JC, meet Abigail Coleman, the sister of Elijah Coleman, aka Benjamin. Abby? This sorry excuse for a gentleman is my cousin, and Nika's older brother, JC Morris. We sometimes refer to him as Junior, but only when we're pissed at him. Which is most of the time."

Abby measured Nika's brother, then inclined her head.

"I'm pleased to meet you, Mr. Morris."

Polite and impersonal, her voice lacked its usual warmth. She kept her hands at her sides.

"Pleasure is all mine, Ms. Coleman. And I am really sorry for before."

"Your apology is accepted." Regal as a queen, Abby nodded at JC. "I didn't know Daisy's bother was visiting."

"Neither did Daisy," Alex added. "It came as a great surprise to all of us."

"Well, it is nice to have family around, especially during a holiday."

"Oh, yeah, we are big on holiday gatherings in our family. Thanksgivings and Christmases are our favorites, aren't they, JC?"

"I—"

"Enough, Alex." *Verochka's* stern rebuttal put an end to his speech. "It won't benefit any of us if we will continue to squabble." Her voice and her eyes warmed up several degrees when she turned to Abby. "Are you okay, my dear?"

"I'm fine, *Verochka*. I'm really sorry for being rude to you, and for running away. I behaved like a spoiled child."

"Never you mind, sweetheart. I understand. You and I, we'll have ourselves a really nice chat later. Okay?" As she turned to her other grandson, a glitter of frost sparkled in her eyes.

"Junior, let's sit on the deck, and you can tell me why you really came here. Alex? Nika? Don't you two have a business to run?"

Alex sniffed at Eli's forgotten mug of tea, before replying, "It's Sunday, *Verochka*." Snatching a cup of coffee from her hands, he managed a couple of slurps.

"So? Go check on some paperwork," *Verochka* removed her cup from her grandson's hands, "or answer emails."

"Gorgeous, I can do all that from home, thanks to the Internet. If you need me to scram, just say so."

"Scram."

"Scramming." A loud kiss and comical lip smacking accompanied Alex's reply.

"As a matter of fact," Daisy interrupted, "I do need to run into town."

"What the heck for? You don't have any appointments today, and the Coleman house is as ready for the senator's arrival as it can be. Don't tell me you want to check on it again."

"No, but... I'm, ah... meeting someone, so I can give you a lift."

"Thanks, Cuz, but I think I'll stick closer to home." Alex cast a quick glance at Abby. "I'll grab a shower, and check my emails. If somebody needs me, holler."

The last was said to the room at large, but Eli had a strong suspicion it was addressed to his sister.

Hmm. Something to ponder later.

"Then I'm going to scram, too. I'll be back in no time."

"Have a nice visit then, my dear." Verochka patted Daisy's cheek, then turned to her other grandson. "Junior? With me."

She sailed out of the room, followed closely by a reluctant JC.

Eli frowned. *Daisy was avoiding his eyes. Was she still peeved?*

"Daisy? Is something amiss?"

"What? Oh, no, not at all. It's just I need to...well, I am meeting a friend, so..."

She was up to something. Why else was she trying so hard to evade the real purpose of her trip to town? Who was she meeting? What friend?

Damn it.

"Should I go with you?"

"No, you should absolutely not. Please Eli. It's something that I need to do on my own. Trust me?"

"With my life." Untarnished truth.

She lifted onto tiptoes and placed a chaste kiss on his chin.

"Talk to Abby," Daisy's whisper teased his ears. "Be sure to grovel."

A flash of a smile and she was gone.

And so, my man, the time has arrived.

The room was deserted but for Abby and him. If Eli ever was more uncomfortable in his life, he had yet to recall that moment. Miserable, with his heart in his throat, he focused on his sister. How long ago did he see her last? Not even a fortnight.

Minute by minute, that day unfolded before his eyes.

He proposed to Daisy, then together they broke the news to the household. Abby was ecstatic, jumping up and down, laughing, clapping her hands in delight.

That was the image of his sister that was etched into his memory. She was a joyful, carefree, elated girl in a long dress with a river of midnight-black hair streaming down her back. The woman that held his gaze now barely resembled that image.

And not just because Abby was dressed in peculiar clothes of this time.

She changed so much that she was more like a stranger who resembled his sister.

A beautiful stranger. When did his baby sister transform into a stunning woman? How did he miss it?

Just fourteen short days...or fourteen long months and a century.

The sun streaming through the windows illuminated Abby's willowy figure, and cast a brilliant halo around her head. Her long tresses were now secured in a twist around her nape. A few unruly wisps escaped the pins, caressing her face.

The contrast between her ink black locks and milky white skin was stark, but somehow endearing. His fingers itched to smooth those strands behind her ears, like he used to do when she was a child. But Abigail was no longer a child. Such a frivolous gesture would not be appropriate. Or welcomed.

And at that precise moment, in the strange place and unknown time, Eli realized he had lost her forever. His baby sister, the child he raised, the girl he loved...

His pang of regret was akin to physical pain.

"Abigail..."

His voice, hollow and lifeless, echoed in the large room. The words of apology were clogging his throat, but his tongue refused to move. As an insult to injury, Eli's eyes started to itch. On the brink of complete humiliation, he steeled his heart, and ordered himself to act like a man. He refused to succumb to a calamity. He squared his shoulders, determined to face his sister's wrath with dry eyes and a high head. And nurse his broken heart later.

"Abby, I..."

She didn't let him finish. Before his brain registered it, she was running toward him, and all but threw herself into his arms.

"Oh, Eli! I missed you so."

"Abby, my little *Papillon*."

Her childhood nickname rolled over his tongue, bringing back memories. And just like that, she was his baby sister again, his sweet, dear butterfly, his Abby.

Just for a moment, time stopped, and he was back home. Eyes shut, Eli held his precious girl in his embrace, unwilling to let go. But soon the unfamiliar fragrance of the woman in his arms shuttered his illusion, and then reality came crushing back. Reluctant to accept the truth, Eli took a step back, but kept Abby's hands in his.

"I am so sorry."

"No, it is me who's sorry, Brother. Will you ever forgive me?"

"Whatever for?"

"For running away, for...for bringing shame and grief on you. For everything."

"You didn't shame me, my dear girl. As for grief? I deserve it and then some, for treating you like a monster."

"Oh, but you weren't, Eli. Well, maybe just a tiniest bit." A tremulous smile twitched her lips, but her eyes were moist and sad. With the unsteady fingers, he wiped the lone tear rolling down her cheek.

"I was a true monster to you, my sweet *Papillon*, and a tyrant. But underneath it all, I swear I was acting out of love. I always loved you. Even if I never spoke of it aloud."

"And I always knew that. I was sure of your love, until you decided to marry me off against my will.'

"I am very sorry about that, Abby. Please know that I had your best interest in mind when I agreed to the engagement with Patrick Carnegie."

"Speaking of the devil, how did the Carnegies react to my disappearance?"

"I've no idea."

"What do you mean?"

"Since your and Daisy's vanishing act fourteen days ago, I was a bit preoccupied. I'll write a formal letter to Mr. Thomas and Ms. Lucy as soon as I'm back."

"Wait, Eli, fourteen days? You said fourteen *days*?"

"Yes, that's what I said."

"Oh, sweet Lord, it's been—"

"I know, longer than a year here. Time apparently moves differently."

"It is so peculiar, isn't it? When we first arrived here, Daisy and I, we have learned that it's been just three days since she had left, so *Verochka* and Alex didn't even notice her disappearance. And she was so torn up about them, remember? Can you imagine her reaction when she learned the truth?"

"It must have been disappointing to her."

"Disappointing? It was a shock, Brother. Brutal shock. Daisy was broken to pieces. But she always believed that you would forgive her, and return the key to its hiding place. She just thought it would have been much sooner, but..." She let out a deep sigh. "I guess we all forgot how time moves differently, here and there. Oh, did Mr. O'Brien explain everything to you? How he gave Daisy the key, right? Please, don't be mad at him, Eli. He tried to help, that's all. And it wasn't his fault that we—"

"William is dead."

"*What?* Oh, goodness! How?"

"It was an unfortunate mishap."

"Oh, Eli, I'm so sorry. No wonder you didn't learn the truth!"

"I did learn the truth, Abby. Three days ago. William confessed on his death bed."

"Wait, three days? But... didn't he explain everything *upon* your arrival?"

"No, he did not." He chose to omit that his best friend not only hid the truth, but was instead spreading ugly lies. Daisy forgave William's deception, but Abby?

He wasn't sure of her reaction. And what was the point of lambasting the dead now?

"But why? I don't understand. He loved you so."

"Yes, he was the most loyal friend. He even died in my stead, Abby, pushing me away from rolling logs. But as to why..." He still couldn't wrap his head around it. The fact that he will never learn the truth was hard to swallow. "I'm afraid we will never know. William took the answer to his grave, God rest his soul."

Confusion was written all over his sister's face. A deep frown marred her forehead, as she tried to come to terms with the troubling news.

"So, until William...until three days ago, you believed... what? That Daisy and I just... ran away?"

And her clever brain latched onto the damning fact with a speed of a hurricane.

Thunderation.

"Yes."

"Are you insane?" Instantly outraged, she yanked her hands from his grip. "Daisy loves you more than life, and would never— ever— betray you! And besides, *where* would we go? You and I, we don't have any family; Daisy came from another time. So, where did you believe we'd run away?"

"Put that way, it does seem foolish of me."

"*Foolish*?" Her voice soared upward, gaining volume. "Brother dear, you truly amaze me! How can you not trust the woman you love?"

Her angry glare condemned him to eternity. Eli fought not to squirm, but failed.

"I know I have no excuse—"

"None whatsoever. Tell me, Eli, what if William didn't perish? If not for the accident, he could've lived and hid the truth for many years. What would you have done then?"

"I..." He never thought of that. What *would* he do? Become bitter, as he grew older, with his anger eating at his soul, or come to his senses, and start searching for the truth? He didn't know, and it shamed him, but Eli was always honest with himself. "I do not know."

She held his eyes for a long moment, then turned away. Like a dark rain cloud, her disappointment hung between them, heavy and suffocating.

"I can only repeat that I'm sorry."

Rather sad than angry, Abby shook her head. "She never stopped believing in you. Never stopped waiting for you."

Guilty as hell, Eli raked his hands through his hair. But she was right, damn it, and that made him more embarrassed and annoyed.

"Abigail, what do you want from me? I'm just a man who made a mistake. Alright, a lot of mistakes." He hurried to add when she speared him with a murderous stare. "But I admit it, and now trying my best to redeem myself. Have a little mercy."

After a moment of silence, Abby said, "Well, since you jumped through time instead of putting the key inside the clock, there is hope for you yet, Brother."

Like a man who was granted a pardon before an execution, Eli whooshed a breath of relief.

"See that you won't repeat that mistake again. Daisy deserves better."

A warning rang loud and clear through Abby's finishing remark. It warmed his heart that all her outrage was not because of his mistreatment of *her*, but Daisy. Abby's feelings always ran deep, and her loyalty to those she loved was infinite. He was never prouder of her than at that moment. Not trusting his voice, Eli inclined his head in agreement.

"Okay, then." Abby's hesitant smile was a healing balm over a wound. "But I am still cross with you."

"And I deserve it." Eli succumbed to temptation, and moving closer, tucked one runaway strand behind Abby's ear. "Enough of me. Now, tell me about yourself. How are you, my dear?"

"I am splendid, Eli. Daisy, *Verochka*, and Alex— they are the best people in the whole world. They accepted me, tended to me, became my family. And now there is Marie Dubois, my mentor, and Rostoffs. Oh, how I wish I could introduce you to all of them! And I'll have my very first showing soon. I'm so excited, and nervous, and I am babbling."

Animated, her face flushed with exhilaration, Abby gripped his hands almost painfully.

Look at her, so lovely, so alive. So happy.

"I will not ask whether or not you are happy, *Papillon*, because it's a silly question." He forced his lips into a smile, while his heart was breaking in two. "Even your hands look happy."

He had never paid attention to Abby's hands before. Long fingered, narrow palmed, they were beautiful and strong, and painfully endearing to him. His thumbs traced some peculiar discoloration of skin.

Going with his heart, Eli pressed his lips onto her open palms, drew in her smell. "They smell happy."

"It's the paints, silly. Hard to remove all the stains, even with a thinner."

"You look radiant, Abby. Beautiful, confident. Content. And that's why I won't insult you by asking the question that's burning my tongue."

"Alex was right." A gentle little smile played at her lips.

"What about?"

"You see, when I saw you this morning, I was first so afraid, that I chickened out, as they say here, and ran away. When he found me, Alex said that I don't have to fret anymore. He said that you wouldn't."

"Wouldn't what?"

"Try to force me to go back."

Morris, it seems that I owe you one more.

"And so I won't. I can clearly see that your place is here."

"Thank you, Eli. Thank you for accepting it, for acknowledging it. It means the world."

Abby flashed him a brilliant smile through her sheen of tears. "When are you going back?"

"Day after Thanksgiving."

"So soon?"

"Yes, *Papillon*. I'm needed at home. And this time jump is...it changes the balance in nature, if only temporarily. So, Daisy and I will take our leave on Friday."

A tiny sound of sorrow broke away before Abby pressed her face to his chest. She held onto him, but only for a moment.

"Well, then, let's not waste a single moment of the time we have left." She rubbed her face with both hands, wiping away the tears. "Tell me about everybody at home, while I make us a sandwich. I don't know about you, Brother, but I am famished."

What a surprise. To him too.

"Abby?"

"Yes?"

Her absent call came from the kitchen area, where she was already busy rummaging through the cupboards.

"I am so proud of you."

She stopped, and turned around to face him.

"You know what I regret most of all, Eli?"

"Tell me."

"That it took us so long to finally find one another."

Closing the distance between them, Eli rested his hands on her shoulders.

"Time is relative, *Papillon*. We both are living proof of that. But love, my sweet, is eternal." His finger traced her face, committing to memory her features.

"I don't want to lose you, Brother."

"And you shall not. I'll live in your heart, as you in mine."

"But we won't ever see each other again."

"Ah, my sweet girl." This time it was he who pressed his face against her hair. "I'll see you time and again, when I look at your garden and see a little butterfly."

"And I'll see you when I look at the Tower. Time and again, and again..."

As he held and rocked his sister in his arms, Eli's thoughts shifted to the old family house where it all began.

The Coleman house.

CHAPTER TWENTY-NINE

Her appointment ran longer than Nika anticipated. Satisfied with her accomplishment, she drove back home, listening with one ear to the hum of the Corvette's engine. The red beauty purred like a well-fed kitten, but under its gleaming hood napped a jangle cat. When fully awake, it growled and ran like a lioness in pursuit of prey. Many a time Nika indulged, drunk on a speed rush and freedom, but that was all in the past now. Time had come to say goodbye to her beloved Coco. God, she loved that car. She hopped Abby might, too.

"You'll be good to your new owner, won't you, sweetie? You'll like her, I promise. I'm sure she'll take excellent care of you."

You're nuts, Nika. Crooning to a car?

"Yeah, so what? It might be our last time together."

Damn, that was depressing. To shake off the blues, she turned on the radio, fiddled with the buttons. Classical or Jazz? Nope, not in the mood for either one. Rock? Maybe. She settled on a station, but after a moment shut the radio off. The husky murmur of Corvette was the best music for her ears.

"Sorry, baby, I guess I'm a little unsettled." Onehanded, Nika patted a dashboard.

A little? And who are you kidding, girl?

"Okay, okay, a lot unsettled. Happy now?"

Chastised, her inner bitch slinked away. Nika was finally alone. Unsettled? Huh. It didn't cover half of it. Sad, conflicted, guilty. Shit.

Her mind danced back to her morning meeting with Vic. The business part of it went well enough, but the personal...Dammit, why did he have to be her friend on top of being her attorney? Her, Alex's, and their company's.

Despite the differences in lifestyles, upbringings, and even appearances, they clicked from the beginning, and that was that.

For eight years Victor Malone was their attorney, their confidante, their friend. They trusted each other, and loved each other like family.

And today, for the first time, she broke that trust. Nika's curse was potent enough to make her Russian ancestors proud. Or horrified.

Unsettled? Try rotten. And she deserved it.

Lying to your friend right to his face while asking him for a personal favor, no less.

And what a doozy that one was: to deed over all she owned in the fastest possible time, and keep it a secret from everybody for several days.

Sure, no problem, girl.

Prepared for questions and arguments from her friend slash attorney, Nika was surprised when Vic didn't blink an eye. A little baffled at his initial reaction, she reminded herself that he was a professional who had probably seen and heard it all. Oh, he was curious, as any sane person would be, as to why she was giving away all her life possessions— her home, business, even her car and truck— like she was about to die tomorrow. And in a manner of speaking, she was, only not tomorrow, but the day after Thanksgiving. But there was no way to tell him.

So she fibbed, hedged, and danced around the truth, all the while cringing inside. The only truthful answer she gave him was the reason for her decision. She was getting married to Elijah Benjamin, whom Vic had met two days earlier, and moving away. All the rest were lies, or a highly abbreviated version of the truth. The place she was moving was far, far away, remote, no Internet or cell connection. And her job? She was exhausted after a full day at work, and decided to take a sabbatical. He didn't say 'bullshit,' didn't have to. His accusing eyes relayed the message instead.

How long she was planning to be away was the question that really made her squirm. Her reply 'I'm not sure' was met with another sardonic stare.

Not sure, my ass. How about forever?

But good old Vic kept his baby-blues cool and steady on her face, and at the end just asked one single question, "Is that all?"

Nika let out a choked laugher. *That's all, indeed.*

When he walked her to the door, Vic's face was a blank mask. The picture of her flamboyant friend with his fluffy companion Maximillian at his feet, both gazing at her in accusation, was not something she would forget anytime soon.

Another loss. How many had she racked up today? Her business, her home, her profession, and a loss of solid friendship to boot. She regretted it more than she could say, but there was no other way.

Dammit, she hated to lie. But how could she tell the truth?

You know, Vic, my fiancé Elijah Benjamin is actually Eli Coleman, the famous Coleman of the Fernandina Beach from 1909. I'm going back in time, where I met him last year, to live in the original Coleman house that I just restored for his great-great-grandson?

Yeah, that's right, sounds much better. That's exactly what she should've said to her attorney to be pronounced loony on the spot.

No, ignorance in this case was better than knowing the truth.

Sorry, my friend.

Sick at heart, Nika navigated the last turn to her home.

Well, it was done, and almost over. Vic, ever the professional even when disgusted with his client, promised to get all the paperwork ready for her signatures on Wednesday. And— *voila*—unencumbered by any earthly possession, Nika was free for her journey back in time. At last.

Free, yes. But ready?

"Shut up, you sneaky piece of miserable shit!"

And that is the best you can come up with?

"Shut the hell up!" Nika banged her fist against the steering wheel.

You're mad because I'm right, and you know it.

"I hate you."

When will that inner bitch take a hint and leave her alone? She *was* ready. She was willing, able, and absofuckinglutely ready, so there!

Okay, so slamming the car door was not the smartest thing to do while courting a pounding headache. As a result, the band of sadistic little drummers inside her head went ballistic. Nika pressed both palms against her temples in an attempt to ease the pain, but that proved to be an exercise in futility. The little fuckers were banging away in a wild frenzy, making her dizzy and nauseated.

Pills. She needed her pills, or she'd end up with a full-blown migraine she had absolutely no time or inclination to deal with. Her rotten luck was holding steady. When she uncapped the prescription bottle, the meds spilled all over her purse. Nika cursed for the umpteenth time, but managed to dig out three escapees, and swallowed them dry. Of course, the pills went the wrong way, scratching her throat, and making her cough. A small price to pay.

What will you do without your meds back there?

The thought popped out of nowhere. She never stopped to think about it. Damn. Can she take enough with her?

She managed to sneak an EpiPen and some trail mix before, but that was a sheer accident. Last year, when she was dropped to 1909, she had no idea what was going on, and whatever she carried on her person, was thrown along with her by default. Now she was going back on purpose, and taking anything through a curtain of time deliberately might be fraught with...what was it again? Oh, yeah, a butterfly effect. A small change in a sensitive dependence of things can result in catastrophic changes later, or something like that. No, cannot risk it.

"Okay, I'll think of something."

Think fast, girl. Time's running out.

As much as she hated it, this time she agreed with her annoying inner bitch.

Yeah, time was always a precious commodity, but especially when one was on the countdown. Like her. Four days. Just four precious days. To turn over her last project as a professional contractor, to spend the last Thanksgiving with her family, to make amends and say her goodbyes. Four days. Eternity for some, blink of an eye for others.

And you are wasting that precious time by standing in the middle of the garage.

True. Enough philosophizing. No more wasted time. Every second was accounted for. Turning to the Corvette, Nika patted it in lieu of an apology. "Sorry, Coco. Didn't mean to bang on you."

The meds were taking their sweet-ass time to work. That band of the little bastards in her head eased off to a steady drum. She'd take it.

Wincing all the way out of the garage, Nika aimed toward the house, but in the middle of the way just stopped and lifted her gaze. God, she loved it. The extravagant, even for Florida octagonal shape of it, the steely Atlases of the beams, the wrap-around deck. The first house they bought. It was home for her and her cousin for eight years. Alex was reluctant at first, but Nika, in love from first sight, badgered him until he agreed to sign his name on the mortgage.

At the beginning, they argued about colors and themes, banisters and flooring, and what's not, but soon they made this house a home. She loved it, was happy in it. And hoped that Alex will be happy living in it for the many years in the future. Because the house was now solely his. Or it would be, as soon as she put her signature on the deed Wednesday.

Home.

But it wasn't her home any longer. She allowed herself a brief moment of regret. A renegade tear, as lonely as the seagull above her head, streaked down.

She was just a human, and there was no one around to witness her distress.

Alone, she closed her eyes, and soaked in the sounds of the ocean and a cry of that lonely seagull. When she opened her eyes, a wave of dizziness she attributed to the effect of her pills blurred her vision. How else to explained the brilliant shimmering, and the image of another house that was taking shape in front of her eyes? White walls, ornate façade, a domineering tower ...

The Coleman house.

Dignified. Striking. Majestic. Her new home. Or the old?

Mesmerized, Nika held her breath. She stared at the image of the brilliant apparition, too stunned to move or blink. Something warm and fuzzy bumped against her hand. Without taking her eyes off the house, Nika scratched the head of the huge shaggy dog. *Belle.* A lick of the rough tongue against her palm, a quiet whimpering...Scent of roses, strong and intoxicating... And a row of the yellow butterflies, flapping their iridescent wings...

Home.

Inhaling deeply, carefree at last, Nika raised her hands, and spanned a wide circle.

"I'm home!"

Where she belonged. Where everything was dear and familiar.

Her home, the Coleman house.

And then everything disappeared. A shimmering curtain of time was yanked back, and once again, Nika was in the middle of her driveway, gaping up at the octagonal form of the house that was no longer her home. A little shaky, she rubbed both hands over her face.

What the hell happened?

What was it? A byproduct of her medication, some kind of a side effect? But if it was just a figment of her imagination, why was her palm still wet from where Belle licked her? More puzzled than confused, Nika brushed her annoying curls out of her eyes, and frowned. Something was... off. Different. But what? She turned her head, squinting at her surroundings, then touched her forehead, and let out a huge sigh of relief. Her headache was gone. Like it never was. Like she dreamed it along with the smells and sounds and the incredible images still dancing in her mind's eye. But she hadn't imagined anything.

How else can she explain a few stray dog's hair still clinging to her jeans?

No, she *was* there. Just for a brief second, Nika was transported back in time. She was dead sure of it. But how? Why? And why now, today of all days?

For those long fourteen months, she beat her head against the wall, searching for answers, anxious to have a tiny glimpse of the other side. Fate refused to allow her that blessing. And all of a sudden, a dramatic show today, with visuals and sound effects. Didn't pull any stops, too. The fragrant aroma of blooming flowers still teased her nostrils. Belle's warm breath was tickling her hand. And the majestic silhouette of the Coleman house flickered in and out of focus. Teasing her, testing her. Torturing her. Well, as shock therapy went, Nika had to admit, this one turned out to be very effective.

"Fate, you fickle bitch."

And what did you expect? Self-doubts, regrets, tears. No wonder she got fed-up and kicked you in the ass. If you ask me, you were long overdue, Nika-Daisy.

"Nobody asked you."

But her inner 'I' was right once again, as much as it grated to admit. That kick in the ass was administered just in time as a reminder. And a warning.

Stop your doubts. Erase your fears and squelch your guilt. Remember who you are.

Nika got the message, loud and clear. Head high, voice strong, she answered from the heart,

"No more doubts, fears, or guilt. I am Daisy Coleman."

And don't you ever *forget it.*

With that stern silent decree ringing in her ears, Nika pivoted toward the house that wasn't her home anymore.

CHAPTER THIRTY

How come it was Tuesday already? Just a moment ago it was Sunday. Nika marveled at the small miracle fate bestowed upon her, reminding her of who and what she was. In the blink of an eye, it was the day of reckoning.

Tuesday, November 24th.

Today, Senator Lauder, with entourage, was expected to fly in to walk through the finished project of his ancestral home, the Coleman house.

Today was the day Nika sweated and labored for ten unimaginable brutal months. The restoration was finished, but her journey that began last September, was approaching its pivotal point. The end of the old chapter, and the beginning of the new one. Today, after she turned the house to the senator, and gave him the keys, her career as a House Whisperer comes to an end. This project was her swan song. After the ceremony today, Nika Morris ceased to exist, and Daisy Coleman will take her place.

She was ready, prepared, and eager to move on.

She was a nervous wreck.

Why was she so jittery? The work she and her crew completed was superb. The house looked the same, if not better, than in its heyday. Who if not Nika should know? After all, she had the privilege of seeing it in situ, so to speak. She lived in it for three months, searched it from top to bottom, and had an intimate knowledge of every nook and cranny. The Coleman house was the best restoration she'd ever done, and then some.

And still...

Nika never was so unsure of herself professionally. Or so afraid. Dammit, she was plain petrified. And that was pissing her off. She kicked the chair, swore, then kick it again. When Alex moved the offending object out of her way, she rounded on him.

"What?"

"Nothing, Cuz. Just making room for you."

The clown had the gall to smirk. Oh, she could kill him for that alone, if only she had time. Time turned into her enemy. Why wasn't it moving?

Unable to keep still, Nika paced the room. Her eyes jumped from the phone she clutched in one hand, to the wall clock, and back. If time was her enemy, the wall clock became an executioner. Dammit, how much longer?

She wasn't paying attention to her family. They all gathered around since early morning under the pretense of having breakfast together. In reality, everyone watched her like she was a bomb about to detonate. Yes, she was on edge. So what?

It was her who would stand in front of the senator in a couple of hours. It was her professionalism at stake, it was...

Dammit, Nika, what are you doing?

What she was doing was driving herself and everybody crazy, behaving like a snooty diva. Or a spoiled brat. She wished she could kick herself.

Everyone was so nice to her, so kind. Even JC.

You ought to be ashamed of yourself.

And she was, honestly, but God, did they have to be so irritating?

Even before *Verochka* and Abby dropped by with an elaborate breakfast from the Ritz, Nika managed to insult JC, yell at Alex, and scowl at Eli.

After one pointed look, *Verochka* opted to leave her alone. Abby, on the other hand, didn't get the hint. Nika's patience held as long as was humanly possible.

After the third cup of coffee and another plate of food foisted on her, she was ready to pull her hair out. On top of everything, Abby, always Nika's champion, started arguing with El about his decision to stay home.

"Why don't you want to come with us?"

"Abby, I explained already."

"Why don't you explain it again?"

"Abby—"

"It is a very important day for Daisy, and her family must be by her side, to show support, and a united front. You, as her future husband, must be present."

"I, as her future husband, will be waiting here, with a bottle of champagne. Be reasonable Abby. I'll be just be in the way. Come to think of it, you all will be in the way."

"Nonsense!"

And so it went, on and on, until Nika was ready to scream. She tried to tune them out. Honest to God. After all, if Eli didn't want to see the newly renovated Coleman house, it was his decision. It irked, but she shrugged it off. God knew, it was not easy to see something familiar and dear through a new set of glasses. Or a prism of time. If it was strange for her, it must be downright painful for him. She got it, she honestly did, but dammit, could they stop arguing about it already? After another round of bickering, her patience, already fried around the edges, just blew up.

"Listen up, you two! One more word from either direction, and I'm going to strangle both of you!"

"There, there," *Verochka*, calm as a cloudless sky, patted Nika's arm. "Why don't you sit down, my dear, and concentrate on breathing."

In response, Nika let loose a sound close to a snarl. One of a large, feral cat.

Unruffled, *Verochka* smiled and addressed the dynamic duo of Coleman siblings, "Abby, sweetie, do leave your brother alone. And Eli? You're going."

"But, Madame—"

"And don't forget to change your shirt." *Verochka* waved her hand at Eli. "This color does not become you."

"Well, I—"

But *Verochka*, a true pro in the sport of handling the opposite sex, rolled over him like the tide over a pebble. "I'm glad, my dear, that you finally changed your mind. You absolutely must see it. After all, it's such a rarity to see your own house in two different centuries during one lifetime."

A businessman, a fearless leader, whose orders were carried out without a qualm or question, Eli gazed at her elegant steamroller of a grandmother in helpless defeat. His face mirrored a mix of emotion, frustration being a dominant one, but as a smart man, he clamped his jaw, and capitulated with a curt nod.

And that was that. If Nika wouldn't be so on edge, she would enjoy a good laugh at his expense. But at the moment she was just grateful for the end of the irritating argument.

Thank God for Verochka.

Her reprieve proved short lived. JC, forgotten by everybody, lifted his head from the cup of coffee he was nursing in silence.

"What do you mean, Grandmother?"

"Hmm?"

"You said 'see his own house in two centuries during one lifetime.' What exactly do you mean by that? And what does Nika's project have to do with Coleman?"

To say that ensued silence was uncomfortable, was an understatement of both centuries combined. All faces, Nika's included, turned toward *Verochka*.

Unusual violet eyes she passed onto her granddaughter stayed clear and innocent as morning dew. Not a hint of discomfort marred her patrician face, while *Verochka* bestowed a patient smile upon her grandson.

"Why, my dear, didn't you know? Our Eli is a descendant of the original Coleman. As to my remark about two centuries, I just…"

The tension in the room rose to the point of a volcano just seconds before its eruption. Everybody held their collective breaths. Everybody, except JC that is.

"I just meant the before and after images of the place. When Eli visited last time, the house was still in great disrepair. A demolition site it was, really. Now he will be able to compare what was and what is. That's all."

"Did he visit that long ago?"

"No, ah… last year."

"Why, then, did you say 'two centuries?'"

"Oh, please, JC." A negligent shrug of *Verochka's* shoulders conveyed annoyance and dismissal at once. "You know me. I exaggerated. Just a manner of speech, really. When I said century, I meant a long period of time, that's all."

"And why did you say 'his own house?' The house belongs to Senator Lauder and his family, isn't it? And what about 'during one lifetime'? Whose lifetime?"

"JC, you making a big deal out of nothing. Stop dissecting words, Counselor."

"But—"

"Enough of that foolishness."

The first notes of impatience crept into *Verochka's* voice. A mild gaze, a slight frown, and Nika's brother got the hint. Still curious, and clearly dissatisfied, JC was too much of his father's son. The current estranged status aside, he was a chip from the old block, so the skill to cut his losses at the right time came to him naturally.

Eyes downcast, JC halted his inquisition, and picked up his coffee mug again. But the sound of wheels turning in his head was deafening, and hard to ignore. Hard or not, Nika ordered herself to do just that. After all, in a couple of days, JC and his curiosity will no longer be a problem. He'd forget all about this conversation, like he forgot about Nika and Alex nine years ago. Because they were not important. JC always focused on the important. Never for a second she believed that his sudden arrival meant anything, except serving his own needs. But whether she wanted or not, JC was family. He was in trouble, and needed help.

Not my problem anymore.

But Alex, poor sap, was in for the duration. Shrugging mentally, Nika allowed herself a deep breath.

"That was a close one."

Alex's muted voice reached her ears, as he too let out a sigh of relief.

"Okay, everybody. Why don't we start moving?" For the emphasis, Verochka clapped her hands. "Abby and I will clear the breakfast, and go to our hotel to change. Boys, you can relax for a while, but don't dawdle. You need showers and a change of clothes. And Nika—"

"I will head out to the location."

As soon as she said that, Nika relaxed.

Should've done that already, and spare the aggravation. Oh, well.

"But it is still too early, my dear. The senator is not expected until noon."

"It's okay. I'll feel better once I'm there."

"But what will you do in the empty house, all alone?"

"I'll walk around one more time, and..."

And just say goodbye, and hello, and try to put my conflicting emotions at rest.

Nika shrugged, avoiding *Verochka's* eyes. "...and make sure everything is ready."

Her grandmother wasn't fooled by her blasé attitude. *Verochka* drew a deep breath, then opened her mouth to reply, but Eli beat her to it, "I'll go with you."

His deep baritone as always sent ripples over Nika's skin. She lifted her eyes at the man who defying nature, science, and logic, burst into her life, and made a myth into reality. Her friend, her lover. Her timeless miracle.

What had she ever done to deserve him? Her heart lurched, trembled, then settled with a gentle sigh. And everything became right with the world.

Humbled, grateful, she walked to him then cupped his face in her palm, and standing on a tiptoe, brushed her lips against his dimpled chin.

"No, my love. Thanks, but no. This is something I need to do on my own."

"Daisy—"

"Eli." She framed his face with both hands. "I'm okay. I really want to be alone in the house for a while. I need to. Have to. Can you understand that?"

"I do." His hand trailed over her hair in a light caress. "Please don't be sad."

"I'm not sad. Or not just sad. It's so much more, I can't explain it."

She leaned forward and breathed him in, then, after a moment, stepped back.

"This is not the end, Daisy. Remember that." Eli dropped his hand, but his eyes maintained their captivating hold.

"I know. It's just the beginning."

With the final glance at Eli, Nika grabbed her purse, and hurried out.

Alex's cheer "well, boys and girls, let's get this show on the road" was the last thing that reached her ears.

...Just the beginning.

Later that night, Nika's own reply echoed in her ears. Famous last words.

And when did you turn into a prophet, Nika-Daisy?

Alone, still off balance after the events of the turbulent day, Nika prowled the house that wasn't her home anymore. Dark. Quiet. Strange.

After a celebratory dinner at Salt, Ritz's posh restaurant, where a little over a year ago she and Alex met for the first time with Senator Lauder, and accepted his proposal for the restoration of the Coleman house, everybody was down for the count. Alex and Eli, both a little tipsy, fell fast asleep. JC, a designated driver, sober and sullen, closed himself into the guest bedroom. *Verochka* and Abby stayed at the hotel where her grandmother retained a suite.

Barefoot, Nika padded to her most favorite place in the house— the second-floor deck. The light breeze danced through her hair, teasing her curls.

She drew in the night air, held it for as long as she could manage, then exhaled with a noisy whooshing sound. Her eyes focused on the picture ahead. The ocean. Ink-black, rumbling and rolling under the waxing moon, it made a perfect backdrop for her mood. Alive, brooding. Infinite.

Could she ever get tired of watching its splendor? Never. The ocean became such an important part of her life, she couldn't imagine being away from it. A breathing, living constant of universe.

A timeless miracle.

Like the inscription Eli put on her grave...Miracle. Time.

Eli.

After a long moment, Nika's gaze shifted to the deck. God, she loved this spot.

Her chair, the coffee table she unearthed from the flea-market, the stripped blue-and-white umbrella... So familiar. So...suddenly alien.

And how strange was that?

Everything around her, everything inside her, was split on before and after. Before her miraculous journey, and after. Before Eli, and after.

Even her name. Nika. Daisy. She lived with this duality for more than a year now, but only recently that line started to shift. The images of two different worlds began to blur and overlap, until she wasn't sure where one ended and another began. This had never troubled her before. Until today.

Until she walked behind Senator Lauder through the newly restored Coleman house; until she handled him the keys from that house, and almost wept with grief. Until today, Nika had no idea how eager she was to get *home*, to her true place and time. To the Coleman house circa 1909.

But fate, that fickle bitch, decided differently.

Once again, Nika's strategic and carefully mapped-out life plan was shot to hell. Because the day that started with stress and anxiety, ended up with a surprise of a lifetime. A shocking discovery of a new owner for the Coleman house.

Nika drew a deep breath, cursed, then laughed without mirth. How many more surprises had that bitch fate kept under her sleeve? Dammit, who could have known Senator Lauder's grandmother left him not one, but two letters written by her father, Elijah B. Coleman, who even now slept the sleep of the innocent in her bed? The first letter that started it all, was addressed to Nika with a specific instruction to be opened in September 2019, and commanded her to 'find the key.' The second one was to Abigail Suzanne Coleman. That letter was actually a duly and lawfully executed deed to the house signed by the familiar handwriting in blue ink, and a short personal message: "Be happy, my little *Papillon*."

Both were more than likely written somewhere between now and their return to 1909, because Eli claimed no prior knowledge of those letters.

And how crazy was that?

And who could ever expect that Margaret Coleman Lauder, the Senator's grandmother and Nika's daughter, had also left him a picture of the beneficiary? The photo was old, faded, with a missing corner, but the image was unmistakable. It was Abby. Standing on the beach, her hair teased by a breeze, she smiled at the camera, happy and carefree. That picture was taken by Alex shortly after their arrival here. Nika remembered that day like it was yesterday.

From the moment Senator Lauder laid his eyes on Abby, he was visibly caught off guard. Eli earned a lot of his curious glances, too, but *Verochka*, who was used to rubbing shoulders with rich and famous, took the reins of the situation. Comfortable in the presence of the sitting U.S. Senator like a fish in water, she made the event flow smooth and easy. She even remembered meeting the Senator's grandmother in New York, a long time ago.

And wasn't that a great surprise, especially for Nika.

So, Verochka *met my daughter some forty years ago. Talk about weird.*

But the announcement that the senator had a grandmother with the middle name Vera, put Nika in a stupor. Until then, she didn't know the full name of her only child.

Margaret Vera Coleman, with her mother's crazy curls and violet eyes.

Nika's hand slid to her abdomen. Too early to tell, just a few days, but call her irrational, or delusional, she was sure that a tiny speckle of life was already pulsing inside of her.

Her own timeless miracle, a baby conceived in the twenty-first century that will be born in 1910. August 14, 1910, to be precise, according to the records in the Fernandina Beach Births and Christenings register. But she didn't need to read the register to know the truth. She was pregnant.

She didn't tell anyone. Who would believe her? Even with the modern technology, it was impossible to detect a five-day pregnancy.

But who needed technology? A mother's heart was the best detector science failed to compete with. No wonder her emotions were out of whack. Dammit, she wanted to go home! Tucking one leg under her, Nika assumed her favorite sitting position.

Her gaze traveled to the horizon where sky and water blended into infinity, even as her mind circled back to the earlier events at the Coleman house...

...Abby was the center of the senator's attention throughout that day. After the end of the house tour, he approached her, and asked for her full name. If Abby was confused, she didn't let it show.

"Abigail Coleman."

"And your middle name?"

"Ah...Suzanne. Why?"

The senator let out a long sigh of relief, "Young lady, you saved me a lot of time and effort looking for you."

And that how the identity of the new owner of the Coleman house came to light.

Without further ado, Abby was given the keys from the estate, and a thick folder with papers confirming her ownership. And that was that.

Deep in her heart, Nika was content. Astonished, but happy, and satisfied.

After all, it was Abby's home before it was hers. She was glad the old Coleman house would be loved, and tended to, and its history respected and preserved.

But if she was happy that her home was in the best possible hands now, she was upset and disappointed that their return trip was delayed until New Year's Day.

Why? Because the new hostess of the Coleman house absolutely refused to give them the access to the grandfather clock, the portal between times, for another month. The little stinker! Her Highness, emboldened by the events of the day and a couple of glasses of Veuve Clicquot, demanded a housewarming gift. She insisted on her brother and his fiancé's presence at her very first showing on December 28th.

"Abby, that's impossible. Eli doesn't have any ID. He won't be able to travel to France. Even if we smuggle him in a private plane, he won't clear customs." But Nika's concern fell on deaf ears.

"France? Who said anything about France? My showing is in California, silly, in Rostoff Gallery in San Francisco."

From the expression on Eli's face the prospect of flying on a plane got him excited to the point of ecstasy.

"*Ma petite*, remember the difference in the flow of time? It is quite possible that one month here will equal to one day there. So, no harm will be done."

"Nik, don't you want to spend one last Christmas with us?" Alex added his two cents to the mix.

"Of course she does." And Verochka closed the debate.

Outnumbered, Nika accepted her defeat. What choice did she have?

Just a month. One month, and then they would be back home where she belonged. All three of them. Patting her flat stomach, she heaved a sigh of resignation.

"It's okay, Button, we still have plenty of time."

But, God, how she wished to be back home.

CHAPTER THIRTY-ONE

The month of November came to an end, but thanks to his tempestuous sister's request, Eli was still in this wondrous time. His lifestyle underwent a miraculous transformation, but not an unpleasant one. What hardship could one find surrounded by so many amazing conveniences? The only pain in his behind continued to be his wardrobe. For one, he found current fashion to be quite revealing, and therefore, embarrassing. But most of all, he still couldn't get over the cost of it. Those blasted things cost as if they were made of pure gold.

Sweet Lord, how much people spend on clothes nowadays! Mindboggling!

How do they manage to pay their way around here, was a mystery to him. Food, supplies, amenities... The prices were horrendous.

But aside from that, the life here was quite amazing. After the first few days, his confusion faded, and Eli began to enjoy himself.

A little thread on tea packets was still befuddling, and the constant noise from so many *gadgets* around the house still startling, but the peal of the diminutive telephone ceased being panicking, and the images in motion on the big black box called television became less shocking. Overall, he was getting the knack of things.

And most important of all, Daisy was always by his side, day or night. Just thinking about her made his chest hurt, and his blood churn.

Daisy, my little ragamuffin, my timeless miracle.

Never a sentimental man, Eli was flummoxed to find himself falling more in love with her by each passing day. Even a month ago he had rejected that notion as impossible, but here he was today, living proof of that phenomenon. At his age, he ought to be embarrassed, but Eli was so outrageously happy he failed to pay any heed to propriety. So what if he was wearing his heart on his sleeve, or smiling without any reason. He loved the most amazing, incredible woman of all times, and his love was reciprocated. Propriety be damned. He was the most fortunate man alive, and wasn't afraid to show it.

Of course, like every couple, they argued at times, and weren't in agreement on every subject, but that was quite normal. He would have been more surprised—disappointed even—if her opinions and beliefs mirrored his. Two such strong personalities like them ought to look at some things differently, and disagree on some matters. Well, to a degree. Secretly, Eli looked forward to their disagreements, because a following make-up session usually involved sex. Sweet as honey, and hot as hell. As his father used to say, a smart man learned to discover his advantages at every state of affairs.

Eli prided himself on being a smart man.

They soon established a daily routine. After breakfast, they drove into town, where Daisy closed herself into her office, to clear up her business matters before their leave, and he, while waiting for her, went for long solitary walks. Sometimes, on the way home, she let him drive her roofless automobile. He lived for those happy moments.

Today downtown Fernandina Beach was quite crowded. Eli's gaze traveled around, skimming along the people all dressed, young and old, in peculiar garments. A closer look took his breath away. Everyone was parading in pajamas! Dear Lord, were his eyes deceiving him, or was today some odd celebration of Morpheus? Then his gaze skipped to the colorful placards dancing all over Centre Street. *Downtown Fernandina Beach Annual Pajama Party.* So, that was what it all meant. Glad his eyes were still in perfect working order, Eli let loose a hearty laugh.

Pajama Party. Why wasn't he surprised? Come to think of it, he stopped being surprised by a great deal of things.

A progress of sorts.

Still chuckling, Eli crossed the narrow street, expertly avoiding bumping into pajama clad pedestrians. Some carted colorful bags, or pushed baby carriages, and almost all were drinking beverages out of paper cups, a practice that still puzzled him. How can you walk and drink at the same time? On top of being unseemly, it was quite uncomfortable. But who was he to challenge modern habits? Shrugging mentally, Eli continued on his way until he reached the Fernandina Beach Train Depot. The diminutive building stood at the same spot, dignified, and untouched by time. The only difference was the absence of trains, since this station served today as a Welcome Center, and the statue of David Yulee, sitting on the bench in front of it. Not for the first time Eli wondered what would his uncle David think of it. He'd object for sure, especially since that statue looked nothing like him. Giving it a mental salute, Eli continued on his way.

There was no hurry, as he still has plenty of time before his rendezvous with Daisy.

So, he kept his pace leisured, his eyes unpeeled, and his brain unencumbered.

Quite naturally, his thoughts turned to the events of the last week: Thanksgiving celebration in the twenty-first century. And what a marvelous experience that turned out to be. The spread was amazing, rich and scrumptious and plentiful. But what made the evening so special, were the people he shared it with. His new *family*.

After Daisy, *Verochka* was his personal favorite of the bunch. Never before did he meet a woman with such a strong, indestructible will and the gentlest, kindest heart. Add to that her clever mind, her glorious looks, quirk wit, and the combination was irresistible. Eli simply adored her.

Alex, despite their turbulent beginning, had earned his respect. That deep protective streak and unshakable loyalty to those he loved were admirable. Eli would be proud to call him friend. But Daisy's favorite cousin stubbornly continued to address him as *Benjamin*, so the irritation factor apparently hadn't run its course yet. *Oh well.*

Even JC, with his furtive glances and sullen attitude became less annoying.

He still treated Eli with an open suspicion, and watched him like a hawk, but that was understandable.

As the only one not privy to his sister fiancé's true identity, JC was at disadvantage. Who would not abhor to be kept in the dark? But trust must be earned, and JC Morris had a long way to go down that road yet.

Eli was given the honor to carve the turkey, the same humongous bird he hauled over to the kitchen a few days ago. He chuckled, as he recalled his astonishment when Alex trusted that frozen ball into his hands and

called it a turkey. That bird, cooked in some wicked-looking apparatus—
deep fryer—tasted like an ambrosia.

Eli was itching to disassemble that apparatus, just to see how it worked.
Maybe I can put together something similar back home.

But for as long as he lived, the memories of that special Thanksgiving
was destined to be among the most cherished in his heart. By Morris's family
tradition, everybody was supposed to announce out loud the single thing
they were most thankful for.

And wasn't that a most humbling experience when everyone declared
'family.' Even JC. When it was his turn, Eli didn't have to think twice. Going
with his overflowing heart, he looked in turn at every member of his new
family and said, "All of you." Just that. The simple truth.

The next day, instead of time-jumping with Daisy back home, Eli found
himself involved in another Morris family tradition, decorating a Christmas
tree.

Never before had Eli participated in such an event. At home, there were
servants who took care of those matters under Mrs. Smith's supervision.

Not anymore.

From now on, Daisy and he will dress their own Christmas tree, starting
a new tradition in the Coleman household.

Lost in thought, Eli continued his midmorning stroll along Centre
Street.

Such a learning experience, to see all the modern establishments, and
compare them with what they used to be. The Palace Saloon, Florida oldest
bar, a playground for rich and famous in his time, was still there, on the
corner of 117 Centre and 2nd North Street. Upon his recent visit, Eli was
pleased and surprised that the ambience stayed almost the same.

The majority of the shops and offices were new to him, even though the
buildings they occupied were old and familiar. But despite that, he easily
found his way around. Here, in the heart of Fernandina Beach, the notion
of displacement was lesser than anywhere else, even in the newly restored
Coleman house. Strange.

No, it was...What was the modern word? Oh, yes, *weird*.

He was getting quite proficient with the new slang. Pleased, Eli mentally patted himself on the back. Pretty soon he'd be conversing like any twenty-first century individual. And wouldn't that be fancy.

As was his habit, Eli stopped at the spot he found himself upon his arrival. That little square held some fondest memories: his first glimpse at the new world, his fear and bewilderment, his meeting with Vic and his peculiar looking little dog, Maximilian. Was it really just a fortnight ago?

He glanced above the almost bare trees, to the impossible blue sky, then skimmed to the building where Daisy was working.

What was she doing? Conversing with people over her miniscule cellphone, or plucking at the keyboard on her computer?

Soon, she'd finish her task, and walk from those doors toward him. Her smile, bright and genuine, will light up the day, and warm his heart. Almost giddy with anticipation, Eli plopped down on the iron bench. He had a little time to kill, so why not spend his waiting in relative comfort? A great deal of fallen leaves covered the seat. Disturbed by Eli's movements, the rust golden layer shifted, and then scattered all over. Bending over, Eli plucked one of the leaves from his shoe. Dry and fragile, lovely and sad, it dissolved into dust in his hands, seeping through his fingers.

Like time.

So, autumn was gone, and winter arrived, but except for the holiday tunes piping from every corner, there was no difference in the big scheme of things.

The weather on Amelia Island was still warm and gentle, with an occasional rain and a mild breeze. The bluest Florida sky and majestic ocean lovingly embraced this little jewel forever frozen in time.

The timeless miracle.

This century, or his own, was almost the same. If not for the amazing technological inventions, Eli wouldn't have known the difference. But, oh, what marvelous inventions they were! His mind, even after a few weeks living here, was still boggled, good and proper.

Dear Lord, talk about miracles!

Tiny telephones, computers, televisions, automobiles. No, *cars*. They were called cars here. As soon as he returned home, Eli decided to buy the most advanced automobile he could get his hands on. Mr. Ford's T? Or maybe, Hudson's Model 20? Of course, after operating—no, driving—Alex's 'Baby,' he was setting himself up for a great disappointment, but still.

And Internet? Fascinated, curious, Eli tried to get to the bottom of that technological wonder, but his brain just refused to cooperate. World Wide Web, invisible connections, sharing information... That Skype thing? Fucking brilliant!

But like an imbecile, he was unable to figure out how it worked.

Thunderation.

Some things were beyond his comprehension, no matter how badly he wanted to understand them. Irritated, frustrated, and ashamed of himself, Eli was even more determined to solve the problem of the mysterious Internet.

I still have time to ponder. Almost a month. No way in hell am I giving up.

Soon he shall be introduced to another miracle of a modern technology: an airplane. Eli could hardly wait. Wasn't it amazing to travel to another part of the country on the plane? From Florida to California. And all it would take just six hours.

Mindboggling.

Eli still had trouble digesting it all. The great progress was more amazing than anything he'd ever read, or dreamt about.

Oh, the miracle of human mind.

And wasn't he the luckiest man alive to be able to witness it firsthand? And wasn't it frustrating as hell that he won't ever be able to share his experience with anyone?

Focusing his eyes on the street scene ahead, Eli soaked up the sounds and pictures of life destined to soon become a distant memory.

People walked, children laughed, music blared. And all sorts of dogs yipped, skipped, and barked. The great number of canines no longer shocked him. Floridians, he learned, considered their dogs members of their family, and didn't keep them chained or caged, a nasty habit he always abhorred. A sudden longing for his own four-legged friend spoiled his jubilation.

Soon, ma Belle, *we'll be home soon.*

"Well, well, look who's here."

The voice that cut into his musings was familiar. Thrown off the path of his thoughts, Eli blinked twice, before his brain registered the newcomer—red-haired, youthful, flamboyant— and connected it to the name.

"Hello, Vic."

"Aww.... you remember me! I'm flattered."

The boy-man he met upon his arrival clapped his hands in obvious delight. A wide grin split his face from ear to ear. Eli smiled in turn. Despite his peculiar manners and odd looks, Red was a very likable person.

"Hard to forget a man such as yourself, Mr. Victor Malone, Esquire."

"Yep, that's me, Mr. Unforgettable." Vic cocked his hip in a playful manner. "And how are you, Mr. Industrialist?"

"I'm quite well, thank you for asking. And where is your trusty companion?"

As if on cue, a joyful yapping announced the arrival of the adorable Maximilian. The miniscule creature was as strange looking as he remembered: long furry ears, hairless body, and a long bushy tail. But the black buttons of its eyes shone with manic joy, and his tiny pinkish tongue began its maneuvers of licking any part of Eli it could reach. Half-prancing, half-shaking on its puny hind legs, poor Maximilian was fighting a losing battle, trying to jump onto Eli's lap. Amused and touched by the dog's adoring antics, Eli picked up the funny ragamuffin.

A mistake.

His brain flashed the warning a tad later than Eli's face was subjected to the ablutions of that tiny but surprisingly enthusiastic tongue.

"There, there." Vic plopped down on the bench, and deftly plucked his manic dog from Eli's hands. "He's just happy to see you. Honestly, you are the only person— beside me, of course— he's positively crazy about. I wonder why."

"I like dogs," Eli patted squiggling Maximilian with one hand, while with the other he whipped the dog's saliva from his face.

Big mistake.

Now his hand was soiled, and a couple of long hair clung to his pinkie.

"Here." Vic's offer of a piece of cloth, moist, soft, with a faint smell of cucumber, came at the most opportune moment. Grateful, Eli accepted, nodded his thanks, and then proceed to clean his hand. The dilemma of what to do with the strange handkerchief —return it or keep it— was quickly solved by Vic. "Toss it...there." His finger pointed at the tall contraption with the swinging top.

A trash collector.

Eli admired those modern conveniences, and was planning to talk to the city major about it when he returned home.

As nonchalant as possible, Eli deposited the soiled square inside the contraption.

Must be some kind of a disposable hanky. Brilliant. No fuss, no need to—

"You are not dressed for the occasion. Why is that?"

Vic's question interrupted his rhapsodizing about modern ingenuity. What was wrong with his attire? Eli's eyes trailed down his own body, then switched to Vic's.

Sweet Lord in heaven!

A one-piece suit in dazzling yellow dotted with the flocks of sheep in all shades of the rainbow, covered the younger fellow's figure from chin to foot. Eli's eyes almost screamed in protest. With a mocking grin, Vic pointed at the nearby sign.

Ah yes, of course. The pajama party.

"No, I'm too old for these festivities."

"You're never too old for fun, my friend. Now, take my uncle Fred. Older than dirt he is, but every year, he's the first one to pull up his pj's and march outside."

"Oh, well. I guess your uncle is more adventurous than I."

"Adventurous?" Vic snorted, but somehow the sound turned out to be almost delicate. "I suppose he is that, but mostly he's just being a live advertisement of his merchandise. You see, Uncle Fred is the owner of Pajama World store. The one on the corner of Centre and 4th North. And this annual party? He started it some forty years ago. Crazy old Uncle Fred, but," pure mischief sparkled in his baby-blue eyes. "You know what they say about us southerners: we don't hide our crazies, we flaunt them."

Not quite sure how to respond to that, Eli opted for a neutral half-smile and a nod.

Undeterred by Eli's reaction, Vic fluffed his wedge of improbable red hair, and crossed his legs in a negligent manner.

"So, Mr. Industrialist, I have to tell you, I have a big—no, make that huge—bone to pick with you."

"What? A... bone?"

"Yep."

Must be another one of the modern sayings. But what does it mean? Thunderation.

"Why?"

"You're the reason our Nika's moving out of the area, that's why. I was so mad at you, let me tell you. Still am." A playful jab of Vic's fist held a surprising punch. Eli's shoulder sang in response. He managed to suppress the urge to rub the spot.

So that's what it meant. Well, hell.

A deep sigh and a frown later, Vic continued in more serious tone of voice, "Are you really taking her to some godforsaken island with no Internet and phone services?"

"Yes."

Since Amelia was a true island, albeit far from *godforsaken,* and there was no Internet or cell connection invented in his time, he supposed it was the truth.

"But why? I mean, what could be so important there that you can't find here?"

The answer was simple, and it was, again, the untarnished truth. "Home. My home is there."

Vic became a picture of an aggrieved person: face drawn and shoulders slouched. His baby blue eyes, clouded with sadness, gazed at Eli with keen reproach.

"I understand. Home is everything, isn't it? It just..." Vic drew a deep sigh, shifted his gaze sideways. Maximillian, sensing his owner's mood, began to whimper. Vic hugged him closer, and proceeded to rub his enormous ears in soothing motions. After a long pause, he continued, "You see, Nika, Alex too, are more than just clients, or friends. They are my family. My only family. And now..." He lifted his shoulders, let them drop.

"I am sorry."

The apology was inadequate, but there was nothing else Eli could do.

"Well, you should be." With an attempt to fall onto his good humor, Vic flashed Eli a grin that was rather strained around the edges. "You're taking away my best girl, and our town celebrity. What are we going to do without our House Whisperer?"

"You are going to live, and enjoy your life," answered the voice of said House Whisperer, who unbeknown to them has joined the party. "And remember her, hopefully fondly."

They both were so engrossed in conversation, they missed Daisy's arrival. Eli surged to his feet, while Vic kept his sitting position and surly disposition.

"Still pissed at me?" Daisy aimed her dazzling smile at Eli, while addressing her friend.

"No, why would I be? It's not like you're hiding something, or lying to your best friend." Vic's negligent shrug accompanied the deep frost in his voice. "Is it?"

"Come on, Red, don't be an ass." And dismissing her friend's verbal jab, Daisy sat on the bench, and shoulder-bumped him. "You can't hold a grudge longer than two seconds."

"Wanna bet?"

"No, but I want to ask you, what are your plans for Christmas?"

"Oh, you know, Maximillian and I are invited to a grand party, then we—"

"Well, I guess my invitation to fly with us on a private jet to California, and spend a holiday with our family and friends is of no interest to you, then."

"What? *What?* California? Christmas in California with you and family? Are you serious?"

"Like the IRS. So, if you're too busy with your previous engagement—"

"What previous engagement?" Rather agitated, Vic jumped up, gave Maximillian a couple of twirls in the air. "We're invited to celebrate Christmas in California, pal of mine!" With sudden concern in his eyes, he turned to Daisy. "He's invited too, right? I'm not going anywhere without Maximillian."

The tiny face with two enormous hairy ears peeked out from the protective hold of Vic's arms.

"Of course, he's invited. He's family, too."

"Fanfuckingtastic!" Vic plopped back onto the bench, and looped his free arm around Daisy and declared magnanimously, "You are forgiven, Curly."

"Oh, what a relief!" In a mocking gesture, Daisy lifted her face heavenward.

"Hey, Mr. Industrialist, what do you think? Mind us tagging along?"

And two pair of eyes, human and canine, aimed their curious gazes in his direction.

CHAPTER THIRTY-TWO

Eli's silence made her twitchy. Dammit, she was so sure that he'd be okay with her idea, but, then again, Vic was such an unusual individual even by most modern standards, plus an additional bonus of a dog, even if a tiny one...

Should've run it by him first, girl. What were you thinking?

Of course, her irritating inner voice butted in at that precise moment. But she was right, the bitch. After all, Vic was Nika's friend, not Eli's, and it was not only a Christmas trip, but Abby's first showing, and—

The sound of a familiar baritone caught her in the middle of her mental debate.

"Your and Maximilian's company during Christmas celebration will be a delightful treat to us all."

Nika let out a breath she was holding. Eli's delayed response was probably caused by translating the meaning of 'tagging along.'

"Aww, listen to that!" Vic's crooning voice dripped honey with every syllable. "I do love how you talk, Tall, Dark and Handsome! Like a freaking aristocrat from the last century, or something. Where did you find this guy, Nika?"

The hell with it. Might as well.

"In the last century."

Eli blanched and recoiled as if she sucker punched him. Vic's reaction, however, was nothing that she expected after such an earthshattering, crazy revelation.

"Huh, you don't say." His ginger-colored brows jumped to his hairline, but that was all. Undeterred, Vic switched his curious gaze from Nika to Eli. "Do you by any chance have any brothers, or cousins, Mr. Industrialist?"

Eli found his voice and regained his composure at the same time. "Ah, no, just a sister."

"Pity. Such a pity, isn't it Maximillian?"

"Why?"

"He's asking why." Vic nuzzled the little dog, then drew in a deep sigh. "Are you really that naïve? If I didn't know better, I'd think you really popped up from the last century."

So, Vic didn't take her seriously.

And what did you expect?

She wasn't sure whether to be relieved or upset, but a more ridiculous situation was hard to imagine. Unable to hold her laughter any longer, Nika doubled over with it, earning a stern glare from Eli, and a mild smirk from Vic.

"I'm sorry, but it's just so...so..." Her mad giggling turned soon to sputtering, then coughing, and still she was powerless to stop it.

Nika, you are out of control. Snap out of it!

"There, there, sweetie."

A couple of sharp slaps on her back, courtesy of her flamboyant friend, cut short her bubbling hysterics. Now her ridiculous merriment was replaced by guilt and shame. In a way, telling the truth in such an offhanded, careless manner, was belittling, like it was nothing of importance. Tears she refused to acknowledged, burned behind her eyelids.

Smothered by chagrin, Nika called herself a thousand names, none of them kind. Apology trembled on her lips, then spilled in a hot whisper, "I'm sorry. God, I am so sorry."

Vic hugged her closer, while Maximillian whined and licked her face.

"Hey, what's that? What are you sorry about?"

"For...everything."

"Okay."

"No, I'm really truly sorry."

"And it's really truly okay."

"No, you don't understand—"

"But I do." Serious now, Vic nudged her chin up with one finger, peered into her eyes. "Hey, it's me, Vic, your BFF and all-around great guy. I love you, Nik. Love means never having to say you're sorry, remember? Good old

Erich Segal sure knew what he was writing about in that heartbreaking book of his."

"But you were so mad at me."

"I was, not any longer. You can't tell everything, even to your BFF. And you know what? You don't have to. Just don't lie."

"I won't. I didn't."

"Well, then. We're good. Are we good?"

"Yes."

"Marvelous. Mr. Industrialist? I think it's time for you to take your girl home."

With the last pat on her hand, Vic unfolded his lanky frame from the bench.

"And Maximillian and I will join the festivities we ignored for far too long. *Au revoir*, my pretties. Pajama party, here we come!"

Focusing on Vic's retreating back, Nika's eyes almost jumped out of their sockets.

He really was dressed in a sort of a pajama, a one-piece kind of deal you put on a baby. But no parent would clad his or her offspring in a screaming yellow onesie with dancing rainbow-colored sheep.

"My Lord, where did he get those nutty pjs?"

"If you mean his outfit, I believe in his Uncle Fred's esteemed establishment."

"Oh, yeah. The Pajama World shop. I knew they were selling some crazy stuff there, but this? Only a lunatic could be tempted to buy it. Or Vic."

"Well, as I was officially notified today, we southerners do not conceal our lunatics — we flaunt them."

"That we do."

Music blared, dogs barked, and children laughed. People milled around, all dressed in pajamas, some sporting glitzy crowns on their heads. The aroma of fried food, burnt sugar, and strong coffee permeated the air.

A carnival atmosphere with a touch of old, dignified class, it was insane, and fun, and unapologetically southern. Nika's heart twisted with love so deep and potent it bordered on pain.

Out of nowhere Vic's scream cut into her merriment. Nika jerked her head in his direction, and froze. Maximillian, his puny hairless body quivering with excitement, broke from Vic's hands, and hurtled across the pavement. Centre Street was mostly pedestrian, but as Murphy's Law would have it, a large black SUV, honking impatiently, was barreling through, toward the tiny dog. Nika sucked on a sharp breath, unable to tear her gaze from the scene unfolding before her eyes. Another moment, and Maximillian was history, smashed under the wide tires of that monster. Helpless, petrified, she pressed both hands against her lips to prevent her own scream.

A lightning fast movement in her peripheral vision penetrated the wall of her shock. She pivoted her head, and stopped dead. In a split second all blood drained from her heart. Constricted by shock, her lungs labored for another breath. A silent cry of horror struck in her throat. Terror, brutal and cold, ripped her to pieces. Her frozen vocal cords refused to function as she watched Eli sprint toward the car and the dog.

Trapped in a real-life nightmare, Nika stood rooted to the spot.

No! Please, God, no!

Suddenly the picture in front of her eyes shimmered and blurred around the edges. Every movement— the speeding car, Eli's run, Maximillian prancing— turned into slow-motion. Every noise muted. Every light dimmed. Mesmerized, she watched Eli picked up the tiny body, and cradle it against his chest. In the next moment he was jogging back with Maximillian in his arms. She had no chance to blink, as everything snapped into focus once again. The black SUV streaked past her. The angry driver blasted his horn and shook his fist. Music blared from the cab with creative swear word combinations screaming out the open window. And Eli, after depositing his precious tiny cargo into Vic's shaking hands, was back, smiling at her. The jerk! She was ready to strangle him, after she kissed him senseless. And then strangle him again.

A split second, that's all it took. A split second that stretched into an eternity, and saved two lives. What the hell happened? Did she cause it? Did she somehow manipulate time?

Think later, Nika. For now, just be grateful.

And like a human missile, she hurtled herself into Eli's arms. Alive. He was alive, safe and sound. That was all that mattered.

A passerby snatched his glittery pointy hat off and then plopped it onto Eli's head. After one hearty laugh and a slap on the back, he continued along his merry way. Eli froze, baffled and shocked at first, then burst into a full-blown laughter.

"Flaunt our crazies? Oh, yes, we definitely do."

CHAPTER THIRTY-THREE

Time flew forward like a maniac on steroids. Nika barely had a chance to catch her breath, as gentle November faded, and boisterous December arrived, armed with bells and whistles. Just yesterday they were celebrating Thanksgiving, gorging on turkey and pecan pie. And in a blink of an eye all of them piled up into the private jet, courtesy of *Verochka's* good friend, Dmitry Rostoff, and headed to California. Christmas was just around the corner, followed closely by Abby's first showing. And on December 31st after traveling back to Florida and welcoming the New Year, she and Eli would start on another journey. Their ultimate trip home.

A little more than a week with her family, to enjoy, to make memories, to be Nika Morris. For the last time.

Nika shook off the sad thoughts when they started to creep her out. She rubbed her palm across her belly gently and, with an effort, switched her thoughts back to the present.

The whole family, including Vic the Flamboyant, and Maximillian the Hairless, were about to embark onto an amazing trip to California. Yippee!

She was excited, if a little apprehensive. New place to stay, new people to meet. Never comfortable with strangers, she had her reservations. But she'd be surrounded by familiar faces, and guarded by one ferocious dog.

Nika smiled. She was glad her friend and his furry companion agreed to this trip. They were family, and what was Christmas without family?

Vic, grateful to Eli for saving Maximillian, became his true champion.

Nika had a strong suspicion her lawyer was a little enamored with her future husband. And who wouldn't? Eli was...well, Eli. She shrugged it off, amused, but not a bit jealous. She was happy little Maximillian was safe and sound, and making the trip with them. As to the matter of his miraculous rescue, she still struggled to come to the terms with it.

As soon as they were back home after that infamous incident, Nika, still reeling, took *Verochka* aside. Her grandmother was the only person in the family she could confide in. After all, hadn't *Verochka* demonstrated some eerie abilities of her own? She called it her precognitive sense.

Precognitive, my butt.

Plain intuition, that's what it was. But whatever you call it, that spooky ability always fascinated Nika, even if she never took it seriously. She wasn't fascinated now. She was now forced to take her own talent seriously. The one she discovered by sheer blind luck.

Her memories took her back to that afternoon.

After she revealed the freaky incident to her grandmother, Verochka, without batting an eyelash, sat her down.

"I had my suspicions long before today, but you just confirmed them. Congratulations, my baby, you just joined the club of Violet Eyes Gift."

"Huh? What the hell's that supposed to mean?"

"Only that you have an extrasensory talent, like me, and your great-grandfather. You see, I inherited my eye color from my father, who had an uncanny sense. In his dreams, he saw the future. Not always, though, and not ever for himself. He predicted, for example, my relocation to the USA, and my marriage to a wealthy man. I have my own little gift, as you know, although not as bright and strong like my father's. He dubbed it the Violet Eyes Gift, and claimed it came to him from his grandmother. And, since I passed his rare eye color to you, I knew the day would come for you to discover you own gift."

"Are you serious?"

"Absolutely."

"And how...how does this thing work?"

"I'm not sure, Daisy-girl. But you obviously can manipulate time. Think about it. Weren't you surprised when you spent three months in 1909, and here it equaled three days? Or last year, when you waited for Eli for fourteen months, but he claimed it was just two weeks in his time?"

"Some gift! If you're right, I should've been able to speed it up, not slow it down last year. I almost didn't survive."

"It just proves my point. When you are experiencing some strong emotion, like fear or love, you are able to make time go slower. Ergo the fourteen months. Or today, when you were afraid for Eli's life."

"But why now? I mean, why couldn't I do it before?"

"Because you never knew what true love was before Eli. Or what true fear is when you almost lost him."

"Huh. And about Alex? He too has your eyes."

"He'll come to his talent when the time is right. And when it is, our dear boy will be in for one hell of a surprise. But we'll let him stumble blind for now. Because each person must discover it on his or her own."

Okay, think of now, girl. Tomorrow will be here soon enough.

And so, the merry bunch of them, including Vic and Maximillian, were flying to San Francisco. The only one who opted out of Christmas in California was JC. Claiming he had lose ends to tie before his final move to Amelia Island, and returned to New York. Maybe he was telling the truth, but Nika had a strong suspicion that Junior decided to mend fences, and appeal to the Twins.

So what? Let it go.

JC was a big boy. Big, self-absorbed, egocentric boy. If he feels like turning his back on her and Alex again? So be it. She had to be content that they were here for Junior when he needed them most, and always will be. Because, whether the selfish jerk wanted it or not, he was family.

The pompous ass.

Enough of that. Time to enjoy the moment. Nika wasn't a big fan of air travel, but this plane took the meaning of flying to a new level. Like stratosphere.

The engines' sound was close to a murmur, lulling, soothing. If she didn't know they were airborne, and moving forward with incredible speed, she'd never guessed it, so soft and smooth was the motion. And sweet Lord, the cabin itself! She looked around. Leather chairs, silky-soft carpet, mahogany desks, crystal vases... What a place! Everything gleamed and sparkled, but in a quiet, classy way. Elegance and grace, the kind that went bone deep, reigned supreme. Wealth, sumptuous and stunning, was quiet and indulgent like a content smile. A palace fit for royalty. Or for the family of one Dmitry Rostoff. Which was essentially the same thing.

Verochka's good friend, the owner of that gorgeous flying fantasy, was a legend, a tycoon in league with Aristotle Onassis or Howard Hughes. Richer than Croesus, and more powerful than the Almighty, Dmitry Rostoff had ruled his jewelry empire for ages. But despite the fact that his name was a synonym for the word 'diamond,' and his handsome patrician face familiar to many, thanks to media, his persona was shrouded in mystery. He was an enigma. But by design, or default? Curious, and yes, intrigued, Nika poked her nose and browsed the Internet, but whatever she found was so damn sketchy, it just whetted her appetite. Who was Dmitry Rostoff?

And what do you care?

She probably shouldn't, but oh, the puzzle was irresistible, and she was determined to solve it. Or, at least, try to. Nibbling on a paper-thin cracker, Nika mentally tallied the info she coaxed out of Google. Dmitry Nikolayevich Rostoff, age seventy-one, son of Russian immigrants, born in San Francisco; married twice, two children. Worth over 170 billion according to Forbs.

Not too shabby.

According to the best source—her grandmother—despite his fame and fortune, the Jewelry Emperor how he was dubbed in the media, was very much a down-to-earth guy, friendly, kind and nice. Philanthropist and humanitarian, he shared his wealth generously and often.

Since Nika hadn't had the pleasure of meeting him yet, the jury was still out on the 'friendly, nice, and kind,' but his generosity was quite obvious.

Chilling bottles of *Dom Perignon* and black Russian caviar on ice-crusted silver plates, Swiss chocolate and Italian olives, German crackers and French chesses were spread on the gleaming table upon their arrival. As a finishing touch of the decadent décor, the exquisite white long-stemmed roses in crystal vases were placed around the cabin.

The crew of five, all dressed in matching uniforms, the trademark Rostoff blue, were efficient, polite, and unobtrusive. A flying paradise if Nika ever saw one.

And since it was her last flight, except for the return flight home, she might as well do it in style.

Nika checked the time on her iPhone. Two hours into the flight, four more to go. Why was it so quiet? What was everybody up to? She craned her neck and looked around.

Abby claimed a small working space in the middle of the cabin, and was sketching furiously on her pad. Vic and Maximillian were napping nearby, cuddled together on the plush loveseat. Eli and Alex both sat near the pilot's cabin, deep in discussion. Eli's facial expression was that of an awestruck child gazing at a new toy. Her cousin, bless his heart, for once was serious, and refrained from joking.

Verochka, who sat next to Nika, was reading something on her iPad.

So, everybody was occupied. Except her. Nika closed her eyes, and willed her brain to give it a rest. Four more hours. She should take a nap.

Yeah, right. Who are you kidding?

Back to the puzzle at hand. She prodded her memory. What else did she know about the elusive Jewelry Emperor? There were two children, a son and daughter. The son was ex-FBI, currently running his own security company. The daughter was a famous painter, one of the most recognizable names in the art world.

They both lived in *Zolotoe Celo,* translated as Golden Village, the family estate where three generations of Rostoffs lived since the dawn of the last century. Now a big part of the estate was dedicated to the art school for unprivileged kids.

So, both offspring stepped away from the family business and made their own paths. Good for them. That was something Nika respected and related to.

What she was still trying to digest, was the fact that the son and daughter of Dmitry Rostoff were married to each other. Obviously, they weren't related. So, what was the story? Time to refresh her memory. And who was the better source than her grandmother?

"*Verochka?*"

"Hmm?" *Verochka* lifted her face from the screen of the iPad.

Since her grandmother's eyes were still a little unfocused, Nika deduced that she pulled her from an engrossing read.

"Sorry to interrupt."

"That's totally fine, sweetie. As a matter of fact, I was about to pause for a drink. How about you?"

Nika slid her palm along her belly. No reason to take any chances. "No, I'm fine, thanks. What are you reading?"

"Harry Potter."

"A ...what? Are you serious?"

"Of course I am. As a matter of fact, I'm re-reading those books for the second time."

"My God, *Verochka*, you never stop to amaze me."

After a delicate sip of champagne, *Verochka* settled back, crossed those skyscraper legs of hers, and smiled. "Good. I hate to be predictable. Now, what is it you wanted, darling?"

For a moment Nika struggled to remember her original question. *Verochka's* reading choice totally threw her off the track. Dammit, what was it again?

Oh, yeah, right. The Rostoff children.

"How come Dmitry's kids are married?"

"Because they are not related."

"Figured. But what's the story?"

"Well, it's a long one. Complicated and quite dramatic."

"Give me the abbreviated version."

"Okay, then. In a nutshell, Kat is Dmitry's daughter, Peter is not his son."

"That's too abbreviated. Come on, Gorgeous, give me some juice."

"Juice? How tawdry, Daisy-girl."

Verochka made a 'tsk-tsk' sound, tucked one exquisite leg under another, and aimed a disapproving scowl toward Nika.

After another dainty sip of champagne, she cleared her throat. "Well, the juice, as you so indelicately put it, my dear, is really... juicy."

And her impeccably mannered, classy, and dressed-to-kill grandmother winked like a mischievous schoolgirl. A rude loud snort erupted before Nika could slap a hand against her mouth. Both Alex and Eli's heads swiveled in her direction. She waved at them. In return to Alex's quizzical gaze, she stuck her tongue, and he laughed. But Eli wasn't amused.

Must be more careful.

No doubt such an unladylike behavior would be frowned upon in 1909, but she was still in this century, so until then, Nika was free to indulge. She ignored them, and turned to *Verochka*.

"God, I simply adore you, Gorgeous!" And Nika mirrored her grandmother's pose by tucking one leg under another. Then she rubbed her hands together. "Okay, then. Gimmy."

"Well, Kat's mother was a Russian ballerina Dmitry was in love with while still married to his first wife, Peter's mother. She— Alina? Polina? whatever her name was— obviously had an affair right before the nuptials, because Dmitry's paternity was never questioned."

"Nice. So, who's the biological father?"

"Some poor relation, and not even on Rostoff's side."

"Hmm. Let me get it straight. Wife number one got pregnant before the wedding, and passed the kid off as her husband's heir. And no one suspected? Hard to believe, but okay. So, when and how Dmitry found out?"

"I'm not sure at what point he learned about it, but he obviously knew long before the kids grew up. Oh, and the Old Bitch, his mother, knew it, too, God rest her evil soul. And that's why she blackmailed Natasha— that's Dmitry's current wife—and, threatened to reveal the truth, made her abandon the kids and Dmitry. You see, Natasha and Dmitry had fallen in love almost at the get go. So, to make her son's life a living hell, the Old Bitch made it look like Natasha took payoff money. You know, your classic pay-off scenario, so it seemed like she betrayed everybody in exchange for moolah."

"Wow, that's too juicy, indeed. Natasha...she was a nanny at first, right?"

"Yes. She's a Professor at Brown University now, but back then she was a nanny to baby Kat."

"So, the old hag threw her out of the house, and made it look like she had abandoned her charge and her lover?"

"Yep."

"That's just so cold and cruel. And wife number one? What happened to her?"

"Hit by a car. Peter was ten or eleven."

"Geez, it does sound like a plot for a gothic novel."

"You're right. And in the middle of that plot was the old hag, like you put it, the cruel, cold, calculating bitch. The woman was evil. But all her manipulations failed at the end, and the truth came to light. Not soon, but still."

"All's well that ends well, then. Oh, but the kids? When did they found out that they weren't related?"

"Oh, that's another chapter. The kids grew up, and Peter fell in love with his sister, as he thought of Kat then. He separated from the family, cut all ties, went to work for the FBI, and relocated to Miami. From what I heard, he took too many risks, deliberately, as if he was punishing himself. Then, one day, after a botched operation, he was shot. Badly. He barely survived. And that's when all the hell broke loose."

"Let me guess. Something about blood, and how his father couldn't be a donor?"

"Bingo." Verochka lifted her flute in a mocked toast and finished the remaining Champagne. "Soon after Peter was healed, the kids were married. And they still live happily ever after."

"Let me repeat: wow."

"Yes, I know. Still gives me goosebumps. So, did I satisfy your curiosity?"

"And then some. No wonder your best buddy Rostoff is so closemouthed about his personal life."

"Dmitry is a very private man, and he values his family above all. And there is nothing he wouldn't do to protect them."

"Sounds ominous."

"Just the plain truth." *Verochka* executed a typical Gaelic shrug only a true Parisian could pull off. She then leaned deeper into the cushions of the chair.

"He's a powerful man, and can be ruthless when it suits him. But with his friends and family... He's a pussycat."

"One with the claws and fangs."

Verochka let out a string of chuckles. "You'll see for yourself soon enough, as we'll be staying in *Zolotoe Celo* for a few days."

"That's another thing I wanted to run by you. Do you think it's okay for all of us stay there? I mean, you and Abby— I get that, but all of us? And Vic and Maximillian?"

"Oh, there will be also Marie Dubois, and her husband."

"My Lord. Maybe we should stay in a hotel as we planned?"

"No, we absolutely should not. Dmitry and Natasha will be offended. They invited everybody, including our flamboyant attorney and his vicious guard dog."

"But—"

"No buts. It's called hospitality, and it's simply impolite to refuse it. Besides, the estate is large enough to accommodate our troupe, and then some. You'll see."

After closing the argument, her grandmother returned to her reading.

Still unconvinced, Nika settled back. There was nothing she could say or do to change the inevitable, or to sway her grandmother.

I guess, we'll see, then.

One thing was clear: their Christmas in California promised to be an adventure.

CHAPTER THIRTY-FOUR

The adventure started as soon as their jet touched the ground. They were ushered outside where an enormous black stretch limo waited in a middle of the tarmac.

A uniformed chauffer, with his back straight, head high, and hands clasped, stood by alert and watchful, like he was on a military parade ground. As soon as their motley troupe disembarked, he stepped forward and greeted them in a polite, but restrained manner, and opened the doors of the limo. Nika admired his speed and efficiency as he dealt with their luggage. Considering there were six people and a dog, they had amassed an impressive amount. Even Maximillian had his own traveling tote. As soon as they all lumbered inside, their chauffer was back at the wheel, maneuvering the beautiful behemoth out of the tarmac.

Smooth as silk, the limo sailed forward, like its wheels hovered above the ground. No sound penetrated from the outside. An almost eerie silence, the same she experienced on the jet, created an impression of being cocooned in a cloud, while the gentle buoyant movement lulled all senses. But this calming effect was lost on Nika, because instead of relaxing, it freaked her out. Must be jet lag. Why else was she so tense and uneasy? After a couple of deep breaths, Nika concentrated on the décor instead.

Mamma mia!

The interior opulence was on par with the jet's leather seats, lacquered accents, crystal glassware, and the munchies. Belgian chocolate, Russian caviar, and five chilling bottles of *Dom Perignon*! Nika blanched and swallowed hard as her stomach roiled.

One bottle per person? Does Rostoff think we are raging alcoholics?

She glanced upward to the winking stars on the limo's ceiling. A smile tugged at her lips. The last time she's been in a Rolls-Royce, she was four or five, but that starlight still held the magic.

Of course, her grandfather's beloved Phantom was a midget compared to this monstrosity, but the feel and smell was the same: splendor and grandeur.

And wealth. With a capital W. Okay, so luxury was obviously the Jewelry Emperor's religion.

So what?

He could afford the best. Good for him.

Nika was not a stranger to riches, considering she was raised a Morris, but all this display of magnificence was setting her teeth on edge.

Get used to it, girl. As a wife of Elijah Coleman, you'll be no pauper yourself.

Dammit, she didn't want to think about Eli's wealth, the Coleman house, her new life as the future Mrs. Coleman. Most of all, she didn't want to think of December 31st and their imminent journey through time. Oh, she wanted to *go* home, but not to *think* about it. And how moronic was that?

So, think of something else. Stop being a jerk. Enjoy your vacation!

Disgusted, Nika's inner I slammed the imaginary door, and left her alone.

That'll teach me.

Being chastised by her bitchy self was a novel experience, and not a very pleasant one, but as slapping goes, it proved to be an effective one.

Her funk forgotten, Nika swept aside all thoughts about future, and concentrated on the present. No one, thank God, has noticed her strange mood, because they were too busy enjoying themselves. Spread all over the place, her merry companions were talking, laughing, or snacking. Everybody was animated to the point of exuberance. *Verochka* chatted with Abby, who was devouring chocolates with an enthusiasm of a three-year-old. Maximillian was in his doggie heaven, sniffing and exploring. Even Eli, usually reserved and subdued, barely contained his excitement. Thank God for Alex, who appointed himself as Eli's guide slash sitter during this trip. Otherwise, her infamous curls would be a distant memory, pulled off by her own hands.

She loved Eli more than life, but, God, all those questions! Half of which Nika didn't know the answer to, because next to her cousin she was technically impaired. Plus, Alex, blessed his heart, had the patience of a saint. She, on the other hand, would never be accused of that trait. Six hours on the plane wiped out the last remnants of her self-restrain.

God, will we ever arrive at the gate?

Unable to sit still, Nika scooted over, and leaned toward the privacy window separating the main cabin from the chauffer.

"How much longer to the estate?"

"Approximately thirty-five minutes, Miss." His voice was clear and strong, each word articulated with military precision.

"Call me Nika. And you are?"

"Ted."

"Nice to meet you, Ted. So, how long you've been working for the emperor?"

Aviator glasses hid half of his face, making his expression unreadable, but for a split moment an amused smile tugged at his chiseled lips. Then it vanished.

"Nine years, six months, and eleven days."

She almost expected to hear the recital of hours and minutes.

"Do you like working for him?"

"Them. I'm employed by the family."

"Alright. Do you like working for *them*?"

"Yes."

Chatty dude. Okay then.

"What branch?"

"Excuse me?"

"What branch of the military were you in before coming to Rostoff's employ?"

Two dark brows shot up, followed by a fleeting glance in the rearview mirror.

"Navy SEAL."

Should've guessed it.

Endurance was written all over Ted's face and body. "You look like it, too."

That earned her another cursory glance via the mirror, and a split-second smile. She'd bet her priceless tool belt that the former member of Sea, Air and Land Special Forces doubled like a bodyguard, and that he won't divulge anything about his employer even under torture.

So much for pumping the information.

"Well, Ted, it was nice talking with you."

"The pleasure's all mine."

Nika slid back to her place, and contemplated her choices. Brooding or eating? No more brooding. Vacations are supposed to be carefree and joyous. Food then. Caviar? No, thanks. She never acquired the taste, despite all *Verochka's* manipulations. Chocolate or champagne? Forget it. She'd just get more restless with the first, and the second was off limits for now. So, what, then?

"Stop fidgeting, Curly. You make Maximillian nervous."

"I'm not fidgeting. I'm thinking."

"You're thinking so loud, I can hear your thoughts. Relax, and turn off that cynical brain of yours."

"Am I that transparent?"

"Only to your BFF. Come on, baby, tell your pal Vic everything. What gives?"

"If only I knew. Everything is so...over the top."

The understatement of any century.

"So?"

"So, it makes me jittery. Am I overreacting?"

"Yes, you are. The million-dollar question is why? You have a guy who's nuts about you, you have your marvelous family. It's Christmas, and on top of it, our Abby's first exhibition. So, I repeat, what gives?"

"I don't know, Vic. Cross my heart and hope to die, I don't really know."

After a long probing gaze, Vic frowned. "Something's bothering you, my girl. Maybe you changed your mind?"

"Changed my mind? What do you mean?"

Instead of a direct answer, Vic slid his baby-blues sideways, and stared at Eli, who was in deep conversation with Alex.

"Oh, no, Vic, no! You couldn't be more wrong. I love Eli! I've waited for him..." *a hundred and eleven years* "...all my life."

Vic turned his laser-sharp eyes back to Nika. For all his flamboyant appearances, he was one of the most serious and level-headed human beings she'd ever met.

Satisfied with what he glimpsed on her face, Vic nodded.

"Perfect. True love is a precious treasure, my girl. And like every treasure, it must be protected, cared for, and respected. It's hard work, a commitment. Or a lifetime sentence, if you will." A quick grin flashed and was gone a second later. "But it's a privilege not too many people are blessed with. So, don't you blow it, Curly."

Vic's voice hit its lower note, so his usual bell clear tenor sounded deep and almost ominous.

Taken aback, Nika blinked a couple of times before she found her own voice.

"Wow, when did you get so wise?"

"I was born that way. And it only improves with age. Like wine."

He winked, and became, once again, good old Vic, funky and funny. The friend she was familiar and comfortable with.

"You are one of a kind, my friend. One of a kind indeed."

"Oh, tell me something I don't already know." Vic's high-pitched chuckle tickled her ears. "By the way, you still didn't explain why I wasn't aware that our Abby is your fiancé's sister? And how come she's Coleman, and he's Benjamin?"

"He's Coleman, too. Benjamin is his middle name."

"Old-fashioned, and impressive. Like the man. There is something about him..."

Vic frowned in concentration. Nika's heart almost stopped in her chest. Damn, he was too perceptive. Then he shrugged, and turned his beguiling smile on her.

"Can't put my finger to it, but your Eli is unusual. It's a shame he's straight, otherwise..." He wiggled his brows comically.

Relaxed at last, Nika smacked playfully at Vic's hand.

"Don't even think about it."

"Can't blame a guy for fantasizing. Just look at him, living breathing eye candy. Yum."

"Well, take your sweet tooth somewhere else. This candy is mine, and I'm not sharing."

"You're so mean and greedy, Curly. But I love you anyway. That's how nice I am. Hey, it's just jumped at me: since Abby is a descendant of our town most famous Coleman, I assume Eli is his relative, too?"

That gave her another unpleasant jolt, but Nika managed to control it. She hoped.

Not missing a beat, she nodded. "Yes," *he is the famous Coleman,* "yes, he is."

"Oh, how delicious! Do tell, my girl."

"There's nothing more to tell, really. When he first arrived—"

"And met me."

"And met you, he decided to use his middle name because..."

"Because?"

"Well, because he didn't want you or anyone to start asking questions. You know."

Lame, so lame, Nika.

"No, I don't, but..." Vic didn't own *Verochka's* panache for shrugging, but his shoulder gesture turned out to be a half decent replica. "If he wanted to be incognito, that's his business. And I can respect that. But why is he still introducing himself as Benjamin? I don't get it."

Now it was her turn to mimic her grandmother's Gaelic shoulder move.

"Habit, I guess. Alex still insists on calling him Benjamin."

"I noticed. Well," and quick as a lightning, Vic snatched Maximillian, preventing his tiny companion from sampling beluga caviar, "what's in a name after all, right?"

"Oh, my goodness!"

Abby's almost reverent exclamation saved Nika from replying.

She turned to the girl whose nose was pressed to the limo's window, her eyes wide as two saucers.

"Welcome to *Zolotoe Celo.*"

Ted's announcement was met with hushed silence, as the passengers leaned closer to the windows, getting their first glimpses of the Rostoff famous domain.

The enormous gates that encircled the estate were the color of a burnished gold, like a manifest to its name. *Zolotoe Celo* meant Golden Village in English, and was it ever! Ten feet high, its sinuous pattern gave an illusion of intricate lace, ethereal and exquisite. A wrought iron masterpiece, it dazzled the eyes and took your breath away. Literally. Nika sucked on a sharp breath, and let it go slowly, while watching the amazing gates slide sideways. The limo turned onto the paved road, and glided forward. She couldn't keep her eyes off those golden lacy gates even after the limo passed through and left it behind. After a long drive through the winding asphalt path, Ted stopped the car in front of the house. More cream than white, a three-story building boasted a majestic portico held by four ornate Corinthian columns. The structure seemed to soar to the sky, fluid, regal, and classy.

The manor.

Her first impression was of grand opulence, but not ostentatious.

During eight years in business, Nika had seen her share of the wealthiest estates, some of which (thanks to her time-traveling journey), she witnessed in situ, but this one surpassed them all. And not because of the magnificent architecture, but its character. Its sheer presence. Goosebumps broke over her skin, Nika's sense of recognition signaled a high alert. This house was special. Alive. And it 'spoke' to her. After all, she was not called House Whisperer for naught.

Nika stepped out of the limo and shivered. The air was cooler than in Florida, but not so cold to warrant her chills. Hugging herself, she focused on the spectacular house, heightening all her senses, trying to intercept any negative energy. No, thank God, nothing. The building was danger-free, healthy, positive, and as people friendly as possible.

You're female.

The Grand Dame of the West was regal, cool, and reserved, but she projected her welcome as if it was written on her facade with huge neon letters.

After a few moments, Nika's muscles relaxed. They will be fine here. A hand placed on her shoulder drew her out of her reverie. Without turning her head, she smiled, and rested her cheek on its welcoming warmth.

"Are you alright, *ma petite*?"

Eli's voice caressed her ears, and sent another kind of chills—of the erotic variety—all over her body. And just like that, she forgot about everything else.

"I'm good, but I missed you."

She nipped on his thumb, a quick and playful bite. The last couple of days before the trip were so hectic, that after dropping into bed, they both were too exhausted for any other activity except exchanging a goodnight kiss.

"I missed you too, enormously so." Eli moved his hand out of the way. "But if you do *that* one more time, I'm afraid I'm going to embarrass our hosts and family."

"Yeah? How?"

"By—"

But whatever erotic scenario Eli was about to whisper into her ear died short as two massive German Shepherds burst from the corner of the house, and galloped toward their group. A large man ran after them, shouting something, but all in vain. The dogs quickly advanced, barking madly. Poor Maximillian froze, gave one pitiful yap, then burrowed inside Vic's jacket, with only his tail sticking out.

Two things happened simultaneously. Eli stepped forward between the dogs and their group as a human barrier, then the main doors to the house flew open, and a slender woman ran out, calling, "*Foo! Nelzia!*"

Both dogs stopped as if they were shot dead. Another shout "*Sidet!,*" and they plunked their quivering butts onto the ground barely two feet in front of Eli.

The furry beasts eyed the approaching woman with something close to adoration. Their tails did a perfect job of swiping the last speckles of dust off the driveway.

"My God, I'm sorry, I'm so sorry..." The running man had finally reached their group. Nika had her first look at the Jewelry Emperor. Imposing man, tall and trim, with a full head of thick white hair. He carried his years like expensive accessories, with panache and careless ease. Even clad in grass-stained jeans and a rumpled polo shirt, Dmitry Rostoff managed to look distinguished and regal.

His face was more striking than handsome, with high Slavic cheekbones, a long narrow nose, and a strong square chin with a deep cleft.

That little endearing dimple reminded her of Eli.

What? Nonsense.

They were as different as the sun and the moon, but still...Something in the way they both carried themselves. Their commanding presence, their imposing statue held everyone's attention even when they were silent. Both men projected strength and power.

Forces to be reckoned with.

Shaking off the thought, Nika concentrated on what their host was saying.

"... two hooligans were playing, and then they took off like a rocket, and I couldn't stop them. I'm so sorry."

"Oh, stop apologizing, Dmitry. We're fine. Come here, you handsome devil."

"*Verochka, golubushka!*" And he enveloped her grandmother in a bear hug, lifting her off the ground, then kissed her on both cheeks before turning to the rest of the group: "Welcome, everybody. Welcome to *Zolotoe Celo*. Sorry again for such an unorthodox greeting. Hope none of you are afraid of dogs. They are harmless, I promise, just fresh and frisky."

The woman who stopped the dogs joined them in time to hear his last words.

"What he meant is young and stupid, but it's not terminal." Then her arresting face lit up with a brilliant smile. "*Verochka,* my dearest!"

Nika debated what was more unusual about the woman: her enormous green eyes, or her deep rich contralto. A mane of mahogany curls was swept from her milk white face, and held at the nape with a pearly clasp. Petite and impeccably put together, she was dressed in a simple long sheath that disguised her figure, but a flare of round hips or swell of generous breasts was hard to hide. If Nika didn't know her true age, she would never have guessed it. Younger than her husband by a decade, she still looked more like a late forty's early fifties than her sixty and small change. A distinct Slavic accent added an endearing charm to the overall picture. After exchanging kisses on both cheeks with her grandmother, she looped one arm around *Verochka's* waist.

"Hello, I am Natasha, and this flustered gentleman who forgot his manners is my husband Dmitry. Welcome to *Zolotoe.*"

"Well, then, allow me to introduce my gang." *Verochka* gestured with one hand, pointing as she went, "My darling girls, Nika and Abigail, our family friend Vic Malone, the adorable baldy is my grandson Alex, and this dashing hottie is Eli, Abby's brother and Nika's fiancé."

"God, *Verochka,* only you!"

After one throaty chuckle, Natasha turned her laughing eyes to the group. "A true pleasure, everybody. I trust your trip was comfortable?"

The dashing hottie stepped forward.

"We thank you for your hospitality, Madame." Eli inclined his head in a formal greeting, raised Natasha's hand, then brushed his lips over her knuckles. He turned to their host. With his eyes directly on the older man's face, Eli addressed him in the best ceremonial manner of his century, "Dear Sir, please accept mine and my family's sincere gratitude over lending us your means of transportations. Our trip was the utmost comfortable in every way indeed. Your generosity in providing us with sumptuous meals and excellent spirits is greatly appreciated."

Nika gritted her teeth. If Rostoff was surprised with such an archaic expression of gratitude, he didn't let it show. His curt nod was no less formal than Eli's speech, but a small smile tugged at the corners of his lips.

"Dmitry Rostoff," he offered his hand, then added, as if an afterthought, "a jeweler."

"Elijah Benjamin Coleman, Industrialist."

Oh, for crying out loud.

CHAPTER THIRTY-FIVE

Mortified, Nika held her breath. No one appeared to be shocked by Eli's slip of a tongue. Or was it her wishful thinking? She squinted at Dmitry Rostoff, but he looked as if nothing out of the ordinary had happened.

Relax, girl. Act normal.

Nika mumbled to her irritating inner self, "Easy for you to say."

The handshake went on and on, during which each man sized up the other.

"Coleman, industrialist, is it?"

Uh-oh. Dammit!

"It is, yes."

"And what industry are you—"

Maximillian, bless his doggy heart, chose that moment to sneeze and stick his nose out of Vic's jacket.

"Aww, and who do we have here?"

And just like that, the attention was switched from Eli to the furry bundle in Vic's hands. Natasha leaned over and with one delicate finger tapped the wet dot of Maximillian's nose. "Don't be afraid, sweetheart. Crested, are you?"

"Yes! Hairless Chinese Crested, to be precise." Vis piped in, delighted to showcase his beloved companion. "Isn't he adorable?"

"He is absolutely precious. What's his name?"

"Maximillian. He's very well behaved, but shy around beautiful females."

Following Eli's example, Vic bowed and kissed Natasha's hand. Not to be outdone, Maximillian stuck his tiny pink tongue and licked her finger in a manifest of doggy gallantry. The rich sound of Natasha's laughter drew twin whimpers from the Shepherds. Nika eyed the pair cautiously.

Jealousy, or excitement? For Vic and Maximillian's sake, she hoped those two were just eager to sniff at their new pal. Not snack on him.

Amused with Maximillian's antics, Natasha scratched between his enormous hairy ears. She seemed to be in no hurry to set free her own dogs that sat nearby, wallowing in their misery. Or plotting revenge.

One way or another, everybody's attention was diverted from Eli's harebrained introduction.

But was it forgotten?

"My apologies again, dear friends. I can only imagine what your first impression of all of us must be. Instead of a proper greeting, almost attacked by the dogs." One stern look from those sparkling green eyes was enough to reduce the almighty Jewelry Emperor to squirming. "But I promise you," Natasha continued in her well-modulated velvety voice, "we have better manners than that, and we'll try to demonstrate it during your stay with us. Let's go inside, and get you settled, shall we? Your baggage will be dealt with shortly."

To Nika's surprise, Ted the driver, and their limo vanished. A tidy row of bags and suitcases graced the driveway.

"Oh, don't bother, we can—" Alex turned to their luggage only to be intercepted by three sturdy young men who gathered the cases and carried them inside.

Natasha slipped one arm through *Verochka's*, and started toward the house.

"What about your dogs, Madame?"

Full of empathy, Eli's gaze was focused on the forgotten German Shepherds.

"Oh, yes. *Olga, Tatyana*," Natasha called over her shoulder, "*domoi*."

Both dogs jumped up and raced toward the house with the speed of a tornado.

"*Olga* and *Tatyana*? Like two sisters in *Eugene Onegin*?"

Surprised pleasure lit up Natasha's face as she turned to Vic. "You know Pushkin?"

"Know and love. I adore Russian poetry. Wish I could read it in the original language."

"Well, then, we must absolutely have a chat. I'll read for you in Russian, if you'd like."

"Oh, how marvelous! I can hardly wait." Excited, Vic trotted after her.

Vic and Russian poetry? Seriously?

Nika wasn't aware he read anything at all except legal documents. Come to think of it, what did she know about Vic's preferences, his likes and dislikes? And the answer was not much. He was her friend and attorney for eight years, and still in many ways, Vic Malone was like a dusty unread book. And now, with her December 31st deadline fast approaching, there was no time to discover any new pages in that fascinating book. And wasn't it just sad?

Too late. Too damn late...

Lost in thought, Nika missed her footing, and stumbled. If not for Dmitry Rostoff, who caught her on the fly, Nika would have had a face to front steps introduction to the excellent marble. Thank God she trailed behind, so no one noticed her less than graceful entrance, except for the Jewelry Emperor. Relieved and embarrassed, Nika nodded in lieu of thanks, and got a mischievous wink in response.

Wow.

Startled, she managed a faint smile. So, the almighty Rostoff had a sense of humor as well as great reflexes. Not to mention the body of an athlete, and a face of a movie star. A beautifully aged and distinguished one.

The man must've been a menace in his heyday. I wonder if Verochka has any old pictures.

Eyeing him askance, broad shoulders and regal posture, it struck her anew how much he reminded her of Eli. And speaking of the devil. Nika swiveled her head, searching for her fiancé. As if he sensed her probing gaze, Eli sent her a smoldering glance and a crooked smile that almost stopped her heart. Then Abby tugged at his hand, and propelled him forward, and the connection was broken. Later, Nika promised herself. She'd have him all to herself, and, by God, she'd have her way with him as soon as she managed to untangle Eli from his sister, her cousin, and their hosts.

Fortified with that, Nika plowed ahead.

The massive double doors were wide open, and Natasha ushered everybody in.

"Welcome to our home."

Nika's jaw dropped to her chest when she got her first glimpse inside.

Holy cow!

If the building's exterior was a statement of grand opulence, the interior was one of hushed splendor and subdued elegance. Regal and classy, with sweeping arches, marble floors, and crystal chandeliers, it was a palace fit for royalty. Rays of sunlight streamed from the domed glass ceiling, bounced off the walls and floors, creating an aura of calmness and reverence. Tall Palladian windows added to the impression of a cathedral. The first floor was an over-sized open space with almost no furniture except for the highbacked chairs and a few settees in Rococo style. A magnificent Christmas tree reigned supreme, decked in sparkling gold and dazzling silver. Its peak, crowned with a feather winged angel, soared upward, almost touching the dome. A mound of wrapped packages under the tree took her breath away. There were enough presents for a small army.

Did they haul the whole department store in here?

Simple red poinsettias, instead of looking out of place in the midst of all that glory, added a touch of intimacy, and brought holiday cheer to the fullest.

Nika's gaze traveled to the sweeping staircase, and her heart almost wept in awe and appreciation. Unblemished white Italian marble of the grand staircase with a polished bronze banister looped fluidly, splitting in two different directions on the second floor. The image was that of a slow and graceful dance.

From her spot Nika had an excellent visual of the second level encircled by the balustrade. Carved marble columns, wide and fluid arches, intricate crown moldings. And the workmanship! The contractor in her was itching to touch and feel. But she held herself together because to sprint to the second floor and start inspecting the nooks and crannies, was impolite at best, and it might be fraught with some consequences. What if the house objected? She might be sick for days, nauseated and dizzy. And wouldn't that be fun.

Well, there's only one way to find out.

Bracing inwardly, Nika closed her eyes, and opened all her senses, probing the energy of the house. A kaleidoscope of emotions, strong and deep and bright.

Underneath the maelstrom of that current was calmness and comfort. *Welcome.*

She smiled, satisfied and content. The Grand Dame was old, a bit snobby, but kind, and despite her obvious splendor, she was *home.* And she welcomed them.

Promising herself a luxury of a thorough inspection later, Nika almost relaxed, when one of the German Shepherds brushed its wet nose against her hand. Startled, Nika tensed and jerked her hand away. She wasn't afraid of dogs, but the sheer size of the furry giant gazing up at her was disconcerting. The dog tilted her head, and barked. Wonderful. Now what? Wary, Nika eyed the pooch. Was she asking for a rub? As if reading Nika's mind, the huge head bumped her hip.

Okay, then, here goes.

And Nika ran her hand over the long fur. At once, the picture before her shimmered and shifted, and here was Belle, her homely face lit up in delight, her tongue lolling playfully. A blink of an eye later, and she was back in Rostoff's manor, her hand laying on the head of the huge German Shepherd.

Nika's heart lurched to her throat. She was sure for a second she was back in 1909, petting her beloved dog. Or else, she was going bonkers.

That's all I need for a full measure of happiness.

Confused and a little dizzy, Nika kneeled, and hugged the huge dog. Only when her face got a mighty lick, she came off of her reverie. A pair of adoring amber eyes met her gaze. A bit steadier, Nika cracked a smile. Up close, she—Olga? Tatyana? —didn't seem so scary, but rather curious. And what a beauty she was. Longhaired coat, almost silver with blue-black streaks, shimmered under the light. Nika peered into the lovely, oddly childlike face.

"You are a real looker, girl."

A doggy agreement came in the form of a deep bark and another lick on the face. Then she jumped up and joined her sister currently courting Eli.

He petted each dog, then laughed as one of the sisters lifted herself up and placed both front paws on his shoulders.

"Good dog, yes, you are. And beautiful, too. But that's enough. Down, girl."

His crooning sent a wave of shivers along Nika's spine.

Really, Nika? Her inner bitched popped up. *Seriously? Hallucination aside, you're getting all hot and bothered in the middle of a crowd!*

What can I do if just the sound of his voice makes me crazy?

Down, girl.

Nika almost yelped as Natasha uttered a sharp command in Russian. One of the dogs plopped down and sat. Her twin, undeterred, kept dancing in circles around Eli, whining and salivating.

I know how you feel.

Natasha repeated her command, and added a sharp hand gesture. Nika could swear she heard a groan of doggy annoyance, but this time they both obeyed.

If only her own lust could be dealt with that easily.

Later, I'll deal with it later.

"Don't mind them, Eli. They are dears, but easily excited. We are still in the process of training, you see," Natasha paused and lifted her humorous gaze to her husband, "but who's training whom sometimes is a question. Dmitry was practicing with them outside today. By the way, darling, did you try to use the command for stop?"

"Command? *Milaya*, for the sake of..." An expression of utter bafflement was written all over his patrician face. "They're still babies!"

"They are female babies, my dear, and already figured out how to manipulate some members of this family, you old softie. They know better with me. Right, girls?"

Two barks and enthusiastic tail wagging was her answer.

"See? They agree."

"Figured. You women tend to stick together, no matter what."

"We sure do. Oh, and the next time? Just try to say *"Nelzia"* or *"Foo"*."

She let out another round of that bewitching laughter. It was so infectious, Nika heard a chorus of answering chuckles, one of which was her own.

"Okay, everybody." Even after her laughter subsided, Natasha's voice still carried some merriment. "Here is the deal, this is your home for as long as your stay. And I mean that. You don't have to ask permission for anything. Feel free to wander, to explore, or rest, and do whatever is it you wish. If you're hungry, the kitchen is this way," a slow graceful gesture to the side, "and you are more than welcome to everything in the fridge. Or ask the cook to make anything you want. Your rooms are in the West wing, and I trust they will be satisfactory. But if you need anything at all, please let us know. We usually dine at six. If you prefer to eat in your rooms, that's fine. A time difference may play havoc with your usual patterns, so feel free to adjust. We are not formal. If the dogs bother you, you are only to tell one of the staff. I will hear about that." The last was said in a firm voice, accompanied by a stern stare aimed at the furry pair.

Is that how Professor Rostoff kept her students in line? Nika wondered. Then again, one glare of those mesmerizing green eyes was enough to make *her* snap to attention. Not to mention all the members of the opposite sex in the room, the almighty Jewelry Emperor included.

CHAPTER THIRTY-SIX

"**F**inally!"

As soon as the door of their room closed behind Eli, Nika pivoted, and shoved him against it. Unprepared, he stumbled, and slammed back, but before he could utter a single sound of protest, she grabbed two fistfuls of his shirt, yanked hard, and took his mouth. Angry, wild and rough, the kiss soon spanned out of control, and became a battle of tongues, lips and teeth. Punishment and rapture, torment and delight.

Dark pleasure spiked with pain, it was a bit mean, and hot as hell.

When they both surfaced for a breath, Nika was pleased to see Eli's flustered face. A slow satisfied smile bloomed on his lips, as he chuckled.

"Hungry, *ma petite*?"

"Yeah, ravenous. Any objections?" She sounded breathless and excited to her own ears.

"None come to mind."

"Splendid. Geez, Coleman, you drive me crazy!"

And she kissed him again, pouring all her suppressed passion into it. God, but she missed him. Eli let her take the lead. After a while, he grabbed under her legs, and hoisted her up, so now they were face-to-face. Screaming inside for satisfaction, Nika nipped at his lower lip, then licked his clefted chin, dipping her tongue into the enticing dent. He went wild, as she expected, and took her mouth almost violently. A low growl deep in his throat reverberated all the way through her body. With their mouths still glued together, he moved, and without ceremony dumped her onto the bed. Panting, trembling, she squinted up at him through the curtains of her curls. A moment went, then another, during which he stood there, gazing down at her. The smoldering fire in his eyes scorched her skin, and set her blood on fire. A low moan stirred the air, sending goosebumps along her arms. To

Nika's utter shock, she realized the sound had come from her. Hard tremors shook her body, and still he stood, as if mesmerized, looking down at her.

"Elijah Benjamin Coleman, if you don't come down here this instant, I swear I—"

But he didn't let her finish. The familiar weight pressed her deeper into the mattress, as Eli dropped on top of her. His marauding mouth covered hers, rough and impatient.

His tongue delved deep.

Ambushed.

Invaded.

Helpless, stripped of all defenses, she was powerless to deflect his passionate attack. No finesse, just scorching heat and brutal need. She reveled in it.

Love.

Frustration

Fear—

All the confusing emotions that had boiled inside her for the past few days erupted like a spewing geyser. Surging upward, she fused both hands into his hair, and shackled her legs around his hips.

Demand.

Invitation.

Instinct to mate overruled all inhibitions. Delirious with it, she grabbed his shirt, cursing her shaking hands. She ripped it apart, sending the buttons flying.

The sound of tearing fabric was music to her ears.

"Now! Don't wait, don't wait, don't—"

Her chant ended on a shrilling note as Eli impaled her, sheathing himself deep. Time stopped. They both stilled. Their eyes collided, held for a dizzying moment, and then the madness broke free.

They napped, or passed out, after a bout of their wonderful, wild, and wicked lovemaking. She tried to recall the last time they both were so out of control in bed. Never. Eli was a most ardent lover, uninhibited and adventurous, but he was always careful with her. Today, however, the reckless beast in him took over.

Yes, she provoked him, almost attacked him, and unleashed the wild animal inside. And she couldn't be happier. Smug, satisfied, Nika resurfaced from her half-swoon, short nap, and curled her lips.

"Pleased with yourself, are you, wench?"

"Hmmm."

"Did I hurt you? Look at me, Daisy."

With great effort, Nika unglued her eyelids, and brought his face into focus. He was adorable! All disheveled, flushed face, frowning. Nika ran her finger over his furrowing brows, then trailed down his nose, tapping his divided chin.

"Have I ever told you how much I love your chin?"

Thrown off balance, Eli blinked. His brows almost disappeared under the fringe of black hair currently falling down his face.

"My...what?"

"Your cute dimpled chin. God, I adore that little cleft." To demonstrate, she dragged herself up, and kissed the dimple in question. Silver grey irises darkened to pewter, even as color drained from his face.

If she wasn't mistaken, she shocked the living lights out of him. Satisfied with the results, Nika plopped back, and inhaled deeply.

"Well," after a long moment of silence, Eli found his voice, "I gather you are fine and in good spirits."

"You gather correct."

"I was afraid...I wasn't careful with you this time. I have no notion how that happens, but..." Eli averted his troubled eyes, "all I felt was this terrible need. I couldn't hear anything, my ears were ringing, or see anything through the haze in my eyes. Like an animal, I just smelled you. And couldn't stop myself from tasting and taking. But that's not an excuse, I know, and I am deeply ashamed of myself."

"Hmmm. I rather liked your animal." Nika brushed dark strands of hair from his eyes. "All that tasting and taking." Shivering from recollection, she licked her lips.

"Stop that. I'm trying to apologize, and you...you make it difficult."

"Apologize? Apologize for what? For the best sex of my life?"

Eli squinted at her. Then a small hesitant smile tugged at his lips. "So, you are not upset?"

"Upset? I'm deliriously happy, and hoping for a repeat performance in the near future, you dolt."

"Dolt, am I?"

The twinkling in his eyes was all too familiar. Nika rolled away, and covered her breasts with a sheet. "Eli—"

"A repeat performance, is it?" His long arm snaked out and tugged the bedclothes, halting her belated attempt at modesty.

"Yes, most definitely, but—" His hand found her breast, molded it.

Oh, God!

"And how nearest a future do you have in mind?"

Dizzy, lost, and shivering, Nika made the last feeble protest, "We'll be late for dinner."

"The hell with dinner."

CHAPTER THIRTY-SEVEN

They were late for dinner, but then so was everyone else.

Nika wasn't sure what excuses the rest of their gang had, but their hosts were gracious enough. Everything was chucked up to the time difference, and waved aside. The dining room was no less spectacular than the rest of the house, but homier. A table that easily sat forty people was currently set for the party of fourteen. When Nika and Eli entered, one and all were chatting, laughing, and having a jolly good time.

"Here you are," Natasha noticed them first. "Come, and meet the rest of the family."

Always a gracious hostess, she made the introductions, "Here are my children, Kat and her husband Peter, and their two kids, my grandbabies, Nick and Lana."

A teenage boy and younger girl scrunched their faces in protest.

"Baba! We are not babies."

"To me, you are. I'll tell you more, your parents will always be my babies, too. So, suck it up, my pretties."

"Okay, people, I don't know about you, but I'm starving."

And with that declaration, the Jewelry Emperor offered the crooks of his elbows to his wife and *Verochka*, leaving the rest of them to follow in his wake.

Nika's cheeks burned when her stomach rumbled. My word, she was famished. Small wonder, considering her latest exercise. She cast her glance askance, and met Eli's laughing eyes.

The rascal.

Nika found herself between Eli and Vic after they all were seated. Abby was sandwiched comfortably between *Verochka* and Alex. All the Rostoffs were on the opposite side of the table. Sitting across, Nika had a perfect visual of their hosts.

Since she already had an impression of the older Rostoffs, she focused all her attention to the younger generation of this unusual family. Kat and Peter intrigued her. They made a striking pair.

With a river of unbound platinum blond hair, willowy slender, Kat Rostoff was one of those women who was born to make men drop to their knees and beg. Any age and sexual orientation included, Nika noted with a rueful smile, as Vic almost swallowed his tongue while gaping at Kat. Her husband, in contrast to her ethereal fairness, was dark, and if Nika's instincts was on point, dangerous.

She was graceful, animated, and open. Peter was quiet, watchful, and restrained. On the surface, they seemed like complete opposites of each other.

Where did she heard or read that the perception of visual surfaces was always the wrong one? Here was the proof.

When Peter looked at his wife, the strength and depth of his feelings were so raw, Nika almost heard his pulsing heart.

"So, tell me, how are your rooms? Is everything okay?" Natasha's polite inquiry was met with the chorus of "fine" and "wonderful."

"Baba, when is Uncle Vlad coming?" Nick interrupted.

"Oh, tomorrow, my darling. He and your Aunty Marie will arrive later in the afternoon."

At the mention of Marie Dubois, her mentor, Abby perked up. Poor girl was so nervous about her upcoming showing, she barely resembled the vibrant strong-willed beauty who jumped through time after Nika to follow her dream.

Pale and hollowed eyed, Abby was like a shadow of her former self. Even Alex's verbal jabs were useless to bring her out of her cocoon. Nika hated that lost look on Abby's face. God knows, she tried— they all did— to slap some sense into the girl, and boost her self-confidence, but the Princess remained captive to her fear.

Let's hope Marie Dubois will be able to bring her around.

"Are they staying here, too?"

That came from Lana, who until then was quiet as a mouse. Her bespectacled dark eyes, just like her father's, surveyed the room unobtrusively, taking notice of everything. And stacking it to memory. Still waters, they say, Nika smiled into her water glass, taking a small sip. That kid was something, alright. The siblings were as different as day and night, and not only on the outside. Grey-eyed, blond, and gregarious Nick was a carbon copy of his mother, while Lana's dark complexion and her watchful demeanor had her father written all over it.

"No, sweetie. They have their new place now, remember? A condo on the beach."

"But that's just a small apartment, and it's like a gazillion miles away!"

"A small apartment?" Natasha shook her head. "You don't know what small is, my peep. When I lived in my old country, that 'small apartment' would have seemed like a royal palace. And a fifteen-minute drive on an intercostal highway is a pleasant and relatively quick trip. Besides, you know how your Uncle Vlad drives."

"Yeah, like a maniac." Dmitry Rostoff chuckled. "The old daredevil thinks he's still eighteen."

"And so do you, my dear."

"Guilty, but it's all your fault. Near you, *milaya*, I always feel like a green youth."

The glance that passed between them was so intimate, Nika felt like an intruder and averted her eyes.

"What are the plans for tomorrow?" Nick, unperturbed by his grandparents' behavior, or more than likely used to it, broke the moment of charged silence.

"Tomorrow? Why, a day before Christmas we should..." Natasha tapped her lips with her fingertip, as a mock frown puckered her forehead, "do whatever the heck we please." She finished on a laugh. "Any suggestions?"

"We can take everybody around town for a tour."

"An excellent idea, Nick." Peter nodded his approval. "Ladies? Gentlemen?"

"I'd love to have a tour." Vic blotted his lips before answering, "I always wanted to see San Francisco's Fisherman's Warf."

"Then you shall. Dad?"

"Count me in, son. I forgot the last time I traveled around the city just for fun."

"Excellent. Anybody else?"

"I'm in." Alex turned to Eli. "Benjamin, care to join?"

"Most definitely, if Daisy has no objections." Eli turned his questioning eyes to her.

"She has not," Nika assured him.

"Why are you calling her Daisy? Isn't her name Nika?"

"Her legal name is Veronika," Eli answered Lana, all serious and polite. "But the first time I met her, she reminded me of a flower. Don't you agree?"

"Hmm." A pair of intense chocolate eyes scanned Nika from the top of her head to her meager bosom. The ridiculous feeling of being X-rayed was mildly irritating.

"I suppose so." With a little careless shrug, the girl returned her eyes to her plate, and the subject was closed.

Little brat. Must keep on my toes with this one.

"Okay, ladies," Natasha interrupted Nika's musings, "and how shall we occupy ourselves while the gentlemen tour the city?" She rubbed her hands together, her eyes dancing with mischief. "Shopping, or a day at a spa?"

"I must head to the gallery in the morning." Kat's voice carried a touch of an apology, as she smiled at her mother. "Just for a couple of hours, I swear, Mama."

"I know your couple of hours, Kitty-Kat." Natasha puckered her brows. "You need to learn to delegate, my girl."

"Kettle, pot," Kat chuckled, and patted her mother's hand. "I promise, I won't be long."

"May I accompany you?"

Abby's hesitant question drew Natasha's attention. "You too, Brutus?"

"Sorry, Mrs. Rostoff, but I must. I'm anxious to find how it all turned out. You see, Facetiming or Skyping is not the same as seeing the exhibit with my own two eyes. This is my very first showing, and I'm..." Abby trailed off, while her hands folded and unfolded the linen napkin.

"Nervous, are you, sweetheart?"

"Horribly so. I'm ecstatic, and happy, but mostly...terrified."

"Oh, don't be." Natasha waved Abby's concerns away. "I'm sure your show will be a smashing success. Marie considers you a very talented young artist, and I trust her judgment unquestionably."

"You are very kind, ma'am. I wish I shared your confidence."

Abby shifted her eyes downcast, but Nika caught a sheen of treacherous mist. Dammit, she was on a verge of tears.

Do something!

Before Nika's brain reacted to her inner voice's command, Natasha's contralto knifed the air, "What's this? Self-doubts? You must stop that. Right this instant."

Hard and stern, her eyes glinted like emeralds, while her words lashed out with all the finesse of a whip, "Don't you dare to question your talent, Abigail! Ever. It's God's gift to you, so you must have a care. A true talent like yours is a precious thing, rare and priceless. Be proud of it. Be worthy of it. Be strong, because that gift will demand so much out of you."

The sudden fury behind her words was startling. Every person around the table froze. All eyes were glued to Natasha. Shocked, Abby focused her unblinking stare on the older woman, but her color began its slow return to her face.

Bravo, Professor. We don't need to wait for Marie Dubois after all.

"And if you won't believe in yourself, my dear, who will?" Natasha added in a gentler voice. "I saw your paintings the other day, and they took my breath away. As a matter of fact, there's one particular watercolor I have my eye on." She turned to her daughter. "You know the one I'm talking about, Kitty-Kat?"

"I know, Mama. *The Timeless.*"

"Mark that one 'sold', will you, girl?" All indulgent, Dmitry smiled at his wife.

"Oh, but...you don't have to, I would be happy just give it to you..." Sputtering, Abby switched her gaze between the Rostoff trio. "Please."

"That's your heart talking, my dear, and your gratitude, and I value both very much. But the artist must have a satisfaction of sale, and a financial reward. Make sure to charge him through the roof," she added matter-of-factly to her daughter, then turned to her husband. "Thank you, my darling."

"You are welcome, *milaya*."

"I don't know what to say." Abby's face was awash with color.

"Say thank you."

"Thank you. Oh, thank you so much, Mrs. Rostoff."

"You are so very welcome, my dear."

"Mrs. Rostoff?" She turned to Kat. "May I accompany you tomorrow, then?"

"Oh, absolutely. Under one condition, you call me Kat. Since there are two Mrs. Rostoffs here, it gets confusing."

"Oh, but surely I cannot—" After a quick glance at Kat's arched brows, Abby capitulated, "Alright, Kat."

"Fantastic. So, while our men will be doing their manly stuff, the two of us will make a quick trip to the gallery. I want your opinion on some adjustments I made. I hope you approve."

"Don't forget to place a 'sold' sign on my watercolor." Natasha reminded.

"I'll go with you, too. I want to see Abby's art." Nick piped in, then looked apologetically at his father. "Sorry, but I saw the Wharf a gazillion times."

"Well, *I* will go with Papa and Deda," Lana aimed her accusing eyes at her brother. "Unlike someone, I'd love to see Fisherman's Warf for a gazillion and a *first* time."

"That's my girl." The older Rostoff beamed at his granddaughter. Peter nodded, his face an unreadable mask.

Gosh, the man must be a helluva poker player.

"Okay, then." Natasha let out a fake dramatic sigh. "If no one wants to stick with a couple old ladies—"

"Old ladies, my ass." The sound of her own voice, clear and loud, was so unexpected, Nika dropped her fork.

Did I really say that out loud?

Verochka's sudden coughing, followed by Alex's muffled laugh and Eli's soft swearing was all the confirmation she needed.

Yep, you really did.

Damn. And now, for damage control. Nika puffed her cheeks, and let out a long breath.

"Sorry, sorry. I didn't mean it. I mean, I meant that— look at you two, both gorgeous, and looking like million bucks— but I shouldn't say it."

Both ladies tilted their heads, all regal and mildly insulted, and fixed identical quizzical expression on their faces.

Really, Nika? Just put a second foot in your mouth, why don't you?

"I mean, I should say it, definitely, but not the word, you know, ah, ass. Sorry."

As apologies went, this one was the most harebrained, if she said so herself.

Double damn.

Now it was Dmitry's turn to cough. Peter applied a couple of hard smacks against his father's back, but his squinting eyes were focused on Nika. Either she was delirious, or the former FBI Special agent Rostoff just cracked a smile.

For the first time that evening.

Yippee.

After a moment of screaming silence, Natasha made a decision. "Not sure about *Verochka*, but I'll take it as a compliment."

"Actually, it was meant as one, bad verbiage and poor delivery notwithstanding." Time to turn the tables. "And besides, what am I? A chopped liver?"

"In what context?"

"In your own. You said that *no one* wanted to stick with the...you two. Forgot about little curly me here, or don't short people count?"

"And that's my girl," *Verochka* declared, and blew Nika a kiss.

"Checkmate," Dmitry chuckled. "Got you there, *milaya*."

"Dear God, I am so sorry, Nika." Distress coated Natasha's voice like molasses poured over heavy cream. "So I did exclude you, didn't I? I didn't mean to, I swear. Of course, you are more than welcome to join us." A sudden grin flashed on her face. "By the way, I envy you your curls, not to mention, your petite size."

Nika almost snorted. Hard to imagine, since the woman had such gorgeous hair, and was just a breath taller than Nika, but... What the heck.

When the Queen apologizes, one must accept it, and be gracious about it.

Especially, after calling said Queen a hypocrite.

"No problem."

Is that your idea of gracious?

"Oh, and any time you wanna swap hair, let me know. I'll be more than happy."

Gosh, girl, you're just racking up major stupidity today!

But Natasha seemed to appreciate her sense of humor. With one of her most engaging smiles, she answered, "Deal," and sealed the truce.

"So, ladies," Natasha steepled her elegant fingers, "what'll it be, then? Spa or shopping?"

"I'm not sure about you, pal of mine, but I have all the shopping I can stomach for now," *Verochka* groaned. "So if you have no objections, why don't we have ourselves a day of pampering? Daisy-girl?"

"Anything but shopping." Nika casted her vote.

"So, spa it is," Natasha concluded. "And I just know the place—"

At that moment, an attractive brunette entered the room, interrupting Natasha in midsentence. Her nervous gait stopped a hair short from a run. Ms. Holms, Nika remembered from their earlier introductions, a twenty-first century version of Mrs. Smith in Louboutin and a sharp mannish suit.

"Mrs. Ro-rostoff?"

"Yes?" Both, Natasha and Kat answered in unison.

"There's a delivery, f-for Mrs. M-morris."

Struggling to conceal her bewilderment, the Rostoff's chief of staff kept her jaw clamed hard, but the slight tremors of her lips and her round eyes betrayed her shock.

"Oh, yes. That must be FedEx." *Verochka* unfolded her long fluid body from the chair. "I forgot, Natasha, I shipped all the Christmas presents by truck."

Dazed, Ms. Holms uttered something close to a moan. Poor woman. Nika clamped her lips together to suppress her smile. When her grandmother said *truck*, she meant exactly that, the whole vehicle. Obviously, no one save Nika and Alex was privy to that little secret.

Well, they'll discover it soon enough.

Hearing the magic word 'presents', both kids perked up.

"We can help." Nick jumped off his chair. "Right, Lana?"

"I suppose so." No less excited than her brother, the little girl still managed to maintain decorum. Barely. "May we be excused?" After permission was granted, both siblings streaked past the adults, giggling like maniacs. Already anticipating the outcome, Nika followed everyone out of the dining room.

"Holy Mother of God."

Dmitry Rostoff's soft exclamation—half-prayer, half-curse—reached her ears seconds before she rounded the corner to the hall, and stopped dead in her tracks.

The majestic Christmas tree with its crowning angel was barely visible. If before the room reminded Nika of a small but organized department store, now it resembled a Santa's workshop after a raid by an army of demented elves.

Chaos ruled. The silence was deafening. Someone hiccupped, then a helpless lone giggle tickled the air, and a chain reaction of laughter broke the floodgates. Nervous at first, then almost hysterical, the merriment grew and expanded like an avalanche. Soon people were bent over hugging their sides, or each other. The Rostoff siblings were running around like two energizer bunnies on steroids, singing their own version of Jingle Bells on the top of their lungs. Disturbed by that outlandish noise, the dogs, who until then were nowhere to be seen, ran in to investigate. Both hairy giants jumped right in the middle, barking like robbers were palming the jewelry, which only increased the general atmosphere of a mayhem. With great surprise Nika noticed the tiny body of prancing Maximillian. His earlier fear evaporated along with his manners as he frolicked and yapped between two mighty Shepherds, having a jolly good time.

And the creator of this chaos, her grandmother, stood aside, surveying that Hollywood scene with an expression of fake innocence. The wicked gleam in her eyes told a different story.

"I just know I forgot something, but..." She shrugged with nonchalance of a true Parisian. "Oh, well."

Wiping tears from his face, the Jewelry Emperor muttered something in Russian that brought another wave of hilarity from his wife.

"Only you, *Verochka*," he managed at last, struggling to catch his breath. "Only you, *dusha moya*."

CHAPTER THIRTY-EIGHT

To say it was the most unusual Christmas in Eli's life, was a significant underplay of the facts.

Not only was he in California, to where he *flew* on an airplane, he was in another century altogether. And who could boast celebrating Christmas sixty some years *after* his demise? Eli shook his head. Funny how fast he acclimated to the newness of his surroundings and the seemingly bizarre situation. But...

Somehow along the way, he stopped wondering, and accepted the truth. He was in the twenty-first century, where he journeyed to find Daisy and fetch her back to 1909. Back home, where both of them belonged.

He acknowledged that he and Daisy were meant to be together a long time ago. He also accepted the fact, not without some difficulty, there were things beyond the realm of human logic. And some of them, like love, was stronger than anything. Even time.

For a man of science like himself, pragmatic and realist, that was the hardest thing to take in. But who was he to argue with the Universe?

Every time he started to question his sanity, there was Daisy, with her amethyst eyes, sunny curls, and wicked smile. His heart always reminded him that even when his eyesight had deceived him at seeing the dirty, disheveled boy, it lurched to his throat and stopped his breath. He hated himself for his depravity, fought his urges like a man possessed, but he was powerless to overcome the hurricane of emotions every time he lay his eyes on the 'boy'.

Cursing God, and himself, he was about to accept the inevitable, when fate intervened. The pitiful street urchin transformed into Daisy, and saved his soul for all eternity.

Daisy, his timeless miracle, his lover. His future wife. His everything.

They were mismatched in every possible way, but their hearts beat in unison, and their souls were mated for life. Partners. Friends. Lovers.

They found each other through time and again, because they were meant to be.

She was the key to his destiny, as he was hers.

The key.

The old brass key from the grandfather clock he wore on a string around his neck lay against his heart. Such a small thing, ordinary, and quite unremarkable. But appearances were deceptive. Especially in this case. Eli palmed the key, ran his thumb along its edge. Was it his imagination, or did the key started pulsing like a living heart?

A reminder. A warning. Eli heeded both.

Soon. Just three more days, and they will tumble through time, going home.

And the Coleman house will welcome its new mistress, Daisy Margaret.

Despite himself, Eli smiled. Such a grand name for a wee thing like her. Then his smile slipped, as his thoughts turned to more troubling matters.

Something was going on with Daisy, and damned if he could figure out what. Distracted and often irritable, she acted rather strange lately like she was on the verge of tears one moment, and fighting hilarity the next. Her skin, always fair and pale, was now almost translucent. And she swooned the other day.

Thunderation.

Scared the bejesus out of him. But of course, as soon as she opened those unholy eyes of hers, she denied it until she was blue in the face.

The hardheaded wench.

But swooning she did. Her appetite was on a sharp decline, and she even stopped drinking her beloved coffee. When he pressed her, Daisy shrugged, claiming that Rostoff's coffee was too strong and fancy for her taste. Fancy he could believe, but strong? Rubbish. Her preferred strength of that distasteful beverage was that of black tar.

Always on the slim and delicate side, her body became almost gaunt. Only last night Eli was taken aback when he ran his fingers along her ribcage. Each bone was so prominent, he could easily count them all.

Damn it all to hell and back.

Had she fallen ill? But of course, his inquiry was a waste of breath. Daisy denied the notion with vehemence, and then laughed until tears sprang to her eyes. Then she kissed him, and Eli forgot everything, his own name included.

Most of the time, though, she was his old feisty Daisy, strong-willed, funny, opinionated. But something was amiss. What, then? Had she decided in favor of staying in her own time? Eli pondered that thought for a moment, but firmly rejected it. No, she was more impatient than he for this California trip to be over, and eager to get back home. Back to 1909 that is.

More than once he heard her grumbling that this journey was Abby's whimsey, an impermissible indulgence they shouldn't have agreed to in the first place. They were needed home, she said, as soon as possible. They must hurry. December 31st couldn't be here soon enough. So, if not for the decision to say in this century, what was troubling his little flower? Because something was, Eli was sure of it.

More than anything he wished Daisy would confide in him. She was the love of his life, and if something was wrong, he must know about it! Together they can overcome any obstacles, or fight any enemies, or—

"Eli, for crying out loud, what takes so long?"

And the love of his life, his little delicate flower flung the shower door open with the force of a lumberjack. Amused, Eli turned, unabashed at his nakedness, and smiled into her glaring eyes.

"Why, Daisy, have you decided to join me after all?"

"Bah. I know you, Coleman, and your indecent invitations."

"Why, *ma petite*, whatever do you mean?" All innocence, Eli faked the affront. "Tsk, tsk, such a dirty mind hides inside that beautiful head. I just wanted to save time and water."

"Ha, pull my other leg."

"I would be more than happy, not to mention privileged, to pull, spread, push, or—"

"Yeah, yeah. I got the picture. Seriously, Eli, do you know what time it is?"

"No, why don't you come closer, and tell me?"

"I can manage it from here, thank you all the same. It's almost five o'clock."

"So?"

"So? Have you forgotten Abby's exhibition? You know, your sister, Abby? Her very first big showing for which we traveled here from Florida? Remember?"

"Now that you mentioned it, it all slowly comes to me."

"Make it come faster!"

"That's not what you were asking of me last night, *ma petite*."

"Dammit, Eli! I'm serious!"

"Me, too. Oh, you mean, Abbigail's showing is tonight? Well, why didn't you say so!"

"For goodness' sake, Coleman..." Growling, glowering, Daisy advanced forward in an attempt to grab his arm. Instead, Eli grabbed her around her waist, and hauled her inside the shower stall. Mad as a wet hen, Daisy sputtered, thrashed, cursed, and made a racket loud enough to wake the people in Alaska. Eli managed to maintain a firm grip, and overcome her protests by the tried and approved method, he kissed her. She bit his lip, and tried to knee him in the groin. Eli pressed her against the shower wall, and continued to argue his case. He succeeded. Soon they were skin to skin, heart to heart, with her legs shackled around his hips like two vises. With their mouths fused together, their tongues began a battle for dominance. The music of moans, the fragrance of passion, the feast of flavors...

Not enough. Not nearly enough.

Hungry, greedy, mad for her, he surged forward, binding them into one entity.

Yes.

The pleasure was almost an agony. The heat became an inferno. Engulfed in flames, they raced each other to the fiery peak...

"We...we are going to be late."

Daisy's declaration was a mere whisper, but since she was sprawled on top of him, with her nose tucked under his ear, Eli had no trouble hearing it. They lay curled together on the floor, where they slid in boneless fashion, unable and unwilling to move. Half-dead after the earthshattering lovemaking, Eli had a revelation. He became quite enamored with the modern structure of a shower stall. Convenience notwithstanding, the advantage of joining ablutions was obvious. And rather rewarding.

As soon as we're back home, I will install a similar one in our bathroom.

How hard could that be? Some reinforced glass, some custom-made large tiles, some —

"Eli?"

"Hmm?"

The design he envisioned in his mind's eye was almost complete, when Daisy's voice accompanied by a slight nudge of her head against his chin, interrupted his musings.

"If we don't move soon, we're going to be late."

"Late... to where?"

"To Abby's showing."

"Oh. Thunderation."

"Well?"

"Well what?"

"Move, for goodness' sake. I can't find my legs, or my arms."

"Not to worry, *ma petite,* I'm pretty sure they are somewhere here, and still attached to you."

"If you say so. Can you get up?"

"I will make every possible effort."

Not as easy a task as he believed, but Eli managed to untangle himself from Daisy's limbs, and pull himself upright. Why was it so slick and slippery? Oh, the water was still gushing from above.

Weak as a kitten, but happy as a hot pig in mud, Eli cut the water off, and squinted at Daisy through the billowing mist. Sure enough, both of her legs and arms were still accounted for.

Oh, what a sight she was! Sopping wet, flushed, disheveled. And if he wasn't mistaken, rather pleased with herself.

The wench.

Since hauling her naked, delightful ass off to bed was not an option at the moment, Eli sent a silent order to his shaft to stay down, and stumbled out to fetch towels for both of them.

"Eli?"

"Yes, my love?"

"I wanted to tell you..." A small frown marred her forehead, but a dreamy smile fluttered on her swollen lips.

"What?"

"Oh, nothing."

And she busied herself with toweling. An alarm went off in his head.

"Daisy, what's wrong?"

"Nothing's wrong. On the contrary. Everything is terrific."

"Then tell me." He removed the towel from her, and stopped her actions. "Please."

She struggled for a moment, but then averted her eyes.

"I will, but not now, okay? We're really going to be late if we don't hurry."

He wanted to press her, to demand, to beg. He wanted nothing more than to drag that confession out of her right here and now. But...Abigail's exhibition was due to start in another hour. There was still the matter of dressing, and driving to the gallery. A special vehicle— *a limo* —would be downstairs in precisely thirty minutes. Daisy was right: they must hurry. Be late for your own party was quite different from being tardy for your sister's opening night.

Abby didn't deserve it. She was a walking wreck as it was. Besides, it was quite impolite and downright insulting to everybody. His own worry must be squelched for now, and Daisy's confession had to wait for a later time.

Thunderation.

CHAPTER THIRTY-NINE

The ride to the gallery progressed at snail speed, or so it seemed to Eli. Or was he just impatient for this event to be done with? And what kind of a brother did that make him? A lousy one, he concluded. But selfish bastard that he was, Eli wished for the evening to be over. Yes, he was very happy for Abigail, and yes, he was proud of her accomplishments. But still. He must get Daisy to tell him what was wrong. Or, according to her, what was so 'terrific' that causes her to act in such a peculiar manner. And it better be soon, because this uncertainty was driving him insane. *She* was driving him insane. Eli closed his eyes and counted to five. Slow and deliberate.

Must keep yourself under control.

What kind of a gentleman falls apart at a time of distress? Damn it. The longer he stays in this time, the softer he becomes. Many conveniences of this amazing century were so contagious, he stopped missing some elemental, basic things such as horse rides.

Sorry, Sultan.

The seduction of modern technology proved to be irresistible, and now he craved an automobile like a man possessed.

The morning paper was obsolete here, and he got into the habit of scrolling the news on a computer screen. Not to mention letters. No one in the twenty-first century wrote handwritten missives anymore, sending e-mails or texts instead. When was the last time *he* wrote a letter?

How about a hundred and eleven years ago?

Genteel. Eli Coleman was getting genteel in his advanced age, dammit all to hell and back. Soon he'd be acting like a damsel needing his smelling salts.

Thunderation.

He needed to get back to his time and place and forget all about cars, and computers, and televisions. Like it never happened. Like it was all a strange dream.

Best of luck with that, pal.

For as long as he lived, Eli will always remember this wondrous journey through time, and cherish the memories. But for the next three days he must remind himself of who he was, and where he came from, and act according to his status. And leave the smelling salts to ladies.

You mean, these ladies? Have you lost your mind?

He eyed the glamorous trio sitting across from him. Since younger Mrs. Rostoff and Abigail departed to the exhibit earlier, there were only *Verochka*, older Mrs. Rostoff, and Daisy. Exquisite, coifed and impeccably put together, they smelled like a spring meadow, and appeared as fragile and delicate as rose petals. Each one of them would put Joan of Arc to shame. Especially his dainty bride.

Three different destinies, three amazing women. Stunning, independent. Strong.

Smelling salts? Huh. How about swords and daggers?

But still. Deep down Eli was convinced that a woman— any woman— even a tough one like Daisy, or a daring one like his sister, needs a man, a home, and a family. First and foremost. So, call him a tyrant, or— what was Daisy's favorite? — oh, yes, a chauvinistic pig. He was a product of his time, and his thoughts were his own. And God help him if any of these three ladies were aware of them. Each would skin him alive.

Was he alone in his convictions, or did the men of this century shared them, too, but learned to hide it better?

Interesting.

Eli switched his gaze at his male counterparts, still pondering this dilemma. No less dashing in their evening attires, the gentlemen sat on his side of the limo. Even young Nickolas was clad in a suit and tie. If he wasn't mistaken, all of them, except the older Rostoff, were none too pleased with the choices of their clothing. Eli, used to the dressing code of his time of a three-piece suit and neckwear, was comfortable enough, but Alex, Peter, and especially Vic, showed signs of mild irritation since they started on their journey.

"Do you think Maximillian will be okay? I've never left him alone before."

"Don't worry, my dear. He'll be fine." Natasha assured Vic for the innumerable time. Lord, the woman had the patience of Jobe. By now Eli was ready to open the door of the limo, and throw the fidgeting Red out. "The girls will take good care of him."

The girls as in two Shepherds, Eli surmised. Enamored with the tiny dog, or vice versa, that canine trio was inseparable for the past couple of days.

But Vic refused to be pacified.

"That's what I'm afraid off."

Amused, Eli turned in time to catch Alex's frowning stare. This one was miserable for totally different reasons. Day or night, his regular preferred attire was shorts, t-shirts, and those ridiculous flip-flops that Eli considered rather indecent.

Now, dressed in a formal black suit, crisp white shirt and a bowtie, Alex was so out of his element, it was almost painful to watch. Despite his better intentions, Eli couldn't prevent a chuckle. Poor chap.

"Enjoying yourself, are you, Benjamin?"

"Well, I am. And if you'd stop squirming, and relax, so would you, Morris."

"Kiss my—"

Verochka's warning glare stopped whatever suggestion Alex was about to voice.

"No, thank you. Kissing any part of you, my friend, no matter how splendid you look, holds no appeal to me."

"Up yours."

Muttered under his breath, Alex's reply still reached his ears.

"In your dreams, pal of mine." And as the coup de grace, Eli patted Alex's knee.

"Glad you're back to your snooty, arrogant self, Benjamin. And here I was getting worried about you."

"Oh? And why is that?"

"Why? Because you were so quiet, I was afraid you lost your mojo."

"My... what?"

"Your irritatingly obnoxious confidence, pal. So, what gives?"

"Well, if you must know, I..." how to say it, without sounding like an imbecile? "I was... concerned."

"Really? Do tell."

"The truth is, it disturbed me that I might be getting... soft." *Idiot.* Put in words, this admission did ring like rubbish even to him.

"Soft? You?" Flabbergasted, Alex blinked a couple of times, then curved his lips into a wicked grin. "Oh, you mean, soft in the head. Yeah, I've noticed."

His smirking retort was like a glass of good whiskey, it punched one in the gut with heat, then jumped to the head with joyful cheer. With his spirits resurrected at last, Eli let go of the last remnants of his gloom.

Damn, but he would miss the man, bald head, sharp tongue, and all.

"Thanks, Morris. I needed that."

"Anytime, man. Anytime at all."

"We're here!"

Nicholas's exclamation brought Eli back to the moment. Along with everyone in the limo, he turned to a window. The first glimpse at the building was an astonishment of major proportions. What an interesting design! Made completely of glass and steel, the multi-layered structure hovered like a stack of cubes. As if put together by an architect who overindulged in his tipples, it leaned precariously over one side, jutting here and there.

The Rostoff Gallery, tucked in between the older traditional buildings, was like a peculiar child, vexing, baffling, but absolutely irresistible. More whimsical than odd, it was presently illuminated from within, like a dazzling beacon of magic in the middle of normal and ordinary.

Amazing. Simply amazing.

"Okay, ladies and gentlemen, let's enjoy some art."

Prompted by Dmitry Rostoff, the exodus began.

CHAPTER FORTY

The moment she was inside, Nika excused herself, and made a beeline for the bathroom. She was not avoiding Eli. Absolutely not. Just delaying the inevitable. Plus, she really needed to pee. All the excitement was finally catching up with her.

More than likely, all that water you guzzled.

Maybe. Probably. When Nika was nervous, she usually became thirsty. She supposed she should be grateful for that. With Alex it was hunger. When excited, he could eat Texas. Come to think of it, lately her cousin's appetite became enormous. So much so it became a subject of anecdotes.

I wonder what he's so nervous about. It's not like he's about to jump through a century, leaving behind his loved ones and his old life forever. And pregnant on top of it. The jerk.

Well, the pregnant part was a bit of an overkill, but the sentiment still stood.

A quick glance in a bathroom mirror didn't produce anything earthshattering. Same face, a bit paler than usual, and a tad peakier, but her own. She continued her inventory, same eyes, same nose, same everything. Even her darn curls, sticking out in every which way. Nika looked so unchanged, so her normal everyday self on the outside, it was impossible to believe that inside of her such a dramatic change was taking place. But it was.

Her hand crept to her stomach. Before her pregnancy was more of a *feeling*, now it became a proven fact. She was knocked up for sure, good and proper.

Even before their trip to California, there was a major sign she chalked up to stress.

Missing her period? Not a big deal. But her irregular cycle aside, all other freaky factors were harder to ignore. First, the smell. Her olfactory glands became so sensitive, some scents just knocked her sideways with a force of a tsunami.

Then, those strange episodes of weakness, when her head swirled, and her knees turned to water. And, as a coup de grace, her inability to stomach coffee.

That was the biggest pisser of them all, and a turning point. She must know for sure. But she was already in *Zolotoe Celo,* away from home and everything familiar.

How hard would it be to find the nearest pharmacy? Not really, but how to get there? They were in California, in this magnificent Rostoff castle, in the middle of the freaking compound. She needed a car. Borrow it from their generous hosts, or call a cab? And how would she explain it?

As fate would have it, on the day of their spa outing, *Verochka* and Natasha had to stop at some boutique to check a new perfume. Nika, unable to step inside of that paradise of fragrance, claimed a headache, and made a mad dash to the nearest CVS. But instead of Tylenol, she grabbed an early pregnancy test. As soon as they were back in *Zolotoe Celo*, she ran to the bathroom. A tiny pink stripe on the testing stick hit her like a sledgehammer in the solar plexus.

She was carrying Eli's baby. She was pregnant.

A tiny light, a new life, a new beginning.

Tears, her new unwelcomed companions, misted her eyes, and clogged her throat.

Dammit, not now. Nika bore down, fighting her emotions. They were so out of whack lately, it was quite disgusting. And humiliating. She will not become a walking fountain no matter what, so there.

Breathe, dammit, just breathe.

She closed her eyes, and counted to five. Then to ten. Okay, better.

More in control, Nika patted her middle, and washed her hands. What now?

And now, Nika-Daisy, you must tell Eli.

No way in hell. What if he's not happy?

Are you kidding, girl? You both know the baby's gender, her name, her date of birth, even her date of death, you imbecile!

"Oh, for goodness' sake, just shut up! Who asked you?"

Talking to yourself again, Nika.

Wincing, she darted her eyes around to make sure that she was still alone in the bathroom. The last thing she needed was to alert some poor art lover.

But no one ventured in while she was debating with her inner bitchy self. Good.

Nika threw the used paper towel in a wastebasket, and contemplated her next step. That was easy. Keep her mouth zipped, and pretend that nothing was out of ordinary. It was hard as hell! She was bursting from joy and excitement and fear. She longed to confide in Eli, to tell her grandmother, and her cousin. She was ready to scream on the top of her lungs to the whole wide world. She was pregnant for the first time!

And the last.

Margaret Vera Coleman would be the only offspring of this marriage. The baby conceived in 2020, and born in 1910. The same one who executed her father's last wish, and hired Nika to restore the Coleman house in 2019.

And if anyone aside from her family would be privy to that, she'd be a prime candidate to the padded room. Hard to cast a blame, since it all seemed too bizarre. But it was her reality, no matter how crazy it sounded.

Call her nuts, or a coward, but she wasn't telling Eli about the pregnancy until they were back home, safe and sound. Back in 1909 that is. Yes, they might both know all the facts, thanks to the amazing circumstances of their time traveling fate, but still.

No matter what time or century, or the damned circumstances, when a woman tells her man about her pregnancy, it's supposed to be a private and intimate occasion. And a happy one. To tell Eli now was a sure way to spoil the moment with worry about their upcoming journey. Or worse, prompt him to stay.

He already leaned toward it, and offered her this choice on several occasions.

Of course, he was excited and curious about all the technological advances of her time, but to stay for good? No way. As much as she was tempted, Nika was firm.

They must go back. He might not get it yet, but for them to stay was dangerous.

Abby's disappearance was one thing, and Nika still wasn't sure what consequences it might cause later on. But for Elijah B. Coleman to vanish into a thin air, and break the course of a history would be a disaster of major proportions.

Talk about butterfly effect!

So, here she was, hiding in the glitzy bathroom of the posh Rostoff Gallery, plotting the way to save history on the evening of Abby's first exhibition.

Time to go outside, and find the culprit of tonight's celebration. After all, tonight was all about Abby. Tomorrow...

Don't think about tomorrow. Don't think about anything but now. You have three days to enjoy your family, to make memories. So, make it count.

In three days, they will be home, in Fernandina Beach, and on New Year's Eve, she and Eli will return back where they belong, to the Coleman house circa1909.

And Nika Morris will became Daisy Coleman, once and forever.

CHAPTER FORTY-ONE

E li wasn't sure what shocked him more: the abundance of paintings, or the striking brunette holding court in the middle of the room.

My Lord...this is impossible.

Rendered mute by realization that all this art were created by his sister, Eli fell in a stupor. In the deafening silence his own ragged breathing thundered in his ears. When that striking brunette tore her gaze away from the man she was conversing with, and flashed him a dazzling smile, he lost his breath.

Abby.

That woman, that stunning beauty, was his baby sister!

The long column of her dress was both regal and sinuous. Or maybe it was the color of it, that deep wanton red the women of the oldest profession colored their lips with. Her smile, like her dress, was both sensual and classy, but at least it was aimed at him. Then she switched her bewitching eyes to the gentleman standing nearby. Shorter by a good foot, and older by a couple of decades, he gazed at Abby like she was his dream come true.

The cad! How dare he!

The desire to break that man's neck with his own two hands was almost irresistible.

Infuriated, Eli snatched a flute of Champagne from the passing waiter, and upended it in one gulp. Because his throat was too tight, the drink went the wrong way, but Eli was beyond caring. The hell with all the proprieties. His baby sister was in the middle of the huge crowd, panted over by every male in the vicinity.

Eli cursed under his breath, as yet another gentleman claimed Abby's attention. This one was older than Moses, but his wrinkled face assumed the same expression of absolute and total rapture.

Thunderation.

Coughing and sputtering, Eli fumed until he was ready to explode. Where was everyone? Where was Daisy, for crying out loud? Why has no one watched over Abigail? Someone administered a couple of whacks on his back, and stuck a napkin in his hand. Without acknowledging, or giving his thanks, Eli strode away.

Better than wringing someone's damned neck.

"Here you are." And *Verochka*, God bless her heart, saved him from further disgrace. Without leaving Eli any choice, she thrust her arm through his, and tugged him away. The woman was relentless, and fearless. Not too many a man would cross his path when Eli was angry. And right now, he was beyond anger: he was hopping mad.

"So, my dear, what do you think?"

Verochka's beatific smile didn't fool him for a second. Clever and sharp as a tack, she sensed that something was amiss.

"They out to be ashamed of themselves."

"What? Who?"

"All these gentlemen flocking Abby. That one is old enough to be her grandfather!"

"Oh, my dear boy," *Verochka's* laughter was like a balm, warm and soothing. "You are so darling. And so predictable." She patted his hand. "I was asking about paintings. What do you think about your sister's art?"

And she swept her incredible violet eyes around the room. Eli followed her gaze.

The paintings.

Pastels, sketches, oils; landscapes, seascapes, portraits...

The canvases surrounded him from all sides. They grabbed his attention, seduced his senses, pleased his eyes. Was it his imagination, or did he hear the music? Something bold and enchanting at the same time.

The phrase 'symphony of color' swirled in Eli's mind. That's it! Yes, Abby's art was music expressed in shades and hues. Staggering. Magnificent. Breathtaking.

Awestruck, Eli allowed *Verochka* to lead him from one painting to another.

All his senses heightened. His body tingled with an eerie energy. Goose bumps rioted along his skin, and the fine hairs on the back of his neck rose to attention. Then it struck him. All the pulsing energy came from the canvases.

He was absorbing it, like a lightning rod, until he was lit from within. And wasn't that the meaning of the art, to light hearts and souls?

"She's... incredible."

"Yes, she is."

"They sing. The paintings. Can you hear the music?"

"I—"

"What are you talking about, *mes amies*?"

An unfamiliar voice that interrupted *Verochka's* reply in a rude fashion, belonged to a female. Frowning, Eli turned, with a stern rebuff hovering on his lips, and lost his breath.

How many shocks can one man withstand through the course of one evening?

The thought flashed in his mind as the face of Botticelli's Venus swam in front of his eyes.

The woman was more striking than beautiful, with the liquid eyes the color of old gold and plum mouth painted in murderous red.

Sweet Lord, have merci.

Eli's heart skipped a bit. He loved Daisy with every drop of blood in him, but he was a human after all. This unexpected, astonishing beauty was almost more than any man could endure without falling to his knees, begging for mercy.

Her hair, a shade darker than her eyes, adorned her bare shoulders in a gleaming cascade. Tall and statuesque, she towered over six feet in her high heels, making them eye-to-eye. On a second glance, the fine lines around her eyes and mouth betrayed her age. She was older, but what did it matter? Eli's tongue and guts were tied in knots so tight it was almost painful. He was sure he was ogling, but damn if he could do anything to stop his embarrassment.

What a woman!

The Venus bestowed a knowing smile upon him, but addressed his companion, "*Verochka, ma cherie.*"

"Marie! Oh, finally! I was looking all over for you."

While the ladies hugged, and exchanged kisses on both cheeks in the European manner, Eli attempted to revive his damaged brain.

So, that was the famous Marie Dubois.

If Eli didn't know her true age, he would never have guessed it. Old enough to be his mother, she looked as vital and vibrant as any woman half her age. Thunderation, did these modern women discovered an elixir of eternal youth? *Verochka*, the older Mrs. Rostoff, and now this incredible French goddess.

"I was with our girl," the Goddess replied in a voice as potent as sin. Her Parisian accent only added to the impression. "And who is this handsome devil?"

"Oh, sorry. Marie, let me introduce you to Abby's brother, Eli Coleman. Eli, this is Marie Dubois, Abigail's mentor, and good friend."

Thank God, Eli managed to untangle his tongue in time for a coherent reply. "Madame, it's an honor, and true pleasure. I've heard so much about you."

Her offered hand was strong, long-fingered, and, when he bent to kiss it, smelled pleasantly of a mixture he was familiar with by now. A combination of fancy perfume and paint. Abby's hands carried the same fragrance. Oddly comforted by it, Eli cradled her hand in his, and curved his lips a genuine smile.

"Good things, I hope, *non*?"

"*Seulement des bonnes choses.* Only good things. But no one mentioned that Abby's mentor was such an astonishing beauty."

"Oh, *mon dieu,* a hottie speaking excellent French, and a charmer! I like him already, *Verochka.*"

"He's my granddaughter's fiancé, you shameless hussy, so behave."

"Such a pity." Arranging that unholy mouth in a pout, Marie feigned a frown, then let out a hearty chuckle that turned several heads in their direction. "But if you're talking about a pixie with curls like sunshine and eyes like violets, I can definitely understand."

"So, you've met our Nika?" *Verochka* switched to French.

"*Oui,* Abby introduced us, but she was calling her... Daisy, *non*?"

"Yes, that's what I called her as a baby, because she resembled a flower. And don't you know it, it's Eli's endearing name for her, too. What do you think, *ma cherie,* isn't she absolutely adorable?"

He doubted Daisy would agree. Even to him, *adorable* sounded more appropriate for a puppy, or a kitten, but not for his fearless time traveling Valkyrie of a bride. But only happy to leave a chatter to the ladies, Eli elected to keep his thoughts to himself.

"She does look like a flower, your adorable fiancé."

And switching back to English, Marie turned her golden eyes on him.

"Thank you, Madame, I think so, too."

"Aww, *mon ami*, you're blushing! So in love with her, are you not?"

Even though he was sure that so-called blushing was a trick of illumination in the room, Eli decided to concede.

"Madly and stupidly."

"*Bon pour vous!* It takes a real man to admit that." And the six-foot Goddess looped her arm around his waist, and bumped him with her hip. Glad he wasn't holding a drink, Eli froze. How to react? Move? Say something? And where, for goodness sakes, to put his arms? But, lo and behold, in the next moment Marie released him, and stepped aside. "So, tell me, Eli, how did you two meet?"

Better if she continued to manhandle him instead of asking questions. *Damn.*

He glances at *Verochka,* and realized no help was forthcoming from that direction. Daisy's grandmother was holding her breath, gazing at him with wide, imploring eyes. He was on his own. Well, what was the better answer than the truth? "She just seemed to drop from the sky, and stopped my heart."

"Aww, how romantic! I am a sucker for good old romance myself."

Verochka's exhale could be heard from the next room.

"So, when is the big day?"

"*Excusez-moi?*"

"The wedding, *mon ami*. The church, guests, vows, flowers?"

"Oh, yes, of course. The wedding." *Thunderation. Now what?* "Ah, we—"

"They haven't decided on the date yet." *Verochka*, God bless her heart, borrowed a page from his 'telling the truth' book just in time to save the moment.

"What the hurry?" Eli asked, struggling for nonchalance. "There's plenty of time."

Just three more days.

Eli and *Verochka* shared a brief glance full of unspoken regret.

"Is there?" Marie's curious eyes switched from Eli to *Verochka*. "I thought..."

"What?"

"Oh. *Non*, nothing. Of course, there's plenty of time between now and...then."

Then? What in the blue blazes does she mean by that? At a loss, Eli frowned.

But the Golden-eyed Goddess shrugged, and switched the subject.

"Well, *mon ami*, what do you think of your sister's art? Tell me."

"I'm not an art critic, Madame."

"Marie, please. Just tell me what first comes to mind."

"It's... incredible. Mindboggling."

"Couldn't have said it better myself."

"It simply defies description. Mere words are so inadequate. The energy, the force of it... just grabs you and holds you captive."

"Better and better. Are you sure you're not an art critic?"

Now it was his turn to shrug, and the heat creeping up his neck and face couldn't be attributed to the any light source. But he'd yet to figure out why was he so embarrassed. Maybe, because he wasn't used to revealing his innermost thoughts to anyone. Or maybe because he was still dealing with the shock. Or maybe because he was a dolt.

"Eli was telling me that he can hear music." *Verochka* added.

"*Oui*! That's exactly it!" Delighted, Marie grabbed his hands. "*Précisément!* She sings with her colors, *non*? I've met only one other artist who could do that, Kat Rostoff. I'm privileged to call both of them my protégées."

"They are both fortunate to have you as their mentor."

"Oh, absolutely. *Tout à fait.*" Marie's smoldering smile was as potent as his father's priceless single malt scotch. "Bet your fine American ass."

"And she's so classy, and modest, too, *non?*" *Verochka* laughed, but the French Goddess didn't take any offence.

"Modesty is highly overrated, *ma cherie*, and I never claimed to have class— just brains and beauty. Well, *mes amies*," closing the personal subject, Marie gazed at them in turn, "what do you say we go and congratulate our artist on her success? She deserves all the accolades, and then some. And Eli, if I may suggest?"

"Yes, Madame?"

"Marie, please. After all we've been through, I think it's time you start calling me Marie." The little devils danced in her golden eyes.

"Yes, Marie." Eli smiled, then chuckled. The woman was something, alright.

"Please tell your sister what you just told me. About her art. Tell her without hiding anything. She needs to hear it." Now her eyes weren't laughing, but censoring. "I'm not sure what happened between you— she didn't confide in me— but she was hurt, and still feeling insecure. So, *mon ami*, you must fix it. Now."

Bristling, and yes, dammit, ashamed, Eli drew the only weapon he had in his arsenal: a cold disdain. Raising his brow, he glared at the woman.

"Orders, Marie?"

She glared back, and almost made him squirm.

"*Non*, Eli. A mere suggestion." Then she disarmed him by cradling his face in the palm of her hand. "You are a man enough to do it. Please."

Brains and beauty, she said earlier. She forgot compassion.

Unbalanced, he took the hand still resting on his cheek, and brought it to his lips. After a brief moment, he let it go. "You ladies go ahead. I want to...peruse a bit more."

And without another word, Eli strode away. Maybe it was rude of him.

No maybe about it, sir. You were rude and unseemly.

He promised himself to apologize later, but for now he needed time to restore his equilibrium before facing Abby.

CHAPTER FORTY-TWO

Alex paced the floor, hands jammed in his pockets, blood boiling. He was way beyond mad: he was enraged. Seething, shaking, cursing, and itching to break something. Especially if it was expensive. He was primed for a good fight. The fact that he was mostly furious at himself didn't make a hellova lot of a difference.

You're behaving like an idiot. A jealous, stupid moron. A crazy person.

Crazy in love, dammit all to fucking hell and back. And whose fault was it?

Who showed up on his doorstep out of the freaking blue, and turned his life upside down? Who looked at him with those doe-like eyes, and called him *sir* in that snooty manner, and transformed his brains to mush? And who stole his breath, along with his stupid heart? Abigail Suzanne Coleman, that's who. And when he all but bent over backwards with an effort to hold himself in check, and act like her freaking older brother, what did she do? Nothing, that's what! Pretend that he was no more than a speck of dust on her canvas, or blob of paint on her brush.

Incorrigible snob!

And today, when he almost swallowed his tongue at the first glance at her, all dressed up and magnificent, how did she react? Ignored him all evening, like he wasn't even there, like he wasn't blown away by her art, and left speechless, helpless, and shattered.

Dear God, but what a gift she has! Astonishing. Staggering. Mind-blowing.

And while he ogled, desperate to pick up his pieces along with his sanity, she just stood there, all glorious and regal, and completely ignored him.

How dare she? Fawned over a crowd of overdressed, overstuffed, over-fucking- everything was one thing. After all, she couldn't help being ridiculously beautiful and talented. But enjoy that fawning? So unabashedly, so in-his-face deliberately? And flirting with some of those idiot peacocks? Oh, the Princess went too far. Way too damned far.

Way over the top. If she thought she can do that, and get away with it, she's better think again.

The uppity brat!

The fact that he was behaving like an overprotective fool enraged him even more.

He was not her brother, or father, or even some twice-removed uncle.

He had no rights, or claims on her. The hell he didn't! And besides, Eli asked him to act in his stead, and watch over her like she was his own sister. Only she wasn't. She was the woman he wanted more than he wanted to breathe, and she acted like she didn't know he was alive. He'd be damned if he let her get away with it.

And what would you do? Fall on your knee and declare your undying love?

Maybe. Probably. But what if she laughed in his face? Or worse, felt sorry for him? Dammit, that would be the ultimate humiliation. He'd never recover from that. He wasn't ready to risk the tentative friendship they shared, and destroy their current relationship, however unsatisfactory and maddening.

Fucking hell.

Fuming, Alex stormed the grounds of the posh Rostoff estate. It was after midnight, but the territory was illuminated throughout. Without any trouble, Alex navigated through the winding path of the rose gardens, pass the pool house, and plunged into the farthest corner, where the small gazebo nestled inside the protective canopies of centennials. When touring the estate earlier, he was told the family dabbed the whimsical white structure *Natasha's Gazebo*, because it was the favorite spot of the older Mrs. Rostoff. Invisible from the main house, surrounded by the magnificent trees and a small brook, it was a perfect hiding place, remote and secluded. And a perfect brooding spot, which suited his current mood just fine. Alex stopped, and surveyed the ethereal structure. He didn't pay much attention to it before, but now the illusion of intricate lace took him by surprise. Curious, he moved closer. Was it his imagination, or did the gazebo shimmered from within?

No, he didn't imagine it. The fragile, flickering light came from the lone lamp in the middle of the tiny table. Someone was inside.

Dammit, who else was restless, and beat him to this perfect secluded spot?

The silhouette of the person was shaded, so the identity of the intruder was vague. Cursing under his breath, Alex started to turn away, when the familiar voice with that unmistakable snooty accent called out, "And how long are you going to stay there, hiding?"

Should've known.

Who else but the Princess was brazen enough to wander the strange premises after midnight? No one was equipped better to spoil his solitary brooding but the one and only Abigail Suzanne Coleman.

Did she do that on purpose? He wouldn't be surprised. The woman was nothing but a thorn in his behind, dammit.

"I'm not hiding," Alex lied, and stepped inside the gazebo. Well, it wasn't a lie per se. He wasn't hiding, just avoiding company. Her company in particular. But...

Fate, you're sneaky bitch.

And here she was. Alex sucked in his breath, then cursed, helpless and defeated.

Tonight, in the gallery, the woman in a long red gown, a spectacular stranger with her elaborate updo hair and made-up face had knocked him down, and smashed him to pieces. The woman standing in front of him now was as different from that image as day and night. Dressed in some shapeless, colorless robe, with the river of mussed hair flowing down her back, scrubbed free of any cosmetics, Abby reminded him of a lost little girl, frightened and fragile. And now she all but destroyed him.

A quiet ache in his heart left him bereft.

"Princess—"

"I hate when you call me that!" She whirled around, but a glimpse of a lone tear running down her face caught his attention. Guilty, helpless, Alex swore.

"God, I'm so sorry, baby. I'll call you anything you want, just please don't cry."

"I'm not crying." The hitch in her voice, accompanied by a loud sniff, betrayed that statement. "And I'm not a baby! I'm a woman grown!"

"Of course, you're a woman." As if he needed any further proof of that after tonight. "Abby...Is that okay? Calling you Abby, I mean? Or do you prefer Abigail?"

"I prefer you stop treating me like a little snotty brat." Abby whipped away her tears, and sniffed again.

"Okay."

"And stop placating me."

"Okay."

"Okay? Is that all you have to say?" She glared at him, magnificent in her anger.

"Dammit, I'm afraid to say anything else and upset you even more."

"I'm not upset!" Quick as a lightning, she pivoted, both hands curled into fists. "Don't you see? I'm furious, and beside myself, and...God, so afraid." Her burst of anger evaporated as fast as it sparked. Pale and miserable, she closed her eyes. "I can't help it."

"My God, Abby, what's wrong?" If someone threatened her, or hurt her...Alex moved forward, then grabbed her by the shoulders. "What happened? Tell me. Tell me, goddamit!"

"Nothing!" Breathing fast, she threw up her arms, and dislodged his grip on her shoulders. "Absolutely nothing. I thought after tonight, everything will be clear. I will know exactly what do to next. But I am at a loss. Complete and utter loss. Can't you see that?"

All he could see that she was agitated, and scared, and mad as hell. Emotions he related to. But he was frustrated because of her. What was she so incensed about?

"I see you're excited, and confused. And sad. Why are you so sad, Abby?"

Undone, he wiped away the lone tear running down her face. God, how he wished to replace his fingers with his lips, and kiss that wet spot.

"Oh, Alex." At once, Abby lost all her fight, and collapsed onto a nearby settee.

To avoid the temptation of dragging her up and into his arms, Alex stuck both hands into the back pockets of his shorts. He was glad of the distance she put between them.

And if you repeated it long enough, you'd believe it. Or not.

"I don't know what to do."

"That makes two of us."

She lifted her tears-streaked face, and broke his heart.

Again. God, she was tearing him apart. The woman was a danger to his system. But Alex bore down on his rampaging desire, and took a seat on the opposite side of the gazebo. One touch, one small graze against her, and he'd explode.

"Abby…" Surprised how normal his voice sounded, Alex paused, then plunged ahead, "I'll do anything for you, fix any problem, but first I need to know what that problem is."

"The problem is in me, Alex. So, no one— not even you, who I consider my dear friend—is able to fix it but myself."

Dear friend, my ass.

"That maybe so, but if you tell me, I might have a suggestion. Like a dear *older* friend." The lopsided grin he managed to pull onto his face was almost painful.

"Older? Did you forget how old *I* am?" A wobbly smile curved her lips. "If anything, I could be your great-great-grandmother."

"Yeah, well. Since you are not, and according to your ID you just turned twenty-one, that makes me older by a decade. And I bet your age, no matter how advanced, in not the reason for your moping."

That was the right button to push. In an instant, Abby forgot all her blues, and glared at him in that insolent manner he was so familiar with. Regal. Snooty as hell.

Damn, do I know you, Princess, or what?

If he wasn't in love with her already, he'd fall hard and fast at that moment.

"Moping? I'll let you know, sir, that Abigail Suzanne Coleman never mopes!"

Yeah, that was exactly the thing to say, but grinning in her furious face was a mistake. Her smack on the shoulder was quite painful, considering the delicate hand it was administered with.

"Ouch."

"You're lucky I didn't box your ears."

"Sorry, sorry, my bad. You never mope." He lifted both palms up in mock surrender. "But seriously, Abby. What's bothering you? Your showing tonight was a smashing success. You sold almost everything, got so many orders, you'll need another decade to finish it all. You've blown away everybody, your brother included. That's a victory with a capital V. So, I repeat, what gives?"

"That's the problem." With a deep sigh, Abby averted her eyes. "You may think I'm silly—"

"Never. Snooty, conceited, stubborn, irritating, beautiful, but never silly."

"You really think so?"

"That you're snooty, and conceited—"

"That I am beautiful."

Her eyes...My God, was there anything more spellbinding than Abby's eyes? Almond shaped, tilted at the corners, they were the color of the rainy clouds pregnant with storm. Or the ocean brewing with hurricane.

And you are about to drown in their depth.

With an effort, he shook himself off, and managed a feeble chuckle.

"Are you fishing for a compliment, by any chance?"

"No, I..." She shrugged. "Never you mind."

"You are the most beautiful woman I've ever met in my life." He was ready to bit his tongue the moment those words jumped out of his mouth. What on earth possessed him to say that? Calling himself a thousand different names for an idiot, Alex managed to hold her gaze. A moment stretched.

"You have a funny way of showing it."

She broke the silence, and kept her eyes focused on his, like she was searching for some answers. God, what did she want from him?

"W-what?"

"Nothing. So, I'm snooty, and stubborn, but not silly?" She tilted her head.

"You forgot conceited and irritating. And beautiful."

Dammit all to hell and back.

Abby rose from the settee, and strode away. Pensive, she gazed into the darkness.

"If you want to know the truth, I feel incredibly lost. Even more than before, when I first came to this time. Then I had a clear purpose: to reach my dream, to paint, and make people recognize and admire my art. But tonight, when my goal was achieved, when people admired and praised my art, when my mentor finally called me an artist, I felt so...disenchanted. Instead of happy, I'm hollowed out. Instead of celebrating, I feel like mourning. If not silly, what it is then?"

"It's a postpartum depression. Well, sort of. You know, when a woman gives birth to a baby she carried inside of her for nine month? Some can't cope with the strain after separation. It's actually quite common, and not silly at all. And you are not alone. Many writers, musicians, and artists experience this phenomenon."

Her expression held doubt, but at least she was looking at him. Inspired, Alex plunged ahead, "It's like an abandonment, or...or some kind of a betrayal, if you wish. Of course, I'm not a creative person by any stretch of imagination, but I think I get it. It's nothing to be afraid, or ashamed of."

She absorbed his every word like her life depended on it. The absolute trust on her face made him uncomfortable, and delirious at the same time.

How he wished she looked at him with ecstasy, or passion instead of rapture. Goddamit, he was just a man, not a deity.

Frustrated all over again, Alex rubbed his bald head with both hands. Dammit, will she say something? When his patience all but ran out, Abby's quiet voice reached his ears.

"Of all the people, only you understand me completely. Only you always say the right words, and find ways to make me feel good. You make me feel whole, Alex, and worthy, and...beautiful. I don't know how I will cope without you."

Lightheaded, Alex gazed at her in wonder, when her last words knifed through the haze of his euphoria.

"You don't have to. I'm always here for you."

"But what will I do without you in California?"

"California? Why California? What are you talking about?"

"Kat Rostoff offered me a position at her art school. You see, I'm not going back to France. Marie informed me that I don't need her mentoring anymore. So, I must decide what to do next."

A claw of panic grabbed him by the throat.

"What's there to decide? You're coming home to Florida with me."

"To do what?"

"Live, paint, enjoy life. It's not like you're hurting for money, and need to work."

"No, but I need to find myself in order to live, and paint, and enjoy life."

"Why can't you find yourself in Amelia Island?" Jesus, he wanted to shake her. Definitely wrong to do to someone you love, but his fist through a wall seemed like a great idea. Two deep breaths and logic took control. "You can open your own school."

"And I've been thinking about that, but I need to make sure that I'm ready. And for that, I need experience to work with children."

"Abby," he was running out of arguments, and cold sweat of fear was pooling down his back. "What about family?"

"What about it? Half of my family will be so far away, come New Year's Eve, I won't see them again, except in my heart and my dreams. *Verochka* is always traveling abroad, so—"

"What about me?"

"You?"

"Yes, me. You know, the dear older friend who always says the right things, and understands you completely?"

She averted her eyes.

"You have your own life, Alex. You need to start a family of your own, you need—"

"Oh, don't you tell me what I need, Princess! You have no idea."

"Why don't you tell me, then?"

I need you! Only you!

But it was selfish of him to speak of his feelings right now. She was young, talented, and vibrant, with the whole world laying at her feet. She was just starting her life journey, testing her wings. Did he have any right to impede that journey? Or clip those fragile wings by tying her up with the family he craved to build with her? She was barely twenty-one, while he had stepped over the line of his big three-o a few months back. No matter what a selfish bastard he was, he couldn't do that to her. He loved her too much for that.

So, he must let her go. Even if it killed him.

But just for a few years, I swear. Goddamit all to hell and back.

The first step away was the hardest.

"You're right, Abby. It's not about me. You must do what's right for you."

Enough was enough.

Get out of here. Now.

Alex turned toward the entrance, but Abby grabbed his arm.

"Alex, wait. You didn't tell me what is it *you* need."

"Right now I need some sleep, and so do you. It was a long and eventful day."

"Alex, please, don't go like that. Tell me what to do: stay in California, or go back to Florida? Please, I need your advice. I'll do whatever you say."

Was it panic, or desperation in her voice? With the last look at her beseeching face, Alex freed his arm from her clutch, and shook his head. Whatever it was, she must deal with it, and come to her own decision.

"Oh, no, Princess. I'm afraid you're on your own. And, by the way, isn't it what your brother did, once upon a time, decided for you on every aspect of your life? And isn't is why you ran away, jumping through time, in order to be free? So, no. I'm not deciding for you. You must make your own choice, Abby. But I promise to honor it, and be there for you no matter what. Always."

Her shattered expression hunted him all the way to his room. Of course it was right to leave the final decision to her. Right and honorable and justified. But, dammit, why did it make him feel like Judas?

Honorable my ass.

Miserable, Alex splashed vodka into a glass, and upended it in a couple of gulps. The burning in his throat was nothing compared to the scorching in his gut.

Idiot, moron! You just destroyed the relationship that meant everything to you!

No, not destroyed. Just soured it, and delayed the happy-ever-after. He was too determined to build his future with Abby to let her run amok for longer than a couple of years. Three tops. When she was twenty-four, he will find her, wherever she might be, and then he'll lay siege.

Dear older friend, my butt.

Anesthetized by alcohol, Alex grunted, then splashed another generous portion into his glass. Drinking wasn't his forte, and he'd suffer for it tomorrow, but what the hell? Right now it was exactly what he needed.

Another glass of vodka made him question the wisdom of his aversion to this marvelous fiery liquid. And to think that he preferred beer.

Idiot.

Sleep was creeping up, making him fuzzy and disoriented. Drunk. He was stinking drunk, but not hurting anymore. Fully dressed, Alex dropped onto the bed.

Must forget about her for a few hours. Must get some sleep. Tomorrow promised to be a doozy. *Princess will be mad. Oh, well. Better mad at me now, than hate me later.*

CHAPTER FORTY-THREE

A more depressing and miserable affair than the journey back home was hard to imagine. The same spectacular Rostoff's plane, the same magnificent spread of snacks and drinks, but Nika and her fellow companions paid no attention to anything. The dazzling luxury was lost on the passengers, as on the morning of December 30th they entered the plane and took their seats.

By the silent agreement, they spread around, occupying different corners, which suited Nika just fine. Eli chose to sit closer to the pilot's door; Alex, whose thunderous expression forbade any conversation, brooded in the opposite corner.

She dropped into a leather chair in the middle, and ignored both of them.

Inside the luxurious cabin the atmosphere was somber and subdued. The only smiley faces belonged to the crew, but their initial efforts to engage the passengers into some small talk turned out to be useless. After a while, even the most accomodating flight attendant left them alone.

A sudden memory of their flight to California flashed in Nika's mind, and a tight fist of grief squeezed around her heart. The difference was staggering. Then it was a happy, merry gang of six people and a tiny dog. Music bleared, conversation flew, Maximillian yapped and sniffed at every corner. They all laughed, and joked, gorged on the generous spread of goodies, and drank a lot of champagne.

Today it was a gloomy party of three: Alex, Eli, and her. The silence in the passenger's cabin was oppressive. All the food sat untouched, a bottle of *Dom Perignon* swam in a pool of thawed ice. No one smiled.

One hour into the flight, and Nika was ready to tear her hair out. Better than to start screaming, she supposed, because once started, she wasn't sure she could stop anytime soon. The mix of impotent rage and fear still bubbled inside.

She wasn't sure how long it would take to flash over the boiling point. And then she would explode.

You're courting a full-blown panic attack, my girl.

Her inner 'I', that nosy, know-it-all bitch was surprisingly absent until now. Glad she finally decided to make an appearance, Nika gritted her teeth, and went on the offensive.

So what? Can you blame me? My family, my sanctuary and stronghold I relied upon, has crumbled in a matter of twenty-four hours.

But her inner bitch was unimpressed.

Don't be a drama queen, Nika. It's not crumbled, just—

Seething, Nika bumped her fist against the armrest of a seat.

Just what? What, dammit?

After a long moment of silence, the quiet voice inside of her delivered the answer, *Changed.*

Yes, everything had changed starting with Abby's staggering announcement at dinner yesterday that she was relocating to San Francisco and taking on a teaching position at Kat's art school. Nika was floored. Blindsided, she gazed at Abby in total confusion. Dammit, she loved the girl like a sister. Heck, they were more than sisters: they were best pals, and confidants, and time-traveling companions. They went through hell and back together, shared everything but clothes, and only because of their different body types. They were family in every sense of the word. And now, just before Nika and Eli's ultimate departure, Abby decided to stay in California instead of spending the last two precious days together. Nika's heart was breaking.

Traitor.

Since most of Abby's possessions were already in *Zolotoe Celo*, there was no point for her to return to Florida. Therefore, she chose to stay in Rostoff manor.

The only one who wasn't surprised by Abby's decision was Alex, who accepted her news with a sardonic little smile, and a curt nod. But his eyes held such sadness that Nika was forced to turn away.

Following that tune, Vic announced his acceptance of an invitation to spend the New Year's Eve in San Francisco. Nika's accusing *'Et tu, Brut?'* glare was lost on her flamboyant friend. Overjoyed, Vic paid no attention to anyone, except his new idol, Natasha. If Nika wasn't positive of Vic's orientation, she'd think that he suddenly developed a passionate crush on the older woman.

His return was pushed to the first week in January. Or so he claimed. But Nika suspected that Vic wasn't coming back to Amelia Island. Ever.

Enamored with the ambiance of San Francisco, he'd taken to the local scene with a glorious abandon. Whether Vic realized it or not, the decision to relocate was formed in his mind as soon as he stepped foot onto California soil. He'd return only to pack his bags, and close his practice.

Alex must find another attorney. Oh, well.

She shook her head. Way too many changes. A twinge of guilt popped through her. She should be happy for Abby and Vic: they found their dreams, their purposes. But God, couldn't they wait another two days? Dammit, it was so unfair. Was it selfish of her? Maybe. Was she acting like a spoiled brat? Probably. So, what? She was about to disappear forever. Was two freaking days too much to ask for?

Nika squirmed, and tried to adjust her body into a more comfortable position. Despite the plush cushions of the chair, she was restless, and couldn't settle down.

Cranky, my girl. You're cranky as a two-year-old pass their bedtime.

She was well beyond cranky. Pissed and hurt and insulted, that's what she was.

Two people she loved and considered best friends abandoned her at the eleventh hour before her ultimate journey. But even that was not the worst.

The real bombshell was dropped this morning by her beloved grandmother.

Verochka's bags were packed, and delivered downstairs, along with everybody's, but instead of a limo, she instructed them to put everything into the truck of a white Mercedes idling nearby. Then she turned to her family with a strained smile on her face.

"I'm not going back to Fernandina, my dears. Late last night I have decided to change plans, and travel to North Sentinel Island instead."

Rendered mute, Nika stared at her grandmother. Her hearing must've been playing some tricks, or else... A following silence was thick enough to cut with the knife.

"Is this a joke, Gorgeous? Because if it is, no one is laughing."

"No, not a joke, Alex. Sorry. I always wanted to visit there, and now seems like a perfect time."

A...a perfect time? Was she kidding?

Her own voice when Nika found it at last, was close to a croak, *"Are you serious?"*

"Absolutely, sweetie." *Verochka's overindulgent, dazzling smile set Nika's teeth on edge.* "You have your own plans, and soon will be traveling far away with your future husband; Alex has his business he needs to get back to. Abby is settled here for now, so..." *That typical Gaelic shrug Nika admired and loved so much now irritated the crap out of her. Tears clouded her vision, but she blinked them away. Damn if she was going to cry.*

Must stay strong, must not fall apart...Oh, the hell with it!

She was never so scared *in her life, not even when she found herself in a middle of the dirty road with the huge black stallion thundering toward her. She never felt so abandoned, not even when she realized that she was transported to 1909, alone and penniless, amongst the strangers who mistook her for a boy.*

No way her grandmother was deserting her now. No way she was leaving Nika alone before her final journey.

Oh, God, please, don't do this to me!

Ready to beg, Nika shrugged off Eli's hand on her shoulder, and broke free of Alex's embrace. She didn't realize they both were holding her.

"Verochka, *please—*"

"Okay, everybody, let's not make our drivers wait."

And, brisk and frighteningly cool, her grandmother started issuing orders right and left, like the commander in chief of this bizarre parade.

Verochka *ignored me!*

She just turned her back, and disregarded Nika like she wasn't even there.

Dumfounded, Nika followed her grandmother with her eyes.

What the hell was going on?

The impression of being stuck in a nightmare, or some weird, surreal play, was overwhelming. Another moment, and she'd waken, and everybody would laugh, and yell: Gotch ya!

But no one was laughing, and this nightmare went on and on, until she was tucked in the Rostoff limo between Eli and Alex, and speeding off to the airport.

If Abby and Vic's decisions cut deep, *Verochka's* ambush almost destroyed her. Nika read once that the saddest thing about betrayal was that it never came from your enemies. No truer words.

Undone, Nika closed her eyes and leaned back into the soft leather chair. God, she was tired. Like marrow deep. The emotional turmoil of the last hours had finally caught up with her, and the last barrier of her resistance was smashed by the flood of recent memories. Nika was still reeling from shock two hours later.

Verochka's sudden decision to travel to some remote island in the middle of the Indian ocean instead of coming back to Florida knocked the wind out of Nika's sails. To say that it was unexpected wasn't saying any-fucking-thing.

Yes, her globetrotter of a grandmother was famous for her traveling adventures, and never spent longer than a few weeks at the same spot. Yes, last year was an anomaly for her, and so it was for Nika, and everybody in the family.

They all had such a challenging year, starting with Nika's disappearance, and ending with Eli's arrival. The last fourteen months was a trial by fire for all. They coped in their own way. They all survived, and each and every one of them ended up a victor. And now, when this unbelievable year was about to come to its conclusion, *Verochka* spoiled everything. Sure, she adjusted her lifestyle for Abby's sake last year. But for her own granddaughter? Oh, no! She couldn't wait another day to travel to some godforsaken island in the middle of nowhere! Dammit, that was so unfair!

Fuming, Nika wished she could turn back the clock to morning.

Instead of standing there like a mummy, she'd rave and scream at *Verochka*: how can you do this to me? You of all people! Can't you give me two days? Just two fucking days, for goodness' sake! Is this too much to ask?

But the only clock that turned back time was in Fernandina Beach, in the Coleman house, and it worked only in between a specific timeframe.

Instead of raving and screaming this morning, she glared at her grandmother in total silence. Did she kiss her? Did she say she loved her?

No, you idiot, you did not. Barely hugged her goodbye, so busy feeling sorry for yourself, wallowing in your misery.

Oh, God, what have I done? What have we both done?

She grabbed her phone to call *Verochka*, but something stopped her. What can she say? Apologize? Too little too late.

Maybe, it's better that way.

Her goodbye letters will be delivered and emailed per her instructions on January 1st to each member of her family. She agonized over every word, and poured her heart and soul into those letters. *Verochka* will get hers, and understand, and forgive.

What about you? Will you understand and forgive?

Afraid that she was on the verge of a major meltdown, Nika closed her eyes, and reminded herself that stress was bad for the baby. She must hold it together for the sake of a tiny life she carried.

I didn't tell Verochka *about the baby.*

Guilt and sorrow pressed on her soul. She checked her phone. Four more hours until landing. God, how will she bear it?

"Excuse me, Ms. Morris?"

With an effort, Nika focused her gaze on the uniformed woman in front of her. The flight attendant held out a folded page of paper to Nika. "There's a letter for you that came via onboard email. Mr. Rostoff instructed the captain to print it out and give it to you."

"For me?"

"Yes, Ma'am."

What on earth? Confused, Nika accepted the folded page.

"Anything I can get you? Coffee? Water? Juice?"

"What? Oh, no, thank you." Without looking up at the woman, Nika shook her head, and opened the letter. As soon as she read the first line, tears she fought all day won the battle of wills.

Alerted by her loud intake of breath, both Eli and Alex turned in her direction, but Nika brought her hand palm up in a silent demand for solitude.

After a moment, she braced herself, and opened the letter again.

My dearest girl,

First of all, I need to ask your forgiveness for my preposterous stunt.

It would probably be best if I just left everything like it is, without explanation, but God help me, I can't. When I looked at you this morning, I almost heard your thoughts: "How can you do this to me? Can't you just wait a couple of days?"

I could feel your pain, and now I have to live the rest of my life, knowing that I caused it. Please, please Nika, forgive this old, selfish lady. My only excuse is that I love you too much.

Oh, Verochka! It's me that has to beg your forgiveness.
Tears rolled down her face, but Nika ignored them and continued to read.

By now, you are probably over your shock, and just feeling hurt, and sad. I am so sorry, Nika, but I can't bear it, I must tell you the truth.

I left because I was afraid. No, terrified. Because I cannot imagine letting you go.

How can I say goodbye, knowing that I never see you again? I just can't, Nika. I'm so sorry, sweetheart. I thought I was prepared for this, that I was ready. Oh, what a fool I was! Darling, if I'd gone to Florida, I would never let you go. And that's the truth. I'd do something stupid, like stealing the clock's key and throwing it in the ocean, or something criminal, like burning to the ground that spectacular house you renovated in order to close that damned portal forever. I'm not kidding. I even googled 'arson'.

Nika chuckled through the mist of tears. *Googled 'arson', for goodness' sake!* Oh, she could believe it.

When I realized it, I became scared, and ashamed of myself. I never knew I could be so selfish, so ruthless. Or so weak. You know how I hate weakness. There is nothing more disgusting that a weak female. Well, maybe a bald man who's trying to cover his naked dome with a toupee.

Verochka, *I simply adore you.*

So, as a punishment for my wicked ways, and yes, to be on a safe side, I've decided to remove myself from the scene completely.

I hate to ruin your long-awaited journey home by the memories of a crying, clinging, and cursing grandmother. And you know my repertoire of curses: it's as colorful as it's infinite.

I'm trying to make you smile, my precious. Did I succeed? I truly hope so.

Nika smiled despite the hollow pain under her left breastbone. Her classy grandmother could—and had on many occasions—let out a string of curses that made the Twins, Nika's father and uncle, cringe and blush. Oh, the precious and bittersweet memories!

She'd cherish them forever. Holding the letter in her shaky hands, Nika took a deep fortifying breath, and read on.

> Please, don't stay mad at me for long, Daisy-girl. You know I love all my grandchildren, but you were always special to me. You hold my heart on the palm of your hand, and always will be. I'll miss you to my very last day. And my only regret is that I will never see that baby you're carrying, and have a chance to spoil her. Yes, I know you're pregnant. Marie is not the only one who noticed your near fainting episode at the gallery, and put two and two together. Kiss that precious baby for me when she's born, promise?

Dammit, how could she be so naïve? If Abby's mentor realized the truth after one brief glance, why did she think that *Verochka* was clueless?

You are a moron, Nika-Daisy.

Of course, her grandmother knew. And never even hinted at it. Oh, God. If guilt had a physical weight, Nika would be buried under the rubble of it by now.

I'm so sorry, Verochka!

There was just one paragraph left in the letter. Reluctant to finish that last epistolary conversation with her grandmother, Nika closed her eyes. After a long moment, she lifted the precious page again.

> Oh, I'm so happy for you, my girl, and for that gorgeous hunk you're marrying. Eli is the best man I've met after your grandfather. Give him my love, will you? Tell him he's one lucky SOB. Hell, you both are

extremely lucky! I hope one day, when you both are older, you will realize just *how* lucky.

Take care of yourself, Daisy-girl, and take care of your new family.

And If I may give you one last advice, woman-to-woman? Learn to compromise. Love, honesty, and compromise—that triumvirate is the real secret to every happy marriage. You have the first two ingredients in abundance, now try to add the third one. I know you can do it, babe. My money is on you.

Bon voyage, my precious.

I love you,

Verochka.

Nika's tears dried, and the enormous weight of guilt was lifted from her soul. And the world turned right side up again.

Nika smiled, kissed the letter, and tucked it into her shirt pocket. As soon as she was back home, she'd put the letter it into a Ziploc bag like she had with Eli's letter. This precious page will be traveling with her back to her new home, and the butterfly effect be damned. After all, Nika was entitled to a single treasure, a memento from her previous life to take with her, wasn't she?

Fortified with that thought, Nika closed her eyes, and leaned her head against the chair's headrest. Her grandmother's face swam in her mind; her voice echoed in Nika's ears.

Bon voyage, my precious. I love you.

No, her grandmother didn't abandon her. She just couldn't face the farewell.

"I love you too, *Verochka*."

Nika opened her eyes. Did she doze off? Huh. How long was she lost in a slumber? She dragged both hands through her hair, checked the time. Almost an hour. Wow. Her dreamless nap left her if not invigorated, but settled. Still sad, but not hurting anymore, Nika smiled, at peace for the first time that day. Languid, almost weightless, she closed her eyes again. A murmur of a nearby conversation reached her ears. Alex and Eli. What were they talking about?

Curious, Nika strained her ears, squinted, and focused her attention on her favorite duo. Alex's voice, soft but grave, matched the expression on his face.

"... afraid I won't be able to make good on my promise."

"What promise is that?"

"You know, to stand in your stead like a brother to Abby."

Interesting.

"And why is that?"

"Because I'm in love with her. I don't know how that happened." Alex heaved a sigh, and rubbed his head. "But I know I can't live without her. It irritates the hell out of me. It's totally crazy, and foolish, and doesn't make any sense. But I love her. End of story. Hence, I can't in good conscience act as her brother."

"Hmm. And what are your intentions toward my sister, Morris?"

"I intend to marry her."

Hot damn, Cuz.

A little butt wiggle while sitting in a chair was a poor substitute for a boogie, but the moment was wrong to jump up and cheer. Besides she was too curious to hear the rest.

Come on, Eli.

"Are you asking for my permission, perchance?"

Yeah, right. She almost snorted, but caught herself in time.

"No, I'm not. No offense, Benjamin, but I don't need your permission. I'm going to marry the Princess no matter what. What I'd rather have is your blessing. It would mean a great deal to me. But I'm telling you frankly, I'm going to marry her with or without your blessing."

"Well, thunderation."

Eli cast his eyes downward, then gazed at her cousin. Nika held her breath.

"Blessing, huh? Well, you have it, Alex. I'm proud to welcome you into the Coleman family." He offered his hand, which Alex accepted.

"Thank you, Eli. I'm honored to be a part of it."

"Do you realize that you just called me by my given name?"

"Yeah, well, you started it: you called me Alex."

"Huh."

"Yeah."

Eli mulled that for a moment. "Does that mean, I stopped irritating you?"

"In your dreams, buddy."

"Just what I thought."

They looked at each other for a moment, both intent and serious, then Alex cracked a smile and delivered a joking punch on Eli's shoulder. Her soon-to-be-husband raised his brow, and answered in turn.

God, was it any wonder she was crazy about them?

Unable to hold still, Nika jumped from her seat, and plopped in between Alex and Eli. With such a snug fit, they were all but glued together, hip to hip, but no one complained. Almost in unison, her bellowed travel companions covered each of her hands. Nika linked their fingers.

Connected. Complete. Content.

With a deep sigh, she leaned back and closed her eyes.

Verochka's letter won't be the only treasure she'd take with her on her journey back in time. This precious moment was yet another one.

CHAPTER FORTY-FOUR

The last day of the year 2020 promised to be clear, sunny, and beautiful. A forecast predicted upper seventies, a perfect weather to roll in a New Year Fernandina style: with all the locals and tourists gathered on Centre Street, cheering, dancing, and enjoying the party. There will be, as always, a lot of music, food and adult beverages, but rarely, if ever, any disorder, or trouble.

The natives of this small, old-fashioned island, even though descendants from badass fishermen and ruthless pirates, took pride in law and order, and frown upon any display of mischief, like destruction of the property, drunkenness, or any disturbance of the town peace. Any major event was taken seriously, planned meticulously, and celebrated with an abandon, like one big and loud family.

And boy, could they party!

New Year's Eve was one heck of an event: the biggest, most anticipated, and clamorous celebration of them all. Nika and Alex participated all nine years they'd been calling Amelia Island home. Last year, Abby and *Verochka* joined them, and they all partied well into the morning, starting in the Palace Saloon in downtown, and ending up on the beach near their home.

The memories of that day— her classy grandmother dancing barefoot in a sand, Abby, a little tipsy, laughing like a loon, and Alex doing his best rendition of *Auld Lang Syne*—were etched into her soul forever.

Another treasure to cherish. Another precious memento to keep.

Nika blinked a couple of times, and turned away from the window. She glanced around, disoriented, like coming out of a trance.

Damn, daydreaming again.

How long had she stood there, staring out, without seeing anything? Her eyes flew to the clock on the wall. God, it was almost afternoon. Where did the time go?

Time.

She had such a limited supply of this precious commodity left—well, in this century that is—that she'd better hurry if she wanted everything to be ready for dinner. They planned to have a quiet dinner at home, just the three of them, and after join the crowd in downtown for fun and drinks. And then...

No, she refused to think about *then*, not yet. There was plenty of time.

First, she needed to make sure that everything was ready for their last dinner together.

The last dinner.

It sounded almost as dire as The Last Supper. Damn it.

To pull herself off the ominous thoughts, Nika concentrated on her to-do list.

A traditional New Year's Olivier Salad was all chopped up and mixed; the baby ribs Alex was so fond of were ready for the oven; a bottle of champagne was chilling. All silverware was polished, and their best china was set on the table. Everything was ready. There was nothing more for her to do but wait. She hated waiting almost as much as she hated crying. Maybe even more so.

She scanned the room. The Christmas tree they traditionally kept until New Year's Day suddenly seemed out of the place, all sad and forlorn. Alex will be taking it down by himself this year. Poor Alex, he'd be living in this huge house all alone, and running the company single-handedly. No doubt he'd take good care of both, but who will take care of him? Remind him to eat, and take his vitamins, and drag him for a walk on the beach, and—

Damn, she was close to tears again.

Not gonna happen. No way.

Alex was a big boy, responsible, independent. He'll do fine. But, God, after tonight she'd never see him again!

Nika closed her eyes, and took several slow, calming breaths. Some pep talk was in order, but where was that argumentative inner bitch when you needed her?

Like a genie, a little voice popped into her head.

Get a grip, Nika-Daisy. It's a day for happiness, for ushering New Year, new life.

But instead of cheering her up, it produced the opposite effect.

"New life? How about a new name, new home, new *everything*?"

Isn't it what you wanted? For fourteen months you longed for this moment.

"Yes, but...what am I going to do there? Be a wife and a mother?"

Isn't that enough?

"Not for me it isn't."

You'll think of something.

"What if I don't?" A sudden panic clawed its way up from her belly, clogging her throat.

Well, there is always an alternative. You can both stay. Eli offered you that choice.

Oh, she was tempted. So tempted! Wouldn't it be wonderful to stay here with Eli, to make their life here, in her time? Yes, wonderful, and simpler, and easier, and—

And that would be just wrong.

Nika plopped onto the sofa and covered her face with both hands. No, she couldn't ask of him to sacrifice his life in order to make hers easier and simpler. There were so many people whose lives would be forever altered—if not destroyed—if she chose the easy way. Mrs. Smith, and Abby, and Senator Lauder, and her baby...And the thousands of workers of Coleman enterprises. What about them, if Eli disappeared from 1909?

And what about the hospital, where Abby was taken with COVID and survived that long, excruciating battle? The same hospital her brother built and donated to the city in 1911.

To ask him to stay and change the course of history was not only wrong, it was selfish, and cruel. And dishonorable. There was no way to forgive herself, and live happily ever after.

Well, then. Here is your answer, Nika-Daisy. Now, get your butt in a gear.

"Okay, pep-talk is over."

Nika shook her head, blew the curls out of her eyes, and got to her feet.

Why was it so quiet? Where were Alex and Eli? Oh, yeah, they went for a drive. Eli's last day in the twenty-first century, and what was he doing? Right, driving around town. Was he agonizing about leaving, and never seeing his sister, or friends he made here? Was he full of regrets, or doubts? Was he thinking about tonight? On, no! He was spending his last hours speeding in a car.

The moron.

Irritated, Nika huffed a breath. No point to get so worked up. But, dammit, was it ridiculous, or what?

Maybe Eli needed a distraction. Did you think of that?

"Yeah, well. We have a different definition of a distraction, then."

The silence grew almost oppressive, until Nika was ready to scream. Desperate for noise— any kind of sound that wasn't her own voice— she contemplated her choices. She could always break something, but then she'll be dealing with a clean-up, or—

"Music. We need music, Maggie-baby. Something with beat and heat. What do you say?" Nika grabbed her iPod. "Springsteen or Queen? Oh, yeah, I know. Kiss."

I Love It Loud wasn't her personal favorite, but it had a beat, and heat, and was loud. Just what the doctor ordered.

Nika turned the volume all the way up, and wiggled her butt. She couldn't dance if her life depended on it, but who cares? She was alone, and if she missed a beat or two, and even stepped on her own foot, so what? She was entitled to dance her heart out on her last day.

The doorbell rang, catching Nika in a middle of her crazy gyration. She tripped, grabbed the chair, and stubbed her little toe on its leg.

"Fuck!"

Her loud curses alternated with pitiful whimpers, as she limped to answer the door. Whoever came to visit better have good health insurance after she dealt with him or her. So help her God.

Nika flung the door open, ready to spew out her wrath.

"JC!"

"Hello, Sis." Cool as a proverbial cucumber, her older brother cocked his brow. "Were you expecting someone else?"

A sudden sense of *deja vu* threw her off track. The last time JC materialized at her door it was Thanksgiving. Today was a New Year's Eve. So, true to the tradition, her brother was about to crash another party he wasn't invited to. Damn.

"I wasn't expecting anyone." She scowled. "Least of all you. What are you doing here?"

"Why, I told you I was coming back, remember?"

"Words are cheap, Counselor, and your track record is really crappy."

"So, you didn't believe me." Without a hint of offence, JC nodded, and leaned against the doorframe. "Hard to blame you, I suppose."

In lieu of an answer, Nika glared at him. Was it her imagination, or had JC lost weight? His cheekbones were more prominent than usual, like sketched with a sharp pencil. Dark smudges under his eyes complemented the picture, and hinted at fatigue. Nika's frown deepened.

"Can I come in?" Even his voice, hollow and blank, held a note of resignation. Something was off. She shrugged. Not her business. JC was a big boy. Big, bad, and selfish. But, dammit, he was her brother.

"Why the hell not."

"Gracious as ever."

JC stepped into the room, stopped in the middle, then racked both hands through his hair. Nika watched him.

Oh, yeah, JC lost weight along with his usual polish. After the first shock of seeing her bother on her doorstep wore off, the small tell-tale signs like his wrinkled shirt and crooked tie, caught her attention. The real red flag, however, was the visible bristle on his face. Either his regular barber was on vacation, or JS skipped several shavings. But instead of rakish, it made him look unkempt and untidy. Something was definitely off. The question was, to mention it, or pretend she didn't notice?

"I didn't know you were a fan of Kiss," JC interrupted her inner debate.

"Huh? Oh, no, not really. It was just—"

"Can you turn it down a bit?"

What was he talking about? Oh, yeah, the volume. Nika forgot she cranked it all the way up. By now, the loud blaring irritated the crap out of her, but hey, it was her crap, after all. Just to annoy him, Nika plastered a fake smile onto her face.

"Why?"

The crescendo of the blasted song reverberated through her skull. Even her teeth started to vibrate.

"Why? Jeez, are you deaf? My eardrums are about to split!"

Not waiting for her reply, JC marched forward, and shut off the iPod. The blessed silence filled the room. Nika almost sighed with relief, but caught herself in the last moment. So, call her a contrary bitch, but she refused to give her brother even that small a satisfaction. Instead, she crossed her arms, and glared at him.

"Okay, your eardrums are safe. Now, why are you really here, JC?"

"Because I'm moving here."

"Oh, yeah? Why?"

"I've decided I like Amelia Island."

"What about New York?"

"There is nothing for me in New York. Not anymore."

Uh-oh. Definitely something's wrong.

"Then why did you skedaddle there for Christmas?"

"Not to celebrate in style, for sure. Just some loose ends I needed to take care of."

"And?"

"And," JC tapped her nose, "I did tie all those lose ends into a nice, fat bow, and came back. This time for good. Why, Sis, aren't you glad to have a new neighbor?"

"I'm ecstatic." To demonstrate, she rolled her eyes, and snorted.

"Oh, I'll grow on you yet, you'll see."

"In your dreams, Junior."

He chuckled. Nika bit the inside of her cheek to hide a grin. Where was the last time they exchanged banter? The answer was never. JC tormented her all throughout her childhood; she did her best to ignore him. The insults? Sure. The taunts? Hell, yeah. But they never shared a joke, or laughed together. His fault? Hers? Did it matter? They both were mature adults now. And they were family. Time to let go of the past. To forgive and forget. And after tonight she'd never see him again.

"Why did you hate me so much?" The question was out of her mouth before she thought better of it. Then again, it was always a mystery to her, the one that irked and baffled. What was the better time to ask than now?

"I never did." His surprise seems genuine. "I always admired your spunk. Heck, I envied you."

Nika snorted. "Yeah, pull my other leg."

"I'm serious. I wished to be as carefree and courageous like you, but never had guts for it. As to all my pranks?" JC shrugged, tugged at his earlobe. "I was duty bound as your older brother to make your life miserable."

"What about Andrew? He was the youngest, but you never tormented him."

"Heck, Andrew was—still is—so damn amiable and gullible, there was no fun in it. Plus, he idolized me, and followed me everywhere like an adoring puppy. You, on the other hand, always ignored me, and preferred Alex's company over your older brother's."

"Don't tell me you were jealous, JC."

"So, what if I was? You were my sister. Ornery, stubborn, a prickly little thorn in my ass, but you were *mine*."

"Oh, JC, you selfish, misguided bastard. You didn't get it: I was my own. Not yours, or Alex's. Or anybody else's."

"Yeah, well. When I finally got it, it was already too late."

"It's never too late to make amends."

"You think so?"

"I know so."

He searched her face for a long moment. "I never hated you, Little Sis. I swear."

"Well, then." Nika spat on the palm of her right hand, offered it to JC. "Welcome home, Big Brother."

He squinted at her, unsure and skeptical, like he was expecting some mischief, then spat on his own palm, and grabbed her hand.

"It's nice to be home. At last."

Flooded with regrets, Nika went with the moment, and hugged JC for the first time in her life. At first he froze, then leaned into her embrace, and burrowed his face in the crown of her head. And broke her heart.

Regrets were useless, as were tears. With an effort, Nika bore down on both, and stepped back. She was getting maudlin.

No way, no how.

Time for a safe subject.

"So, you really moving down here?"

"Yep." Visibly relieved, JC plopped onto the sofa, crossed his legs. "Any objections?"

"Not a single one. As a matter of fact, your timing is perfect. You can stay here with Alex, until you find your own place."

"I can? Well, that's mighty generous of you, Sis."

"Kiss my—"

"Okay, okay." He brought both palms up, chuckling. "Don't fly off your handle." His gaze grew serious. "What about you?"

"What about me?"

"You said 'stay with Alex'. So, I repeat: what about you?"

"Oh, I'm going away. Did you forget I'm getting married?"

"No, but I thought you were planning to live here, in this house."

"Nope. Eli and I...we're leaving. Tonight, as a matter of fact."

"Tonight? Kid, in case you forgot, it's New Year's Eve."

"So? We'll celebrate together, then we're going to... visit his family."

"Huh. I though he was local, no?"

"He is, but his folks...they live in...in another place."

And time.

"Okay, Nika, what are you hiding?"

"What do you mean?"

"Do you think I forgot your habits? You just wrinkled your nose, and tugged your hair. And you're stuttering."

"So?"

"So, you did exactly that as a child when you wanted to get rid of me."

Damn, forgot how astute JC was. My mistake.

Nika let out a sigh, and sat beside him on the sofa. "The thing is, I'm going away with Eli, and I'm never coming back."

"Why?"

"Because I can't."

"I repeat, why?"

"Trust me, you'd better not knowing."

He mulled that for a moment, then cursed, and raked both hands through his hair.

"Is Eli in trouble with the law?

"What?"

"You heard me. Are you running away with him?"

As preposterous as it sounded, that was the perfect and easy way out, but...It was a lie. Not a fib, but a lie all the way. She shook her head.

"No, JC, that's not it. He's not in any trouble, trust me, especially with the law. And we are not running away. We're just...going on a journey. A long one."

But JC wasn't convinced. With a skepticism written all over his face, he leaned over, and grabbed her hand.

"Sis, if you need any help, just tell me. I know I wasn't there for you all these years, but I'll do whatever I can to help. I swear."

The honesty and care written on his face clenched her heart. How had they lost all those years? And now it was too late to make amends.

"Oh, JC." Moved beyond words, Nika lay her head on his shoulder. "Thank you. If I ever need help, I'll let you know." Then she did something she'd never done before: she kissed her brother's cheek. And stunned them both.

After a brief pause, JC cleared his throat. "Promise?"

"Cross my heart and hope to die."

To lighten the mood, Nika sent him a crooked grin. In response, JC curved his lips in a small smile. The dimple that popped into his cheek was as shocking as it was adorable. Come to think of it, he was a real hunk. Handsome, polished, classy. Not in Eli's league handsome, but, then again, who was?

"You know what? You're one hot number, Junior Morris."

He grimaced. "Hot? My ex-wife would disagree. She called me a coldblooded bastard most of the time."

"Ex? Gosh, JC, you got married like a minute ago!"

"Two years ago, to be precise, and yes, the divorce was finalized just before Christmas."

So, that what it was. Damn.

"What happened?"

"You may say we grew so far apart, it became difficult, if not impossible, to find each other, even when we were in the same room."

"It may not seem like that yet, JC, but everything happens for the best."

"If you say so. Anyway, what's done is done. Lesson learned."

"What lesson?"

He squinted at her. "Not everybody's cut out for marriage. Or able to love."

"Oh, that's not true! You just didn't meet the right girl, that all."

"Right." JC rose from the sofa. "Hey, where is everybody?"

Nika cursed under her breath, unsettled and sad.

Case dismissed. Dammit.

"Alex and Eli are driving around town; Abby decided to stay in San Francisco. And *Verochka* flew to North Sentinel Island."

"Our grandmother is true to herself." JC's brow creased for a moment, then he tilted his head. "And what are the plans for New Year's Eve?"

"Dinner at home, then a night on the town."

"Is there a room for a prodigal bother?"

"Absofuckinglutely."

"Fanfuckingtastic."

They bumped fists, something else they'd never done before. The last day of the year 2020 turned out to be the day of many 'firsts' for Nika. She vowed to cherish them all forever.

CHAPTER FORTY-FIVE

Historic downtown Fernandina Beach was a sight to behold. The New Year's party was at the full swing. People danced, cheered, sang, were exuberant and carefree. Just a few minutes young, the year 2021 was welcomed with the brilliant explosion of fireworks. The loud wishes of happiness, health, and prosperity rang here and there, accompanied by hugs and kisses among total strangers. This unconstrained, unhindered jubilation was a novel experience to Eli.

Then again, everything in this wondrous time was new, refreshing, and amazing.

He learned a lot of things here: about miraculous inventions, and people, and his hometown. But most important of all, he learned some new things about himself. Some of his views and beliefs underwent rather drastic transformation, some just altered a bit. But sure as day was long, Eli Coleman was a different man today. Somehow, this mindboggling journey had changed him. For the better? *We shall see.* Caught in the moment of contagious exhilaration, he almost missed a tap on his hand.

"Eli."

A bit annoyed at the interruption, he shifted his focus. But as soon as Daisy's somber face filled his vision, Eli's annoyance dissipated. Pale and intent, she gazed upon him with something close to grief in her eyes. In an instant, his mood plummeted, chased off by dark and cold apprehension. Daisy was hurting, but why? Just a moment ago they exchanged their first New Year's kiss. She was happy, and brimming with joy. What happen between then and now? What caused such sorrow? Something was amiss. Eli's disquiet turned to fear.

"Daisy, what is it, *ma petite?*"

"It's time." Her voice came out almost in a whisper.

Befuddled, Eli blinked several times. What was she talking about?

"Time for what?"

Without elaborating, she repeated in more insistent manner, "It is *time*, Eli."

Confusion turned to shock. Was she referring to...? Impossible. He must have misunderstood her meaning. But Daisy's bewitching eyes held him spellbound, as they transmitted their silent message. After a long moment, she spurred into action. Pulling him by hand, Daisy plowed her way in between the partygoers.

"Daisy, wait. Where are we going?"

"Where else? To the Coleman house."

"Now? But...what about Alex and JC?"

"They're big boys. They'll find their way home."

"But..." Bewildered, he let her propel him farther away.

Their prior, agreed upon plan was to spend a couple of hours in town, then return home for their old-fashioned clothes, and after that proceed to the Coleman house. Alex was the designated driver. The plan left JC at home under some false pretense. He was clueless still, and after some deliberation, they've decided to keep it that way. But all of a sudden, his bride has decided to change the course of action.

Infuriating wench. Just look at her! Maneuvering between people with sure purpose, and dragging me along like a puppy on a leash. Thunderation. What's got into her?

Eli had enough. If nothing else, she owed him an explanation.

"Daisy, stop this!"

She stopped, and pivoted. Defiant, poised for a fight, she met his eyes straight on. The raw anguish on her face contested her battling stance. His heart squeezed.

More than anything he wished to touch her, to take her into his arms.

But she wouldn't let him, not now. Instead, he asked in a gentle voice, "What's going on, *ma petite*? Why are we running away?"

"Because it's better this way."

"For whom?"

"For everybody. What's the point of prolonging the inevitable? We said our good-byes. We all know what's going to happen tonight. Why wait? You have the keys from the house and the clock, so, let's just go. Please."

Abandoning her fighting stance, Daisy stepped closer, and put her hand on his arm. Moist and misty, her violet eyes implored and begged.

"I can't do this, Eli. Don't you understand? It hurts so much."

Eli tore his gaze from her beseeching eyes.

She was tearing him apart. Why was he so reluctant to concede? He wanted to return home, to his place and time. An hour or two won't make any difference. He was ready. Or was he?

Thunderation.

Eli would rather die than admit that temptation to stay was there all along.

He resented it, ashamed, and appalled. He reminded himself, time and again, that he was but a guest here. As miraculous as this century was, it wasn't his place.

But, dear God, the seduction of it!

Daisy was right. They must go right now. The sooner they get back, the better for everybody. His last argument, although valid, was a mere exercise in futility. "Do you realize that we're still wearing our modern clothes? How are we going explain that?"

"We'll think of something."

"Like what?"

"Like whatever. We'll deal with it when we have to."

"Okay, but if we take the automobile, the guys will be left stranded."

"Car. It is called a car, Eli." Impatience rang in her voice. "And it's not like we're leaving them in the middle of a deserted island. They'll be fine."

Without waiting for his reply, she turned, and marched where they parked her car. What choice did he have but to follow? When Daisy made up her mind, she was unstoppable. Eli heaved a deep sigh. Of course, she was right.

A single clean amputation was better than a repetition of small cuts.

But, damn, why did he feel like a traitor?

With a last look over his shoulder at the cheering crowd, Eli slid into the passenger seat, and buckled up. And not a moment too soon. Daisy took off like a maniac, with the tires screeching in a feeble protest.

The initial movement threw him back against the seat. Not ashamed to clutch the door handle, Eli held on with all his might. She always operated her automobile fast but sure. Now she drove like all the demons of Hades were chasing them.

The little car flew over the night city like a red bullet, and in a blink of an eye, they were at the gates of the Coleman house.

All of his misgivings evaporated like a fog.

Home.

He was home. At last.

The urge to get inside was irresistible. Shaken, overwhelmed, Eli bore down, and balled his hands. A true gentleman must squelch his excitement, and act in a calm and dignified manner.

The hell with manners!

Like a green youth, he was bursting from exhilaration, almost shaking with it.

Home.

Unaware of his eagerness, Daisy disengaged the engine, and sat there, quiet and pensive. Eli dropped a glance at her. Lost in her own thoughts, Daisy focused on the regal white structure.

"I loved it from the get-go. It pulled at me, talked to me. Once it even snarled at me, back when I was afraid to open your letter. But I was always drawn to it, and didn't understand why."

She fell silent, then, as if coming to her senses, shook her head, and smiled.

"Now I do." Then she turned to face him. "Let's go home, Eli."

CHAPTER FORTY-SIX

From his vantage point Alex had a panoramic view of the city he called home. Alone, sober and somber, he watched the event with the detachment of a journalist. As if sensing his mood, the hugging, kissing, and cheering crowd gave him a wide berth. And that was fine with Alex. He didn't feel like celebrating, or hugging a complete stranger. The only person he wished to hug was half a world away.

Abby.

What was she doing? Was she celebrating? Was she happy? And who did she kiss first when the New Year rolled in?

Stop torturing yourself.

Easier said than done. As if to add to his torment, his treacherous mind conjured her face. God, she was so beautiful, she took his breath away. Exquisite, elegant, classy as hell.

The Princess.

Alex cursed under his breath, and rubbed both hands over his bald crown. Dammit, he should've called her.

Why didn't you?

The answer was simple: he was afraid. What if she was happy there, and didn't have any regrets? What if she planned to stay in California for good?

No way, no how.

There was not a single doubt in his mind that she belonged here. With him. She just didn't realize it yet. Or did she? Maybe, she was just acting out of sheer stubbornness? Wouldn't surprise him. What if she was waiting for him to change her mind? What if she *wanted* to? Dammit, instead of giving her free reins, he should've put his foot down, and insist on her coming back.

Are you freaking nuts? Orders? To Abby?

That would have been the biggest mistake he ever made. Eli tried that route before, and look where he landed. What he should've done, was to tell her he loved her. But like a coward, he kept his mouth shut. And regretted it ever since.

What's done is done. Regrets will get him nowhere. Time to get his act together, and go get the girl.

Perked up a little, Alex contemplated his choices. To wait awhile, or jump on the next plane to San Francisco? To bide time, or to ambush?

Damn.

As much as it galled him, Alex needed advice. And who knew the Princess better than her older brother? He turned around, searching the crowd. Where was his soon-to-be brother-in-law, and his cousin?

Sometime after midnight their small group got separated, but Alex was sure he heard Nika's laughter and Eli's unmistakable baritone just a few minutes ago.

With so many people milling around, it was hard to find a specific person in the melee. Alex disregarded the first twinges of concern. Yes, Nika was a shorty, but Eli's height and his statue made him quite distinguishable amongst the crowd. He'd find them without a problem. He hurried to the spot where he last saw Nika and Eli, shoving and pushing aside the partygoers. That earned him glares and few rude remarks. Alex ignored it all. But when he reached the area, there was no sign of them.

Panic grabbed him by the throat. *Stay calm.* Either he made a mistake, or they just migrated to another location. Alex moved around, called their names, but deep down he already knew. He wouldn't find them. They were gone.

Without a word, or last good-bye, they slipped away while he was too busy contemplating his love life dilemma. Guilt knifed him in the gut; grief twisted the blade.

Goddamit.

Defeated, Alex shut his eyes. He didn't hug Nika one last time, or tell Eli that the poor bastard stopped irritating him long time ago. Too late now. He lost them both. Not to death, but to time. Somehow it was even more devastating.

Goddamit all to fucking eternity.

Helpless, he scrubbed his face with both hands. A vicious headache stabbed behind his eyes, and reverberated through his skull. He welcomed it. Anything to take his mind off the moment.

Alex was about to turn, when a bump from behind propelled him forward, face first into a nearby tree.

Fuck.

The impact was solid, and brutal, and emptied his mind of everything except his stinging cheek.

Be careful what you wish for.

"Sorry, buddy, didn't mean to. Happy New Year!"

And the tipsy stranger, unsteady on his feet, stumbled forward.

Alex gingerly touched his injured face. A smear of blood on his fingers added the final drop that broke the floodgates. He let out a string of curses.

Where was Nika with her first aid kit when he needed her? She was gone, and he must now tend to his own wounds and hurts. Some was easily mended, like his scraped cheek, but what about his bruised heart?

And feeling sorry for yourself will get you nowhere, brother.

Deflated like a freaking balloon, hurting all over, Alex dropped to the iron bench, and closed his eyes.

He lost all sense of time, alone and isolated in his secluded little spot on the corner. How long had he sat there? With no idea what time it was, Alex opened his eyes, and looked around. The smell of recent fireworks clung to the air like fuzzy Spanish moss to the oaks. The starless dome of the sky over the city was unrelieved and stark black. Music, muted and soft, still poured from the open doors of the bars and cafés on both sides of Centre Street. The boisterous crowd had thinned and moved indoors for the last leg of the festivities. Just a few groups of young and adventurous were gathered here and there still, laughing and clowning around.

Dawn was hours away, but the new day of the year of 2021 had spread its tender wings over Amelia Island.

The holiday was over. Time to get back to reality.

"Alex!"

Startled, he turned around. Damn, he forgot all about JC. That son of a bitch was now his responsibly. A major pain in the ass, more accurate. Like he needed it.

Too beat to drum up even a small dollop of irritation, Alex accepted the inevitable. What was the point in resentment? He let go of the hard feelings toward his older cousin long ago. To hold grudges was silly and unproductive, a total waste of time and energy. So, what if JC was a dick? No one's perfect. And for better or worse, he was family.

One thing Alex knew for sure: everything happened for a reason. If that fickle bitch fate dropped JC into his life now, then there was a reason for that. And who was he to argue with providence? After all, last year it brought him Abby.

"H-happy New Year, C-Cousin!"

Geez, the bastard was drunk as a skunk. Despite his current mood, Alex laughed. His injured cheek protested with the vengeance, but he ignored the pain.

My God, this is hysterical.

As comic relief went, this one was a doozy. Tipsy, overdressed in his wilted three-piece suit and a tie, JC stumbled forward, sporting a pointed hat on his head, and humongous plastic eyeglasses on his face with 20 and 21 glued to the sides.

A string attached to a withered balloon of undetermined color was clutched in his hand. Like an old tired whore who didn't give a shit and just went with the motions, this half-deflated, dingy balloon trailed behind JC, bored and lazy.

What a picture!

With a dopey grin the former CLO of New York Morris Bank dropped beside him on the bench.

"What h-happened to your f-face, Cuz? Did you get into a f-fight?"

"Yea, something like that."

"Cool. Who w-won?"

"The tree."

"Huh? What tree?"

"I think it was an oak, but I can't be sure."

"I'm s-serious, Alex."

"Me too."

"Huh." JC squinted at him through the plastic lenses of his ridiculous glasses. They were pink, for crying out loud. Geez. "Looks nasty. Prob'ly have a scar."

All business, he nodded, like he just delivered a winning argument in court. The motion sent his pointy hat further askew. The more ridiculous image was hard to imagine. Alex swallowed another laugh.

"You know what they say about men and scars."

For some incomprehensible reason, JC found this statement hilarious, and burst into a laughter.

"You're f-funny, Cuz."

"Yep, that's me, an all-around funny guy. Tell me, Counselor, where did you get this, ah, get-up?"

"Oh, someone g-gave it to me. Like it?"

"Love it. It's so... you."

"Thought so. Hey," animated, JC turned to face Alex, "let's make a selfie, you and m-me!"

"Let's not."

"'Kay." With a shrug, he finally let go of a stupid balloon, then yawned. "I'm totally wiped out."

"You're totally wasted."

"B-both. But, Lord, it was so worth it! Hadn't have so much f-fun since...f-forever." JC shut his eyes, and dropped his head. "Let's go home, Cuz. What do you say?"

"I say *yipikayay*, Counselor." Alex rose from the bench, and grabbed JC under his arms. The son of a gun weighted a ton despite his skinny appearance. He removed the hat and the eyeglasses from JC, and dumped them in the nearest waste can.

"Bossy," JC hiccupped once, then frowned. "Hey, where is Nika and Eli?"
A million-dollar question.

"Left."

"Left? Where did they go?"

"Home."

"B-but, wait—" JC shrugged Alex's arms, and dug into his heels. "H-how...w-when? We were s-suppose to..."

"Change of plans. They left earlier. So, are you going with me, or staying here?"

"G-going. But I don't like it."

"For once, we're in total agreement."

Without elaborating, Alex half dragged, half carried his inebriated cousin away.

CHAPTER FORTY-SEVEN

The Coleman house was eerily quiet. Since his arrival to this century, Eli got used to the little noises made by the modern appliances. Wasn't it strange that the absence of those sounds bothered him more now than the initial presence of them?

Everything inside was just as it was in his time: the furniture, the décor, even the smell of it. Daisy made him proud. Such a marvelous job! If he didn't know better, he'd think that he just stepped into his own house moments after he left.

Moments?

He spent more than fortnight in the twenty first century. Eli wondered how long it equated in his own time, since time evolved differently here and there. Had a day passed? A week, or maybe a year? But that was worry for another day. The main challenge now was to wake up the grandfather clock, and get back. How did this blasted time-jumping thing work, anyway?

Too late to wonder about it. Eli dropped an imperceptible glance at Daisy. What was going on in her mind? After he opened the house, and they stepped in, she hadn't uttered a single word. If he was the judge, he'd say his bride was calm and determined. Familiar with the layout of the house, she didn't need his guidance to navigate. He followed in her steps, and soon they both faced the Coleman's prized grandfather clock. The mysterious guard of the house. The portal between times. Their only hope to return where they belong. Will it work, or refuse them the safe passage home?

Only one way to find out.

The grandfather clock's golden hands were poised at twelve, with its pendulum swaying in a hypnotic rhythm. Eli frowned. He was sure the hour was later, way past midnight. But the clock disagreed. Well, then. He braced himself before removing the cord from beneath his shirt.

The familiar weight of the small brass key in the palm of his hand brought some sense of reassurance. Calmer now, he lifted the key, and offered it to Daisy.

"Go ahead, *ma petite*. You know what to do."

Her violet eyes sparkled with excitement, but her hand that accepted the key was steady and sure. Without a moment's hesitation, Daisy inserted it into its slot. But then she turned to him.

"Together. Let's do it together this time."

He stepped behind her, and covered her right hand with his.

The first evolution of the key in the slot went effortless, but bore no results. They exchanged brief glances. Eli held his breath as their joint hands turned the key again. Nothing. Was the damn thing dead?

Thunderation.

While he was traipsing around this century, the old grandfather clock just stopped working. Dear Lord, now what? A small crease marred Daisy's forehead.

With a deep breath, she blew the ringlets from her face, and looked at him.

"One more time. Ready?"

In lieu of an answer, he nodded, and concentrated all his attention on the blasted key.

At the third revolution, the clock awakened.

A deep and resonant chime filled the room. That *bong*ing sound reverberated through every bone in Eli's body. Daisy tensed, but didn't release her hold on the key. Ghostly light illuminated the face of the clock. The spectral rays of unimaginable colors exploded around the room. Like an otherworldly ballet, they danced and shimmered. An invisible electricity hissed and fizzled. All fine hairs on Eli's neck lifted at once. Goose bumps broke out over his body.

What in the blazes?

In the next moment, a brutal invisible force swept around the room, and hugged them into its savage embrace. Eli's body contracted and folded into itself. Dear Lord, what was happening? He didn't remember the searing pain, or the blazing heat that set his insides on fire.

The last and only time he turned the key in this clock, he was thrown through the centuries as fast as a blink.

His ears popped.

His eyes stung and watered.

His limbs went numb.

And all the while, the clock's incessant chimes boomed around like a macabre chant. Mad from this noise, unable to withstand the immeasurable pull of an unseen force, Eli cried out, "*Daisy!*"

He more sensed than heard her response. "Don't... let... go... of the key!"

Key?

They were about to be blown to smithereens, and she was worrying about the blasted key? He'd laugh if his breath wouldn't be squeezed out of his chest. The key can go to hell for all he cared, but he'd be damned if he let go of her.

With a herculean effort of will, Eli enfolded Daisy into his embrace, shielding her from the unbridled frenzy that churned all around. And together they were sucked into a giant invisible tunnel.

CHAPTER FORTY-EIGHT

Being alone never bothered Alex before. But being alone was a light year apart from being lonely. The difference was humongous. Everybody had abandoned him. Except JC that is. By the irony of Fate, he was now Alex's only companion.

Yippee.

Hey, better than nothing. At least he was a breathing, living body, albeit an annoying one. What the hell? They'll bunk together for the time being, and see where it goes. The vast emptiness of the house was more intolerable than the presence of his stuck-up, dick of a cousin.

And wasn't that pathetic?

But pathetic or not, it beat being totally alone.

After the Uber ride home, Alex deposited JC, wrinkled three-piece suit minus shoes, into bed. He'd be damned if he'd undress the Counselor, but the dirty wingtips on clean sheets? A definite no-no. And he'd be double damned to play babysitter.

As soon as JC came to his senses, they'd have a talk, and establish some ground rules. If he wanted to share the place with Alex, there would be no more drunken binges, period. And he must pull his weight around the house, or hit the road.

Tomorrow. He'd deal with everything tomorrow.

Alex grabbed a bottle of beer he didn't want, and stepped onto the deck.

The predawn ocean was spectacular in its splendor. Nika always loved this hour of the day. How many times they greeted the new day on this deck together, drinking coffee, or just shooting air? Alex swore under his breath. Damn, he missed her already.

He was tired to the marrow, but sleep was out of the question. Restless, he turned his eyes to the beach, deserted at this hour. Maybe a long walk will help? But the prospect of putting on shoes, or doing any kind of physical activity was daunting. Instead, Alex plopped into his chair, and brooded.

Happy fucking New Year.

In slow-motion, like an old-time movie, the memories of the last evening swam in his mind. Burst of laughter, snippets of conversation, flickers of candles...Happiness. Joy.

Togetherness.

He almost blocked it. Wouldn't it be better just to drink himself to a stupor, and go to bed? Probably. But it wouldn't change anything, and overindulgence in hard liquor would only bring him the misery of a hangover. Since his injured face already hurt like a mother, adding more pain was pure masochism. Thanks, but no thanks.

Alex closed his eyes, braced himself against the heartache, and let the memories unfold...

Everybody was doing their best to act nonchalant, like nothing special was going to happen after midnight. Everybody, that is, except JC. Although clueless, he kept Nika and Eli in his focus all evening. Alex got the impression that JC sensed something was off, but couldn't put his finger on it. Or was he projecting?

After dinner, he roped him and Eli into cleaning up. Nika's protest fell on deaf ears.

"She who cooked, doesn't clean."

"But they might break Verochka's *best china!"*

"The hell with it. I need to show you something important."

"Gosh, Alex, can it wait? Just let me—"

"No, it cannot. Come with me." He tugged her away from the table and into the sanctuary of his room.

"Computer? You wanted to show me a freaking computer? Seriously?"

"No, not the computer, Brat." He laid his hands on her shoulders and pushed her into the desk chair. "Look at the screen. Look and weep."

"Okay, I'm weeping." Nika made a production of blotting up imaginary tears from her eyes. "Golly, the copy of Nicholas Benjamin's The History of Amelia Island Homes and Mansions!" Then she rounded on him. "Are you kidding me? I know that book by heart!"

"Do you? Do you really?"

"Of course I do, you moron. I have a copy of it here, and in the office. Those photos have been the best reference for all my restoration projects."

"I'm aware of that. But what do you know about the author of that book?"

"No one knows anything about the elusive Mr. Benjamin. Not even the Historical Society of Amelia Island. He's been somewhat of a hermit."

"Humor me."

"Okay, alright. If memory served, he insisted on communicating by mail only, and refused to meet with people, even with his publisher. No one knows how old he was, or what he looked like, because he was never photographed, or interviewed during his lifetime." She started to stand but Alex kept his hands firmly in place.

"Have you ever wondered why?"

"Why would I? So, the man didn't like publicity, and valued his privacy. So what? I'm grateful for his meticulous notes and detailed photographs; I've studied his book, used it in my restorations, and that's all."

"Okay, Nik. Now look at the dedication page."

"Alex, I have no time—"

"I think you want to make time. Trust me."

She was so darn cute when she was grumbling and scowling, but Alex valued his sensitive body parts too much to point it out. Nika had a wicked right hook, not to mention her killer knee. He'd been on the receiving part of that deceptively tiny joint a couple of times, and wasn't partial for a repeat experience. He leaned over her then scrolled all the way to the page in question. Then he pointed at the screen. *"Read."*

To my cousin Alex who was right before and after, time and again.

After one sharp intake of breath, Nika read it again aloud. When she turned to look at him, her eyes were sparkling with hope.

"What does it mean?"

"I think you know. In your heart you figured it out. Don't you?"

"Do you mean...are you sure—"

"Yes. You've worried what you're going to do there. That's what."

"Oh, Alex..." Nika flew into his arms. *"Thank you, Cuz!"*

"Hey, don't thank me. You've managed it by yourself!"

"Not without you, I wouldn't. Thank you, thank you so much!"

"You are very welcome, Mr. Nicholas Benjamin."

With a start, Alex opened his eyes. He could swear he smelled Nika's faint perfume, and heard her voice. Had she returned? Have they lost the key again? Or maybe the clock got stuck, or broken, and the portal didn't open?

But her chair sat empty, and only his rapid breathing and the faint murmur of the ocean disturbed the predawn silence.

Shake it off, buddy.

With the last glance at Nika's vacant chair, Alex left the deck, and stepped inside.

His gaze traveled around the room. Empty, quiet. Forlorn. Just like him.

Even the Christmas tree had lost its spark, despite the glitter of garlands and ornaments.

Damn, the Christmas tree!

Alex swore under his breath. The chore to take it down was not so much painstaking, as sad. He always hated it. Nika called him a tenderhearted fool, and a softy, but never laughed at his feelings. For the past nine years, they'd always done it together, with Nika cheering him on, or kicking his butt, whichever worked best. But this time he must do it alone.

What was Eli's favorite curse?

Thunderation.

A loud snore from the guest room crashed his pity party. Alex cringed. Sheesh, the Counselor was a champion snorer.

Eureka!

Alex brightened. He'd dump the chore onto JC. That'd keep his cousin occupied and out of Alex's hair. Perfect.

A win-win for everybody. Well, maybe not so much for JC, but who cares? And, besides, he must carry his fair share of chores around the house, so why not start with the Christmas tree? Alex cracked a smile as he eyed the half-withered evergreen, pleased with the solution. He almost missed a lone package hidden under the tree. Odd. Alex was positive it wasn't there before.

Curious, he picked it up. Small, but weighty, wrapped in a plain piece of paper, it was addressed to *Alexander Morris*. The handwritten cursive was precise, bold, and elegant at the same time.

What on earth…? Only one way to find out.

As soon as he unfolded the small parcel, his heart almost stopped. Nestled inside, lay the familiar golden watch incrusted with diamonds and sapphires.

Eli's pocket watch.

Stunned, Alex stared at it, afraid to touch, afraid to breathe. After a moment, his lungs screamed in protest, and he gulped some air. A folded page inside the package caught his attention at last. With unsteady hands, Alex opened the note.

My dearest Alex,

You refused to accept this item as payment for your hospitality. I hope you will agree to accept it as a token of my sincere appreciation and friendship. If it is not to your liking, then safe keep it for your firstborn as the family heirloom. After all, he'll be a Coleman too, even if in half. I wish you and Abby all the happiness in the world. And if I may give you the last advice? Do not wait until my obstinate sister comes to her senses. Go after her, Alex. Now. Bring her where she belongs.

Oh, and as to your statement you made on the airplane? Remember? You said that love doesn't make any sense? Well, my friend, it is true. Love per se does not make any sense, but it infuses everything else in the world with it.

Farewell, brother.

Always yours,

Elijah B. Coleman.

"Ah, Eli, you shmuck."

Unashamed of tears misting his vision, Alex cradled the priceless Coleman watch in the palm of his hand. He'll wear it until his firstborn will be old enough to understand and appreciate his inheritance. Damn straight he'll be half Coleman!

"Farewell, brother."

Careful not to damage it, Alex folded the note, and tucked it inside his shirt pocket. He'll borrow Nika's example, and put it into a Ziploc bag later. Another heirloom, even more valuable than the antique pocket watch. One day, he'll tell his son all about his uncle. But to make sure he does have a son, first he must go get Abby, haul her ass home, and marry her. Not necessarily in that order.

They can get hitched in California, or Nevada, for all he cared. An express wedding in Las Vegas, with an Elvis impersonator crooning "Love Me Tender?"

Why the hell not?

So, what are you waiting for? Time's awasting, Nika's voice whispered in his ear.

As earlier on the deck, her unmistakable perfume wafted through the air, but Alex didn't question his sanity anymore. The bard was right when he wrote Hamlet, there are more things in heaven and earth. And who was he to question the Universe?

"Thanks, Cuz."

Energized, Alex grabbed his iPhone. A couple of clicks later the local airport app flashed on his screen. For once, that fickle bitch fate was on his side. A JetBlue flight from Fernandina to San Francisco was departing in five hours. Fantastic. Another set of clicks, and he booked his seat. Okay, done. With great care, Alex flipped open his new heirloom watch, and checked the time. Just enough for a quick shower. Already on the move, he removed his shirt and shorts, dumping them helter skelter along the way. A loud snore hampered his progress.

Damn, he forgot about JC. Shit. Should he wake his cousin up? Better not. What if he decides to tag along?

No way in hell.

A note. Yes, a short note was the perfect solution.

Satisfied, Alex resumed his mad dash to the bathroom.

The Counselor was a big boy. He can fend for himself for a couple of days. Three at the most. After all, how long will it take to convince the Princess that they were destined for each other?

CHAPTER FORTY-NINE

"Eli, wake up! Open your eyes. Please, darling, look at me."

Like the buzz of a tiny insect, the sound irritated more than angered.

Go away, leave me be.

But the urgent buzz continued, increasing in volume and urgency.

"Don't you dare scare me like that! Open your eyes. Now!"

No, not a buzz, but a ...voice. Familiar. Scared. But, oh dear Lord, so loud.

Just go away, please.

Still wrapped in a bliss of numb darkness, Eli disregarded the urgent plea. The hell with it. He was too comfortable, too cozy, too —

"Ouch! Thunderation!"

A slap in the face was impossible to ignore. Who was brazen enough to administer such an insult? Whoever it was, better run for the hill, or there will be a hell to pay.

His thoughts were jumbled, but his rage cut thought the haze in his brain. Whenever he gets his hands on the offender, he'll kill the bastard. Fueled by bubbling anger, Eli gathered all his willpower, and dragged his eyes open.

Gliding in and out of focus, a comely face filled his vision.

I know that face.

The boy, that pitiful street urchin he picked up from the dirty road. No, he was not a boy, but...

Daisy!

In a flash, all the events of the past came tumbling in like an avalanche.

William's death, discovery of betrayal, his journey through time.

Daisy.

He found her at last. But what happened next? His memories were still vague.

The last thing Eli remembered was a New Year's celebration. And then nothing.

"My God, Daisy. What happened?"

"What happened? He's asking what happened! You scared the hell out of me, that's what happened, Eli Coleman!" Her little fists flew in a blur, and landed, quite painfully, upon his chest. "Don't you dare to do that again! Ever!"

Disheveled, with her ringlets sprouting in a mad fashion, she glared at him with blazing anger.

Amethyst eyes.

Such a unique color. Just like the gem he put on her finger. Eli smiled. His mind was afloat above his head, but he didn't mind the sensation. Pleasant. Strange, but enjoyable.

Then his focus became sharper, and he noticed an ugly bump crowning Daisy's forehead. She was injured!

"Ah, *ma petite*, you're hurt."

But when he tried to touch her, his hand disobey his brain orders.

Thunderation. Weak as a newborn babe.

Was he sick? And why, for crying out loud, was he sprawled on the floor? With a tremendous effort of will, Eli brought his body to a sitting position. The movement sent his head swimming and his gut churning, but he ground his teeth, and managed to stay upright.

"Daisy—"

She sniffed, then laughed, then covered her face with both hands, and dissolved into tears. Thunderation. Daisy never cried. But to cry and laugh in turns? She must be hurt more than he thought. Eli's attempt to scoot closer failed, so he used his most gentle voice to croon to her.

"It's okay, baby, don't cry. Tell me how badly are you hurt."

"I'm not. I'm perfectly okay. Just...I thought you were dead." And she carried on with her hysterics, until he was beside himself with worry.

"Why would I die? I'm strong, and healthy. But your head..." Carefully he reached out and touched the offensive knot. "How did that happen?"

"Just a rough landing, nothing to worry about."

"Landing? What landing?"

"Don't you remember?"

"I..." Flashing snippets of images and sensations, but still not a complete picture. Eli raked his fuzzy brain. They were in the middle of the celebratory crowd, then Daisy tagged him away, then the fast ride in her red automobile, and then....

The Coleman house!

"I remember entering the house, and the grandfather clock. I remember inserting the key. It didn't work at first, and then..." And the fog dissipated at last.

The loud chime, the pain, the force of the hurricane sucking everything inside its invisible tunnel. And the sensation of tumbling.

Afraid to hope, Eli squinted at his surroundings. Everything was familiar and dear, and just as he remembered. But was it his old house, or the restored one? He closed his eyes, and listened. No noise of any kind, no hum of the appliances—just silence. Elated, he glanced at the newel post. And here it was. A peculiar little hat with the golden letters *B&A* on its front. He left it there for safekeeping before his time jump. In November of 1909. They were home. At last.

"Dear God! We are...we're back!"

A wicked grin split Daisy's face, as she looped her arms around his neck.

"Bet you fine aristocratic ass, we are!"

"I told you before, and I'm repeating again, you are not a lady, *ma petite.*"

"And thank God for that!"

With the force that put to shame any hurricane, she flung herself into his arms. Eli's heart summersaulted, then went into overdrive.

Her kiss was more enthusiastic than carnal, but he was okay with that. For a minute that is. Then he tilted his head, and in turn crushed her lips under his.

When she came up for a breath of air, Daisy scrunched her forehead, as if she just remembered something.

"Forgot to ask, do you happen to have a camera?"

Taken aback, Eli blinked. The woman just scrambled his brain with unrestrained passion, and now she's asking for a... camera? His hearing must be affected, or... "A photographic camera?"

"Yes, that."

I'll be damned.

Dumbfounded, Eli rubbed his chin. "As a matter of fact, I own a Brownie."

"Fantastic!"

And with renowned enthusiasm, Daisy planted another kiss onto his lips that wiped his brains clean of any coherent thought.

The maddening, infuriating creature.

No wonder he was insane about her. But as much as kissing on the floor was invigorating, it soon ceased being enough. Before he succumbed to his more primitive urges, and forget all about propriety, Eli rose from the floor, and dragged Daisy after him. They were running to the stairs, but unsatisfied with the speed of their progress, he picked up Daisy into his arms, and carted her all the way to his bedroom. And there at last, he let go of the beast clawing its way out.

When the gentle dawn kissed the lavender sky, Eli gazed at his sleeping bride. His flower, his timeless miracle. His Daisy.

Flushed and rumpled, she was a picture of a well content feline that overindulged in a full bowl of a cream. He grinned. She'd skin him alive for such a comparison.

Delighted, satisfied, and happy to the point of delirium, Eli placed a soft kiss upon her bare shoulder. Daisy stirred. With a little purring sound, she finally opened her eyes.

"Welcome home, *ma petite.*"

A drowsy little smile trembled upon her puffy lips. Still not awakened fully, she yawned, flopped onto her back, and stretched her arms.

"Damn, it's good to be home."

When she squinted at him next, her amethyst eyes were dancing with a familiar mischief. Eli braced himself, and not a moment too soon. Swift as a cat, Daisy rolled over, and took his mouth with the renowned fervor. Through the rush of blood in his ears, he heard the resonant *bong* of the old grandfather clock. The sound of it broke the hushed stillness of the Coleman house, announcing the arrival of the new day.

Eli's last lucid thought was: hell yes, it was good to be home.

And then he ceased thinking altogether.

AKNOWLEDGEMENTS

TO COME UP WITH A STORY and write it down is easy. To make it into a book—now that's entirely different story.

The creative process is a lonely road, sometimes straight and smooth, often like a hike in the hills, but always solitary. And that's how it should be. But every road, no matter how long or hilly, comes to an end, and then...

...you realize that it's not the end— far from it! — but a crossroads, and you need to choose carefully where to turn, or how to proceed and not to get completely disoriented. You need help to choose the right path, a map to orient yourself, a guidance and a gentle nudge (or a mighty push) to start moving again. In short, you need other people. Then, the real adventure begins.

I've been truly blessed. By the time I came to my crossroads, I was so lost, I was about to turn back. But fate decided differently: she sent me Sloane Taylor, my editor, who very soon became my mentor and my guardian angel. She took me by my hand and dragged me to the right path, showing me the way. And all the time while I stumbled along the thorny path, she was walking behind me, cheering me on, whipping my tears, or kicking my behind. I've never had so much fun, or been so frustrated, in my life, but every second of it was worth it.

Thank you, Sloane Taylor, for sticking up and not giving up on me. Thank you for everything. This book is as much yours as it is mine. Without you it wouldn't see the light of a day.

Special thanks to a fellow writer Tina Ruiz for test-reading my book, and all her valid suggestions. I greatly appreciate it.

My heartfelt thanks to Justine Alley Dowsett, who created such a beautiful cover.

And as always, my sincere gratitude to the men in my life, my husband Leo and my son George. Thank you for believing in me, guys.